THE SIL[ENT WORLD] OF NICHOLAS QUINN

&

SERVICE OF ALL THE DEAD

Colin Dexter has won many awards for his novels including the CWA Gold Dagger and Silver Dagger awards. In 1997 he was presented with the CWA Cartier Diamond Dagger Award for outstanding services to crime literature. Colin's thirteenth and final Inspector Morse novel, *The Remorseful Day*, was published in 1999. He lives in Oxford.

ALSO BY COLIN DEXTER

COLIN DEXTER

THE SILENT WORLD
OF NICHOLAS QUINN

&

SERVICE OF ALL
THE DEAD

PAN BOOKS

The Silent World of Nicholas Quinn first published 1977 by Macmillan.
First published in paperback 1978 by Pan Books.
Service of All the Dead first published 1979 by Macmillan.
First published in paperback 1980 by Pan Books.

This omnibus first published 2008 by Pan Books
an imprint of Pan Macmillan Ltd
Pan Macmillan, 20 New Wharf Road, London N1 9RR
Basingstoke and Oxford
Associated companies throughout the world
www.panmacmillan.com

ISBN 978-0-330-45782-8

1 3 5 7 9 8 6 4 2

A CIP catalogue record for this book is available from
the British Library.

Printed and bound in Great Britain by
Mackays of Chatham plc, Chatham, Kent

THE SILENT WORLD
OF NICHOLAS QUINN

For Jack Ashley

Rear Car Park

Mr Quinn

Miss Height

Corridor

Mr Martin

Dr Bartlett

Cloak Room

Cloak Room

Registry

Entrance Hall

Mr Ogleby

Front Car Park

PROLOGUE

'WELL? WHAT DO you think?' The Dean of the Foreign Examinations Syndicate addressed his question directly to Cedric Voss, the Chairman of the History Committee.

'No, no, Dean. I think the Secretary should be the first to have his say. After all, it's the permanent staff who'll have to work with whoever we appoint.' In slightly less distinguished company, Voss would have added that he didn't give two monkeys which of them got the job. As it was, he reassumed a characteristically somnolent posture in his comfortable blue leather chair, and prayed they'd all get their fingers out. The meeting had already lasted almost three hours.

The Dean turned to the person sitting on his immediate left, a small twinkling man in his middle or late fifties, who blinked boyishly behind his rimless spectacles. 'Well, Dr Bartlett, let's hear what you've got to say.'

Bartlett, permanent Secretary of the Foreign Examinations Syndicate, glanced good-naturedly round the tables before looking down briefly at his neatly written notes. He was used to this sort of thing. 'It seems to me, Dean, that generally speaking, by and large' (the Dean and several senior members of the Syndicate visibly winced) 'and on the whole, we would all agree that the short list has been a very good one. All the applicants seemed pretty competent, and most of them sufficiently

1

experienced to take on the work. But—' He looked down again at his notes. 'Well, to be truthful, I would not myself wish to appoint either of the two women. The one from Cambridge was, I thought, a little, er, a little *strident*, shall we say?' He beamed expectantly round the Appointments Committee and a few heads nodded fairly vigorous assent. 'The other woman I thought just a *little* inexperienced, and I, er, didn't feel much inner surge of conviction about some of her answers.' Again there was no visible sign of dissent from the silent tables, and Bartlett stroked his ample belly with mild satisfaction. 'So. Let's come to the three men. Duckham? Just a little vague, I thought. Nice chap and all that, but I wonder if he's got quite the snap and zip that I'd welcome in the Humanities Department here. He's third, in my book. Then there's Quinn. I liked him: honest, intelligent fellow; firm views; clear brain. Not quite the ideal experience, perhaps, and then— Well, let me be quite honest about it. I think that, er, I think his, er – *handicap* may be a bit too much of a liability here. You know what I mean: phone calls, meetings, that sort of thing. It's a pity, but there it is. Anyway, I'd put him second. That leaves Fielding, and he's the man I'd go for every time: damn good schoolmaster; excellent results from his pupils; just the right age; modest; likeable; and a First in History from Balliol. References quite outstanding. I don't honestly think we could have hoped for a better applicant, and he's my first choice, Dean, without the slightest doubt.'

Not unostentatiously the Dean closed his appointments

folder and gently nodded his agreement, noting with gratification that several other heads were nodding too. Including the Dean himself, the full complement of Syndics was present. Twelve of them, each a prominent fellow of his or her college within the University of Oxford, and each called upon to attend the meetings held twice a term at the Syndicate building for the purpose of formulating official examination policy. None of them was on the permanent staff of the Syndicate, and none was paid a penny (apart from travelling expenses) for attendance at these meetings. Yet most of them took an active part on the various Subject Committees, were happy to adopt a policy of enlightened self-interest towards the profitable procedures of public examinations, and during the months of June and July, after their own undergraduates had departed for the long vac, acted as chief examiners and moderators in the GCE Ordinary- and Advanced-level examinations. Of the permanent officers of the Syndicate only Bartlett was automatically invited to participate in the counsels of this governing body (though even he was not entitled to cast a vote), and it was Bartlett who brought the number in the room up to thirteen. Thirteen ... Yet the Dean was not a superstitious man, and he looked round the committee with a degree of mild affection. Tried and trusted colleagues almost all of them, although one or two of the younger dons he'd not yet got to know particularly well: hair rather too long, and one of them had a beard. Quinn had a beard, too ... Come on! The appointment would be settled very quickly now, and with a bit of luck he could be back in Lonsdale College before six. Tonight was a 'gaudy' and . . . Get it over with! 'Well, if I'm right in assuming that the committee agrees to the appointment of Fielding, there's only the matter of his starting salary to settle. Let's see, he's thirty-four. I should think the bottom of the B Lecturers' Scale might—'

'Could I just make one point before you go on, Dean?' It was one of the younger dons. One of the long-haired ones. The one with the beard. A chemist from Christ Church.

'Yes, of course, Mr Roope. I didn't mean to give the impression—'

'If I may say so, I think you're presuming that we all agree with the Secretary's views; and, of course, it may be that everyone else does. But *I* don't, and I thought the whole purpose of this meeting—'

'Quite so, quite so, Mr Roope. As I say, I'm sorry if I gave you the impression that, er – you know . . . I certainly didn't mean to do that. It was just that I thought I sensed a feeling of general agreement. But we're in your hands. If you feel—'

'Thank you, Dean. I do feel strongly about this, and I just can't agree with the order of merit the Secretary has given. If I'm going to be frank about it, I thought that Fielding was too much of a yes-man, too much of a smoothie for me. In fact if he got the job, it wouldn't be so much a matter of taking the rough with the smooth as taking the smooth with the smooth.' A gentle murmur of amusement rippled round the tables, and the slight tension, perceptible only a minute before, was visibly relaxed. And as Roope continued, some of his senior colleagues listened to him with slightly more interest and attention. 'I agree with the Secretary about the rest, though I can't say I completely agree with his reasons.'

'You mean you'd put Quinn first, is that it?'

'I would, indeed. He's got sound views on examinations, and he's got a good mind. But what's more important, I reckon he's got a genuine streak of integrity, and these days—'

'You didn't feel the same about Fielding?'

'No.'

The Dean ignored the Secretary's audible mumble of 'Nonsense!' and thanked Roope for his views. His eyes swept vaguely over the committee, inviting comments. But none was immediately forthcoming. 'Anyone else wish to, er—?'

'I think it quite unfair for us to make too many cosmic character-judgements on the strength of a few brief interviews, Dean.' The speaker was the Chairman of the English Committee. 'We must all make our own assessments of these people; of course we must. That's the only reason we're here. But I agree with the Secretary. My order of merit was the same as his: exactly so.'

Roope leaned back and stared at the white ceiling, a yellow pencil balanced between his teeth.

'Anyone else?'

The Vice-Dean sat shuffling uneasily in his chair, profoundly bored, and anxious to be on his way. His notes consisted of an extraordinarily intricate doodle of whorls and scrolls; and he added a further florid curve to the flowing tracery as he made his first and final contribution to the day's deliberations: 'They're both good men, that's obvious. Doesn't seem to me to matter much which we go for. If the Secretary wants Fielding, I want Fielding. A quick vote, perhaps, Dean?'

'If that's, er, that's, er . . .'

A few members of the committee interjected their muted bleats of approval, and in a vaguely disconsolate voice the Dean called the division lobbies. 'All right. A show of hands, then. All those in favour of appointing Fielding, please?'

Seven or eight hands were being raised when Roope suddenly spoke again, and the hands were slowly lowered.

'Just before we vote, Dean, I would like to ask the Secretary for some information. I'm quite sure he'll have it at his fingertips.'

From behind his spectacles the Secretary eyed Roope with chill distaste, and several committee members could scarcely conceal their impatience and irritation. Why had they co-opted Roope? He was certainly a brilliant chemist and his two years with the Anglo-Arabian Oil Co. had seemed a decided asset in view of the Syndicate's commitments. But he was too young, too cocky; too loud and splashy, like a vulgar speedboat churning through the placid waters of the Syndicate regatta. This wasn't the first time he'd clashed with the Secretary, either. And he didn't even serve on the Chemistry Committee; didn't do a scrap of examining. Always said he was too busy.

'I'm sure the Secretary will be glad to, er— What were you thinking of, Mr Roope?'

'Well, as you know, Dean, I've not been with you very long yet, but I've been looking at the Syndicate's Constitution, and as it happens I've got a copy with me here.'

'Oh God!' mumbled the Vice-Dean.

'In paragraph 23, Dean – would you like me to read it?' Since half the committee had never even seen a copy of the Constitution, let alone read it, it seemed wholly inappropriate to dissemble any phoney familiarity, and the Dean nodded reluctant assent.

'Not, er, too long, I hope, Mr Roope?'

'No, it's very brief. Here's what it says, and I quote: "The Syndicate will endeavour at all times to remember that, wholly dependent as it is for its income on public monies, it owes and must seek to discharge a corresponding responsibility both to society at large and to its own permanent employees. Specifically, it will undertake to employ in its services a small percentage of persons who are variously handicapped, should the disabilities of such persons prove not substantially to interfere with the proper discharge of the duties entrusted to them."' Roope closed the slim document and put it aside. 'Now, my question is this: can the Secretary please tell us how many handicapped people are at present employed by the Syndicate?'

The Dean turned once more to the Secretary, whose customary *bonhomie* had now apparently returned.

'We used to have a one-eyed fellow in the packing

department—' In the ensuing laughter the Vice-Dean, whose own particular handicap was a weak bladder, shuffled out of the room, where Roope was pursuing his point with humourless pedantry.

'But presumably he's no longer employed here?'

The Secretary shook his head. 'No. Unfortunately he turned out to have an uncontrollable weakness for stealing toilet rolls, and we—' The rest of the sentence was drowned in a ribald cackle of lavatory laughter, and it was some little while before the Dean could bring the meeting to order again. He reminded the comittee that paragraph 23 was not, of course, a statutory injunction – merely a marginal recommendation in the interests of normal civilized, er, living. But somehow it was the wrong thing to say. Far wiser to have allowed the Secretary a few more anecdotes about his less-than-fortunate experiences with the unfortunately afflicted few. As it was, the subtle shift had been made. The man with the handicap was coming into the betting once more, his odds shortening further as Roope pressed his point neatly and tellingly home.

'You see, Dean, all I really want to know is this: do we feel that Mr Quinn's deafness is going to be a significant liability in the job? That's all.'

'Well, as I said,' replied Bartlett, 'there's the telephone for a start, isn't there? Mr Roope perhaps isn't fully aware of the vast number of incoming and outgoing telephone calls here, and he must excuse me if I suggest that I know slightly more about this than he does. It's a very tricky problem when you're deaf—'

'Surely not. There are all sorts of gadgets these days.

You can wear one of those behind-the-ear things, where the microphone is—'

'Does Mr Roope actually know someone who's deaf and who—?'

'As a matter of fact, I don't but—'

'Then I suggest he is in real danger of underestimating the sort of problems—'

'Gentlemen, gentlemen!' The exchanges were becoming increasingly tetchy, and the Dean intervened. 'I think we all agree that it would be *something* of a problem. The real question is – how much of one?'

'But it's not just the telephone, is it, Dean? There are meetings – dozens and dozens of 'em a year. A meeting like this one, for instance. You get stuck in a meeting with somebody on the same side of the table, sitting three or four places away . . .' Bartlett warmed to the point, and made his case without interruption. He was on safer ground, he knew that. He was getting just a little deaf himself.

'But it's not beyond the wit of man to arrange the seating of a meeting—'

'No, it isn't,' snapped Bartlett. 'And it's not beyond the wit of man either to rig up a convenient little system of headphones and microphones and God knows what else; and we could all learn the deaf-and-dumb alphabet, if it came to that!'

It was becoming increasingly obvious that there was a festering, strangely personal antipathy between the two men, and few of the older Syndics could understand it. Bartlett was usually a man of wonderfully equable temperament. And he hadn't finished yet: 'You all saw the report from the hospital. You all saw the audiographs. The fact of the matter is that Quinn is very deaf. *Very* deaf.'

'He seemed to be able to hear us all perfectly well, didn't he?' Roope spoke the words quietly, and if Quinn himself had been there he would almost certainly have missed them. But the committee didn't, and it became perfectly clear that Roope had a point. A strong point.

The Dean turned again to the Secretary. 'Mm. You know it's amazing that he *did* seem to hear us so well, isn't it?'

A desultory discussion broke out, gradually drifting further and further away from the immediate decision that still remained to be taken. Mrs Seth, the Chairman of the Science Committee, thought about her father . . . He had gone deaf very quickly when he was in his late forties and when she was only a schoolgirl; and he had been dismissed from his job. Redundancy money, and a meagre disability pension from his firm – oh yes, they'd tried to be sympathetic and fair. But he'd had such a clear brain, and he'd never worked again. Confidence irreparably shattered. He could still have done a whole host of jobs infinitely more efficiently than half the layabouts sitting idling on their backsides on office stools. It made her so very sad and so very cross to think of him . . .

Suddenly she was aware that they were voting. Five hands went up almost immediately for Fielding, and she thought, as the Secretary did, that he was probably the best of the bunch. She would vote for him too. But for some curious reason her hand remained on the blotting paper in front of her.

'And those for Quinn, please?'

Three hands, including Roope's, were raised; and then a fourth. The Dean began counting from the left: 'One, two, three ... four ...' Another hand, and the Dean started again: 'One, two, three, four, five. It looks—' And then, slowly and dramatically, Mrs Seth raised her own hand.

'Six.'

'Well, you've made your decision, ladies and gentlemen. Quinn has been appointed. Close vote: six-five. But there it is.' He turned rather awkwardly to his left. 'Are you happy, Mr Secretary?'

'Let's just say we all have our own views, Dean, and the view of the Appointments Committee is not mine. But, as you say, the committee has made its decision and it's my job to accept that decision.'

Roope sat back once more staring vaguely at the ceiling, the yellow pencil once more between his teeth. He may have been inwardly gloating over his minor triumph, but his face remained impassive – detached almost.

Ten minutes later the Dean and the Secretary walked side by side down the flight of stairs that led to the ground floor and to Bartlett's office. 'You really think we've made a bad mistake, Tom?'

Bartlett stopped and looked up at the tall, grey-haired theologian. 'Oh, yes, Felix. Make no mistake about that. We have!'

Roope pushed his way past them on the stairs and volunteered a vague 'Cheerio'.

'Er – goodnight,' said the Dean; but Bartlett remained darkly silent, and watched Roope go before slowly walking down the few remaining stairs and entering his office.

Above his door was a twin-coloured light, similar to the sort found in hospitals, which was operated from two switches on the desk inside. The first switch turned on a red light, signifying that Bartlett was in session with someone, and did not wish to be (and would not be) disturbed; a second switch turned on a green light, indicating that one was free to knock and enter. When neither switch was depressed, no light showed, and the conclusion thence to be drawn was that the room was empty. Since his appointment to the Secretaryship, Bartlett had firmly maintained that if anyone wished to discuss a matter of importance with him, he himself should have the courtesy to ensure an uninterrupted, confidential chat; and his staff fully appreciated and almost invariably observed the arrangement. On the very few occasions that the rule had been infringed, Bartlett had displayed quite uncharacteristic anger.

Once inside the Secretary snapped down the red switch before opening a small cabinet and pouring himself a glass of gin and dry vermouth. Then he sat down behind his desk, opened a drawer and took out a packet of cigarettes. He never smoked at meetings, but he lit one now, inhaled deeply, and sipped his drink. He would send a telegram to Quinn in the morning: it was too late to send one now. He opened his appointments folder once more and reread the information on Quinn. Huh! They'd picked the wrong fellow – of course they had! All because of Roope, the bloody idiot!

He put the papers away neatly, cleared his desk and sat back in his chair – a curious half-smile forming on his lips.

WHY?

CHAPTER ONE

WHILST THE OTHER four took their seats in the upstairs lounge of the Cherwell Motel, he walked over to the bar and ordered the drinks: two gins and tonics, two medium sherries, one dry sherry – the latter for himself. He was very fond of dry sherry.

'Put them all down to the Foreign Examinations Syndicate, will you? And we shall be having lunch. If you can tell the waiter we're here? Sitting over there.' His north-country accent was still noticeable, though less so than it had been.

'Have you booked a table, sir?'

He enjoyed the 'sir'. 'Yes. The name's Quinn.' He grabbed a handful of peanuts, took the drinks over on a tray, and sat down with the other members of the History Committee.

It was his third Revision meeting since joining the Syndicate, and there were several others fixed for later in the term. He sat back in the low leather chair, drained half his sherry at a gulp, and looked out at the busy lunchtime traffic along the A40. This was the life! A jolly good meal to come – wine, coffee – and then back for the afternoon session. Finish with a bit of luck about five or even earlier. The morning session had been a concentrated, unremitting slog; but they'd done well. Question papers covering the periods from the Continental Crusades to the English Civil War had now assumed the final and definitive form in which they

17

would appear before the following summer's Advanced-level History candidates. Just the five papers left, from the Hanoverians to the Treaty of Versailles; and he felt much more at home with the recent periods. At school History had been his favourite subject, and it was in History that he had won his exhibition to Cambridge. But after Prelims he'd changed over to English, and it had been as an English teacher that he had been subsequently appointed to the staff of Priestly Grammar School, Bradford, only twenty-odd miles from the Yorkshire village in which he was born. Looking back on it, he realized how lucky the switch to English had been: the advertisement for the post with the Syndicate had stressed the need for some qualification in both History and English, and he'd realized that he might stand a pretty good chance, although even now he couldn't quite believe that he had landed the job. Not that his deafness . . .

'Your menu, sir.'

Quinn had not heard the man approach, and only when the inordinately large menu obtruded itself into his field of vision was he aware of the head waiter. Yes, perhaps his deafness would be slightly more of a handicap than he'd sometimes assumed; but he was managing wonderfully well so far.

For the moment he sat back, like the others, and studied the bewildering complexity of permutations on the menu: expensive – almost all the dishes; but as he knew from his two previous visits, carefully cooked and appetizingly garnished. He just hoped that the others wouldn't plump for anything *too* exotic, since Bartlett had quietly mentioned to him after the last jollification that perhaps the bill was a *little* on the steep side. For himself, he decided that soup of the day, followed by gammon and pineapple would not be beyond the Syndicate's means – even in these hard days. A drop of red wine, too. He knew it would be red wine whatever happened. Many of them drank red wine all the time in Oxford – even with Dover sole.

'We've got time for another drink, haven't we?' Cedric Voss, Chairman of the History Committee, passed his empty glass across the table. 'Drink up, men. We shall need something to keep us going this afternoon.'

Quinn dutifully collected the glasses and walked over to the bar once more, where a group of affluent-looking executives had just arrived and where a five-minute wait did nothing to quell the vague feeling of irritation which had begun to fester quietly in a corner of his mind.

When he returned to the table, the waiter was taking their orders. Voss, after discovering that the cherries were canned, the peas frozen, and the steak delivered the previous weekend, decided that he would revise his original ideas and go for the escargots and the lobster, and Quinn winced inwardly as he noted the prices. Three times his own modest order! He had pointedly *not* bought a second drink for himself (although he could have tossed another three or four back with the greatest relish) and sat back rather miserably, staring at the vast aerial photograph of central Oxford on the wall beside him. Very impressive, really: the quads of Brasenose and Queen's and—

'Aren't you drinking, Nicholas, my boy?' Nicholas! It was the first time that Voss had called him by his Christian name, and the irritation disappeared like a lizard's eyelid.

'No, I er—'

'Look, if old Tom Bartlett's been griping about the expense, forget it! What do you think it cost the Syndicate to send him to the oil states last year, eh? A month! Huh! Just think of all those belly-dancers—'

'You wanted wine with your meal, sir?'

Quinn passed the wine list over to Voss, who studied it with professional avidity. 'All red?' But it was more a statement than a question. 'That's a nice little wine, my boy.' He pointed a stubby finger at one of the Burgundies. 'Good year, too.'

Quinn noted (he'd known it anyway) that it was the most expensive wine on the list, and he ordered a bottle.

'I don't think one's going to be much good, is it? With five of us—'

'We ought to have a bottle and a half, you think?'

'I think we ought to have two. Don't you, gentlemen?' Voss turned to the others and his proposal was happily approved.

'Two bottles of number five,' said Quinn resignedly. The irritation was nagging away again.

'And open them straight away, please,' said Voss.

*

In the restaurant Quinn seated himself at the left-hand corner of the table, with Voss immediately to his right, two of the others immediately opposite, and the fifth member of the party at the top of the table. It was invariably the best sort of arrangement. Although he could see little of Voss's lips as he was speaking, he was just about near enough to catch his words; and the others he could see clearly. Lip-reading had its limitations, of course: it was of little use if the speaker mumbled through unmoving lips, or held a hand over his mouth; and absolutely useless when the speaker turned his back, or when the lights went out. But in normal circumstances, it was quite wonderful what one *could* do. Quinn had first attended lip-reading classes six years previously, and had been amazed to discover how easy it was. He knew from the outset that he must have been blessed with a rare gift: he was so much in advance of the first-year class that his teacher had suggested after only a fortnight, that he should move up to the second-year class; and even there he had been the star pupil. He couldn't really explain his gift, even to himself. He supposed that some people were talented in trapping a football or in playing the piano: and he had a talent for reading the lips of others, that was all. Indeed, he had become so proficient that he could sometimes almost believe that he was in fact 'hearing' again. In any case, he hadn't completely lost his hearing. The expensive aid at his right ear (the left was completely nerveless) amplified sufficient sound at reasonably close quarters, and even now he could hear Voss as he pronounced the benediction over the escargots just placed before him.

'Remember what old Sam Johnson used to say? "The fellow who doesn't mind his belly can't be trusted to mind anything." Well, something like that.' He tucked a napkin into his waistband and stared at his plate with the eyes of a Dracula about to ravish a virgin.

The wine was good and Quinn had noticed how Voss had dealt with it. Quite beautifully. After studying the label with the intensity of a backward child trying to get to grips with the Initial Teaching Alphabet, he had taken the temperature of the wine, lightly and lovingly laying his hands around the bottle-neck; and then, when the waited had poured half an inch of the ruby liquid into his glass, he had tasted not a drop, but four or five times sniffed the bouquet suspiciously, like a trained alsatian sniffing for dynamite. 'Not bad,' he'd said finally. 'Pour it out.' Quinn would remember the episode. He would try it himself next time. 'And turn the bloody music down a bit, will you,' shouted Voss, as the waiter was about to depart. 'We can't hear each other speak.' The music was duly diminished a few decibels, and a solitary diner at the next table came over to express his thanks. Quinn himself had been completely unware that any background music was being played.

When the coffee finally arrived Quinn himself was feeling more contented, and a little befuzzled. In fact, he couldn't quite remember whether it was Richard III on the First Crusade or Richard I on the Third Crusade. Or, for that matter, whether either Richard had been on either Crusade. Life was suddenly very good again. He thought of Monica. Perhaps he would call in – just for a second – before they started the business of the afternoon. Monica . . . It must have been the wine.

They finally arrived back at the Syndicate building at twenty minutes to three; and whilst the others were making their leisurely way back to the Revision Room upstairs, Quinn himself walked quickly along the corridor and gently knocked on the furthest door on the right, whereon the nameplate read MISS M. M. HEIGHT. He tentatively opened the door and looked in. No one. But he saw a note prominently displayed beneath a paperweight on the neatly cleared desk, and he stepped inside to read it. 'Gone to Paolo's. Back at three.' It was typical of their office life together. Bartlett never minded his staff coming and going just when and how they liked, so long as their work was adequately done. What he did insist upon, however (almost pathologically), was that everyone should keep him informed about exactly where they could be found. So. Monica had gone to have her comely hair coiffured. Never mind. He didn't know what he would have said, anyway. Yes, it was just as well: he would see her in the morning.

He walked up to the Revision Room, where Cedric Voss was leaning back in his chair, his eyes half-closed, an inane grin upon his flabby, somnolent features. 'Well, gentlemen. Can we please try to turn our attention to the Hanoverians?'

CHAPTER TWO

BY THE MIDDLE of the nineteenth century radical reforms were afoot in Oxford; and by its end a series of Commissions, Statutes, and Parliamentary Bills had inaugurated changes which were to transform the life of both Town and Gown. The University syllabuses were extended to include the study of the emergent sciences, and of modern history; the high academic standards set by Benjamin Jowett's Balliol gradually spread to other colleges; the establishment of professorial chairs increasingly attracted to Oxford scholars of international renown; the secularization of the college fellowships began to undermine the traditionally religious framework of university discipline and administration; and young men of Romanist, Judaic, and other strange persuasions were now admitted as undergraduates, no longer willy-nilly to be weaned on Cicero and Chrysostom. But, above all, university teaching was no longer concentrated in the hands of the celibate and cloistered clergymen, some of whom, as in Gibbon's day, well remembered that they had a salary to receive, and only forgot that they had a duty to perform; and many of the newly appointed fellows, and some of the old, forswore the attractions of bachelor rooms in the college, got themselves married, and bought houses for themselves, their wives, their offspring, and their servants, immediately outside the old spiritual centre of Holywell and the High, the Broad and St Giles'; especially did they venture north of the great width of tree-lined St Giles', where the Woodstock and the Banbury Roads branched off into the fields of North Oxford, towards the village of Summertown.

A traveller who visits Oxford today, and who walks northward from St Giles', is struck immediately by the large, imposing houses, mostly dating from the latter half of the nineteenth century, that line the Woodstock and the Banbury Roads and the streets that cross their ways between them. Apart from the blocks of weathered yellow stone round the white-painted window frames, these three-storeyed houses are built of attractive reddish brick, and are roofed with small rectangular tiles, more of an orange-red, which slope down from the clustered chimney stacks aslant the gabled windows. Today few of the houses are occupied by single families. They are too large, too cold, and too expensive to maintain; the rates are too high and salaries (it is said) are too low, and the fast-disappearing race of domestic servants demands a colour telly in the sitting-room. So it is that most of the houses have been let into flats, converted into hotels, taken over by doctors, by dentists, by English Language schools for foreign students, by University faculties, by hospital departments – and, in the case of one large and well-appointed property in Chaucer Road, by the Foreign Examinations Syndicate.

The Syndicate building stands some twenty yards back from the comparatively quiet road which links the busy Banbury and Woodstock thoroughfares, and is modestly sheltered from inquisitive eyes behind a row of tall horse-chestnut trees. It is approached from the front (there is no back entrance) by a curving gravelled drive, allowing space sufficient for the parking of a dozen or so cars. But the Syndicate staff has grown so much of late that this space is now inadequate, and the drive has been extended along the left-hand side of the building, leading to a small concreted yard at the rear, where it has become the custom of the graduates themselves to park their cars.

There are five graduates on the permanent staff of the Syndicate, four men and one woman, severally superintending the fields of study corresponding, in the main, to the disciplines which they had pursued for their university degrees, and to the subjects taught in their subsequent careers. For it is an invariable rule that no graduate may apply for a post with the Syndicate unless he (or she) has spent a minimum of five years teaching in schools. The names of the five graduates are printed in bold blue letters at the top of the Syndicate's official notepaper; and on such notepaper, in a large converted bedroom on the first floor, on Friday, 31st October (the day after Quinn's deliberations with the History Committee), four of the five young shorthand typists are tapping out letters to the headmasters and headmistresses of those overseas schools (a select, but growing band) who are happy to entrust the public examination of their O- and A-level candidates to the Syndicate's benevolence and expertise. The four girls pick at their typewriters with varying degrees of competence; frequently one of them leans forward to delete a misspelling or a careless transposition of letters; occasionally a sheet is torn from a typewriter carriage, the carbon salvaged, but the top sheet and the under-copies savagely consigned to the wastepaper basket. The fifth girl has been reading *Woman's Weekly*, but now puts it aside and opens her dictation book. She'd better get started. Automatically she reaches for her ruler and neatly crosses through the third name on the headed notepaper. Dr Bartlett has insisted that until the new stocks are ready the girls shall manually correct each single sheet – and Margaret Freeman usually does as she is told:

T. G. Bartlett, PhD, MA Secretary
P. Ogleby, MA Deputy Secretary
~~G. Bland, MA~~
Miss M. M. Height, MA
D. J. Martin, BA

Beneath the last name she types 'N. Quinn, MA' – her new boss.

After Margaret Freeman had left him, Quinn opened one of his filing cabinets, took out the drafts of the History question papers, deciding that a further couple of hours should see them ready for press. All in all, he felt quite pleased with life. His dictation (for him, a completely new skill) had gone well, and at last he was beginning to get the knack of expressing his thoughts directly into words, instead of first having to write them down on paper. He was his own boss, too; for Bartlett knew how to delegate, and unless something went sadly askew he allowed his staff to work entirely on their own. Yes, Quinn was enjoying his new job. It was only the phones that caused him trouble and (he admitted it) considerable embarrassment. There were two of them in each office: a white one for internal extensions, and a grey one for outside calls. And there they sat, squat and menacing, on the right-hand side of Quinn's desk as he sat writing; and he prayed they wouldn't ring, for he was still unable to quell the panic which welled up within him whenever their muted, distant clacking compelled him to lift up one or other (he never knew which). But neither rang that morning, and with quiet concentration Quinn carried through the agreed string of amendments to the History questions. By a quarter to one he had finished four of the question papers, and was pleasantly surprised to find how quickly the morning had flown by. He locked the papers away (Bartlett was a martinet on all aspects of security) and allowed himself to wonder whether Monica would be going for a drink and a sandwich at the Horse and Trumpet – a pub he had originally misheard as the 'Whoreson Strumpet'. Monica's office was immediately opposite his own, and he knocked lightly and opened the door. She was gone.

In the lounge bar of the Horse and Trumpet a tall, lank-haired man pushed his way gingerly past the crowded tables and made for the furthest corner. He held a plate of sandwiches in his left hand, and a glass of gin and a jug of bitter in his right. He took his seat beside a woman in her mid-thirties who sat smoking a cigarette. She was very attractive and the appraising glances of the men who sat around had already swept her more than once.

'Cheers!' He lifted his glass and buried his nose in the froth.

'Cheers!' She sipped the gin and stubbed out her cigarette.

'Have you been thinking about me?' he asked.

'I've been too busy to think about anybody.' It wasn't very encouraging.

'I've been thinking about *you*.'

'Have you?'

They lapsed into silence.

'It's got to finish – you know that, don't you?' For the first time she looked him directly in the face, and saw the hurt in his eyes.

'You said you enjoyed it yesterday.' His voice was very low.

'Of course I bloody well enjoyed it. That's not the point, is it?' Her voice betrayed exasperation, and she had spoken rather too loudly.

'Shh! We don't want everybody to hear us, do we?'

'Well – you're so silly! We just can't go on like this! If people don't suspect something by now, they must be blind. It's got to stop! You've got a *wife*. It doesn't matter so much about me, but—'

'Couldn't we just—?'

'Look, Donald, the answer's "no". I've thought about it a lot – and, well, we've just got to stop, that's all. I'm sorry, but—' It *was* risky, and above all she worried about Bartlett finding out. With his Victorian attitudes . . .

They walked back to the office without speaking, but Donald Martin was not quite so heart-broken as he appeared to be. The same sort of conversation had taken place several times before, and always, when he picked his moment right, she was only too eager again. So long as she had no other outlet for her sexual frustrations, he was always going to be in with a chance. And once they were in her bungalow together, with the door locked and the curtains drawn – God! What a hot-pants she could be. He knew that Quinn had taken her out for a drink once; but he didn't worry about that. Or did he? As they walked into the Syndicate building at ten minutes to two, he suddenly wondered, for the first time, whether he *ought* perhaps to be a fraction worried about the innocent-looking Quinn, with his hearing aid, and his wide and guileless eyes.

Philip Ogleby heard Monica go into her office and gave her no second thought today. He occupied the first room on the right-hand side of the corridor, with the Secretary's immediately next door, and Monica's next to that – at the far end. He drained his second cup of coffee, screwed up his thermos flask, and closed an old copy of *Pravda*. Ogleby had been with the Syndicate for fourteen years, and remained as much a mystery to his present colleagues as he had done to his former ones. He was fifty-three now, a bachelor, with a lean ascetic face, and a perpetually mournful, weary look upon his features. What was left of his hair was grey, and what was left of his life seemed greyer still. In his younger days his enthusiasms had been as numerous as they were curious: Morris dancing, Victorian lampposts, irises, steam-locomotives and Roman coins; and when he had come down from Cambridge with a brilliant First, and when he had walked directly into a senior mathematics post in a prestigious public school, life had seemed to promise a career of distinguished and enviable achievement. But he had lacked ambition, even then; and at the age of thirty-nine he had drifted into his present position for no other reason than the vague conviction that he had been in one rut for so long that he might as well try to climb out and fall as gently as possible into another. There remained but few joys in his life, and the chief of these was travel. Though his six weeks' annual holiday allowed him less time than he would have wished, at least his fairly handsome salary allowed him to venture far afield, and only the previous summer he had managed a fortnight in Moscow. As well as deputizing for Bartlett, he looked after Mathematics, Physics and Chemistry; and since no one else in the office (not even Monica Height, the linguist) was his equal in the unlikelier languages, he did his best to cope with Welsh and Russian as well. Towards his colleagues he appeared supremely indifferent; even towards Monica his attitude seemed that of a mildly tolerant husband towards his mother-in-law. For their part, the rest of the staff accepted him for what he was: intellectually superior to them all; administratively more than competent; socially a nonentity. Only one other person in Oxford was aware of a different side to his nature . . .

At twenty past three Bartlett rang extension five.

'Is that you, Quinn?'

'Hullo?'

'Come along to my office a minute, will you?'

'I'm sorry. I can't hear you very well.'

'It's Bartlett here.' He almost shouted it into the phone.

'Oh, sorry. Look, I can't quite hear you, Dr Bartlett. I'll come along to your office right away.'

'That's what I asked you to do!'

'Pardon?'

Bartlett put the phone down and sighed heavily. He'd have to stop ringing the man; and so would everybody else.

Quinn knocked and entered.

'Sit down, Quinn, and let me put you in the picture. When you were at your meeting yesterday, I gave the others some details of our little, er, jamboree next week.'

Quinn could follow the words fairly easily. 'With the oil sheiks, you mean, sir?'

'Yes. It's going to be an important meeting. I want you to realize that. The Syndicate has only just broken even these last few years, and – well, but for these links of ours with some of the new oil states, we'd soon be bankrupt, like as not, and that's the truth of the matter. Now, we've been in touch with our schools out there, and one of the things they'd like us to think about is a new History syllabus. O-level only for a start. You know the sort of thing: Suez Canal, Lawrence of Arabia, colonialism, er, cultural heritage, development of resources. That sort of thing. Hell of a sight more relevant than Elizabeth the First, eh?'

Quinn nodded vaguely.

'The point is this. I want you to have a think about it before next week. Draft out a few ideas. Nothing too detailed. Just the outlines. And let me have 'em.'

'I'll try, sir. Could you just say one thing again, though? Better than "a list of metaphors", did you say?'

'Elizabeth the First, man! Elizabeth the First!'

'Oh yes. Sorry.' Quinn smiled weakly and left the room deeply embarrassed. He wished Bartlett would occasionally try to move his lips a little more.

When Quinn had gone, the Secretary half-closed his eyes, drew back his mouth as though he had swallowed a cupful of vinegar, and bared his teeth. He thought of Roope once more. Roope! What a bloody fool that man had been!

33

CHAPTER THREE

THROUGHOUT THE MONTH of October the health of
the pound sterling was a topic of universal, if melancholy, interest. Its effective devaluation against the
dollar and against other European currencies was sol-
emnly reported (to two points of decimals) in every
radio and TV news bulletin: the pound had a poor
morning, but recovered slightly in later dealings; the
pound had a better morning, but was later shaky against
its Continental competitors. The pound, it seemed,
occasionally sat up in its sick bed to prove to the world
that reports of its death had been somewhat exaggerated; but almost invariably the effort appeared to have
been overtaxing and very soon it was once more lying
prostrate, relapsing, slipping, falling, collapsing almost
– until finally it struggled up on to its elbow once more,
blinked modestly around at the anxious foreign finan-
ciers, and moved up a point or two in the international
money market.

Yet although, during that autumn, the gap in the
balance of payments grew ever wider; although the
huge oil deficit could be made up only by massive loans
from the IMF; although the number of the unemployed
rose sickeningly to unpredicted heights; although the
bankruptcy courts were enjoying unprecedented business; although foreign investors decided that London
was no longer a worthy recipient for their ever-
accumulating cash surpluses – still, in spite of it all,

there remained among our foreign friends a firm and charming faith in the efficiency and efficacy of the British educational system; and, as a corollary to this, in the integrity and fair-mindedness of the British system of public examinations. Heigh-ho!

On the night of Monday, 3rd November, many were making their ways to hotel rooms in Oxford: commercial travellers and small business men; visitors from abroad and visitors from home – each selecting his hotel with an eye to business expenses, subsistence allowances, travellers' cheques or holiday savings. Cheap hotels and posh hotels; but mostly of the cheaper kind, though they (Lord knew) were dear enough. Rooms where the cisterns groaned and gurgled through the night; rooms where the window sashes sagged and the floorboards creaked beneath the flimsy matting. But the five emissaries from the Sheikdom of Al-jamara were safely settled in the finest rooms that even the Sheridan had to offer. Earlier in the evening they had eaten gloriously, imbibed modestly, tipped liberally; and each in turn had made his way upstairs and slipped between the crisp white sheets. Domestic problems, personal problems, health problems – certainly any or all of these might ruffle the waters of their silent dreams; but money was a problem which worried none of them. In the years immediately after the Second World War, oil, of high quality and in large accessible deposits, had been discovered beneath their seemingly barren sands; and a benevolent and comparatively scrupulous despot, in the person of the uncle of Sheik Ahmed Dubal, had not only secured American capital for the exploitation of the wells, but had immeasurably enriched the lives of most of the inhabitants of Al-jamara. Roads, hospitals, shopping centres, swimming pools and schools had not only been planned – but built; and in such an increasingly westernized society the great demand of the wealthier citizens was for the better education of their children; and it was now five years since the first links with the Foreign Examinations Syndicate had been forged.

The two-day conference started at 10.30 a.m. on Tuesday the 4th, and at the coffee session beforehand there was much shaking of hands, many introductions, and all was mutual smiles and general bonhomie. The deeply tanned Arabs were dressed almost identically in dark-blue suits, with sparklingly laundered white shirts and sober ties. Quinn had earlier viewed the day with considerable misgivings, but soon he found to his very great relief that the Arabs spoke a beautifully precise and fluent brand of English, marred, it was true, by the occasional lapse from purest idiom, but distinct and (to Quinn) almost childishly comprehensible. In all, the two days passed rapidly and delightfully: plenary sessions, individual sessions, general discussions, private discussions, lively conversations, good food, coffee, sherry, wine. The whole thing had been an enormous success.

On Wednesday evening the Arabs booked the Disraeli

suite at the Sheridan for a farewell party, and all the Syndicate's permanent staff, together with wives and sweethearts, and all the Syndicate's governing council, were invited to the junketing. Sheik Ahmed himself, resplendent in his Middle-Eastern robes, took his seat beside a radiant Monica Height, exquisitely dressed in a pale-lilac trouser suit; and Donald Martin, as he sat next to his plain-looking little wife, her white skirt creased and her black jumper covered with dandruff, was feeling progressively more miserable. The Sheik had clearly commandeered the fair Monica for the evening and was regularly flashing his white and golden smile as he leaned towards her – intimate, confiding. And she was smiling back at him – attentive, flattered, inviting ... Quinn noticed them, of course, and as he finished his shrimp cocktail he watched them more closely. The Sheik was in full flow, but whether his words were meant for Monica alone, Quinn was quite unable to tell.

'As one of your own Englishmen told me one day, Miss Height,

"Oysters is amorous,
Lobsters is lecherous,
But Shrimps – Christ!"'

Monica laughed and said something close beside the Sheik's ear which Quinn could not follow. How foolish he had been to harbour any hope! And then he was able to follow another brief passage of their conversation, and he knew that the words must certainly have been whispered *pianissimo.* He felt his heart beat thicker and faster. He must surely have been mistaken . . .

Towards midnight the party had dwindled to about a third of its original number. Philip Ogleby, who had drunk more than anyone, seemed the only obviously sober one amongst them; the Martins had left for home some time ago; Monica and Sheik Ahmed suddenly reappeared after an unexplained absence of over half an hour; Bartlett was talking rather too loudly, and his large solicitous wife had already several times reminded him that gin always made him slur his words; one of the Arabs was in earnest negotiation with one of the barmaids; and of the Syndics, only the Dean, Voss, and Roope appeared capable of sustaining the lively pace for very much longer.

At half past midnight Quinn decided that he must go. He felt hot and vaguely sick, and he walked into the Gentlemen's, where he leaned his head against the coolness of the wall mirror. He knew he would feel rough in the morning, and he still had to drive back to his bachelor home in Kidlington. Why hadn't he been sensible and ordered a taxi? He slapped water over his face, turned on the cold tap over his wrists, combed his hair, and felt slightly better. He would say his thank-yous and good-byes, and be off.

Only a few were left now, and he felt almost an interloper as he re-entered the suite. He tried to catch Bartlett's eye, but the Secretary was deep in conversation with Sheik Ahmed, and Quinn stared rather fecklessly around for a few minutes before finally sitting down and looking again towards his hosts. But still they talked. And then Ogleby joined them; and then Roope walked over, and Bartlett and Ogleby moved away; and then the Dean and Voss went across; and finally Monica. Quinn felt almost mesmerized as he watched the changing groupings and tried to catch the drift of what they were talking about. He felt a simultaneous sense of guilt and fascination as he looked at their lips and followed their conversation, as though he were standing almost immediately beside them. He knew instinctively that some of the words must have been whispered very quietly; but to him most of them were as clear as if they were being shouted through a megaphone. He remembered one occasion (his hearing had been fairly good then) when he had picked up a phone and heard, on a crossed line, a man and his mistress arranging a clandestine rendezvous and anticipating their forthcoming fornication with lascivious delight . . .

He felt suddenly frightened as Bartlett caught his eye and walked over, with Sheik Ahmed just behind him.

'Well? You enjoyed yourself, my boy?'

'Yes, indeed. I – I was just waiting to thank you both—'

'That is a great pleasure for us, too, Meester Queen.' Ahmed smiled his white and golden smile and held out his hand. 'We shall be meeting you again, we hope so soon.'

Quinn walked out into St Giles'. He had not noticed how keenly one of the remaining guests had been watching him for the past few minutes; and it was with considerable surprise that he felt a hand on his shoulder and turned to face the man who had followed him to his car.

'I'd like a word with you, Quinn,' said Philip Ogleby.

At 12.30 the following day, Quinn looked up from the work upon which, with almost no success, he had been trying to concentrate all morning. He had heard no knock, but someone was opening the door. It was Monica.

'Would you like to take me out for a drink, Nicholas?'

CHAPTER FOUR

ON FRIDAY, 21ST November, a man in his early thirties caught the train from Paddington back to Oxford. He found an empty first-class compartment with little difficulty, leaned back in his seat, and lit a cigarette. From his briefcase he took out a fairly bulky envelope addressed to himself ('If undelivered please return to the Foreign Examinations Syndicate'), and extracted several lengthy reports. He unclipped his ballpoint pen from an inside pocket, and began to make sporadic notes. But he was left-handed, and with an ungenerous margin, and that only on the right of the closely-typed documents, the task was awkward; and progressively so, as the Inter-City train gathered full speed through the northern suburbs. The rain splashed in slanting parallel streaks across the dirty carriage window, and the telegraph poles snatched up the wires ever faster as he found himself staring out abstractedly at the thinning autumn landscape; and even when he managed to drag his attention back to the tedious documents he found it difficult to concentrate. Just before Reading he walked along to the buffet car and bought a Scotch; then another. He felt better.

At four o'clock he put the papers back into their envelope, crossed out his own name, C. A. Roope, and wrote 'T. G. Bartlett' on the cover. Bartlett, as a man, he disliked (he could not disguise that), but he was honest enough to respect the man's experience, and his flair for administration; and he had promised to leave the papers at the Syndicate that afternoon. Bartlett would never allow a single phrase in the minutes of a Syndicate Council meeting to go forward before the relevant draft had been circulated to every member who had attended. And (Roope had to admit) this meticulous minuting had frequently proved extremely wise. Anyway, the wretched papers were done now, and Roope snapped his briefcase to, and looked out at the rain again. The journey had passed more quickly than he could have hoped, and within a few minutes the drenched grey spires of Oxford came into view on his right, and the train drew into the station.

Roope walked through the subway, waited patiently behind the queue at the ticket barrier, and debated for a second or two whether he should bother. But he knew he would. He took the second-class day-return from his wallet and passed it to the ticket collector. 'I'm afraid I owe you some excess fare. I travelled back first.'

'Didn't the ticket inspector come round?'

'No.'

'We-ll. Doesn't really matter then, does it?'

'You sure?'

'Wish everybody was as honest as you, sir.'

'OK then, if you say so.'

Roope took a taxi and after alighting at the Syndicate tipped the driver liberally. Rectangles of pale yellow light shone in the upper storeys of nearby office blocks, and the giant shapes of the trees outside the Syndicate

building loomed black against the darkening sky. The
rain poured down.

Charles Noakes, present incumbent in the key post of
caretaker to the Syndicate, was (for the breed) a comparatively young and helpful man, whose soul was yet to
be soured by years of cumulative concern about the
shutting of windows, the polishing of floors, the management of the boiler, and the setting of the burglar
alarm. He was replacing a fluorescent tube in the
downstairs corridor when Roope entered the building.

'Hello, Noakes. The Secretary in?'

'No, sir. He's been out all the afternoon.'

'Oh.' Roope knocked on Bartlett's door and looked
in. The light was on; but then Roope knew that the
lights would be on in every room. Bartlett always
claimed that the mere switching-on of a fluorescent
tube used as much electricity as leaving it on for about
four hours, and consequently the lights were left on all
day throughout the office – 'for reasons of economy'.
For a brief second Roope thought he heard a noise
inside the room, but there was nothing. Only a note on
the desk which read: 'Friday p.m. Off to Banbury.
Maybe back about five.'

'Not there, is he, sir?' Noakes had descended the
small ladder and was standing outside.

'No. But never mind. I'll have a word with one of the
others.'

'Not many of 'em here, I don't think, sir. Shall I see
for you?'

'No. Don't worry. I'll do it myself.'

He knocked and put his head round Ogleby's door. No Ogleby.

He tried Martin's room. No Martin.

He was knocking quietly on Monica Height's door, and leaning forward to catch any response from within, when the caretaker reappeared in the well-lit, well-polished corridor. 'Looks as if Mr Quinn's the only graduate here, sir. His car's still out the back, anyway. I think the others must have gone.'

When the cat's away, thought Roope . . . He opened Monica's door and looked inside. The room was tidiness itself, the desk clear, the leather chair neatly pushed beneath it.

It was the caretaker who tried Quinn's room, and Roope came up behind him as he looked in. A green anorak was draped over one of the chairs, and the top drawer of the nearest cabinet gaped open to reveal a row of buff-coloured file cases. On the desk, placed under a cheap paperweight, was a note from Quinn for his typist's attention. But Quinn himself was nowhere to be seen.

Roope had often heard tell of Bartlett's meticulous instructions to his staff not only about their paramount duty for ensuring the strictest security on all matters concerning question papers, but also about the importance of leaving some notification of their whereabouts. 'At least he's left a note for us, Noakes. More than some of the others have.'

'I don't think the Secketary would be very happy

44

about this, though.' Noakes gravely closed the top drawer of the cabinet and pushed in the lock.

'Bit of a stickler about that sort of thing, isn't he, old Bartlett?'

'Bit of a stickler about everything, sir.' Yet somehow Noakes managed to convey the impression that if he were on anyone's side, it would be Bartlett's.

'You don't think he's too much of a fusspot?'

'No, sir. I mean, all sorts of people come into the office, don't they? You can't be too careful in a place like this.'

'No. You're absolutely right.'

Noakes felt pleasantly appeased, and having made his point he conceded a little to Roope's suspicions. 'Mind you, sir, I reckon he might have picked a warmer week for practising the fire drill.'

'Gives you those, does he?' Roope grinned. He hadn't been on a fire drill since he was at school.

'We had one today, sir. Twelve o'clock. He had us all there, standing in the cold for something like a quarter of an hour. Freezing it was. I know it's a bit too hot in here but . . .' Noakes was about to embark on an account of his unequal struggle with the Syndicate's antiquated heating system, but Roope was far more interested in Bartlett, it seemed.

'Quarter of an hour? In *this* weather?'

Noakes nodded. 'Mind you, he'd warned us all about it earlier in the week, so we had our coats and everything, and it wasn't raining then, thank goodness, but—'

'Why as long as that, though?'

'Well, there's quite a lot of permanent staff now and we had to tick our names off a list. Huh! Just like we was at school. And the Secketary gave us a little talk . . .'

But Roope was no longer listening; he couldn't stand there talking to the caretaker all night, and he began walking slowly up the corridor. 'Bit odd, isn't it? Everybody here this morning and nobody here this afternoon!'

'You're right, sir. Are you sure I can't help you?'

'No, no. It doesn't matter. I only came to give this envelope to Bartlett. I'll leave it on his desk.'

'I'm going upstairs for a cup o' tea in a minute, sir, when I've fixed this light. Would you like one?'

'No, I've got to be off. Thanks all the same, though.'

Roope took advantage of the Gentlemen's lavatory by the entrance and realized just how hot it was in the building: like walking into a Turkish bath.

Bartlett himself had been addressing a group of Banbury headmasters and headmistresses on the changing pattern of public examinations; and the last question had been authoritatively (and humorously) dispatched at almost exactly the same time that Roope had caught his taxi to the Syndicate. He was soon driving his pride and joy, a dark brown Vanden Plas, at a steady sixty down the twenty-odd-mile stretch to Oxford. He lived out at Botley, on the western side of the city, and as he drove he debated whether to call in at the office or to go straight home. But at Kidlington he found himself beginning to get caught up in the regular evening paralysis, and as he negotiated the roundabouts on Oxford's northern perimeter he decided to turn off right along the ring-road instead of carrying straight over towards the city centre. He would call in the office a bit later, perhaps, when the evening rush-hour had abated.

When he arrived home, at just gone five, his wife informed him that there had been several phone calls; and even as she was giving him the details the wretched thing rang again. How she wished they had a number ex-directory!

On Saturday, 22nd November (as on most Saturdays), the burglar alarm system was switched off at 8.30 a.m., one hour later than on weekdays. During the winter months there were only occasional Saturday workings, and on this particular morning the building was, from all appearances, utterly deserted. Ogleby was on foot, and let himself in quietly. The smell of floor polish, like the smell of cinema sets and old library books, took him back tantalizingly to his early schooldays, but his mind was on other things. Successively he looked into each room on the ground floor in order to satisfy himself that no one was around. But he was aware of this instinctively: there was an eerie, echoing emptiness about the building which the quiet clickings-to of the doors served merely to re-emphasize. He went into his own room and rang a number.

'Morning, Secretary. Hope I didn't get you out of bed? No? Ah, good. Look, I know it sounds a bit silly, but can you remind me when the alarm's turned off on Saturday mornings? I've got to . . . 8.30? Yes, I thought so, but I just wanted to make sure. I didn't want . . . No. Funny, really. I'd somehow got it into my head that there'd been some change . . . No, I see. Well, sorry to trouble you. By the way, did the Banbury meeting go off all right? . . . Good. Well, I'll be off.'

Ogleby walked into Bartlett's room. He looked around quickly and then took out his keys. Botley was at least twenty minutes' drive away: he could probably allow himself at least half an hour. But Ogleby was a cautious soul, and he allowed himself only twenty minutes.

Twenty-five minutes later, as he was sitting at his own desk, he heard someone enter the building, and almost immediately, it seemed, his door was opened.

'You got in all right then, Philip?'

'Yes, thanks. No bells ringing in the police station this morning.'

'Good.' Bartlett blinked behind his spectacles. 'I've, er, got a few things I want to clear up myself.' He closed the door and walked into his own office. He knew what had been happening, of course. For a clever man, Ogleby's excuse about the burglar alarm had been desperately thin. But what had he been looking for? Bartlett opened his cabinets and opened his drawers; but everything was in order. Nothing seemed to have been taken. What *was* there to take? He sat back and frowned deeply: the whole thing was strangely disturbing. He walked up the corridor to Ogleby's room, but Ogleby had gone.

CHAPTER FIVE

MORSE LOOKED DIRECTLY into the large mirror in front of him, and there surveyed the reflection of the smaller hand mirror held behind him, in which, in turn, he considered the occipital regions of what he liked to think of as a distinguished skull. He nodded impassively as the hand mirror was held behind the left side of his neck, nodded again as it was switched to the right, declined the suggested application of a white, greasy-looking hair oil which stood on the surface before him, arose, like a statue unveiled, from the chair, took the proffered tissue, rubbed his face and ears vigorously, and reached for his wallet. That felt much better! He was never happy when his hair began to grow in untidy, curling profusion just above his collar, and he wondered sadly why it now failed to sustain such luxuriance upon the top of his head. He tipped the barber generously and walked out into Summertown. Although not so cold as in recent days, it was drizzling slightly, and he decided to wait for a bus up to his bachelor flat at the top of North Oxford. It was 10.15 a.m. on Tuesday, 25th November.

It would be unlikely that anything of importance would require his immediate attention at HQ, and he had to call in home anyway. It was a ritual with Morse. As a young recruit in the army he had been driven almost mad by the service issue of prickly vests, prickly shirts, and prickly trousers. His mother had told him that he had an extremely sensitive skin; and he believed her. It was always the same after a haircut. He would take off his shirt and vest, and dip his head into a basin full of hot water. Bliss! He would shampoo his hair twice, and then flannel his face and ears thoroughly. He would then rub his back with a towel, dry his hair, wash down the short, black hairs from the sides of the basin, select a clean vest and shirt, and finally comb his hair with loving care in front of the bathroom mirror.

But this morning it *wasn't* quite the same. He was just about to rinse off the second application of medicated shampoo when the phone rang. He swore savagely. Who the hell?

'Hoped I might find you at home, sir. I couldn't find anyone who'd seen you at the office.'

'So what? I've had a haircut. Not a crime, is it?'

'Can you get here straight away, sir?' Lewis's tone was suddenly grave.

'Give me five minutes. What's up?'

'We've got a body, sir.'

'Whereabouts are you?'

'I'm phoning from the station. Do you know Pine-wood Close?'

'No.'

'Well, I think you'd be best to call here first anyway, sir.'

'OK. Wait for me there.'

Chief Superintendent Strange was waiting for him, too. He stood impatiently on the steps outside the Thames

51

Valley Police HQ in Kidlington, as Morse hurriedly parked the Lancia and jumped out.

'Where have you been, Morse?'

'Sorry, sir. I've had a haircut.'

'You *what*?'

Morse said nothing, not the slightest flicker of guilt or annoyance betraying itself in the light grey eyes.

'A fine advertisement, eh? Citizens under police care and protection getting themselves bumped off, and the only Chief Inspector I've got on duty is having his bloody hair cut!'

Morse said nothing.

'Look, Morse. You're in charge of this case – is that clear? You can have Lewis here if you want him.' Strange turned away, but suddenly remembered something else. 'And you won't get another haircut until you've sorted this little lot out – that's an order!'

'Perhaps I shan't need one, sir.' Morse winked happily at Lewis and led the way into his office. 'What's it look like from behind?'

'Very nice, sir. They've cut it very nicely.'

Morse sat back in his black leather armchair and beamed at Lewis. 'Well? What have you got to tell me?'

'Chap called Quinn, sir. Lives on the ground floor of a semi-detached in Pinewood Close. He's been dead for a good while by the look of him. Poisoned, I shouldn't wonder. He works' ('worked', muttered Morse) 'at the Foreign Examinations Syndicate down the Woodstock Road somewhere; and one of his colleagues got worried about him and came out and found him. I got the call about a quarter to ten, and I went along straight away with Dickson and had a quick look round. I left him there, and came back to call you.'

'Well, here I am, Lewis. What do you want me to do?'

'Knowing you, sir, I thought you might want me to arrest the chap who found him.'

Morse grinned. 'Is he here?'

'In the Interview Room. I've got a rough statement from him, but it'll need a bit of brushing up before he signs it. You'll want to see him, I suppose?'

'Yes, but that can wait. Got a car ready?'

'Waiting outside, sir.'

'You've not called the path boys in yet, I hope?'

'No. I thought I ought to wait for you.'

'Good. Go and get your statement tarted up and I'll see you outside in ten minutes or so.'

Morse made two phone calls, combed his hair again, and felt inordinately happy.

Several faces peeped from behind ground-floor lace-curtained windows as the police car drove into Pinewood Close, a small, undistinguished crescent wherein eight semi-detached houses, erected some fifty years previously, stood gently fading into a semi-dignified senescence. Most of the wooden fences that bordered the properties managed to sustain only a precarious pretence to any upright posture, the slats uncreosoted and insecure, the crossrails mildewed, sodden with rain, and rotten. Only at each end of the crescent had the original builder left sufficient sideroom for the erection of any garage, and it was at the house at the extreme left that the bulky figure of Constable Dickson stood, stamping his feet on the damp concrete in front of a prefabricated unpainted garage, and talking to a woman in her early fifties, the owner of the property and rentier of some half a dozen other houses in the neighbourhood. But whatever other benefits her various incomes conferred upon her, her affluence appeared not to be reflected in her wardrobe: she wore no stockings and was pulling a shabby old coat more closely over a grubby white blouse as Morse and Lewis stepped out of the car.

''Ere come the brains, missus,' muttered Dickson, and stepped forward to greet the Chief Inspector. 'This is Mrs Jardine, sir. She owns the property and she's the one who let us in.'

Morse nodded a friendly greeting, took the Yale key from Dickson, and instructed him to take Mrs Jardine to the police car and get a statement from her. He himself stood for a while in silence with his back to the house, and looked around him. In a kerbed oval plot, a thick cluster of small trees and variegated bushes sheltered the houses from the main road and gave to the crescent the semblance of partial privacy. But the small curved stretch of road itself was poorly maintained and unevenly surfaced, with a long, irregular black scar, running parallel to the pavement, where the water mains had recently been dug up again. The gutter was full of sopping brown leaves, and the lamppost immediately outside No 1 had been vandalized. The front door of the next house opened a few inches and a middle-aged woman directed inquisitive eyes towards the centre of activity.

'Good morning,' said Morse brightly.

The door was closed in a flash, and Morse turned round to survey the garage. Although the claw of the lock which secured the doors was not pushed home, he touched nothing, contenting himself with a quick glance through the glass panels at the top. Inside he saw a dark blue Morris 1300 which allowed little more than a foot of space between the wall and the driver's door. He walked over to the front porch and inserted the key. 'Good job he doesn't drive a Cadillac, Lewis.'

'Didn't,' corrected Lewis quietly.

The front door of No 1 Pinewood Close opened on to a narrow hallway, with a row of clothes pegs at the foot of the staircase which climbed the wall to the left. Morse stood inside and pointed to the door immediately to his right. 'This the one?'

'Next one, sir.'

The door was closed and Morse took out his pen and depressed the handle carefully. 'I hope you haven't left your prints all over the place, Lewis?'

'I opened it the same way as you, sir.'

Inside the room the electric light was still turned on; the dull-orange curtains were drawn; the gas fire was burning low; and lying in a foetal posture on the carpet was the body of a young man. The fire was flanked by two old, but comfortable-looking armchairs; and beside the one to the right, on a low french-polished coffee table, stood a bottle of dry sherry, almost full, and a cheap-looking sherry glass, almost empty. Morse bent forward and sniffed the pale, clear liquid. 'Did you know, Lewis, that about eighteen per cent of men and about four per cent of women can't smell cyanide?'

'It *is* poison, then?'

'Smells like it. Peach blossom, bitter almonds – take your pick.'

The dead man's face was turned towards them, away from the fire, and Morse knelt down and looked at it. A small quantity of dry froth crusted the twisted mouth, and the bearded jaw was tightly clenched in death; the pupils of the open eyes appeared widely dilated, and the skin of the face was a morbid, blotchy blue. 'All the classic symptoms, Lewis. We hardly need a post-mortem on this one. Hydrocyanic acid. Anyway the path boys should be here any minute.' He stood up and walked over to the curtains, which had obviously shrunk in a not particularly recent wash, and which gaped open slightly towards the top. Outside Morse could see the narrow garden, with its patchy, poor-quality grass, a small vegetable plot at the far end, and a section of fencing missing on the left. But the view appeared to convey little of significance in his mind, and he turned his attention back to the room itself. Along the wall opposite the fire were a dozen or so bundles of books, neatly tied with stout cord, and a dark mahogany sideboard, the left-hand door of which gaped open to reveal a small collection of assorted tumblers and glasses, and an unopened bottle of whisky. Everywhere seemed remarkably clean and tidy. A small wastepaper basket stood in the shallow alcove to the left of the fire; and inside the basket was a ball of paper, which Morse picked out and smoothed gently on the top of the sideboard:

> Mr Quinn. I can't do all the cleaning this afternoon because Mr Evans is off sick and I've got to get him a prescription from the doctor. So I'll call back and finish just after six if that's convenient for you.
> A. Evans (Mrs)

Morse handed the note over to Lewis. 'Interesting.'

'How long do you think he's been dead, sir?'

Morse looked down at Quinn once more and shrugged his shoulders. 'I dunno. Two or three days, I should think.'

'It's a wonder someone didn't find him earlier.'

'Ye-es. You say he just has these downstairs rooms?'

'So Mrs Jardine says. There's a young couple living upstairs usually, but she's in the John Radcliffe having a baby, and he works nights at Cowley and he's been staying with his parents in Oxford somewhere.'

'Mm.' Morse made as if to leave, but suddenly stopped. The bottom of the door had been amateurishly planed to enable it to ride over the carpet and a noticeable draught was coming beneath it, occasionally setting the low, blue gas jets flickering fitfully into brighter yellow flames.

'Funny, isn't it, Lewis? If I lived in this room I wouldn't choose the armchair immediately in line with the draught.'

'Looks as if he did, sir.'

'I wonder, Lewis. I wonder if he did.'

The front-door bell rang and Morse sent Lewis to answer it. 'Tell 'em they can start as soon as they like.' He walked out of the room and through into the kitchen at the back of the house. Again, everywhere was tidy. On a red Formica-topped table stood a stack of recently purchased provisions: half a dozen eggs in their plastic container; $\frac{1}{2}$ lb butter; $\frac{1}{2}$ lb English Cheddar; two generous slices of prime steak under a cellophane wrapper; and a brown paper bag full of mushrooms. Beside the groceries was a curling pay-out slip from the Quality supermarket, and a flicker of excitement showed in Morse's grey eyes as he looked it through.

'Lewis!'

Nothing else here looked particularly interesting: a sink unit, a gas cooker, a fridge, two kitchen stools, and by the side of the back door, filling the space under the stairs, a small larder. Lewis, who had been chatting to the police surgeon, appeared at the door. 'Sir?'

'What's going on in there?'

'Doc says he's been poisoned.'

'Amazing thing – medical science, Lewis! But we've got other things to worry about for the minute. I want you to make a complete inventory of the food in the fridge and in this larder here.'

'Oh.' Lewis was almost thinking that a man of his own rank and experience should be above such fourth-grade clerical chores; but he had worked with Morse before, and knew that whatever other faults he had the Chief Inspector seldom wasted his own or other people's time on trivial or unnecessary tasks. He heard himself say he would get on with it – immediately.

'I'm going back to the station, Lewis. You stay here until I get back.'

Outside, Morse found Dickson and Mrs Jardine standing beside the police car. 'I want you to drive me back to HQ, Dickson.' He turned to Mrs Jardine. 'You've been very kind and helpful. Thank you very much. You've got a car?'

The landlady nodded and walked away. In truth, she felt disappointed that her small part in the investigation seemed now to be over, and that she had warranted no more than a cursory question from the rather abrupt man who appeared to be in charge. But as she drove away from the crescent her thoughts soon veered to other, more practical considerations. Would anyone be over-anxious to move into the rooms so lately rented by that nice young Mr Quinn? People didn't like that sort of thing. But as she reached the outskirts of Oxford she comforted herself with the salutary thought that the dead are soon forgotten. Yes, she would soon be able to let the rooms again. Just give it a month or so.

Morse read the statement aloud to the youngish man seated rather nervously at the small table in Interview Room No 1.

I have known Nicholas Quinn for three months. He came to work at the Foreign Examinations Syndicate as an assistant secretary on 1st September this year.

On Monday, 24 November, he did not appear at the office and did not ring in to say that anything was wrong. It is not unusual for the graduates to take a day or two off when they can, but the Secretary, Dr Bartlett, always insists that he should be kept fully informed of any such arrangement. None of my colleagues saw Mr Quinn on Monday, and no one knew where he was. This morning, Tuesday, 25th November, Dr Bartlett came to my ofice and said that Mr Quinn had still not arrived. He said that he had tried to phone him, but that there was no reply. He then asked me to drive round to Mr Quinn's house and I did so, arriving at about 9.30 a.m. The front door was locked and no one answered the doorbell. I could see that Mr Quinn's car was still in the garage, so I proceeded to the back of the house. The light was on in the ground-floor room and the curtains were drawn; but there was a gap in the curtains and I looked inside. I could see someone lying quite still on the floor in front of the fireplace, and I knew that something was seriously wrong. I therefore rang the police immediately from the public call box in the main street, and was told to wait at the house until the police came. When Sergeant Lewis arrived with a constable, they discovered who owned the house. The landlady turned up with the key about ten minutes later. The police then proceeded into the house for a short while, and when Sergeant Lewis came out he told me that I must prepare myself for a shock. He said that Mr Quinn was dead.

'You happy to sign this?' Morse pushed the statement across the table.

'I didn't use the word "proceeded".'

'Ah, you must forgive us, sir. We never "go" anywhere in the force, you know. We always "proceed".'

Donald Martin accepted the explanation with a weak smile and signed the statement with nervy flourish.

'How well did you know Mr Quinn, sir?'

'Not very well really. He's only been with us—'

'So you say in your statement. But why did the Secretary send you – not one of the others?'

'I don't know. I suppose I knew him as well as any of them.'

'What did you expect to find?'

'Well, I thought he was probably ill or something, and couldn't let us know.'

'There's a phone in the house.'

'Yes, but it could have – well, it could have been a heart attack, or something like that.'

Morse nodded. 'I see. Do you happen to know where his parents live?'

'Somewhere in Yorkshire, I think. But the office could—'

'Of course. Did he have a girlfriend?'

Martin was aware of the Inspector's hard grey eyes upon him and his mouth was suddenly very dry. 'Not that I know of.'

'No pretty fillies he fancied at the office?'

'I don't think so.' The hesitation was minimal but, for Morse, sufficient to set a few fanciful notions aflutter.

'I'm told such things are not unknown, sir. He was a bachelor, I take it?'

'Yes.'

'You a married man, sir?'

'Yes.'

'Mm. Perhaps you've forgotten what it's like to be single.' Morse would have been happier if Martin had told him not to talk such drivel. But Martin didn't.

'I don't quite see what you're getting at, Inspector.'

'Oh, don't worry about that, sir. I often don't know what I'm getting at myself.' He stood up, and Martin did the same, fastening his overcoat. 'You'd better get back to the office, or they'll be getting worried about you. Tell the Secretary I'll be in touch with him as soon as I can – and tell him to lock up Mr Quinn's room.'

'You've no idea—?' said Martin quietly.

'Yes, I'm afraid I have, sir. He was almost certainly murdered.' The sinister word seemed to hang on the air, and the room was suddenly and eerily still.

CHAPTER SIX

DURING THE PREVIOUS decade the Foreign Examinations Syndicate had thrown its net round half the globe; and for its hundred or so overseas centres the morning of Tuesday, 25th November, had been fixed for the 'retake' of the Ordinary-level English Language papers. For the vast majority of the foreign candidates involved, the morning afforded the chance of a second bite at the cherry; and such was the importance of a decent grade in English Language, either for future employment or for admission to higher education, that there were very few of the candidates who were treating the two question papers (Essay and Comprehension) with anything but appropriate respect. Only those few who had been ill during the main summer examination were taking the examination for the first time; the remainder were the 'returned empties' who, either through some congenital incapacity or a prior history of monumental idleness, had yet to succeed in persuading the examiners that they had reached a standard of acceptable competence in the skills of English usage.

At 11.55 a.m. this same morning, in strict accord with the explicit instructions issued by the examining body, invigilators in Geneva, in East and West Africa, in Bombay, and in the Persian Gulf, were reminding their candidates that only five minutes remained before scripts would be collected; that all candidates should ensure that their full names and index numbers appeared on each sheet of their work; and that all sheets must be handed in in the correct order. Some few candidates were now scribbling furiously and for the most part fruitlessly; but the majority were having a final look through their answers, shuffling their sheets into order, and then leaning back in more relaxed postures, shooting the occasional grin at fellow examinees who sat at desks (the regulation five feet apart) in commandeered classrooms or converted gymnasiums.

At twelve noon, in an air-conditioned, European-style classroom in the Sheikdom of Al-jamara, a young Englishman, who was invigilating his first examination, gave the order to stop writing. There were only five pupils in the room, all Arabs, all of whom had finished writing several minutes previously. One of the boys (not a pupil of the school, but the son of one of the sheiks) had in fact finished his work some considerable time earlier, and had been sitting back in his chair, arms folded, an arrogant, self-satisfied smirk upon his dark, semitic features. He was the last of the five candidates, and handed in his script without saying a word.

Left alone, the young Englishman filled in the invigilation form with great care. Fortunately, no candidate had failed to turn up for the examination, and the complexities of the sections dealing with 'absentees' could be ignored. In the appropriate columns he filled in the names and index numbers of the five candidates, and prepared to place the attendance sheet, together with the scripts, in the official buff-coloured envelope. As he did so his eye fell momentarily upon the work of Muhammad Dubal, Index Number 5; and he saw immediately that it was very good – infinitely better than that of the other four. But then the sheik's son had doubtless had the privilege of high-class private tuition. Ah well. There would be plenty of opportunity for him to try to jack up the standards of his own pupils a bit before next summer . . .

He left the room, licking the flap of the envelope as he did so, and walked through to the school secretary's office.

It was just after noon, too, that Morse returned to Pinewood Close. He made no effort to move on the curious crowd who thronged the narrow crescent, for he had never understood why the general public should so frequently be castigated for wishing to eye-witness those rare moments of misfortune or tragedy that occurred in their vicinity. (He would have been one of them himself.) He threaded his way past the three police cars, past the ambulance, its blue light flashing, and entered the house once more. There were almost as many people inside as outside.

'Sad thing, death,' said Morse.

'*Mors, mortis,* feminine,' mumbled the ageing police surgeon.

Morse nodded morosely. 'Don't remind me.'

'Never mind, Morse. We're all dying slowly.'

'How long's he been dead?'

'Dunno. Could be four, five days – not less than three, I shouldn't think.'

'Not too much help, are you?'

'I shall have to take a closer look at him.'

'Have a guess.'

'Unofficially?'

'Unofficially.'

'Friday night or Saturday morning.'

'Cyanide?'

'Cyanide.'

'You think it took long?'

'No. Pretty quick stuff if you get the right dose down you.'

'Minutes?'

'Much quicker. I'll have to take the bottle and the glass, of course.'

Morse turned to the two other men in the room who had been brushing the likeliest-looking surfaces with powder.

'Anything much?'

'Seems like his prints all over the place, sir.'

'Hardly surprising.'

'Somebody else's, though.'

'The cleaner's, most likely.'

'Just the one set of prints on the bottle, sir – and on the glass.'

'Mm.'

'Can we move the body?'

'Sooner the better. I suppose we'd better go through his pockets, though.' He turned again to the surgeon. 'You do it, will you, doc?'

'You getting squeamish, Morse? By the way, did you know he wore a hearing aid?'

*

At one minute to two, Morse got to his feet and looked down at Lewis.

'Time for another if you drink that up smartish.'

'Not for me, sir. I've had enough.'

'The secret of a happy life, Lewis, is to know when to stop and then to go that little bit further.'

'Just a half, then.'

Morse walked to the bar and beamed at the barmaid. But in truth he felt far from happy. He had long since recognized the undoubted fact that his imagination was almost invariably fired by beer, especially by beer in considerable quantities. But today, for some reason, his mind seemed curiously disengaged; sluggish even. After the body had been removed he had spent some time in the downstairs front room, used by Quinn as a bedroom-cum-study; he had opened drawers, looked through papers and folders, and half-stripped the bed. But it had all been an aimless, perfunctory exercise, and he had found nothing more incriminating than the previous month's copy of *Playboy*; and it was whilst sitting on the uncovered mattress scanning a succession of naked breasts and crotches that Lewis, after completing his tedious inventories, had found him.

'Anything interesting, sir?'

'No.' Morse had guiltily returned the magazine to the desk and fastened up his overcoat.

Just as they were about to leave, Morse had noticed the green anorak on one of the clothes pegs in the narrow hallway.

CHAPTER SEVEN

BARTLETT KNEW THAT the man had been drinking and found himself feeling surprised and disappointed. He had been expecting the call all the afternoon, but it had not come through until half past three. The four of them had been seated in his office since lunchtime (the red light on outside) talking in hushed voices amongst themselves about the shattering news. Graphically Martin had recounted again and again the details of his morning discovery, and had taken some muted pleasure, even in these grim moments, at finding himself, quite unprecedentedly, at the centre of his colleagues' attention. But invariably the conversation had reverted to the perplexing question of who had been the last to see Quinn alive – and where. They all agreed, it seemed, that it had been on Friday, but exactly when and exactly where no one seemed able to remember. Or cared to tell . . .

Monica Height watched the Inspector carefully as he came in, and told herself, as they were briefly introduced, that his eyes held hers a fraction longer than was strictly necessary. She liked his voice, too; and when he informed them that each would be interviewed separately, either by himself or by Sergeant Lewis (standing silently by the door), she found herself hoping that in her case it would be him. Not that she need have worried on that score: Morse had already mentally

allocated her to himself. But first he had to see what
Bartlett could tell him.

'You've locked Quinn's door, I hope, sir.'

'Yes. Immediately I got your message.'

'Well, I think you'd better tell me something about
this place: what you do, how you do it, anything at all
you think may help. Quinn was murdered, sir – little
doubt about that; and my job's to find out who murdered him. There's just a possibility, of course, that his
murder's got nothing at all to do with this place, or with
the people here; but it seems much more probable that
I may be able to find something in the office here that
will give me some sort of lead. So, I'm afraid I shall be
having to badger you all for a few days – you realize
that, don't you?'

Bartlett nodded. 'We shall all do our best to help
you, Inspector. Please feel completely free to carry out
whatever inquiries you think fit.'

'Thank you, sir. Now, what can you tell me?'

During the next half-hour Morse learned a great
deal. Bartlett told him about the purpose, commitments, and organization of the Syndicate, about the
personnel involved at all stages in the running of public
examinations. And Morse found himself surprised and
impressed: surprised by the unexpected complexities of
the operations involved; and, above all, impressed by
the extraordinary efficiency and grasp of the Pickwick-
ian little Secretary sitting behind his desk.

'What about Quinn himself?'

Bartlett opened a drawer and took out a folder. 'I looked this out for you, Inspector. It's Quinn's application for the job here. It'll tell you more than I can.'

Morse opened the folder and his eyes hurriedly scanned the contents: curriculum vitae, testimonials, letters from three referees, and the application form itself, across the top of which Bartlett had written: 'Appointed w.e.f. 1st Sept.' But again Morse's mind remained infuriatingly blank. The cogs in the machine were beginning to turn all right, but somehow they refused to engage. He closed the folder, defensively mumbling something about studying it later, and looked again at Bartlett. He wondered how that clear and supremely efficient mind would be tackling the problem of Quinn's murder, and it appeared that Bartlett could almost read his thoughts.

'You know that he was deaf, don't you, Inspector?'

'Deaf? Oh yes.' The police surgeon had mentioned it, but Morse had taken little notice.

'We were all very impressed by the way he coped with his disability.'

'How deaf was he?'

'He would probably have gone completely deaf in a few years' time. That was the prognosis, anyway.'

For the first time since Bartlett had been talking the merest flicker of interest showed itself in Morse's eyes. 'Little surprising you appointed him, perhaps, sir?'

'I think it's you who would have been surprised, Inspector. You could hardly tell he was deaf, you see.

Apart from dealing with the phone, which *was* a problem, he was quite remarkable. He really was.'

'Did you, er, did you appoint him, you know, because he *was* deaf?'

'Did we feel sorry for him, you mean? Oh no. It seemed to the, er, the, er, committee that he was the best man in the field.'

'Which committee was that?'

Did Morse catch a hint of guardedness in Bartlett's eyes? He wasn't sure. What he did know was that the teeth of the smallest cog had now begun to bite. He sat back more happily in his chair.

'We, er, had all twelve Syndics on that committee – plus myself, of course.'

'Syndics? They're, er—?'

'They're like governors of a school, really.'

'They don't work here?'

'Good gracious, no. They're all university dons. They just meet here twice a term to see if we're doing our job properly.'

'Have you got their names here?'

Morse looked with interest down the typed list that Bartlett handed to him. Printed beside the name of each of the Syndics were full details of university, college, degrees, doctorates and other academic honours, and one name in the list jumped out at him. 'Most of them Oxford men, I see, sir.'

'Natural enough, isn't it?'

'Just one or two from Cambridge.'

'Ye-es.'

'Wasn't Quinn at Magdalene College, Cambridge?' Morse began to reach for the folder, but Bartlett immediately confirmed the fact.

'I see that Mr Roope was at the same college, sir.'

'Was he? I'd never noticed that before.'

'You notice most things, if I may say so.'

'I always associate Roope with Christ Church, I suppose. He's been appointed a fellow there: "student", rather, if we want to be pedantic, Inspector.' His eyes were utterly guileless now, and Morse wondered if he might earlier have been mistaken.

'What's Roope's subject?'

'He's a chemist.'

'Well, well.' Morse tried to suppress the note of excitement in his voice, but realized that he wasn't succeeding. 'How old is he? Do you know?'

'Youngish. Thirty or so.'

'About Quinn's age, then?'

'About that.'

'Now, sir. Just one more thing.' He looked at his watch and found that it was already a quarter to five. 'When did you last see Quinn? Can you remember?'

'Last Friday, sometime. I know that. But it's a funny thing. Before you came in, we were all trying to think when we'd last seen him. Very difficult, you know, to pinpoint it exactly. I certainly saw him late on Friday morning; but I can't be sure about Friday afternoon. I had to go to a meeting in Banbury at three o'clock, and I'm just not sure if I saw him before I went.'

'What time did you leave the office, sir?'

'About a quarter past two.'

'You must drive pretty fast.'

'I've got a fast car.'

'Twenty-two, twenty-three miles?'

Bartlett's eyes twinkled. 'We've all got our little weaknesses, Inspector, but I try to keep within the speed limits.'

Morse heard himself say he hoped so, and decided it was high time he saw Miss Monica Height. But before he did so he had a very much more urgent call to pay. 'Where's the nearest Gents? I'm dying for—'

'There's one right here, Inspector.' He got up and opened the door to the right of his desk. Inside was a tiny lavatory with a small wash basin tucked away behind the door; and as Morse blissfully emptied his aching bladder, Bartlett was reminded of the mighty outpourings of Niagara.

After only a few minutes with Monica Height, Morse found himself wondering how the rest of the staff could ever manage to keep their hands off her, and cynically suspected that perhaps they didn't. The bright-green, flower-pattered dress she wore was stretched too tightly across her wide thighs, yet somehow managed to mould itself softly and suggestively around her full breasts. Biddable, by the look of it – and eminently beddable. She wore little make-up, but her habit of passing her tongue round her mouth imparted a moist sheen to her slightly pouting lips; and she exuded a perfume that seemed to invite instant and glorious gratification. Morse felt quite sure that at certain times and in certain moods she must have proved well-nigh irresistible to the young and the susceptible. To Martin, perhaps? To Quinn? Yes, surely the temptation must always have been there. Morse knew that he himself, the middle-aged and the susceptible . . . But he pushed the thought to the back of his mind. What about Ogleby? Or even Bartlett, perhaps? Whew! It was a thought! Morse recalled the passage from Gibbon about one of the tests designed for the young novitiate: stick him in a sack all night with a naked nun and see if . . . Morse shook his head abruptly and passed his hand over his eyes. It was always the same when he'd had a lot of beer.

'Do you mind if I just ring my daughter, Inspector?' (Daughter?) 'I'm usually on my way home by this time, and she'll probably wonder where I've got to.' Morse listened as she rang a number and explained her whereabouts.

'How old is your daughter, Miss, er, er, Miss Height?'

She smiled understandingly. 'It's all right, Inspector. I'm divorced, and Sally's sixteen.'

'You must have married young.' (Sixteen!)

'I was foolish enough to marry at eighteen, Inspector. I'm sure you had much more sense than that.'

'Me? Oh yes, em, no, I mean. I'm not married myself, you see.' Their eyes held again for a brief second and Morse sensed he could be living dangerously. It was time he asked the fair Monica a few important questions.

'When did you last see Mr Quinn?'

'It's funny you should ask that. We were only . . .' It was like listening to a familiar record. She'd seen him on Friday morning – quite sure of that. But Friday afternoon? She couldn't quite remember. It was difficult. After all, Friday was – what? – five days ago now. ('Could have been four, five days' hadn't the police surgeon said?)

'Did you like Mr Quinn?' Morse watched her reaction carefully, and suspected that this was one question for which she hadn't quite prepared herself.

'I haven't known him all that long, of course. What is it? Two or three months? But I liked him, yes. Very nice sort of person.'

'Did he like you?'

'What do you mean by that, Inspector?'

What *did* he mean? 'I just thought – well, I just thought—'

'You mean did he find me attractive?'

'I don't suppose he could help that.'

'You're very nice, Inspector.'

'Did he ever ask you out with him?'

'He asked me out to the pub once or twice at lunchtimes.'

'And you went?'

'Why not?'

'What did he drink?'

'Sherry, I think.'

'What about you?'

Her tongue moistened her lips once more. 'I've got slightly more expensive tastes myself.'

'Where did you go?'

'The Horse and Trumpet – just at the end of the road. Nice, cosy little place. You'd love it.'

'Perhaps I'll see you in there one day.'

'Why not?'

'Your tastes are expensive, you say?'

'We could work something out.'

Again their eyes met and the danger bells were ringing in Morse's brain. He stood up: 'I'm sorry to have kept you so long, Miss Height. I hope you'll apologize for me to your daughter.'

'Oh, she'll be all right. She's been home a lot of the time recently. She's retaking a few O-levels, and the school lets her go home when she hasn't got an examination.'

'I see.' Morse stood at the door, and seemed reluctant to leave. 'We shall be seeing each other again, no doubt.'

'I hope so, Inspector.' She spoke pleasantly and quietly and – damn it, yes! – sexily.

Her last words re-echoed in Morse's mind as he walked abstractedly down the corridor.

'At last!' muttered Lewis to himself. He had been sitting in the entrance foyer for the past twenty minutes with Bartlett, Ogleby and Martin. All three had their overcoats and briefcases with them but were obviously reluctant to depart until Morse came and said the word. The death of Quinn had obviously thrown a pall of gloom over everything, and they had little to say to each other. Lewis had liked Ogleby, but had learned little from him: he'd remembered seeing Quinn the previous Friday morning, but not in the early afternoon; and to each of Lewis's other questions he had appeared to answer frankly, if uninformatively. Martin, though, had seemed a completely different proposition: intense and nervous now, as the shock of the whole business seemed to catch up with him, he'd said he couldn't really remember seeing Quinn at all on Friday.

Rather awkwardly, Morse thanked them for their co-operation, and gathered from Bartlett that it would be perfectly in order for himself and Lewis to stay in the building: the caretaker would be on the premises until at least 7.30 p.m., and naturally the building would be kept open for them as long as they wished. But before handing over the keys to Quinn's office and to his filing cabinets, Bartlett gave the policemen a stern-faced little lecture on the strictly confidential nature of most of the material they would find; it was of the greatest import-ance therefore that they should remember . . . Yes, yes, yes, yes. Morse realized how he would have hated working under Bartlett, a man for whom the sin against the Holy Ghost was clearly that of leaving filing cabinets unlocked whilst nipping out to pee.

After they had gone, Morse suggested a quick stroll round the block, and Lewis responded willingly. The building was far too hot, and the cool night air was clean and refreshing. On the corner of the Woodstock Road they passed the Horse and Trumpet and Morse automatically consulted his watch.

'Nice little pub, I should think, Lewis. Ever been in?'

'No, sir, and I've had enough beer, anyway. I'd much rather have a cup o' tea.' Relieved that it still wanted ten minutes to opening time, he told Morse of his interviews, and Morse in turn told Lewis of his. Neither of them, it seemed, felt unequivocally convinced that he had stared into the eyes of a murderer.

'Nice-looker, isn't she, sir?'

'Uh? Who do you mean, Lewis?'

'Come off it, sir!'

'I suppose she is – if you go for that sort.'

'I notice you kept her all to yourself.'

'One o' the perks, isn't it?'

'I'm a bit surprised you didn't get a bit more out of her, though. Of the lot of 'em she seemed to me the one most likely to drop her inhibitions pretty quickly.'

'Drop her knickers pretty smartish, too, I shouldn't wonder.'

Lewis sometimes felt that Morse was quite unnecessarily crude.

CHAPTER EIGHT

QUINN'S OFFICE WAS large and well furnished. Two blue leather chairs, one on each side, were neatly pushed beneath the writing desk, the surface of which was clear, except for the in- and out-trays (the former containing several letters, the latter empty) and a large blotter, with an assortment of odd names and numbers, and meaningless squiggles scribbled round its perimeter in black biro. Lining two complete walls, right up to the ceiling, were row upon row of History texts and editions of the English classics, with the occasional yellow, red, green and white spine adding a further splash of colour to the brightly lit and cheerful room. Three dark green filing cabinets stood along the third wall, whilst the fourth carried a large plywood notice board and, one above the other, reproductions of Atkinson Grimshaw's paintings of the docks at Hull and Liverpool. Only the white carpet which covered most of the floor showed obvious signs of wear, and as Morse seated himself magisterially in Quinn's chair he noticed that immediately beneath the desk the empty wastepaper basket covered a patch that was almost threadbare. To his right, on a small black-topped table stood two telephones, one white, one grey, and beside them a pile of telephone directories.

'You go through the cabinets, Lewis. I'll try the drawers here.'

'Are we looking for anything in particular, sir?'

'Not that I know of.'

Lewis decided to plod along in his own methodical manner: at least it promised to be a bit more interesting than listing tins of rice pudding.

Almost immediately he began to realize what an enormous amount of love and labour went into the final formulation of question papers for public examinations. The top drawer of the first cabinet was stuffed with bulky buff-coloured folders, each containing copies of drafts, first proofs, first revises, second revises – even third revises – of papers to be set for the Ordinary-level English syllabuses. 'I reckon I could get a few quick O-levels this way, sir.'

Morse mumbled something about not being worth the paper they were printed on, and carried on with his own desultory investigation of the top right-hand drawer of Quinn's desk, wherein it soon became abundantly clear that he was unlikely to make any cosmic discoveries: paper-clips, bulldog-clips, elastic bands, four fine-pointed black biros, a ruler, a pair of scissors, two birthday cards ('Love, Monica' written in one of them – well, well!), a packet of yellow pencils, a pencil sharpener, several letters from the University Chest about the transfer of pension rights to the University Superannuation Scheme, and a letter from the Centre for the Deaf informing Quinn that the lip-reading classes had been transferred from Oxpens to Headington Tech. After poking haphazardly around, Morse turned to the books behind him and found himself in the middle of the M's. He selected Marvell's *Collected Poems,* and as if someone else had recently been studying the same page, the book fell open of its own accord at the poem written 'To His Coy Mistress', and Morse read again the lines which had formed part of his own mental baggage for rather more years than he wished to remember:

'The grave's a fine and private place,
  But none, I think, do there embrace . . .'

Yes, Quinn was lying in the police mortuary, and Quinn had hoped his hopes and dreamed his dreams as every other mortal soul . . . He slotted the book back into its shelf, and turned with a slightly chastened spirit to the second drawer.

The two men worked for three-quarters of an hour, and Lewis felt himself becoming progressively more dispirited. 'Do you think we're wasting our time, sir?'

'Are you thirsty, or something?'

'I just don't know what I'm looking for, that's all.'

Morse said nothing. He didn't either.

By seven o'clock Lewis had looked through the contents of two of the three cabinets, and now inserted the key into the third, whence he took a further armful of thick folders and once again sat down to his task. The first file contained many carbons of letters, stretching back over two years, all marked GB/MF, and the replies from various members of the Syndicate's English Committee, all beginning 'Dear George'.

'This must be the fellow Quinn took over from, sir.'

Morse nodded cursorily and resumed his study of a black Letts desk diary which was the only object of even minimal interest he had so far unearthed. But Quinn had obviously shown no inclination to emulate an Evelyn or a Pepys, and little more than the dates and times, of various meetings had been entered. 'Birthday' (under 23rd October), and 'I owe Donald £1' seemed to form the only concession to an otherwise autobiographical blank. And since he could think of nothing more purposeful to pursue, Morse idly counted the meetings: ten of them, almost all for the revisions of various question papers, within twelve weeks or so. Not bad going. And one or two other meetings: one with the English Committee on 30th September and one, a two-day meeting, with AED – whatever that was – on the 4th and 5th November.

'What's AED stand for, Lewis?'

'Dunno, sir.'

'Have a guess.'

'Association of Eccentric Dentists.'

Morse grinned and shut the diary. 'You nearly finished?'

'Two more drawers.'

'Think it's worth it?'

'Might as well go through with it now, sir.'

'OK.' Morse leaned back in the chair, his hands behind his head, and looked across the room once more. Not a particularly memorable start to a case, perhaps; but it was early days yet. He decided to put a call through to HQ. The grey telephone seemed the one used for outside calls, and Morse pulled it towards him. But as soon as he had picked up the receiver he put it down again. Underneath the orange code book he saw a letter which had escaped his notice hitherto. It was written on the official notepaper of the Frederic

Delius School, Bradford, and was dated Monday, 17th
November:

> Dear Nick,
> Don't forget me when you sort out your examining
> teams for next year. I trust you've had the form back
> by now. Gryce wasn't all that co-operative about the
> testimonial at first, but you'll have noticed that I'm
> 'a man of sound scholarship, with considerable
> experience of O- and A-level work'. What more can
> you ask for? Martha sends her love, and we all hope
> you'll be up here on your old stamping ground this
> Christmas. We've decided we can't please both lots
> of parents, and so we are going to please neither –
> and stay at home. By the way, old sour-guts has
> applied for the headship of the new Comprehensive!
> O tempora! O mores!
> As ever,
> Brian.

The letter was ticked through in black biro, and Morse
considered it carefully for a moment. Had Quinn rung
up his friend? A former colleague, possibly? If so, when?
It might be worth while finding out.

But it was Lewis who, quite accidentally, was to stumble
through the trip-wire and set off the explosive that blew
the case wide open, although he himself was quite
unaware at the time of his momentous achievement. As
he was about to jam the latest batch of files back into its
cabinet he caught sight of an envelope, squashed and
crumpled, which had become wedged beneath the

moveable slide designed to keep the file cases upright. He worked it out and took the single sheet of paper from the envelope. 'I can tell you what AED stands for, sir.' Morse looked up without enthusiasm and took the letter from him. It was an amateurishly-typed note, written on the official, headed notepaper of the Al-jamara Education Department, and dated 3rd March.

Dear George,
Greetings to all at Oxford. Many thanks for your
letter and for the summer examination package.
All Entry Forms and Fees Forms should be ready
for final dispatch to the Syndicate by Friday
20th or at the very latest, I'm told, by the 21st.
Admin has improved here, though there's room
for improvement still; just give us all two or three
more years and we'll really show you! Please
don't let these wretched 16+ proposals destroy
your basic O- and A-pattern. Certainly this
sort of change, if implemented immediately,
would bring chaos.
Sincerely yours,

Apart from the illegibly scrawled signature, that was all.

Morse frowned slightly as he looked at the envelope, which was addressed to G. Bland, Esq, MA, and marked 'STRICTLY PRIVATE AND CONFIDENTIAL' in bold red capitals. But his face quickly cleared, and he handed the letter back to Lewis without a word. It really was time they went.

Idly he opened the Letts diary again and his eyes fell upon the calendar inside the front page. And suddenly the blood began to freeze in his arms, and from the quiet, urgent tone of his voice Lewis immediately realized that the Inspector was strangely excited.

'What's the date of the postmark on that envelope, Lewis?'

'Third of March.'

'This year?'

Lewis looked again. 'Yes, sir.'

'Well, well, well!'

'What is it?'

'Funny, wouldn't you say, Lewis? Friday the 20th, it says in the letter. But *which* Friday the 20th?' He looked down at the calendar again. 'Not March. Not April. Not May. Not June. Not July. And it must refer to entry forms for last summer's examinations.'

'Somebody could have made a mistake over the date, sir. Could have been using last year's—'

But Morse wasn't listening. He picked up the letter again and studied it for several minutes with a fierce intensity. Then he nodded slowly to himself and a quiet smile spread over his face. 'Lewis, my boy, you've done it again!'

'I have, sir?'

'I'm not saying we're much nearer to finding out the identity of the person who murdered Nicholas Quinn, mind you. But I'll tell you one thing: I'm beginning to think we've got a pretty good idea *why* he was murdered! Unless it's a cruel coincidence—'

'Hadn't you better explain, sir?'

'Look at the letter again, Lewis, and ask yourself why such a seemingly trivial piece of correspondence was marked "Strictly Private and Confidential". Well?'

Lewis shook his head. 'I agree, sir, that it doesn't seem very important but—'

'But it *is* important, Lewis. That's just the point! *We* start reading from the left and then go across, agreed? But they tell me that some of these cockeyed foreigners start from the right and read down!'

Lewis studied the letter once more and his eyes gradually widened. 'You're a clever old bugger, sir.'

'Sometimes, perhaps,' conceded Morse.

At 7.35 p.m. the caretaker knocked deferentially and put his head round the door. 'I don't want to interrupt, sir, if—'

'Don't then,' snapped Morse, and the door was quietly reclosed. The two policemen looked across the table at each other – and grinned happily.

WHEN?

CHAPTER NINE

MORSE HAD NEVER been in the slightest degree interested in the technicalities of the science of pathology, and on Wednesday morning he read the reports before him with the selectivity of a dedicated pornophilist seeking out the juciest crudities. 'The smallest dose which has proved fatal is a ½ drachm of the pharmacopoeial acid, or 0.6 gram of anhydrous hydrocyanic acid ... rapidly altered in the body after death, uniting with sulphur...' Ah, here we are: '... and such in this instance were the post-mortem appearances that there is reason to believe that death must have occurred almost immediately ... fruitless, in the absence of scratches or abrasions, to speculate on the possibility of the body having been moved after death...' Interesting. Morse skipped his way along. '... would suggest a period of between 72–120 hours before the body was discovered. Any greater precision about these time limits is precluded in this case...' As in *all* cases you ever have, muttered Morse. He had never ceased to wonder why, with the staggering advances in medical science, all pronouncements concerning times of death remained so disconcertingly vague. For that was the real question: *when* had Quinn died? If Aristotle could be believed (why not?) the truth would probably lie somewhere in the middle: 94 hours, say. That meant Friday lunchtime or thereabouts. Was that possible? Morse put the report aside, and reconsidered the little he as yet knew of Quinn's whereabouts on the previous Friday. Yes. Perhaps he should have asked Quinn's colleagues where *they* were on Friday, not when they had last seen Quinn. But there was plenty of time; he would have to see them all again soon, anyway. At least one thing was clear. Whoever had tinkered with Quinn's sherry bottle had known something about poison – known a great deal about poison, in fact. Now who . . .? Morse went to his shelves, took down Glaister and Rentoul's bulky and definitive tome on *Medical Jurisprudence and Toxicology*, and looked up 'Hydrocyanic Acid' (page 566); and as he skimmed over the headings he smiled to himself. The compiler of the medical report he had just read had beaten him to it: some of the sentences were lifted almost verbatim. Why not, though? Cyanide wasn't going to change much over the years . . . He recalled Hitler and his clique in the Berlin bunker. That was cyanide, wasn't it? Cyanide. Suicide! Huh! The obvious was usually the very last thing that occurred to Morse's mind; but he suddenly realized that the most obvious answer to his problem was this: that Quinn had committed suicide. Yet, come to think of it, that was no real answer either. For if he had, why on earth . . .?

Lewis was surprised when half an hour later Morse took him to his home in North Oxford. It was two years since he had been there, and he was pleasurably surprised to find how comparatively neat and clean it was. Morse disappeared for a while, but put his head round the door and told Lewis to help himself to a drink.

'I'm all right, sir. Shall I pour one for you?'

'Yes. Pour me a sherry. And pour one for yourself.'

'I'd rather—'

'Do as you're told for a change, man!'

It wasn't unusual for Morse suddenly to turn sour, and Lewis resigned himself to the whims of his superior officer. The cabinet was well-stocked with booze, and Lewis took two small glasses and filled them from a bottle of medium sherry, sat back in an armchair, and wondered what was in store for him now.

He was sipping his sherry effeminately when Morse reappeared, picked up his own, lifted it to his lips and then put it down. 'Do you realize, Lewis, that if that sherry had been poisoned, you'd be a goner by now?'

'So would you, sir.'

'Ah, no. I've not touched mine.'

Lewis slowly put down his own glass, half-empty now, and began to understand the purpose of the little charade. 'And there'd be my prints on the bottle and on the glass . . .'

'And if I'd carefully wiped them both before we started, I've just got to pour my own sherry down the sink, wash the glass – and Bob's your uncle.'

'Somebody still had to get into Quinn's place to poison the sherry.'

'Not necessarily. Someone could have given Quinn the bottle as a present.'

'But you don't give someone a bottle that's been opened! You'd have a hell of a job trying to reseal a sherry bottle. In fact, you couldn't do it.'

'Perhaps there wasn't any need for that,' said Morse slowly; but he enlightened Lewis no further. For a moment he stood quite still, his eyes staring into the hazy past where a distant memory lingered on the threshold of his consciousness but refused the invitation to come in. It was something to do with a lovely young girl; but she merged into other lovely young girls. There had been so many of them, once . . . Think of something else! It would come. He drained his sherry at a gulp and poured himself another. 'Bit like drinking lemonade, isn't it, Lewis?'

'What's the programme, sir?'

'Well – I think we've got to play things a bit delicately. We might be on to something big, you must realize that; but it's no good rushing things. I want to know what all of 'em in the office were doing on Friday, but I want 'em to *know* what I'm going to ask them.'

'Wouldn't it be better—?'

'No. It wouldn't be fair, anyway.'

Lewis was getting lost. 'You think one of the four of them murdered Quinn?'

'What do you think?'

'I don't know, sir. But if you let them know before-hand—'

'Yes?'

'Well, they'd have something ready. Make something up—'

'That's what I want them to do.'

'But surely if one of them murdered Quinn—?'

'He'd have an alibi all ready, you mean?'

'Yes.'

Morse said nothing for a few seconds and then suddenly changed tack completely. 'Did you see me last Friday, Lewis?' Lewis opened his mouth and shut it again. 'Come on! We work in the same building, don't we?' Lewis tried hard, but he couldn't get hold of the problem at all. Friday. It seemed a long way away. What had he done on Friday? Had he seen Morse?

'You see what I mean, Lewis? Not easy, is it? We ought to give 'em a chance.'

'But as I say, sir, whoever killed Quinn will have something pretty good cooked up for last Friday.'

'Exactly.'

Lewis let it go. Many things puzzled him about the chief, and he felt even more puzzled as Morse pulled the front door to behind him: 'And what makes you so sure that Quinn was murdered on Friday?'

Margaret Freeman was unmarried – a slim, rather plain girl, with droopy eyelashes, who had worked for the Syndicate for just over three years. She had earlier been confidential secretary to Mr Bland, and had automatically been asked to transfer her allegiance to Mr Quinn. She had slept little the previous night, and not until the late grey dawn had she managed to rein in the horses of her terror. But Morse (who thought he understood such things) was still surprised when she broke down and wept after only a few minutes of gentle interrogation. She had certainly seen Quinn on Friday morning. He had dictated a whole sheaf of letters to her at about 10.45, and these had kept her busy until fairly late that same afternoon, when she had taken them into Quinn's office and put them in the in-tray. She hadn't seen him that Friday afternoon; yet she'd had the feeling that he was about somewhere, for she could almost positively recall (after some careful prodding) that Quinn's green anorak had been draped over the back of one of the chairs; and yes! there had been that little note for her, with her initials on it, MF, and then the brief message ('Dr Bartlett liked them to leave messages, sir'); but she couldn't quite remember . . . something like . . . no. Just something about 'going out', she thought. About being 'back soon', perhaps? But she couldn't really remember – that was obvious.

Morse had interviewed her in Quinn's office, and after she had gone he lit a cigarette and considered things anew. It was certainly interesting. Why wasn't the note still there? Quinn must have come back, crumpled up the note . . . But the wastepaper basket was empty. Cleaners! But Quinn had been alive at about 11 or 11.15 that Friday morning. That was something to build on, anyway.

To Lewis was entrusted the task of finding the caretaker and of discovering what happened to the Syndicate's rubbish. And for once the luck was with him. Two large, black plastic sacks of wastepaper were standing in a small loading bay at the side of the building, awaiting collection, and the job of sifting through the papers was at least a good deal more congenial than delving into rubbish bins. Comparatively quick, too. Most of the wastepaper was merely torn across the middle, and not screwed into crumpled balls: outdated forms mostly and a few first drafts of trickier letters. No note from Quinn to his confidential secretary, though, and Lewis felt disappointed, for that was the prime object of the search. But there were several (identical) notes from Bartlett, which Lewis immediately sensed might well be of some interest; and he took them along to Quinn's office, where the receiver that Morse held to his ear was emitting the staccato bleeps of the 'engaged' signal. He further smoothed out one of the notes, and Morse put down the receiver and read it:

Mon, 17th Nov

Notice to all Staff

PRACTICE FIRE DRILL

The fire alarm will ring at 12 noon, on Friday, 21st Nov, when all staff must immediately stop working, turn off all fires, lights and other electrical appliances, close all windows and doors, and walk through the front door of the building and out into the front parking area. No one is to remain in the building for *any reason*, and normal work will not be resumed until everyone is accounted for. Since the weather seems likely to be cold and wet, staff are advised to take their coats, etc., although it is hoped that the practice will take no longer than ten minutes or so. I ask and expect your full co-operation in this matter.

Signed T. G. Bartlett (Secretary)

'He's a careful soul, isn't he, Lewis?'
'Seems pretty efficient, sir.'
'Not the sort to leave anything to chance.'

'What's that supposed to mean?'

'I was just wondering why he didn't tell me about this fire drill, that's all.' He smiled to himself, and Lewis knew that that *wasn't* all.

'Perhaps he didn't tell you because you didn't ask him.'

'Perhaps so. Anyway, go along and ask him if there was a roll-call. You never know – we may be able to postpone Quinn's execution from 11.15 to 12.15.'

The red light showed outside Bartlett's office, and as Lewis stood undecided before the door, Donald Martin walked past.

'That light means he's got somebody with him, doesn't it?'

Martin nodded. 'He'd be very annoyed if any of the staff interrupted him, but – I mean . . .' He seemed extremely nervous about something, and Lewis took the opportunity (as Morse had instructed him) of disseminating the news that Quinn's colleagues would all soon be asked to account for their whereabouts the previous Friday.

'But what—? He can't really think—'

'He thinks a lot of things, sir.'

Lewis knocked on Bartlett's door and went in. Monica Height turned round with some annoyance on her face, but the Secretary himself, smiling benignly, made no reference whatsoever to the infraction of the golden rule. In answer to his query, Lewis was informed that he'd better see the chief clerk upstairs, who had been in charge of the whole operation and who almost certainly would have kept the register of all those who had been present for the fire drill.

After Lewis had left the room, Monica turned around and looked hard at Bartlett. 'What's all that about, pray?'

'You know you mustn't blame the police for trying to find out when Mr Quinn was last seen alive. I must admit I'd not mentioned the fire drill—'

'But he was alive last Friday *afternoon* – there's not much doubt about that, is there? His car was here until about twenty to five. So Noakes says.'

'Yes, I know all about that.'

'Don't you think we ought to tell the police straight away?'

'I've got a strong suspicion, my dear, that Chief Inspector Morse is going to find out far more than some of us may wish.'

But whatever might have been the cryptic implication of this remark, Monica appeared not to notice it. 'Don't you agree it may be very important, though?'

'Certainly. Especially if they think that Mr Quinn was murdered last Friday.'

'Do *you* think he was murdered on Friday?'

'Me?' Bartlett looked at her with a gentle smile. 'I don't think it matters very much what I think.'

'You haven't answered my question.'

Bartlett hesitated and stood up. 'Well, for what it's worth the answer's "no".'

'When—'

But Bartlett held up his finger to his lips and shook his head. 'You're asking as many questions as they are.'

Monica rose to her feet and walked to the door. 'I still think you ought to let them know that Noakes—'

'Look,' he said in a kindly way. 'If it'll make you happier, I'll let them know straight away. All right?'

As Monica Height left the room, Martin came up to her and said something urgently into her ear. Together they disappeared into Monica's office.

The chief clerk remembered the fire drill well, of course. Everything had gone according to plan, and the Secretary had scrutinized the final list himself before allowing his staff to resume their duties. Of the twenty-six permanent staff, only three had not ticked themselves off. But all had been accounted for: Mr Ogleby was down at the Oxford University Press; one of the typists had flu; and one of the junior clerks was on holiday. Against Quinn's name was a bold tick in black biro. And that was that. Lewis walked downstairs and rejoined Morse.

'Have you noticed how everyone in this office uses black biro, Lewis?'

'Bartlett's got 'em all organized, sir – even down to the pens they use.'

Morse seemed to dismiss the matter as of no importance, and picked up the phone once more. 'You'd have thought this bloody school would have more than one line, wouldn't you?' But this time he heard the ringing tone, and the call was answered almost immediately. Morse heard a cheerful north country voice telling him that she was the school secretary and asking if she could help. Morse explained who he was and what information he required.

'Friday, you say? Yes, I remember. From Oxford, that's right ... Oh, must have been about twenty past twelve. I remember I looked on t'timetable and Mr Richardson was teaching until a quarter to one ... No, no. He said not to bother. Just asked me to give him t'message, laik. He said he would be inviting Mr Richardson to do some marking this summer ... No, I'm sorry. I can't remember t'name for the minute, but Mr Richardson would know, of course ... Yes. Yes, I'm sure that was it. Quinn – that's right. I hope there's nothing ... Oh dear ... Oh dear ... Shall I tell Mr Richardson? ... All right ... All right, sir. Goodbye.'

Morse cradled the phone and looked across at Lewis. 'What do you think?'

'I think we're making progress, sir. Just after eleven he finishes dictating his letters; he's here for the fire drill at twelve; and he rings up the school at twenty past.' Morse nodded and Lewis felt encouraged to go on. 'What I'd really like to know is whether he left the note for Miss Freeman *before* or *after* lunch. So perhaps we'd better try to find out where he had a bite to eat, sir.'

Morse nodded again, and seemed to be staring at nothing. 'I'm beginning to wonder if we're on the right track, though, Lewis. You know what? I wouldn't be at all surprised if—'

The internal phone rang and Morse listened with interest. 'Well, thank you for telling me, Dr Bartlett. Can you ask him to come along straight away?'

When the sycophantic Noakes began his brief tale, Morse wondered why on earth he had not immediately sought the caretaker's confidence; for he knew full well that in institutions of all kinds throughout the land it was the name of the caretaker which should appear at the top of all official notepaper. Wherever his services were called upon (including Police HQ) it seemed to be the caretaker, with his strangely obnoxious combination of officiousness and servility, whose goodwill was prized above all; whose co-operation over rooms, teas, keys and other momentous considerations was absolutely indispensable. On the face of it, however, Noakes seemed one of the pleasanter specimens of the species.

'Yes, sir, his coat *was* there – I remember it distinct like, because his cabinet was open and I closed it. The Secketary wouldn't 'ave wanted that, sir. Very particular he is, about that.'

'Was there a note on his desk?'

'Yes, we saw that as well, sir.'

'"We", you say?'

'Mr Roope, sir. He was with me. He'd just—'

'What was he doing here?' said Morse quietly.

'He wanted to see the Secketary. But he was out, I knew that, sir. So Mr Roope asked me if any of the assistant secketaries was in – he had some papers, you see, as he wanted to give to somebody.'

'Who did he give them to?'

'That's just it. As I was going to say, sir, we tried all the other secketaries' offices, but there was nobody in.'

Morse looked at him sharply. 'You're quite sure about that, Mr Noakes?'

'Oh yes, sir. We couldn't find anybody, you see, and Mr Roope left the papers on the Secketary's desk.'

Morse glanced at Lewis and his eyebrows rose perceptibly. 'Well, well. That's very interesting. Very interesting.' But if it was as interesting as Morse would have the caretaker imagine, it prompted no further questions. At least not immediately so. The plain truth was that the information was, for Morse, completely unexpected, and he now regretted his earlier (stupidly theatrical) decision of allowing word to be spread on the office grapevine (it had surely got round by now?) that he would be asking all of them to account for their movements on Friday afternoon. The last thing he had expected was that they'd *all* need an alibi. Bartlett, he knew, had been out at Banbury. But where had the others been that fateful afternoon? Monica, Ogleby, Martin, and Quinn. *All of them out of the office.* Whew!

'What time was all this, Mr Noakes?'

''Bout half-past four, sir.'

'Had any of the others left a note?'

'I don't think so.'

'Could any of them have been upstairs, do you think?'

'Could 'ave been, sir, but – well, I was here quite a long while. I was in the corridor, you see, fixin' this broken light when Mr Roope came in.'

Morse still seemed temporarily blown off course, and Lewis decided to see if he could help. 'Could any of them have been in the lavatory?'

'Must have been in there a long time!' It was quite clear from the slightly contemptuous smirk that crossed Noakes's face that he was not prepared to pay any particular respect to the suggestions of a mere sergeant, and the almost inevitable 'sir' was noticeably absent.

'It was raining on Friday afternoon, wasn't it?' said Morse at last.

'Yes, sir. Rainin', blowin' – miserable afternoon it was.'

'I hope Mr Roope wiped his feet,' said Morse innocently.

For the first time Noakes seemed uneasy. He passed his hands one over the other, and wondered what on earth *that* was supposed to mean.

'Did you see any of them at all – later on, I mean?'

'Not really, sir. I mean, I saw Mr Quinn leave in his car about—'

'You *what?*' Morse sat up and blinked at Noakes in utter bewilderment.

'You saw him *leave*, you say?'

'Yes, sir. About ten to five. His car was—'

'Were there any other cars here?' interrupted Morse.

'No, sir. Just Mr Quinn's.'

'Well, thank you, Mr Noakes. You've been very helpful.' Morse got up and walked to the door. 'And you didn't see anyone else – anyone at all – after that?'

'No, sir. Except the Secketary himself. He came back to the office about half-past five, sir.'

'I see. Well, thank you very much.' Morse had scarcely been able to hide his mounting excitement and he fought back the strong impulse to push Noakes out into the corridor.

'If I can be of any help any time, sir, I hope you . . .' He stood fawning at the door like a liegeman taking leave of his lord. But Morse wasn't listening. A little voice within his brain was saying 'Bugger off, you obsequious little creep,' but he merely nodded good-naturedly and the caretaker finally sidled through the door.

'Well, Lewis? What do you make of that little lot?'

'I expect we shall soon find somebody who saw Quinn in a pub on Friday night. About chucking-out time.'

'You think so?' But Morse wasn't really interested in what Lewis was making of it. The previous day the cogs had started turning all right, but turning, it now appeared, in the wrong direction; and whilst Noakes had been speaking they'd temporarily stopped turning altogether. But they were off again now, in forward gear, with two or three of them whirring furiously. He looked at his watch, and saw that the morning was over. 'What swill do they slop out at the Horse and Trumpet, Lewis?'

CHAPTER TEN

FEW OF THE buildings erected in Oxford since the end of the Second World War have met with much approval from either Town or Gown. Perhaps it is to be expected that a public privileged with the daily sight of so many old and noble buildings should feel a natural prejudice against the reinforced concrete of the curious post-war structures; or perhaps all modern architects are mad. But it is generally agreed that the John Radcliffe Hospital on Headington Hill is one of the least offensive examples of the modern design – except, of course, to those living in the immediate vicinity who have found their expensive detached houses dwarfed by the gigantic edifice, and who now view from the bottom of their gardens a broad and busy access road instead of the green and open fields of Manor Park. The seven-storeyed hospital, built in gleaming, off-white brick, its windows painted chocolate brown, is set in spacious, tree-lined grounds, where royal-blue notice boards in bold white lettering direct the strangers towards their destinations. But few are strangers here, for the John Radcliffe Hospital is dedicated to the safe delivery of all the babies to be born beneath the aegis of the Oxfordshire Health Authority, and in it almost all the pregnant mums have suffered their precious embryos to be coddled and cosseted, turned and tested many many times before. Joyce Greenaway has. But with her ('one in a thousand', they'd said) things have not gone quite according to the gynaecological guarantee.

Frank Greenaway had Wednesday afternoon free and he drove into the hospital car park at 1 p.m. He was feeling much happier than he had done, for it now looked as if everything was going to be all right after all. But it still annoyed him that the incompetent nitwit of a foreman at Cowley had not been able to get the message to him the previous Friday evening, and he felt that he had let his wife down. Their first, too! Not that Joyce had been over-worried: when things seemed to her to be getting to the critical stage, she had shown her usual good sense and contacted the hospital direct. But it still niggled a bit; he couldn't pretend it didn't. For when he had finally arrived at the hospital at 9.30 p.m., their underweight offspring – some three weeks premature – was already putting up its brave and successful little fight in the Intensive Care Unit. It wasn't *his* fault, was it? But for Frank (who had little imagination, but a ready sympathy) it was something like arriving ten minutes late for an Oxford United fixture and finding he'd missed the only goal of the match.

He, too, was no stranger now. The doors opened for him automatically and he walked his way confidently down the wide, blue carpeted entrance hall, past the two enquiry desks, and made straight for the lift, where he pressed the button and, with a freshly laundered nightie, a box of Black Magic, and a copy of *Woman's Weekly*, he ascended to the sixth floor.

Both Joyce and the baby were still isolated – something to do with jaundice ('Nothing to worry about,

Mr Greenaway'), and Frank walked once more into Private Room 12. Why he felt a little shy, he could hardly begin to imagine; but he knew full well that he had every cause for continued apprehension. The doctors had been firmly insistent that he should as yet say nothing whatsoever about it. ('Your wife has had a pretty rough time, Mr Greenaway.') She would have to know *soon*, though; couldn't *help* getting to know. But he had willingly agreed to play the game, and the sister had promised to have a word with each of Joyce's visitors. ('The post-natal period can be very difficult, Mr Greenaway.') No *Oxford Mail* either, of course.

'How are we then, love?'

'Fine.'

'And the little one?'

'Fine.'

They kissed, and soon began to feel at ease again.

'Has the telly-man been yet? I meant to ask you yesterday.'

'Not yet, love. But he'll fix it – have no fear.'

'I should hope so. I shan't be in here much longer – you realize that, don't you?'

'Don't you worry about that.'

'Have you put the cot up yet?'

'I keep telling you. Stop *worrying*. You just get on your feet again and look after the little feller – that's all that matters.'

She smiled happily, and when he stood up and put his arm around her she nestled against his shoulder lovingly.

'Funny, isn't it, Frank? We'd got a name all ready, if it was a girl. And we were so sure it would be.'

'Yeah. I been thinking, though. What about "Simon"? Nice name, don't you think. "Simon Greenaway" – what about that? Sounds sort of – distinguished, if you know what I mean.'

'Yeah. Perhaps so. Lots of nice names for boys, though.'

'Such as?'

'Well. You know that chap downstairs – Mr Quinn? His name's "Nicholas". Nice name, don't you think? "Nicholas Greenaway." Yeah. I quite like that, Frank.' Watching his face closely, she could have sworn there was *something* there, and for a second she felt a surge of panic. But he *couldn't* know. It was just her guilty conscience: she was imagining things.

The Horse and Trumpet was quite deserted when they sat down in the furthest corner from the bar, and Lewis had never known Morse so apparently uninterested in his beer, over which he lingered like a maiden aunt sipping homemade wine at a church social. They sat for several minutes without speaking, and it was Lewis who broke the silence. 'Think we're getting anywhere, sir?'

Morse seemed to ponder the question deeply. 'I suppose so. Yes.'

'Any ideas yet?'

'No,' lied Morse. 'We've got to get a few more facts before we start getting any fancy ideas. Yes ... Look,

Lewis. I want you to go along and see Mrs What's-her-name, the cleaner woman. You know where she lives?'
Lewis nodded. 'And you might as well call on Mrs Jardine – isn't it? – the landlady. You can take my car: I expect I'll be at the Syndicate all afternoon. Pick me up there.'

'Anything particular you want me to—'

'Christ, man! You don't need a wet nurse, do you? Find out all you bloody well can! You know as much about the case as I do!' Lewis sat back and said nothing. He felt more angry with himself than with the Inspector, and he finished his pint in silence.

'I think I'll be off then, sir. I'd just like to nip in home, if you don't mind.'

Morse nodded vaguely and Lewis stood up to go. 'You'd better let me have the car keys.'

Morse's beer was hardly touched and he appeared to be staring with extraordinary intensity at the carpet.

Mrs Evans had been cleaning the ground floor of No 1 Pinewood Close for several years, and had almost been part of the tenancy for the line of single men who had rented the rooms from Mrs Jardine. Most of them had been on the lookout for something a little better and had seldom stayed long; but they'd all been pleasant enough. It was chiefly the kitchen that would get so dirty, and although she dusted and hoovered the other rooms, her chief task always lay in the kitchen, where she usually spent half a hour cleaning the stove and another half-hour ironing the shirts, underwear and handkerchiefs which found their weekly way into the

local launderette. It was just about two hours' work –
seldom more, and often a little less. But she always
charged for two hours, and none of the tenants had
ever demurred. She liked to get things done whilst no
one was about; and, with Quinn, 3–5 p.m. on Fridays
was the regularly appointed time.

It was about poor Mr Quinn, she knew that, and she
invited Lewis in and told him the brief story. She had
usually finished and gone before he got back home. But
the previous Friday she had to call at the Kidlington
Health Centre for Mr Evans, who had bronchitis and
was due to see the doctor again at 4.30 that day. But the
weather was so dreadful that she thought he ought to
stay in. So she went herself to get Mr E another
prescription, called in at the dispensing chemist, and
then went home and got the tea. She got back to
Quinn's house at about a quarter past six and stayed
about half an hour to do the ironing.

'You left a note for him, didn't you, Mrs Evans?'

'I thought he'd wonder why I hadn't finished.'

'That was at about four o'clock, you say?'

She nodded, and felt suddenly nervous. Had poor Mr
Quinn died on *Friday night*, just after she'd left, perhaps?
'We found the note in the wastepaper basket, Mrs
Evans.'

'I suppose you would, sir. If he screwed it up, like.'

'Yes, of course.' Lewis found himself wishing that
Morse was there, but he put the thought aside. A few
interesting ideas were beginning to develop. 'You left
the note in the lounge?'

'Yes. On the sideboard. I always left a note there at

the end of the month – when me four weeks' cleaning was up, like.'

'I see. Can you remember if Mr Quinn's car was in the garage when you got back?'

'No, Sergeant. I'm sorry. It was raining, and I was on me bike and I just got in as fast as I could. Anyway, why should I look in the garage? I mean—'

'You didn't see Mr Quinn?'

'No, I didn't.'

'Ah well. Never mind. We're obviously anxious—'

'You think he died on Friday night, then?'

'No, I wouldn't say that. But if we could find what time he got back from the office – well, it would be a great help. For all we know, he didn't get back home at all on Friday night.'

Mrs Evans looked at him with a puzzled frown. 'But *I* can tell you what time he got home.'

The room was suddenly very quiet and Lewis looked up tensely from his notes. 'Will you say that again, Mrs Evans?'

'Oh yes, Sergeant. You see, I left this note for him and he must have seen it.'

'He *must* have done, you say?'

'Must have done. You just said it was in the waste-paper basket.'

Lewis sank back in the sofa, his excitement ebbing away. 'He could have found the note any time, I'm afraid, Mrs Evans.'

'Oh no. You don't understand. He'd seen the note before I got back at quarter past six.' Lewis was sitting very still again and listening intently. 'You see, he left a note for me, so—'

'*He left a note for you?*'

'Yes. Said he'd gone shopping, or something. I forget exactly – but something like that.'

'So you—' Lewis started again. 'You left the note at four o'clock and went back there at quarter past six, you say?'

'That's right.'

'So you think he must have got home – when? About five?'

'Well, yes. He usually got home about then, I think.'

'You're sure the note was for you?'

'Oh yes. It got me name on it.'

'Can you – can you remember *exactly* what it said?'

'Not really. But I tell you what, Sergeant: I might have still got it. I probably put it in me pinny, or something. I always wear—'

'Can you try to find it for me?'

As Mrs Evans went out into the kitchen, Lewis found himself praying to the gods that for once they would smile upon him, and he felt almost sick with relief when she came back with a small folded sheet of paper, and handed it to him. He read it with the awesome reverence of a druid brooding on the holy runes:

Mrs E,
Just off shopping – shan't be long. NQ

It couldn't have been much briefer and it puzzled him a little; but he was fully aware of its huge importance.

'"Shopping", he says. Funny time for shopping, isn't it?'

'Not really, sir. The supermarket's open till nine of a Friday night.'

'The Quality supermarket, is that?'

'Yes, sir. It's only just behind the house, really. There's a pathway by the side of the crescent, and now that the fence is down you can get on to it from the side of the garden.'

Five minutes later Lewis thanked her fulsomely and left. By Jove, old Morse was going to be pleased!

It was just after one then Monica walked into the lounge bar. She spotted Morse immediately (though he appeared not to notice her) and after buying a gin and Campari she walked across and stood beside him.

'Can I get you a drink, Inspector?'

Morse looked up and shook his head. 'I seem to be off the beer today.'

'You weren't yesterday.'

'I wasn't?'

She sat down beside him and brought her lips close to his ear. 'I could smell your breath.'

'You smelled pretty good, too,' said Morse, but he knew that this was not to be a time for high romance. He could read the signs a mile away.

'I thought I might find you here.'

Morse shrugged non-committally. 'What have you got to tell me?'

'You don't beat about the bush, do you?'

'Sometimes I do.'

'Well, it's – it's about Friday afternoon.'

'News gets around.'

'You wanted to know what we were all doing on Friday afternoon, is that right?'

'That's it. Seems none of you were in the office, wherever else you were.'

'Well, I don't know about the others – no, that's not quite true. You see – Oh dear! You don't make it very easy for me. I was out all the afternoon and, well – I was with somebody else; and I suppose sooner or later you'll have to know who I was with, won't you?'

'I think I know,' said Morse quietly.

Monica's face dropped. 'You can't know. Have you already spoken—?'

'Have I spoken to Mr Martin? No, not yet. But I shall be doing so very soon, and I suppose he'll tell me the whole story, with the usual dose of reluctance and embarrassment – perhaps with a bit of anxiety, too. He *is* married, isn't he?'

Monica put her hand to her forehead and shook her head rather sadly. 'Are you a clairvoyant?'

'I'd solve all my cases a bit quicker if I were.'

'Do you want to hear about it?' She looked at him unhappily.

'Not now. I'd rather hear it from your boyfriend. He's not a very good liar.' He stood up and looked down at her empty glass. 'Gin and Campari, was it?'

She nodded, and thanked him; and as Morse walked over to the bar, she lit another cigarette and inhaled deeply, her immaculately plucked eyebrows narrowing into a worried frown. What on earth was she going to do if . . .?

Morse was soon back again, and placed her drink neatly on to a beer mat. 'I see what you mean about expensive tastes, Miss Height.'

She looked up at him and smiled feebly. 'But – aren't you going to join me?'

'No. Not now, thank you. I'm a bit busier than usual this week, you know. I've got a murder to investigate, and I don't usually mix much with tarts, anyway.'

After he had gone Monica felt utterly miserable, her thoughts a pallid multitude that drifted along the sunless waters. How cruel he had been just now! Only yesterday she had experienced an unwonted warmth of pleasure in his company. But how she hated him now!

Morse, too, was far from happy with himself. He shouldn't really have treated her as callously as that. How stupid it was, anyway – feeling so childishly jealous! Why, he'd only met her once before. He could go back, of course, and buy her another drink . . . and say he was sorry. Yes, he could do that. But he didn't; for interwoven with the jealousy motif was something else: he sensed intuitively that Monica had lied to him.

CHAPTER ELEVEN

APART FROM THE fact that Mrs Greenaway, the upstairs tenant, had been delivered of a baby boy the previous Friday evening, Lewis had learned nothing much of interest from Mrs Jardine. She was unable to add anything of substance to the statement made to Constable Dickson the previous day, and Lewis had stayed with her no more than ten minutes. But he'd had his earlier triumph. Oh yes! And as that same afternoon he recounted to Morse his interview with Mrs Evans – and presented his prize – he felt very pleased with himself indeed. Yet Morse's reactions seemed decidedly lukewarm; certainly he'd looked long and hard at Quinn's brief note, but in general he appeared preoccupied with other things.

'You don't seem very happy with life, sir.'

'The majority of men lead lives of quiet desperation.'

'But if this doesn't cheer you up—'

'What? Don't be daft!' Almost physically Morse tried to shake off his mood of temporary gloom, and he looked down at the note once more. 'I couldn't have done much better myself.' He said it flippantly, but Lewis knew him better.

'Let's have it, sir.'

'What do you mean?'

'What would you have asked her?'

'Just what you did – I told you.'

'What else?'

Morse appeared to consider the question carefully. 'Perhaps one or two other things.'

'Such as?'

'Perhaps I'd have asked her if she'd looked in the wastepaper basket.'

'Really?' Lewis sounded unimpressed.

'Perhaps I'd have asked her if Quinn's anorak was there.'

'But—' Lewis let it ride.

'I'd certainly have asked her if the gas fire was on.'

Lewis began to catch the drift of Morse's mind, and he nodded slowly to himself. 'I suppose we'd better see her again, sir.'

'Oh, yes,' said Morse quietly. 'We shall have to see her again. But that's no problem, is it? The main thing is that we seem to have got Quinn alive till about six o'clock. I wonder . . .?' His thoughts floated away again, but suddenly he sat upright and took out his Parker pen. 'There's still a good deal to do here, though, Lewis. Nip and see if he's back from lunch.'

'Who do you mean, sir?'

'I just told you — Martin. You going deaf?'

As Martin painfully corroborated Monica's story, Morse's facial expression was that of a man with a rotten egg stuck just beneath his nose. The pair of them had left the office at about 1.10 p.m. No, not together – in separate cars. Yes, to Monica's bungalow. Yes, to bed.

(Putrescent, fetid egg!) That was all really. (All! Christ! That was *all*, he'd said.)

'What time did you leave?'

'About a quarter to four.'

'And you didn't come back to the office at all?'

'No. I went straight home.'

'Nice little surprise for your wife.'

Martin was silent.

'Lewis! Go and see Miss Height. You've heard what this man says. Get her story, and see if it fits.'

After Lewis had gone Morse turned to Martin and looked him hard in the eyes. 'You're a cock-happy young sod, aren't you?'

The young man shook his head sadly. 'I'm not really, you know, Inspector. I've only been unfaithful with Monica, never anyone else.'

'You in love with her?'

'I don't know. This business has – I don't know, Inspector. She's – Ah, what's it matter now!'

'Why did you leave so early?'

'There's Sally – that's Monica's daughter. She usually gets home from school about quarter past four.'

'And you didn't want her to find you shagging her mother, is that it?'

Martin looked up miserably. 'Haven't you ever been unfaithful, Inspector?'

Morse shook his head. 'No, lad. I've never had to be faithful, you see.'

'There's – there's no need for all this to come out, is there?'

'Not really, no. Unless—'

'Unless what?' A look of alarm sprang into Martin's eyes, and Morse did nothing to dispel it.

'Tell me. This girl Sally: is she at school in Oxford?'

'Oxford High School.'

'Bit awkward with examinations, isn't it? I mean, with her mother—'

'No. You don't quite understand, Inspector. This Board doesn't examine in England at all.'

'Who examines Oxford High?'

'Oxford Locals, I think.'

'I see.'

After Martin had gone, Morse rang HQ and gave Constable Dickson his instructions; and he was smiling contentedly to himself when Lewis returned.

'She confirms what Martin says, sir.'

'Does she now?'

'You sound a bit dubious.'

'Do I?'

'You don't believe 'em?'

'For what it's worth, Lewis, I think they're a pair of bloody liars. But I may be wrong, of course. As you know, I often am.' He had that deprecatingly conceited look on his face which many found the Chief Inspector's least attractive trait, and Lewis was determined not to demean himself by trying to delve further into that cocky logic. For his part, he believed them, and high-and-mighty Morse could mumble away as he pleased.

'Didn't you hear me, Lewis?'

'Pardon, sir?'

'What the hell's up with you today, man? I said go and get Ogleby. Can you do that small thing for me?'

Lewis slammed the door behind him and walked out into the corridor.

Morse had spoken no more than half a dozen words to Ogleby when they had been formally introduced the previous day, yet he had felt an instinctive liking for the man; and his impression was confirmed as Ogleby began to chat informatively and authoritatively about the work of the Syndicate.

'What about security?' asked Morse cautiously, like a timid skater testing the ice.

'It's a constant problem, of course. But everyone's conscious of it, and so in an odd sort of way the problem solves itself – if you see what I mean.'

Morse thought he did. 'I gather the Secretary's pretty keen on that side of things.'

'Yes, I suppose you could say that.'

Morse eyed him sharply. Had there been a tinge of irony – or even jealousy, perhaps – in Ogleby's reply? 'Is there *never* any malpractice?'

'Oh, I wouldn't say that. But that's a completely different question.'

'Is it?'

'You see if a candidate decided to cheat in the examination room, either by taking notes in with him or copying from someone else, then we've just got to rely on the invigilators keeping a very careful eye on things, and reporting anything suspicious directly to us.'

'That happens, does it?'

'Two or three times a year.'

'What do you do about it?'

'We disqualify the candidates concerned from every subject in the examinations.'

'I see.' Morse tried another angle. 'You send out the question papers before the examination, don't you?'

'Wouldn't be much good holding the examinations if we didn't, would it?'

Morse realized what a stupid question he'd asked, and continued rather hastily. 'No. I mean – if one of the teachers was dishonest, or something?'

'The question papers are sent out directly to examination departments, and then distributed to heads of centres – not to individual teachers.'

'But let's take a headmaster, then. If he was a crook – let's say he opened a particular package of question papers and showed them to his pupils—'

'It's as good a way as any for the headmaster to slit his throat.'

'You'd know, you mean?'

Ogleby smiled. 'Gracious, yes. We've got examiners and awarders who'd smell anything like that a mile away. You see we've got records going back over the years of percentage passes for all the subjects examined, and so we know the sort of pupils we're examining, the types of schools – all that sort of thing. But that's not really the point. Like all the examining Boards we inspect our centres regularly after they've been accepted, and they have to meet pretty high standards of integrity and administrative competence before they're recognized in the first place.'

'The schools are regularly inspected then?'

'Oh yes.'

'Is that the sort of job Mr Bland does in Al-jamara?'

Morse watched Ogleby carefully, but the deputy sailed serenely on. 'Among other things, yes. He's in charge of the whole administrative set-up there.'

Morse decided that he might as well tackle the problem from the other end, and he delicately tiptoed his way over the ice again.

'Would it be possible for an outsider, one of the cleaners, say, to get into the cabinets in this office? And get the papers he wanted?'

'Technically, I suppose, yes. If he had the keys, knew where to look, knew the complicated system of syllabus numbering, had the intelligence to understand the various amendments and printing symbols. Then he'd have to copy what he'd got, of course. Every page of proofs and revises is carefully numbered, and no one could get away with just pinching a page.'

'Mm. What about examiners? Let's say they put a high mark down for a particular candidate who's as thick as a plank.'

'Wouldn't work, I'm afraid. The arithmetic of every single script is checked against the marksheet.'

'Well, let's say an examiner gives high marks for all of the answers on the script – even if they're rubbish.'

'If an examiner did that, he would have been kicked

out years ago. You see the examiners are themselves examined by a team of what we call "awarders", who report on all the members of the various panels after each examination.'

'But the awarders could . . .' No, Morse, let it go. He began to see that it was all far more complex that he had imagined.

But Ogleby finished the thought for him. 'Oh, yes, Inspector. If one of the people *at the top* was crooked, it would be very easy. Very easy indeed. But why are you asking me all this?'

Morse pondered a while, and then told him. 'We've got to find a motive for Quinn's murder, sir. There are a hundred and one possibilities, of course, but I was just wondering if – if perhaps he'd found some er some suggestion of jiggery-pokery, that's all. Anyway, you've been very helpful.'

Ogleby stood up to go, and Morse too rose from his chair. 'I've been asking the others what they were doing last Friday afternoon. I suppose I ought to ask you too. If you can remember, that is.'

'Oh, yes. That's easy enough. I went down to the Oxford University Press in the morning, had a pretty late lunch at the Berni place there with the chief printer, and got back here about, oh, about half-past three, I should think.'

'And you spent the rest of the afternoon in the office here?'

'Yes.'

'Are you sure about that, sir?'

Ogleby looked at him with steady eyes. 'Quite sure.'

Morse hesitated, and debated whether to face it now or later.

'What is it, Inspector?'

'It's a bit awkward, sir. I understand from, er, from other sources that there was no one here in the latter part of Friday afternoon.'

'Well, your sources of information must be wrong.'

'You couldn't have slipped out for a while? Gone up to see the chief clerk or something?'

'I certainly didn't go out of the office. I might have gone upstairs, but I don't think so. And if I had, it would only have been for a minute or two, at the very outside.'

'What would you say, then, sir, if someone said there was no one here on Friday afternoon between a quarter past four and a quarter to five?'

'I'd say this someone was mistaken, Inspector.'

'But what if he insisted—?'

'He'd be a liar, then, wouldn't he?' Ogleby smiled serenely, and gently closed the door behind him.

Or *you* would, thought Morse, as he sat alone. And although you don't know it, my good friend Ogleby, there are two someones who say you weren't here. And if you weren't here, where the hell *were* you?

Chapter Twelve

THE POLICE CAR, white with a broad, pale blue stripe along its middle, stood parked by the pavement, and Constable Dickson knocked at the spruce detached bungalow in Old Marston. The door was immediately opened by a smartly dressed, attractive woman.

'Miss Height?'

'Yes?'

'Is your daughter in?'

Miss Height's features crumpled into a girlish giggle. 'Don't be silly! I'm only sixteen!'

Dickson himself grinned oafishly, and accepted the young lady's invitation to step inside.

'It's about Mr Quinn, isn't it? Ever so exciting. Coo. Just think. He worked in the same office as Mummy!'

'Did you ever meet him, miss?'

'No, worse luck.'

'He never came here.'

She giggled again. 'Not unless Mummy brought him here while I was slaving away at school!'

'She wouldn't do that, would she?'

She smiled happily. 'You don't know Mummy!'

'Why aren't you at school today, miss?'

'Oh, I'm taking some O-levels again. I took them in the summer but I'm afraid I didn't do too well in some of them.'

'What subjects are they?'

'Human Biology, French and Maths. Not that I've got much chance in Maths. We had Paper Two this morning – a real stinker. Would you like to see it?'

'Not now, miss. I er – I was just wondering why you weren't at school, that's all.' It wasn't very subtle.

'Oh, they let us off when we haven't got an exam. Great really, I've been off since lunchtime.'

'Do you always come home? When you're free, I mean?'

'Nothing else to do, is there?'

'You revise, I suppose?'

'A bit. But I usually watch telly. You know, the kiddies' programmes. Quite good, really. Sometimes I don't think I've grown up at all.'

Dickson felt he shouldn't argue. 'You've been here most days recently, then?'

'Most afternoons.' She looked at him innocently. 'I shall be here again tomorrow afternoon.'

Dickson coughed awkwardly. He'd done the bit of homework that Morse had told him to. 'I watched one of those kiddies' films, miss. About a dog. Last Friday afternoon, I think it was.'

'Oh yes. I watched that. I cried nearly all the way through. Did it make *you* cry?'

'Bit of a tearjerker, I agree, miss. But I mustn't keep you from your revising. As I say, it was your mother I really wanted to see.'

'But you said – you said you wanted to see *me*!'

'I got it a bit muddled, miss, I'm afraid. I sort of thought—' He gave it up and got to his feet. He hadn't done too badly at all really, and he thought the Chief Inspector would be pleased with him.

At 7 p.m. the same evening Morse sat alone in his office. A single tube of white strip-lighting threw a harsh unfriendly glare across the silent room, and a single yellow lamp in the yard outside the uncurtained window did little more than emphasize the blackness of the night. Occasionally, especially at times like this, Morse wished he had a home to welcome him, with a wife to have his slippers warmed and ready. It was at times like this, too, that murder seemed a crude and terrifying thing . . . Dickson had reported on his visit to Sally Height, and the silhouettes on the furthest walls of the darkened cave were now assuming a firmer delineation. Monica had lied to him. Martin had lied to him. It was odds-on that Ogleby had lied to him. Had Bartlett lied as well? Stocky, cautious little Bartlett, meticulous as a metronome. If *he* had murdered Nicholas Quinn . . .

For half an hour he let his thoughts run wild and free, like randy rabbits in orgiastic intercourse. And then he put a stop to it. He needed a few more facts; and facts were facing him, here and now, in the dark blue plastic bag containing the items found in Quinn's pockets, in Quinn's green anorak, and in Lewis's inventories. Morse cleared the top of his desk and set to work. Quinn's pockets had thrown up little of surprise or interest: a wallet, a grubby handkerchief, half a packet of Polos, a diary (with not a single entry), 43½p, a pink comb, one half of a cinema ticket, two black biros, a strip of tired-looking Green Shield stamps, and a statement from Lloyds Bank (Summertown branch), showing a current account balance of £114.40. That was the lot, and Morse arranged each item neatly before him and sat surveying them for minutes, before finally taking a sheet of notepaper and listing each item carefully. Ye-es. The thought had flashed across his mind a few minutes earlier. Decidedly odd . . . Next he picked up the anorak and took a further selection of objects from each side pocket: another grubby handkerchief, car keys, a black key case, two ancient raffle tickets, a further 23p, and an empty white envelope addressed to Quinn, with the word 'Bollox' written on the flap in pencil. 'Well, well,' mumbled Morse to himself. His randy rabbits could have a field day with *that*, but he decided to give them no chance. Again he listed each item with great precision and again sat back. It was just as he had thought, but it was too late to go back to the lonely rooms in Pinewood Close that night. A bit too creepy, anyway.

Having completed a synoptic review of the evidence before him, Morse systematically tackled each item severally. The wallet first: a driving licence, RAC membership card, Lloyds Bank cheque card, an outdated NHS prescription for Otosporin, the previous month's pay-slip, a blue outpatients' appointment card for the ENT department at the Radcliffe Infirmary, one five-pound note, three one-pound notes, and a Syndicate acknowledgement card on which were written two telephone numbers. Morse picked up the phone and dialled the first, but his ears were greeted only by a continuous high-pitched monotone. He dialled the second.

'Hello? Monica Height here.'

Morse hastily put down the receiver. It was naughty of him, he knew, but he had the feeling that Monica would not be very happy with him for the moment. Or with Constable Dickson. Yet it made him wonder exactly what the pattern of cross-relationships in the Syndicate had been.

It was the buff-coloured right-hand half of the cinema ticket which next attracted Morse's attention. Across the top were the numbers 102, beneath them the words 'Rear Lounge', and along the right edge, running down, the numbers 93550. On the back of the ticket was the design of a pentagram. Sombody must know which cinema it was, he supposed. Job for Lewis, perhaps . . . And then it struck him. Fool of a fool! It wasn't 102 across the top at all. There was just the slightest gap between the o and the 2 and Morse saw the name of the cinema staring up at him: STUDIO 2. He knew the place – in Walton Street. Morse had bought a copy of the previous day's *Oxford Mail* (wherein the Quinn murder had been briefly reported) and he turned the pages and found that Tuesday was the critics' day for reporting to the citizens of Oxford on the quality of the entertainments currently available. Yes, there it was:

It is all too easy to see why *The Nymphomaniac* has been retained for a further week at Studio 2. The afficionados have been flocking to see the Swedish sexpot, Inga Nielsson, dutifully exposing her 40″ bosom at the slightest provocation. Flock on.

Morse read the review with mixed feelings. Clearly, the critics hadn't yet gone metric, and this particular aficionado couldn't even spell the word. Yet big Inga seemed to Morse a most inviting prospect; and doubtless to many another like him. Especially perhaps when the boss was away one Friday afternoon . . .? He flicked through the telephone directory, found the number, and asked to speak to the manager who surprisingly turned out to be the manageress.

'Oh yes, sir. All our tickets are traceable. Buff, you say? Rear lounge? Oh yes. We should be able to help you. You see all the blocks of tickets are numbered and a record is kept at the start of each matinée, and then at six o'clock, and then at ten o'clock. Have you got the number?'

Morse read out the number and felt curiously excited.

'Just one minute, sir.' It turned into three or four, and Morse fiddled nervously with the directory. 'Are you there, sir? Yes, that's right. Last Friday. It's one of the first tickets issued. The doors opened at 1.15 and the programme started at 1.30. The first rear lounge number is 93543, so it must have been issued in the first five or ten minutes, I should think. There's usually half a dozen or so waiting for the doors to open.'

'You quite sure about this?'

'Quite sure, sir. You could come down and check if you wanted to.' She sounded young and pretty.

'Perhaps I will. What film have you got on?' He thought it sounded innocent enough.

'Not quite your cup of tea, I don't think, Inspector.'

'I wouldn't be too sure about that, miss.'

'*Mrs*. But if you do come, ask for me and I'll see you get a free seat.'

Morse wondered sadly how many more gift horses he'd be looking in the mouth. But it wasn't that at all really. He was just frightened of being seen. Now if she'd said . . .

But she said something else, and Morse jolted upright in his chair. 'I think I ought to mention, Inspector, that someone else asked me the very same sort of thing last week and . . .'

'*What?*' He almost screamed down the phone, but then his voice became very quiet. 'Say that again, will you, please?'

'I said someone else had—'

'When was this, do you remember?'

'I'm not quite sure; sometime – let's see, now. I ought to remember. It's not very often—'

'Was it Friday?' Morse was excited and impatient.

'I don't know. I'm trying to remember. It was in the afternoon, I remember that, because I was doing a stint in the ticket office when the phone rang, and I answered it myself.'

'Beginning of the afternoon?'

'No, it was much later than that. Just a minute. I think it was . . . Just a minute.' Morse heard some chattering in the background, and then the manager-ess's voice spoke in his ear once more. 'Inspector, I think it was in the late afternoon, sometime. About five, perhaps. I'm sorry I can't—'

'Could have been Friday, you think?'

'Ye-es. Or Saturday, perhaps. I just—'

'A man, was it?'

'Yes. He had a nice sort of voice. Educated – you know what I mean.'

'What did he ask you?'

'Well, it was funny really. He said he was a detective story writer and he wanted to check up on some details.'

'What details?'

'Well, I remember he said he'd got to put some numbers on a ticket his detective had found, and he wanted to know how many figures there were – that sort of thing.'

'And you told him?'

'No, I didn't. I told him he could come round to see me, if he liked: but I felt a bit – well, you know, you can't be too careful these days.'

Morse breathed heavily down the phone. 'I see. Well, thank you very much. You've been extremely kind, I think, as I say, I shall probably have to bother you again—'

'No bother, Inspector.'

Morse put down the phone, and whistled softly to himself. Whew! Had someone else found Quinn's body and the cinema ticket before Tuesday morning? Long before? Saturday; the manageress had said it might have been Saturday. And it couldn't have been Friday, could it? About five, she'd said. Morse looked quickly again at the *Oxford Mail* and saw the times: *The Nymphomaniac.*

1.30 to 3.20 p.m. Until twenty past three on Friday Quinn had been feasting his eyes on Inga Nielsson's mighty bosom and few things, surely, would have dragged him out of Studio 2 before the film had finished. Unless, of course . . . At long last it struck him: *the pretty strong probability that Quinn had not been sitting alone in Studio 2 that Friday afternoon.*

CHAPTER THIRTEEN

As MORSE STOOD with Lewis in Pinewood Close at
2 p.m. on the following afternoon, awaiting the arrival
of Mrs Jardine, he tried with little success to draw a veil
over the harrowing events of the morning. Mr and Mrs
Quinn had trained down from Huddersfield, and somewhere amid the wreckage of their lives, somewhere
amid the tears and the heartbreak, they had managed
to find reserves of quiet dignity and courage. Morse had
accompanied Mr Quinn senior to the mortuary for the
formal identification of his son, and then spent over an
hour with them both in his office, unable to tell them
much, unable to offer anything except the usual futile
words of sympathy. And as Morse had watched the
tragic couple climb into the police car for Oxford, he
felt great admiration – and even greater relief. The
whole interview had upset him, and apart from a few
brief minutes with a reporter from the *Oxford Mail*, he
had not been in the mood to grapple with the perpetually multiplying clues to the last hours lived by Nicholas
Quinn.

Two men were repairing the street lamp in front of
No 1, and Morse strolled over to them. 'How long
before they come and smash it up again?'

'You never know, sir. But, to be truthful, we don't get
too much vandalism round 'ere, do we, Jack?'

But Morse had no chance of hearing Jack's views on
the local yahoos, for Mrs Jardine drew up in her car

and the three of them disappeared into the house, where for half an hour they sat together in the front room. Mrs Jardine told them as much as she knew about her former tenant: about his coming to see her in mid-August; about her chat with Bartlett (Quinn's choice as referee); about his tidy habits and his punctuality in paying his rent; about his usual weekend routine; and about any and every thing Morse could think of asking her that might add to his picture of Mr Quinn alive. But he learned nothing. Quinn had been a model tenant, it seemed. Quiet, orderly, and no gramophone. Girl-friends? Not that she knew of. She couldn't stop that sort of thing, of course, but it was much better if her tenants – well, you know, *behaved* themselves. The others – upstairs? Oh, they got along well with Mr Quinn, she thought, though she couldn't really *know*, could she? What a good job Mrs Greenaway hadn't been there on Tuesday, though! You could never tell – with the *shock*. Yes, that had been a real blessing.

It was another chilly afternoon, and Morse got up to light the fire, turning the automatic switch on the side as far as he could. But nothing happened.

'You'll have to use a match, Inspector. Those things never seem to work. How the manufacturers get away with it—'

Morse struck a match and the fire exploded into an orange glow.

'Do you make any extra charge for gas and electricity?'

'No. It's included in the rent,' replied Mrs Jardine. But as if to dispel any possible suspicion of excessive generosity, she hastily added that the tenants had to share the telephone bill, of course.

Morse was puzzled. 'I don't quite follow you.'

'Well, there's a shared line between them, you see. There's a phone upstairs in the Greenaways' bedroom and one here in this room.'

'I see,' said Morse quietly.

After the landlady had left them, Morse and Lewis went into the room where Quinn had been found. Although the curtains were now drawn back, it seemed no less sombre than when they were in it last; and certainly colder. Morse bent down and tried turning the switch on the gas fire. He tried again; and again. But nothing.

'Probably no batteries in it, sir.' Lewis unfastened the side panel, and produced two stumpy Ever Ready batteries, now covered with a slimy, mildewed discharge.

The same Thursday morning Joyce Greenaway had been moved from the Intensive Care Unit at the John Radcliffe Hospital; and when one of her old school-friends came to see her at 2.30 p.m. she was in a pleasant ward, two storeys below, in the company of three other recently delivered mothers. Conversation was babies, babies, babies, and Joyce felt buoyant. She should be out in a few days, and she felt a strangely satisfying surge of maternal emotions developing deep within herself. How she loved her darling little boy! He was going to be fine – there was no doubt of that now. But the problem of what to call him remained unresolved. Frank had decided that he didn't really like 'Nicholas' all that much, and Joyce wanted *him* to make the choice. She herself wasn't all that smitten with the name, anyway. It had been awfully naughty of her to mention the name in the first place. But she'd just *had* to see if Frank had suspected anything, and despite her earlier fears she now felt convinced that he hadn't. Not that there was *much* to suspect.

It had started just after Nicholas had come, at the beginning of September, when he'd always seemed to be running out of matches, or sugar, or milk tokens; and he'd been so grateful, and so attentive towards her – and she over six months gone! Then that Saturday morning when *she* had been out of milk, with Frank on one of his everlasting shifts, and she had gone down in her nightie and housecoat, and they had sat for a long time drinking coffee together in the kitchen, and she had longed for him to kiss her. And he had, standing beside her with his hands on her shoulders, and then, after delicately unfastening her housecoat, putting his right hand deep inside her nightie and gently fondling her small firm breasts. It had happened three times after that, and she'd felt a deep tenderness towards him, for he made no other demands upon her body than to pass the tips of his fingers silkily over her legs and over her swollen belly. And just that once she had done more than passively lean back and surrender herself to the exquisite thrill that his hands could bring to her. Just the once – when so diffidently and so lightly, her outstretched fingers had caressed him. Oh yes, so very, very lightly! She had felt an enormous inner joy as he had finally buried his head on her shoulder, and the things she'd whispered to him then were now the focus of her conscience-stricken thoughts. But Frank would never know, and she promised herself that never, never again would she . . . would she . . .

She was awoken by the clatter of cups at four o'clock, and a quarter of an hour later the trolley came round with books and newspapers. She bought the *Oxford Mail.*

Morse was a few minutes early for his appointment, but the Dean of the Syndicate was ready for him in his oak-panelled rooms on the Old Staircase in the inner quad, and the two men were chatting vaguely of this and that when at five past four a scout knocked and came in with a tray.

'I thought we'd have a drop of Darjeeling. All right with you?' The voice, like the man, was syrupy and civilized.

'Lovely,' said Morse, wondering what Darjeeling was.

The white-coated scout poured the dark brown liquid into bone china cups, embossed with the crest of Lonsdale College. 'Milk, sir?'

Morse watched it all with an amused detachment. The Dean, it seemed, always had a slice of lemon, and one half-teaspoonful of sugar, which the scout himself measured out, almost to the grain, and stirred in with high seriousness. The old boy probably got his scout to tie his shoelaces up for him! Cloud-cuckoo-land! Morse took a sip of the tea, sat back, and saw the Dean smiling at him shrewdly.

'You don't really approve, I see. Not that I blame you. He's been with me almost thirty years now, and he's almost – But, I'm sorry, I'm forgetting. You've come to see me about Mr Quinn. What can I tell you?'

The Dean was clearly a sensitive and cultured soul: he was due to retire in one year's time, at sixty-five, and was clearly saddened that the tragedy of Quinn's murder should have clouded a long and distinguished connection with the Syndicate. To Morse, it seemed a curiously self-centred commiseration.

'Would you say the Syndicate is a happy sort of place, sir?'

'Oh yes. I think everybody would tell you that.'

'No hostility? No, er, personal animosities?'

The Dean looked a little uneasy, and it was clear that he might have one or two reservations – minor ones, of course. 'There are always a few er difficulties. You find them in every, er—'

'What difficulties?'

'Well – basically, I think, there'll always be just a little, er, friction, shall we say, between the older generation – my generation – and some of the younger Syndics. You always get it. It was just the same when I was their age.'

'The younger ones have their own ideas?'

'I'm glad they have.'

'Are you thinking of any particular incident?'

Again the Dean hesitated. 'You know the sort of thing as well as I do, surely? One or two people get a bit hot under the collar now and again.'

'Has this got anything to do with Mr Quinn?'

'Quite honestly, Chief Inspector, I think not. You see,

one of the incidents I'm thinking of happened before Quinn was appointed – in fact it happened when we were appointing him.' He gave a brief account of the interviewing committee's disagreement over the choice of candidates, and Morse listened with deep interest.

'You mean Bartlett didn't want to appoint Quinn?'

The Dean shook his head. 'You misunderstand me. The Secretary was quite happy about him. But, as I say, personally he would have given the job to one of the others.'

'What about you, sir? What did you feel?'

'I, er, I thought the Secretary was right.'

'So Mr Roope was the fly in the ointment?'

'No, no. You still misunderstand me. Quinn was appointed by the *committee* – not by Roope.'

'Look, sir. Please be quite frank with me. Would I be right in saying that there's not much love lost between Bartlett and Roope?'

'Aren't you enjoying your tea, Chief Inspector? You've hardly touched a drop yet.'

'You're not going to answer my question, sir?'

'I really do think it would be fairer if you asked *them*, don't you?'

Morse nodded, and drained the lukewarm liquid. 'What about the permanent staff? Any, er, friction there?'

'Amongst the graduates, you mean? N-o, I don't think so.'

'You sound a bit dubious.'

The Dean sat back and slowly finished his own tea, and Morse realized he would have to push his luck a bit.

'Miss Height, for instance.'

'A lovely girl.'

'You mean we can't blame the others too much if . . .'

'If there's any of, er, of that sort of thing going on, I can only say that I know nothing about it.'

'Rumours, though?'

'We've all got more sense than to listen to rumours.'

'Have we?' But it was clear that the Dean was not to be drawn, and Morse switched the line of his questioning once more. 'What about Bartlett? Is he well liked?'

The Dean looked at Morse keenly, and carefully poured out more tea. 'What do you mean?'

'I just wondered if any of the other graduates had any cause to – to, you know—' Morse didn't know what he wondered; but the Dean, it seemed, did.

'I suppose you're thinking of Ogleby?'

Morse nodded sagely, and tried to ooze omniscience. 'Yes, it was Mr Ogleby I was wondering about.'

'That's ancient history, though, isn't it? It's a long time ago, now. Huh! I remember at the time thinking that Ogleby was potentially the better man. In fact, I voted for him. But with hindsight I'm sure that Bartlett was the wiser choice, and we were all very glad that Ogleby was willing to accept the post of Deputy Secretary. Very able man. I'm quite sure that if he'd wanted to, he . . .' The Dean talked freely now, and Morse felt his own attention drifting further and further away. So. Bartlett and Ogleby had applied for the Secretaryship together, and Ogleby had been turned down; and perhaps the slight had rankled on and on over the years – might still be rankling on. But what on earth could that have to do with the murder of Quinn? If Bartlett had been murdered – or even Ogleby – yes! But . . .

The Dean stood at the window and watched Morse walk briskly around the quad. He knew that for the last ten minutes his words had fallen on deaf ears, and for the life of him he was completely unable to fathom the look of quiet contentment which had so suddenly appeared on the Chief Inspector's face.

Lewis finished his own cup of tea and was leaving the police canteen as Dickson walked in.

'I see you're appealing for help, Sarge. Old Morse stuck, is he?'

He handed Lewis the *Oxford Mail* and pointed to a paragraph at the bottom of the front page:

MURDER INQUIRY

Police investigating the murder of Mr N. Quinn, 1 Pinewood Close, Kidlington, whose body was found on Tuesday morning by a colleague from the Foreign Examinations Syndicate, are appealing to anyone who may have seen the murdered man on either the evening of Friday, 21st November, or on Saturday, 22nd November, to come forward. Chief Inspector Morse, who is heading the inquiry, said today that any such information could be vital in establishing the time of Mr

Quinn's death. An inquest will be held next Monday.

Lewis looked at the photograph beside the article, and handed the paper back to Dickson. In his inside pocket was the original which Morse had asked the Quinns to bring with them from Huddersfield. Sometimes, he had to agree, Morse *did* take on the dirty work; compared to which his present little assignment was a doddle.

He soon found the young manager and learned that the flimsy short roll of paper he had brought with him was a richly-seamed mine of information: the date at the top; the 'customer-reading' number on the right; the items purchased each classified according to the various departments, and designated by one of the Roman numerals I-IV; the number of the till at the bottom. 'Customer flow' (Lewis learned) was fairly constant on Fridays, with high takings for most of the day, and (though the manager refused to be precise) the items listed had doubtless been purchased in the late afternoon or early evening. If he had to guess? Well, between 5 and 6.30 p.m. Unfortunately, however, the plump waddling little woman who was summoned in her capacity as i/c Till 3 could remember nothing, and failed to register even the vaguest recollection of ever having seen the face on the photograph she was shown. It was the goods she always watched, you see; seldom the faces.

Ah well!

Lewis thanked the manager and left the Kidlington premises of the Quality supermarket. Morse wouldn't be too pleased, perhaps, but all the clues seemed to be fitting into a firm, clear pattern.

'But why why *why* didn't you tell me? You must have realized—'

'Come off it, Joyce! You *know* why. It would have upset you, and we've—'

'It wouldn't have been half such a shock as reading about it in the paper!'

He shook his head sadly. 'I just thought I was doing right, luv. That's all. Sometimes you just can't win, can you?'

'No, I suppose not.' She understood all right, but she knew that *he* didn't. How could he?

'As I say, there's no need to worry about *anything*. When you're better again, we can talk about things. But not now. It'll soon all blow over – you see; and we're all fixed up for the time being.'

No, he couldn't begin to understand. He was trying hard not to put it into so many words, but he'd got it all wrong. The fact was that she hadn't as yet given a single thought as to whether they should go back to live in Pinewood Close or not. No. There was something much more urgent on her mind for the minute, and of that she would tell him nothing. Not yet anyway.

CHAPTER FOURTEEN

CHRISTOPHER ROOPE HAD willingly agreed to meet Morse, on Friday just after 12 noon, at the Black Dog in St Aldates, just opposite the great portal of Christ Church. Roope had mentioned that he might be a few minutes late – he had a tutorial until twelve – but Morse waited happily with a pint of beer in front of him. He looked forward to meeting the young chemist, for if any outsider was involved in the murder of Quinn, he'd decided that Roope was the likeliest candidate, and already he had gleaned a few significant facts about him. First, he had learned that Roope had spent some time with one of the Gulf Petroleum companies, and might therefore have been in some sort of liaison with the men of power. For a deal there must have been at some stage, doubtless (though later) involving Bland at the Oxford end, in a perverse, though infinitely profitable, betrayal of public trust. It was certainly a possibility. Second, Roope was a chemist: and whoever had murdered Quinn had a great deal of technical knowledge about the fatal dosages of cyanide. Who better than Roope? Third, it was Roope who had suddenly materialized in the Syndicate building at a very, very crucial time – 4.30 p.m. or thereabouts (according to Noakes) on the previous Friday; and it was Roope who had looked into the rooms of each of the graduate staff in turn. What exactly had he been doing there? And what had he done after Noakes had gone upstairs for tea...? Fourth, there was the strange animosity that existed between Roope and Bartlett, and it appeared to Morse that the explanation for such animosity probably lay deeper, far deeper, than any temporary clash of views over the appointment of Quinn. Yes ... It was interesting that the clash had been over *Quinn*. And that fitted well with the fifth fact, which Morse had patiently unearthed earlier that morning in the University Registry: the fact that Roope had been educated at a public school in Bradford, the city where Quinn had lived almost all his short life, first as a pupil and then as a teacher. Had the two men known each other before Quinn was appointed to the Syndicate? And why had Roope been so obviously anxious to get Quinn appointed? (Morse found himself dismissing the Dean's charitable view of his colleague's social conscience.) Why, then? Now, Quinn had been thirty-one and Roope was thirty, and if they had been friends ... Yet where was the logic in that? One didn't go around murdering one's friends. Unless, that is—

A trio of laughing, long-haired, bearded undergraduates came into the bar, T-shirted and bejeaned, and Morse pondered on the changing times. He had worn a scarf and a tie himself – and sometimes a blazer. But that seemed a long time ago. He drained his glass and looked at his watch.

'Chief Inspector Morse?' It was one of the bearded trio and Morse realized that he was a good deal further out of touch than he had imagined.

'Mr Roope?'

The young man nodded. 'Can I get you a refill?'

'I'll get them—'

'No, no. My pleasure. What are you drinking?'

Over their beer a somewhat bemused Morse explained as much of the situation as he deemed prudent, and stressed the importance of trying to fix the exact time of Quinn's death. And when he came to ask about the visit to the Syndicate on the previous Friday, Morse was pleasantly impressed to find how carefully and indeed (if Noakes could be believed) how accurately Roope retraced his steps from the moment he had entered the building. All in all, Roope and Noakes appeared to corroborate each other's evidence neatly at almost every juncture. Yet there were several points on which Roope's memory seemed somewhat less than clear, and on which Morse immediately pressed him further.

'You say there was a note on Quinn's desk?'

'Yes. I'm sure the caretaker must have seen it too. We both—'

'But you don't remember exactly what it said?'

Roope was silent for a few seconds. 'Not really. Something about – oh, I don't know – being "back soon", I think.'

'And Quinn's anorak was on one of the chairs?'

'That's right. Over the back of the chair behind his desk.'

'You didn't notice if it was wet?'

Roope shook his head.

'And the cabinets were open, you say?'

'One of them was, I'm sure of that. The caretaker pushed it to and locked it.'

'Bit unusual for a cabinet to be left open – with Bartlett around, I mean?' Morse watched the chemist closely, but discerned no reaction.

'Yes.' And then Roope grinned disarmingly. 'Bit of a sod, you know, old Bartlett. Keeps 'em all on their toes.' He lit himself a cigarette and put the spent match carefully back into the box with his left hand.

'How do *you* get on with him, sir?'

'Me?' Roope laughed aloud. 'We don't see eye to eye, I'm afraid. I suppose you've heard—?'

'I gathered you weren't exactly bosom pals.'

'Oh, I wouldn't put it like that. You mustn't believe everything you hear.'

Morse let it ride. 'Mr Ogleby wasn't in his room, you say?'

'Not while I was there.'

Morse nodded, and believed him. 'How long *were* you there, sir?'

'Quarter of an hour, I suppose. Must have been. If Ogleby or any of the others were there – well, I just didn't seen them, that's all. And I'm pretty sure I would have done if they *had* been there.'

Morse nodded again. 'I think you're right, sir. I don't think anyone was there.' His mind drifted off, and for a brief second one of the silhouettes on the cavern wall focused in full profile – a profile that Morse thought he could recognize without much difficulty . . .

Roope interrupted his thoughts. 'Anything else I can tell you?'

Morse drained his beer and said there was. He asked Roope to account for his activities during the whole of the previous Friday, and Roope gladly obliged: he had caught the 8.05 to London; arrived at Paddington at 9.10; caught the Inner Circle tube to Mansion House; conferred with his publishers about the final proofs of a forthcoming opus on Industrial Chemistry; left about 10.45; had a chicken salad in the Strand somewhere; spent an hour or so in the National Portrait Gallery in Trafalgar Square; and then returned to Paddington, where he'd caught the 3.05 for Oxford.

Morse himself couldn't have specified the reason, but suddenly he became convinced that somehow, somewhere, Roope was lying. It was all too pat, too slick. A good deal of it must be true (the bit about the publishers, for instance). Mm. He'd obviously gone to London all right; but exactly when had he returned? Roope said he'd left his publishers at about 10.45 a.m. A taxi to Paddington, perhaps? Easy! *Roope could have been back in Oxford before lunchtime.* 'Just as a matter of interest, sir' (he asked it very mildly) 'do you think you could prove all that?'

Roope looked at him sharply. 'I don't suppose I could, no.' The eyes were steady and steely.

'You didn't meet anyone you knew in London?'

'I told you. I went to see—'

'Of course. But I meant later.'

'No, I didn't.' The words were slow and evenly spaced, and Morse sensed that in spite of his slim build and his rather mannered trendiness, Roope was probably considerably tougher, both physically and mentally, than he appeared to be. One thing was sure: he wasn't very happy when his word was questioned. Was that perhaps why he and Bartlett . . .?

'Well, never mind that now, sir. Tell me something else, if you will. Did you know Quinn before he came to Oxford?'

'No.'

'You came from that part of the country though, don't you?'

'You mean I haven't got an Oxford accent?'

'I'd put you down as a Yorkshireman.'

'You've done your homework, I see.'

'That's what they pay me for, sir.'

'I'm from Bradford, and so was Quinn. But let me spell it out. I'd never set eyes on him before he came before the interviewing committee. Do you believe that?'

'I believe everything you tell me, sir. Why shouldn't I?'

'You'd be a fool to believe everything some people told you.' There was little pretence now at masking the hostility in his voice, and Morse was beginning to enjoy himself.

'I think you ought to know,' said Morse quietly, 'that whatever else I am, I'm not a fool, sir.'

Roope made no reply and Morse resumed his questioning. 'Have you got a car?'

'No. I used to have, but I only live just up the Woodstock Road—'

'That's the bachelor flats, isn't it?'

Roope suddenly relaxed and smiled ingenuously.

'Look, Inspector, why don't you ask me something you *don't* know?'

Morse shrugged his shoulders. 'All right. Tell me this. Was it raining when you came back from London?'

'Raining like hell, yes. I—' Suddenly the light dawned in his eyes. 'Yes. I got a *taxi* from the station – straight to the Syndicate! There'll be a record of that some-where, surely?'

'Do you remember the driver?'

'No. But I think I remember the cab firm.'

Roope was right, of course. It shouldn't be all that difficult. 'We could try to—'

'Why not?' Roope got to his feet and picked up a pile of books. 'No time like the present, they say.'

As they walked up to Carfax and then left into Queen Street, Morse felt that he had gone wrong somewhere, and he said nothing until they reached the railway station, where a line of taxis was parked alongside the pavement. 'You'd better leave it to me, sir. I've got a bit of experience—'

'I'd rather do it myself, if you don't mind, Inspector.'

So Morse left him to get on with it; and stood there waiting under the 'Buffet' sign, feeling (he told himself) like the proverbial spare part at a prostitute's wedding.

Five minutes later a crestfallen Roope rejoined him: it wasn't going to be so easy as he'd thought, though he'd still like to do it himself, if Morse didn't mind, that was. But why should Morse mind? If the young fellow was as anxious as all that to justify himself . . . 'Like another beer?'

They walked through the ticket area and came to the barrier.

'We only want a beer,' explained Morse.

''Fraid you'll need platform tickets, sir.'

'Ah, bugger that,' said Morse. He turned to Roope: 'Let's walk down to the Royal Oxford.'

'Just a minute!' said Roope quietly. His eyes were shining again, and he retraced his steps and tapped the ticket collector on the shoulder. 'Do you remember me?'

'Don't think so, mate.'

'Were you here on duty last Friday afternoon?'

'No.' Dismissive.

'Do you know who was?'

'You'd have to ask in the office.'

'Where's that?'

The man pointed vaguely. 'Not much good now, though. Lunchtime, isn't it?'

Clearly, it wasn't Roope's day, and Morse put a sympathetic hand on his shoulder, and turned to the ticket collector. 'Give us two of your platform tickets.'

Half an hour later, after Roope had left him, Morse sat deep in thought and, to the teenaged couple who came to sit opposite him at the narrow buffet table, his face seemed quite impassive. Yet had they looked more carefully at him, and rather less eagerly towards each other, they might just have spotted the mildest hint of a satisfied smile trying to hide itself around the corners of his mouth. He sat quite still, his grey eyes staring unblinkingly into some great blue beyond, as the unresting birds of thought winged round and round his brain . . . until the London train came lumbering massively alongside the platform and finally broke the spell.

The young couple got up, kissed briefly but passionately, and said their fond farewells.

'I won't come on the platform,' he said. 'Always makes me miserable.'

'Yeah. You ge' off now. See you Sat'day.'

'You bet!'

The girl walked off in her high-heeled boots towards the door leading to Platform 1, and the boy watched her as she went, and fished for his platform ticket.

'Don't forge'. *I'll* bring the drinks this time.' She almost mouthed the words, but the boy understood and nodded. Then she was gone; and Morse felt the icy fingers running down from the top of his spine. *That* was the memory that had been eluding him. Yes! It all came back in a rushing stream of recollection. He'd been an undergraduate then and he'd invited the flighty little nurse back to his digs in Iffley Road and she'd insisted on bringing a bottle because her father kept a pub and she'd asked him what his favourite drink was and he'd said Scotch and she'd said it was hers too not so much because she enjoyed the taste but because it made her feel all sexy and . . . Christ, yes!

Morse shut off the distant, magic memories. The main silhouette was growing blurred again; but others now appeared upon the wall of the darkened cave, and together they fell into a more logical grouping. Much more logical. And as Morse handed in his platform ticket and walked out into the bright afternoon, he was more firmly convinced than ever that *someone else* had been in Studio 2 that Friday afternoon. He looked at his watch: 1.45 p.m. Tempting. By Jove, yes! The cinema was only three or four minutes' walk away, and Inga would be showing 'em all a few tricks. Ah well.

He signalled for a taxi: 'Foreign Examinations Syndicate, please.'

CHAPTER FIFTEEN

'I DON'T CARE what you ask her,' snapped Morse. 'When I've fetched her in here, just keeping her talking for ten minutes, that's all I ask.' Lewis, who half an hour previously had been summoned to the Syndicate building once more, looked inordinately uncomfortable. 'What do you want me to find out, though?'

'Anything you like. Ask her what her measurements are.'

'I wish you'd try to be serious, sir.'

'Well, ask her whether gin goes straight to her tits, or something.'

Lewis decided he would get nowhere with Morse in such a mood. What had happened go him? Something, surely; for suddenly he seemed as chirpy as a disc jockey.

Morse himself crossed the corridor, knocked on Monica's door, and went in. 'Can you spare a minute, Miss Height? Won't take long.' He escorted her politely to Quinn's office, showed her to the chair that faced Lewis, her reluctant interlocutor, and himself stood idly aside.

The phone went a few minutes later and Lewis answered it. 'For you, sir.'

'Morse here.'

'Ah, Inspector. Can I see you for a minute? It's, er, rather important. Can you come along straight away?'

'I'm on my way.'

Both Lewis and Monica had heard the voice plainly, and Morse excused himself without further explanation.

Once inside Monica's office, he worked swiftly. First, the bulky sheepskin jacket hanging up in the wall cupboard. Nothing much in either pocket – nothing much of interest, anyway. Next, the handbag. It would surely be here, if anywhere. Make-up, cheque book, diary, Paper-mate pen, comb, small bottle of perfume, pair of ear-rings, programme for a forthcoming performance of *The Messiah*, packet of Dunhill cigarettes, matches – and a purse. His hands trembled slightly as he opened the catch and poked his fingers amidst the small change and the keys and the stamps and – *there it was*. Ye gods. He'd been right! He was breathing nervously and noisily as he closed the handbag, placed it carefully back in its former position, left the room, closed the door quietly behind him, and stood alone in the corridor. He saw the implications – the extraordinarily grave implications – of the discovery he had just made. Certainly he'd been fairly sure that with a bit of luck he might find something. Yet now he'd found it, he knew there was something wrong, something that rang untrue, something that had not occurred to him before. Still, there was a quick way of finding out.

He hadn't been away for more than two or three minutes, and Lewis was relieved to see him back so soon. He sat on the corner of the table and looked at her. There were times (not very frequent, he admitted) when he seemed to lose all interest in the female sex, and this was one of them. She might as well have been a statue cast in frigid marble for all the effect she was having on him now. It happened to all men – or, at least, so Morse had heard. The womenopause, they called it. He took a deep breath. 'Why did you lie to me about last Friday afternoon?'

Monica's cheeks flushed a deep crimson, but she was not, it appeared, excessively surprised. 'It was Sally, wasn't it? I realized, of course, what your man was up to.'

'Well?'

'I don't know. I suppose it sounded less – less sordid, somehow, saying we went to my place.'

'Less sordid than what?'

'You know – motoring around, stopping in lay-bys and hoping no one else would pull in.'

'And that's what you did?'

'Yes.'

'Would Mr Martin back you up?'

'Yes. If you explained to him why—'

'You mean *you* haven't done that already?' The tone of Morse's voice was becoming increasingly harsh, and Monica coloured deeply again.

'Don't you think we ought to ask him?'

'No I don't! You've got him round your little finger, woman! Anyone can see that. I'm not interested in your web of lies. I want the truth! We're investigating a murder – not a bloody parking offence!'

'Look, Inspector. I can't do much more than tell you—'

'Of course you can! You can tell me the *truth.*'

'You seem terribly sure of—'

'And so I am, woman! What the hell do you think *that* is?' He banged his right hand furiously on the top of the desk, and revealed the torn-off half of a cinema ticket. Across the top were the letters I0, and almost immediately after them the number 2; beneath were the words 'Rear Lounge', and along the right-hand edge, running downwards, were the numbers 93556.

Monica looked down at the ticket as if mesmerized.

'Well?'

'I suppose it was *you* who arranged the little charade on the phone with Dr Bartlett?'

'I've done worse in my time,' said Morse. And suddenly, and quite inexplicably, he felt a surge of sympathy and warmth towards her, and his tone softened as he looked into her eyes: 'It'll come out in the end – you know that. Please let me have the truth.'

Monica sighed deeply. 'Do you mind getting me a cigarette, Inspector? As I think you know, mine are in my handbag.'

Yes (she said) Morse had been right. With Sally back from school that afternoon, there was no chance of going home, and she wasn't that keen, in any case. The whole thing was her fault quite as much as Donald's, of course; but recently she had been increasingly anxious to end the futile and dangerous affair. It was Donald who suggested they should go to the cinema and she had finally agreed. It would be an unnecessary risk to be seen going in together, and so it was arranged that he should go in at twenty past one, and she a few minutes later. They would each buy a ticket separately, and he would sit on the back row of the rear lounge in Studio 2 and watch out for her. And that's what they'd done. Everything had gone as planned, and they had left the cinema at about half-past three. They'd each taken their car, and hers had been parked in Cranham

Terrace, at the side of the cinema. She herself had gone straight home afterwards, and so, for all she knew, had Donald. Naturally they'd both been worried when they heard that the police wanted to know their whereabouts on Friday afternoon, and so they'd foolishly – well, Morse knew what they'd done. It wasn't all that far from the truth, though, was it? But, yes, they'd lied about that Friday afternoon. Of course, they had.

'Do you mind if we get your boyfriend in?' asked Morse.

'I think it would be better if you did.' She looked a little happier now, in spite of the jibe – certainly happier than Morse.

Pathetically Martin himself began to repeat the unauthorized version, but Monica stopped him. 'Tell them the truth, Donald. I just have. They know exactly where we both were on Friday afternoon.'

'Oh. Oh, I see.'

Morse felt his morale sagging ever lower as Martin stumbled his way through the same cheap little story. No discrepancy anywhere. He, like Monica it seemed, had gone straight home afterwards. And that was that.

'One more question.' Morse got up from the edge of the table and leaned against the nearest cabinet. It was a vital question – *the* vital question, and he wanted to witness their immediate reactions. 'Let me ask you both once again – did either of you see Mr Quinn on Friday afternoon? Please think very, very carefully before you answer.'

But it seemed that neither of them had any wish to think unduly carefully. Their faces registered blank. They shook their heads, and with apparent simplicity and earnestness they said that they hadn't.

Morse took another deep breath. He might as well tell them, he thought – that is, if they didn't know already. 'Would it surprise you both if I told you that . . .' (Morse hesitated – dramatically, he hoped) 'that there was another of your colleagues in Studio 2 last Friday afternoon?'

Martin turned deathly pale, and Monica opened her mouth like a chronic asthmatic fighting for breath. Morse (as he later realized) would have been wiser if he had allowed his little speech to take its full effect. But he didn't. 'You may well look surprised. You see, we know exactly where Mr Quinn was on Friday afternoon. He was sitting along with the pair of you – in the rear lounge of Studio 2!'

Martin and Monica Height stared at him in stupefied astonishment.

After they had gone, Morse turned to Lewis: 'That'll give 'em something to think about.'

But Lewis was feeling far from happy, and he said so. 'I hope you'll forgive me, sir, but—'

'C'mon, Lewis. Out with it!'

'Well, I don't think you handled it very well.' He sat back and waited for the explosion.

'Nor do I,' said Morse quietly. 'Go on.'

'You see, sir, I had the impression that when you said

one of the others was in the cinema – well, they didn't seem *surprised* at all. It was almost as if—'

'I know what you mean. It was almost as if they expected me to say someone else, wasn't it?'

Lewis nodded vigorously. 'But they really *were* surprised when you said it was Quinn.'

'Ye-es. You're right. And there's only one other person it could have been, isn't there? Bartlett was in Banbury that afternoon.'

'We haven't checked on that.'

'I don't think we shall have much trouble in finding a few headmasters to back up his alibi. No. I don't think there's much doubt where Bartlett was that afternoon.'

'That leaves Ogleby, then, sir.'

Morse nodded.

'Shall I go and fetch him, sir?'

'What do you think?' His customary confidence had deserted him, and Lewis got up and walked to the door. 'No, Lewis. Leave it a while, please. I want to think things through a bit more carefully.'

Lewis shrugged his shoulders with some impatience and sat down again. Morse didn't seem quite the man he had been, one way or another; but Lewis knew from previous experience that it wouldn't be long before something happened. Something was always happening when Morse was around.

And even as Lewis righteously reviewed the perfectly valid points he had just been making, Morse himself was conscious of an even greater failure in his own powers of logical analysis. Clown of a clown! Martin and Monica Height! Why had they ever told that abject lie in the first place? There was every risk (with Sally home so often) that even a moderately competent detective would pretty soon ferret out the truth about that. Why, then? And suddenly the answer presented itself, pellucidly clear: *there was an even greater risk about telling the truth.* If they had gone to the cinema together, why not say so? It seemed an infinitely less reprehensible piece of behaviour than the sordid liaison to which they had both been prepared to admit. People *did* go to the pictures together. It would cause a bit of talk – of course it would – if someone saw them. But . . . The silhouetted figures once again reformed, and they were all now grouping around one man. Arnold Philip Ogleby.

'You're right, you know, Lewis. Go and fetch him straight away.'

After they had left Quinn's office, Donald and Monica had stood silent for a few seconds in the polished corridor. 'Come in a second,' whispered Monica. She closed her own office door behind her, and looked at him fiercely. She spoke clearly and quietly, and with a force that was impressive. 'We don't say a word about it. Is that clear? *Not a single word!*'

CHAPTER SIXTEEN

OGLEBY LOOKED TIRED, and Morse decided he might as well be short and sharp. He knew he was taking a risk, but he'd played longer shots before – *and* won.

'You say, sir, that you came back to the office after lunch last Friday afternoon?'

'We've been over that before.'

Morse ignored him and continued. 'But you lied to me. You were seen outside this office last Friday afternoon. To be precise, you were seen going into Studio 2 in Walton Street.'

Ogleby sat placidly in his chair. He seemed in no way surprised. Indeed, if anyone were surprised it was Morse, who expected almost anything except the answer he received. 'Who saw me?'

'You don't deny it?'

'I asked you who it was that saw me.'

'I'm afraid I can't tell you that, sir. I'm sure you understand why.'

Ogleby nodded disinterestedly. 'As you wish.'

'We also have evidence, sir, that Mr Quinn was in Studio 2 that afternoon.'

'Really? Did somebody see him, too?'

Morse felt progressively less at ease with the man. It was one of the troubles with lies – his own lies; but he solved the problem by ignoring it. 'What time did you go to the cinema, sir?'

'Don't you know?' (There it was again!)

162

'I'd like your own statement.'

For a few seconds Ogleby appeared to be weighing the pros and cons of coming clean. 'Look, Inspector. In a way I suppose I lied to you a little.' (Lewis was scribbling as fast as he could.) 'We finish here, officially that is, at five. I try to put in my time as honestly as I can, and I think anyone you speak to here will confirm that. I'm never late, and I often work well after the rest have gone. On Friday, I agree, I left a bit early. I should think about a quarter to five, or so.'

'And you went to Studio 2.'

'I live in Walton Street, you know. It's not far away.'

'You went there?'

Ogleby shook his head. 'No.'

'Will you tell me why you went?'

'I didn't.'

'Have you ever been?'

'Yes.'

'Why?'

'I'm a lecherous old man.'

Morse switched his line of attack. 'Were you still here when Mr Roope came into the building?'

'Yes. I heard him talking to the caretaker.'

Again it was the answer that Morse had least expected, and he felt increasingly bewildered. 'But you weren't in your room. Your car—'

'I didn't come in a car on Friday.'

'You didn't see Quinn – in the cinema, I mean?'

'I wasn't in the cinema.'

'Did you see Miss Height and Mr Martin there?'

Surprise certainly registered now. 'Were *they* there?'

Morse could have sworn that Ogleby had not known of *that*, at any rate, and in a blindingly perverse sort of way, he felt very tempted to believe the man. 'Did you enjoy the film, sir?'

'I didn't see it.'

'You enjoy pornographic films, though?'

'I've sometimes thought that if I were a film producer I'd make something *really* erotic, Inspector. I think I've got the right sort of imagination.'

'You didn't keep your ticket?'

'I didn't have a ticket.'

'Will you look for it, sir?'

'Not much point, is there?'

Whew!

Morse decided that he might as well go the whole hog now. Few secrets could be kept for long in a place like the Syndicate, and he realized that he would be losing nothing – might, in fact, be gaining – by coming out into the open.

With Ogleby gone, he invited Bartlett along to Quinn's office, and told him what he had learned that afternoon: told him of the deserted office he had left behind him when he'd gone to Banbury; told him of the mammary magnetism of Miss Inga Nielsson; told him of his difficulties in establishing the whereabouts of everyone on that Friday afternoon; told him indeed, most of what he knew, or suspected, to be true. It wasn't really giving much away for most of it would have to come out in the wash fairly soon anyway. Finally, he told Bartlett that he would be grateful of a more accurate timetable of *his* movements; and all in all Bartlett hadn't taken things too badly. He could (he said) so very easily establish his own whereabouts; and there and then he rang the Head of Banbury Polytechnic and put him straight on to Morse. Yes, Bartlett had addressed a meeting of Heads; had arrived about five to three; together they had taken a glass of sherry; and the meeting was over about twenty, twenty-five past four. That was that, it seemed.

Bartlett asked if he was allowed to make his own observations on what he'd been told, and it was quite obvious that he was a far shrewder judge of his fellows than Morse had given him credit for. 'I'm not *all* that surprised, Inspector, about Miss Height and Martin. She's a very attractive girl: she's attractive to me, and I'm getting an old man; and Martin hasn't had the happiest of marriages, so I'm led to believe. There have been the occasional rumours, of course; but I've said nothing. I hoped it was just one of those brief infatuations – we've all had them in our time, and I thought it best to let it blow itself out. But – but, I must be honest, I'm very surprised by what you told me about Ogleby. It just doesn't seem to fit in. I've known him many years now, and he's – well, he's not like that.'

'We've all got our little weaknesses, sir.'

'No, you misunderstand me. I didn't mean whether he'd want to go to a sexy film or not. I've often . . . Well, never mind about that. No. It was about him saying he was *here*. You see, he's just not the sort of man who lies about things, and yet you say he insists that he was here when Roope came.'

'That's what he says.'

'And Roope says he wasn't in his own office, or anywhere around?'

'The caretaker backs him up.'

'He might have been upstairs.'

'I don't think so. Mr Ogleby himself says he heard Roope come in.'

Bartlett shook his head slowly and frowned. 'What do the girls say?'

'What girls?'

'The girls who collect the out-trays.'

Morse mentally kicked himself. 'What time are the trays collected?'

'Four o'clock every afternoon. The Post Office van is usually here about four-fifteen, and we like to have everything ready before then.'

I bet you do, thought Morse.

Bartlett rang through to the Registry and almost immediately a young, fair-haired girl came in and tried to keep her head as Morse questioned her. She had collected the trays on Friday afternoon. Yes, at four o'clock. And no one was there. Neither Ogleby, nor Miss Height, nor Martin, nor Quinn. No, she was *quite* sure. She'd mentioned to the other girls how odd it seemed.

Bartlett watched her distastefully as she left. He was wondering exactly how much work the 'other girls' had been doing when his back was turned.

Morse, as he walked slowly up the corridor with Bartlett, realized how very little he knew about the tangled complexity of relationships within the office. 'I'd like to have a long chat with you sometime, sir – about the office, I mean. There are so many things—'

'Why not come out and have a meal with us? My wife's a jolly good cook, you'll find. What about it?'

'That's very kind of you, sir. When do you suggest?'

'Well. Any time, really. Tonight, if you like.'

'Your wife—'

'Oh, don't worry about that. Leave it to me.' He disappeared into his office, and returned a couple of minutes later. 'Do you like steak, Inspector?'

As they walked to the car, both Lewis and Morse were deep in thought. The case was throwing up enough clues to solve a jumbo crossword, but somehow they wouldn't quite fit into the diagram.

'Nice fellow, Bartlett,' ventured Lewis, as they drove along the Woodstock Road towards the ring-road perimeter.

Morse did not reply. Bit too nice, perhaps, he was thinking. Far too nice, really. Like one of those suspects in a detective story who like as not turns out to be the crook. Was it possible! Was there any way in which the sturdy, shrewd, efficient little Secretary could have contrived the murder of Nicholas Quinn? As Lewis picked up speed down the long hill towards Kidlington, Morse began to see that there *was* a way. It would have been fiendishly clever; but then for all Morse knew . . . Oxford was full of clever people, wasn't it? And all at

once it occurred to Morse that he was in very real
danger of underestimating *all* of those he'd interviewed
so far. Why, even now, perhaps, they were all sitting
there quietly laughing at him.

Chapter Seventeen

Morse sat alone in his office. It was over two and a half hours before he was due at the Bartletts' and he welcomed the solitude and the chance to think.

The groceries which Quinn had purchased and the list of the provisions found in his kitchen proved more interesting than Morse had expected. Two pieces of steak and a bag of mushrooms, for instance. Bit extravagant, for one person? Might it have been for *two*? Two lovers? Morse pictured again the girl at the buffet door that led to Platform 1, and she merged into the figure of Monica Height. Could it have worked? Monica now admitted going to the cinema – with Martin, though. Could he forget Martin? Spineless creature. And so besotted with Monica that he'd say anything – if she told him to, or bribed him to. Think on, Morse! Monica and Quinn, then. Back row of the rear lounge; awkward unfastenings and frenetic fondlings, with the promise of still more glorious things in store – later. Later, yes. But where? Not at her place: impossible with Sally around. Why not at *his*? He could get some food in (steak? mushrooms?), and she would cook it for him. She'd love to. 'And don't forget, Nick, *I'll* bring the drinks this time. Sherry, isn't it? Dry sherry? I like that, too. And I'll bring a bottle of Scotch, as well. It always does things to me . . .' Possible. A starting point anyway.

Morse looked at the two lists again, and noticed a fact he'd missed before. Quinn already had two half-pound

169

packs of butter in his fridge, yet for some reason he'd bought another. Different brand, too. Very odd. Like a few other facts. He took a piece of paper and wrote them down:

(a) Position of Quinn's coffee table indicated that he'd probably been sitting in the draught. (Steady, Sherlock!)

(b) No spent matches found in either kitchen or living room; no matches found in Quinn's pockets. (Remember: Mrs E had already cleaned; she'd only returned for the ironing and had *not* cleared the wastepaper basket again.)

(c) More butter bought, when plenty in stock. (Forget it?)

(d) Note left by Quinn for Mrs E: vague enough to fit virtually any occasion? (Not *all* that vague though.)

Morse sat back and looked at his handiwork. Individually each point seemed pretty thin; but collectively – did they add up to something? Something like assuming that *Quinn did not return from work at all that Friday evening*? Had it been somebody else who lit the fire, and bought the groceries, and wrote a note for Mrs Evans? Think on, Morse! Think on, my boy! It was possible. Another starting point. Could the mysterious somebody have been Monica? (His mind kept coming back to her.) But she must have gone home to Sally sometime. (Job for Lewis – check.) Martin? He must have gone home to his wife some time. When? (Job for Lewis – check.) And anyway, neither of them knew enough

about cyanide, did they? Poisoning was a highly specialized job. (A woman's weapon, though.) Now, Roope
was a chemist. And Ogleby knew enough . . . Roope or
Ogleby – a much likelier pair to choose from. But
Roope was out of Oxford until about 4.15 p.m. (Or so
he said.) And Ogleby went home a bit early. (Or so he
said.) Mm. And what about Bartlett? Kidlington was on
the main road from Banbury, and the main road passed
no more than thirty yards from Pinewood Close. If he'd
left Banbury at 4.25 p.m. and really pushed it, 70 mph
say, he could have been in Kidlington by, well, ten to
five? Opportunity enough for any of them really. For if
Quinn had discovered that one of the four . . .

Morse knew he wasn't getting very far. It was the
method he couldn't fathom. But one thing was becoming
an ever firmer conviction in his mind: whoever had
come to Pinewood Close that Friday evening, *it hadn't
been Nicholas Quinn.* Leave it there for the minute,
Morse. Think of something else. Always the best way,
and there was one thing he could check on straightaway.

He called in Peters, the handwriting pundit, showed
him the note written to Mrs Evans, and gave him one
of the sheets of Quinn's writing taken from Pinewood
Close.

'What do you think?'

Peters hesitated. 'I'd need to study—'

'What's stopping you?'

Nothing had ever been known to hurry or ruffle Peters,
an ex-Home Office pathologist, who in his younger days
had made a considerable name and a considerable
income for himself by disobeying the two cardinal rules

for success – of thinking quickly and of acting decisively. For Peters thought at the speed of an arthritic tortoise and acted with the decisiveness of a soporific sloth. And Morse knew him better than to do anything but sit quietly and wait. If Peters said it was, it was. If Peters said that Quinn had definitely written the note, Quinn had definitely written the note. If he said he wasn't sure, he wasn't sure: and no one else in the world would be sure.

'How long will you be, Peters?'

'Ten, twelve minutes.'

Morse therefore knew that in about eleven minutes he would have his answer, and he sat quietly and waited. The phone went a few minutes later.

'Morse. Can I help you?'

It was the switchboard. 'It's a Mrs Greenaway, sir. From the John Radcliffe. Says she wants to talk to the man in charge of the Quinn murder.'

'That's me,' said Morse, without much enthusiasm. Mrs Greenaway, eh? The woman above Quinn. Well, well.

She had read the report in the *Oxford Mail* (she said) and felt that she ought to ring the police. Her husband wouldn't be very happy but— (Come on, girl, come on!) Well, she wasn't to have the baby until December, but she'd known – about four o'clock on Friday. The contractions— (Come on, girl!) Well, she'd rung up the works where Frank ('my husband, Inspector'), where Frank worked, and tried to get a message to him. But something must have gone wrong. She'd sat there by the window, watching and waiting, but no one came; and then she'd rung the works again about a quarter to five. She wasn't really worried, but she'd feel happier if

Frank ... Anyway she could always ring the hospital herself. They would send an ambulance straightaway; and she wasn't *absolutely* sure. It could have been just— (Come *on*!) Anyway, she saw Quinn come in, in his car, just after five.

'You *saw* him?'

'Yes. About five past five, it must have been. He drove in and put his car in the garage.'

'Was anybody with him?'

'No.'

'Go on, Mrs Greenaway.'

'Well, there's nothing else, really.'

'Did he go out again?'

'I didn't see him.'

'*Would* you have seen him?'

'Oh yes. As I say, I was looking out of the window all the time.'

'We think he went out to the shops, Mrs Greenaway. But you say—'

'Well, he could have gone out the back way, I suppose. You can get through the fence and on to the path, but—'

'But you don't think he did?'

'Well, I didn't hear him, and he wouldn't have gone over the back. It's ever so muddy.'

'I see.'

'Well, I hope—'

'Mrs Greenaway, are you absolutely sure you *saw* Mr Quinn?'

'Well, perhaps I didn't actually ... I *heard* him on the phone, though.'

'You *what?*'

'Yes. We've got a shared line, and it was just after he came in. I was really getting worried, and I thought I'd try the works again; but I couldn't get through, because Mr Quinn was using the phone.'

'Did you listen to what he was saying?'

'No, I'm sorry, I didn't. I'm not nosy like that.' (Of course not!) 'You see I just wanted him to get off the line, that's all.'

'Was he talking for long?'

'Quite a while. I picked up the phone two or three times and they were still—'

'You don't remember a name, *any* name, that Mr Quinn used? Christian name? Surname? Anything at all that could help us?'

Joyce Greenaway was silent for a minute. There *was* a very vague recollection, but it slipped away from her. 'I— No, I can't remember.'

'Not a woman, was it?'

'Oh no. It was a man all right. Sounded an educated sort of man – well, you know what I mean, it wasn't a common sort of voice.'

'Were they having a row?'

'No. I don't think so. But I didn't listen in. I didn't *really*. I was just getting impatient, that's all.'

'Why didn't you go down and tell Mr Quinn what the situation was?'

Joyce Greenaway hesitated a little, and Morse wondered exactly why. 'Well, we weren't, you know, as friendly as all *that.*'

'Look, Mrs Greenaway. Please think very hard. It's

vitally important – do you understand? If you could remember – even the slightest thing.'

But nothing would come, although the outline of that name still lurked subliminally. If only—

Morse did it for her. 'Ogleby? Mr Ogleby? Does that ring any bells?'

'No-o.'

'Roope? Mr Roope? Bartlett? Dr Bartlett? Mar—'

Joyce's scalp tingled. She'd been fishing for a verbal shape like 'Bartlett'. Could it have been? She wasn't really listening to Morse now. 'I can't be sure, Inspector, but it might have been Bartlett.'

Whew! What a turn-up for the books! Morse said somebody would be in to see her, but it would have to be the next day; and Joyce Greenaway, feeling a strange mixture of relief and trepidation, walked slowly back to the maternity ward.

Peters had been sitting quite motionless for the past two or three minutes, openly listening to the conversation, but he made no comment. 'Well?' said Morse.

'Quinn wrote it.'

Morse opened his mouth, but closed it again. Any protestation was futile. Peters said it was; so it *was*. Why not go with the evidence, Morse and fling your flimsy fancies aside? Quinn got back home about five; he wrote a note for Mrs Evans; and he rang somebody up – a well-spoken somebody, whose name may have been Bartlett.

CHAPTER EIGHTEEN

MRS BARTLETT WAS something of a surprise. She was three or four inches taller than her husband, and she ordered him around as if he were a naughty but lovable little schoolboy. There was another surprise, too. No one had mentioned to Morse that the Bartletts had a son, and the rather slovenly dressed, sullen-looking, bearded young man who was introduced as Richard seemed not particularly anxious to make an immediately favourable impression. But whilst the four of them sat rather awkwardly drinking their sherry, it became apparent that under his skin young Richard had a pleasant and attractive personality. As the ice thawed, he spoke with an easy humour and a total lack of self-consciousness; and as he and Morse discussed the respective merits of the Solti and Furtwängler recordings of *The Ring*, Mrs Bartlett slipped away to push a cautious fork into the Brussels sprouts and summoned her husband to open the wine. The table was immaculately set for the four of them, the silver cutlery winking and sparkling on the white tablecloth in the dimly lit room. The vegetables were almost ready.

Bartlett himself refilled Morse's glass. 'Nice little sherry, isn't it?'

'Indeed,' said Morse. He noticed that the label was different from that on the sherry bottle found in Quinn's rooms.

'Any more for you, Richard?'

'No.' It sounded oddly abrupt, as though there lurked some dark and hidden enmity within the Bartlett clan.

The soup was ready now, and Morse tossed back the last of his sherry, got to his feet, and walked across the wide room rubbing his hands together.

'Come on then, Richard.' His mother said it pleasantly, but Morse could hear the underlying note of tension.

'Don't worry about me. I'm not hungry.'

'But you *must*, Richard. I've—'

The young man stood up, and a strange light momentarily blazed in his eyes. 'I've just told you, mother, I'm not hungry.'

'But I've got it all ready for you. Just have a—'

'I don't want any bloody food. How many times do you want telling, you stupid woman?' The words were cruel and harsh, the tone one of scarcely repressed fury. He stalked out of the room, and almost immediately the front door slammed with a thudded finality.

'I'm awfully sorry, Inspector.'

'Don't worry about me, Mrs Bartlett. Some of the youngsters these days, you know—'

'It's not that, Inspector. You see . . . you see, Richard suffers from schizophrenia. He can be absolutely charming, and then – well, he gets like you saw him just now.' She was very near to tears and Morse tried hard to say the right things; but inevitably the incident had cast its shadow deep across the evening, and for a while they ate in awkward silence.

'Can it be treated?'

Mrs Bartlett smiled sadly. 'Good question, Inspector. We've spent literally thousands, haven't we, Tom? He's a voluntary patient at Littlemore at the moment. Sometimes he comes home at the weekends, and just occasionally, like tonight, he'll drop in and sit around or have something to eat.' Her voice was wavering and her husband patted her affectionately on the shoulder.

'Don't worry about it, my dear. We didn't ask the Inspector along to talk about *our* problems. He's got enough of his own, I should think.'

Only when Mrs Bartlett was washing the pots were the two men able to talk, and Morse's earlier impression that the Secretary knew exactly what was going on in his own office was cumulatively confirmed: if anyone had any ideas about who had been prepared to prostitute the integrity of the Syndicate, Morse felt it would be Bartlett. But he didn't, it seemed. With every subtlety he knew, Morse tried to draw out any suspicion of secret doubts; but the Secretary was deeply loyal to his staff, and Morse knew that he was tiptoeing too delicately. He decided the time had come.

'What did Mr Quinn want when he rang you up?'

Bartlett blinked behind the window frames; and then looked down at his coffee, and was silent for a while. Morse knew perfectly well that if Bartlett denied that Quinn had spoken to him, that would be the end of it, for there was no hard evidence on the point. Yet the longer Bartlett hesitated (surely Bartlett must realize it?), the more obvious it became.

'You know that he did ring me, then?'

'Yes, sir.' He might as well push his luck a little.

'Do you mind telling me how you know?'

It was Morse's turn to hesitate, but he decided to come reasonably clean. 'Quinn's telephone is on a shared line. Someone overheard you.'

Did Morse catch a sudden flash of alarm behind the friendly lenses? If he did, it was gone as quickly as it had appeared.

'You want me to tell you what the conversation was about?'

'I think you should have told me before, sir. It would have saved a great deal of trouble.'

'Would it?' Bartlett looked the Inspector in the eye, and Morse suspected that he was still a long, long way from reaching to the bedrock of the mystery.

'The truth's going to come out some time, sir. I honestly think you'd be sensible to tell me all about it.'

'Haven't you got that information, though? You say someone was listening in? Despicable attitude of mind, isn't it? Eavesdropping on other people—'

'Perhaps it is, sir; but, you see, the, er, person wasn't really listening in at all – just trying to get a very important call through, that's all. There was no question of deliberately—'

'So you *don't* know what we were talking about?'

Morse breathed deeply. 'No, sir.'

'Well, I'm er I'm not going to tell you. It was a very personal matter, between Quinn and myself—'

'Perhaps it was a personal matter that led to him being murdered, sir.'

'Yes, I realize that.'

'But you're not going to tell me?'

'No.'

Morse slowly drained his coffee. 'I don't think you realize exactly how important this is, sir. You see, unless we can find out where Quinn was and what he was doing that Friday evening—'

Bartlett looked at him sharply. 'You said nothing about Friday before.'

'You mean—?'

'I mean that Quinn rang me up one evening last week, yes. But it wasn't Friday.'

Clever little bugger! Morse had let the cat out of the bag – about not really knowing what the conversation had been about – and now the cat had jumped away over the fence. Bartlett was right, of course. He *hadn't* actually mentioned Friday, but—

Mrs Bartlett came through with the coffee pot and refilled the cups. She appeared quite unaware of breaking the conversation at a vital point, sat down, and innocently asked Morse how he was getting on with his inquiries into the terrible terrible business of poor poor Mr Quinn.

And Morse was game for anything now. 'We were just talking about telephone calls, Mrs Bartlett. The curse of the times, isn't it? I should think you must get almost as many as I do.'

'How right you are, Inspector. I was only saying last week – when was it, Tom? Do you remember? Oh yes. It was the day you went to Banbury. The phone kept ringing all the afternoon, and I said to Tom when he came in that we ought to get an ex-directory number and – do you know what? – just as I said it, the wretched thing rang again! And you had to go out again, do you remember, Tom?

The little Secretary nodded and smiled ruefully. Sometimes life could be very unfair. Very unfair indeed.

Just after 8.15 p.m. that same evening a man was taking the lid off the highly polished bronze coal scuttle when he heard the knock, and he got slowly to his feet and opened the door.

'Well, well! Come on in. I shan't be a minute. Take a seat.' He knelt down again by the fire and extracted a lump of shiny black coal with the tongs.

In his own head it sounded as if he had taken an enormous bite from a large, crisp apple. His jaws seemed to clamp together, and for a weird and terrifying second he sought frantically to rediscover some remembrance of himself along the empty, echoing corridors of his brain. His right hand still held the tongs, and his whole body willed itself to pull the coal towards the bright fire. For some inexplicable reason he found himself thinking of the lava from Mount Vesuvius pouring in an all-engulfing flood towards the streets of old Pompeii; and even as his left hand began slowly and instinctively to raise itself towards the shattered skull, he knew that life was ended. The light snapped suddenly out, as if someone had switched on the darkness. He was dead.

CHAPTER NINETEEN

MRS BARTLETT GOT up to answer the phone at a quarter to eleven and Morse realized that it would be as good an opportunity as he would get of taking a reasonably early leave of his hosts.

'It's probably Richard,' said Bartlett. 'He often feels a bit sorry later on, and tries to apologize. I shouldn't be surprised if—'

Mrs Bartlett came back into the room. 'It's for you, Inspector.'

Lewis told him as quickly and as clearly as he could what had happened. The Oxford City Police had been called in about nine o'clock – Chief Inspector Bell was in charge. It was only later that they realized how it might all tie in, and they'd tried to get Morse, and had finally got Lewis. The man had been killed instantly by a savage blow with a poker across the back of the skull. No prints or anything like that. The drawers had been ransacked, but not in any methodical way, it seemed. Probably the murderer had been interrupted.

'I'll see you there as soon as I can manage it, Lewis.'

As Morse came back into the room his face was pale with shock and he tried to keep his voice steady as he told the Bartletts the tragic news. 'It's Ogleby. He's been murdered.'

Mrs Bartlett buried her head in her hands and wept, whilst the Secretary himself, as he showed Morse to the front door, had difficulty in putting his words together coherently. He suddenly seemed an old man, shattered and uncomprehending. 'You asked about Quinn – when he rang – when he rang me – you asked about it – I said—'

Morse put his hand gently on the little man's shoulders. 'Yes. You tell me.'

'He said that – he said that he'd found out something I ought to know – he said that – that someone from the office was deliberately leaking question papers.'

'Did he say who it was?' asked Morse.

'Oh yes, Inspector. *He said it was me.*'

When Morse arrived at the neat little terraced house in Walton Street, Lewis was engaged in low conversation with Bell. It was an ugly sight, and Morse turned his head away, closed his eyes, and felt the nausea rising in his gorge. 'Look, Lewis. I want you to get on to one or two things straight away. Phone, if you like, or go around to see 'em – but I want to know exactly where Roope was tonight, where Martin was, where Miss Height was, where—'

Bell interrupted him. 'I've just been telling the Sergeant. We know where Miss Height was. She was here. She was the one who found him.'

It was not what Morse had expected, and the news appeared to confound whatever provisional procedure he had planned. 'Where is she now?'

'She's in a pretty bad way, I'm afraid. She rang through on a 999 call and then fainted, it seems. Somebody found her slumped by the public telephone box just up the road. She's been seen by the doc and they've taken her to the Radcliffe for the night.'

'She's got a young daughter.'

Bell put his hand on Morse's shoulder. 'Relax, old boy. We've seen to all that. Give us a *bit* of credit.'

Morse sat down in an armchair and wondered about himself. He seemed to be losing his grip. He closed his eyes again, and breathed deeply several times. 'Do as I tell you, anyway, Lewis. Get on to Roope and Martin straight away. And there's something else. You'd better go up to the Littlemore hospital sometime, and find out what you can about Richard Bartlett – got that? Richard Bartlett. He's a volunteer patient there. Find out what time he got in tonight – *if* he got in, that is.'

Morse forced himself to look once more at the liquid squelch of brains and blood commingled on the carpet, beyond which the fire was now no more than an ashen glow. 'And try to find out if any of them changed their clothes, tonight. What do you think, Bell? Blood must have spurted all over the place, mustn't it?'

Bell shrugged his shoulders. 'The girl had blood on her hands and sleeves.'

'I'd better see her,' said Morse.

'Not tonight, old boy, I'm afraid. Doc says she's to see nobody. She's in a state of deep shock.'

'Why did she come here? Did she say?'

'Said she wanted to talk to him about something important.'

'Was the door unlocked?'

''No. She says it was locked.'

'How the hell did she get in then?'

'She's got a key.'

Morse let it sink in. 'Has she now! She certainly spreads the joys around, doesn't she?'

'Pardon?' said Bell.

It was in the early hours of Saturday morning that Morse found what he was looking for and he whispered incredulously. Only he and Lewis remained, apart from the two Oxford City constables standing guard outside.

'Come here, Lewis. Look at this.' It was the diary found in Ogleby's hip pocket. Bell had earlier flipped cursorily through it, but had found no entries whatsoever, and had put it down again. It was a blue University diary with a small flap at the back which could be used for railway tickets and the like. And as Morse had prised open the flap, he could hardly believe his eyes. It was a ticket, torn roughly in half, with IO 2 printed across the top, 'Rear Lounge' beneath it, and along the right edge, running down, the numbers 93592.

'What do you make of it?'

'He *was* there after all, then, sir.'

'*Four* of them. Just think of it. Four out of the five!'

Lewis himself picked up the diary and looked with his usual thorough care at every page in turn. It was clear that Ogleby had never used the diary during the year. But on a page headed 'Notes' at the back of the diary, Lewis saw something that made his eyeballs bulge. 'Sir!' He said it very quietly, as though the slightest noise might frighten it away. 'Look at this.'

Morse looked at the diary, and felt the familiar constriction of the temples as an electric charge seemed to flash across his head. There, drawn with accuracy and neatness, was a small diagram:

```
┌─────────┬────┐
│ IO 2    │ 9  │
│         │ 3  │
│ Rear    │ 5  │
│         │ 5  │
│ Lounge  │ 0  │
└─────────┴────┘
```

'My God!' said Morse. '*It's the same number as the ticket we found on Quinn.*'

Half an hour later, as the two policemen left the house in Walton Street, Morse found himself recalling the words of Dr Hans Gross, one-time Professor of Criminology at the University of Prague. He had them by heart: 'No human action happens by pure chance unconnected with other happenings. None is incapable of explanation.' It was a belief that Morse had always cherished. Yet as he stepped out into the silent street, he began to wonder if it were really true.

No more than fifty or sixty yards down the street he saw the building which housed both Studio 1 and Studio 2. The neon lighting still illuminated the white boards above the foyer, the red and royal-blue lettering garish and bright in the almost eerie stillness: *The Nymphomaniac X* (Strictly Adults Only). Was she trying to tell him something? He walked down to the cinema with Lewis and stood looking at the stills outside.

She was certainly a big and bouncy girl, although a series of five-pointed stars had been superimposed by some incomparable idiot over the incomparable Inga's nipples.

CHAPTER TWENTY

MORSE WAS IN his office at 7.30 a.m. the next morning, tired and unshaven. He had tried to catch a few hours' sleep, but his mind would give him no rest, and he had finally given up the unequal struggle. He knew that he would be infinitely better able to cope with his problems if he had a complete change. But while there was no chance of that, at least he could sharpen his brain on the crossword; and he folded over the back page of *The Times*, looked at his watch, wrote the time in the left-hand margin, and began. It took him twelve and a half minutes. Not his best, this week; but not bad. And barring that one clue, he would have been within ten minutes: *In which are the Islets of Langerhans* (8). –A–C–E–S had been staring him in the face for well over two minutes before he'd seen the answer. He'd finally remembered it from a quiz programme on the radio: one contestant had suggested the South China Sea, another the Baltic, and a third the Mediterranean; and what a laugh from the radio audience when the question master had told them the answer!

During the morning the seemingly endless flood of news poured in. Lewis had managed to see Martin who (so he said) had felt restless and worried the previous evening, gone out about 7.30 p.m., and got back home at about a quarter to eleven. He had taken his car, called at several pubs near Radcliffe Square, and on his return had been banished by his wife to the doghouse. Roope (so he said) had been at home working all evening. No callers – seldom did have any callers. He was preparing a series of lectures on some aspect of Inorganic Chemistry which Lewis had been unable to understand at the time, and was unable to remember now. 'So far as I can see, sir, they're both very strongly in the running. The trouble is we seem to be running out of suspects. Unless you think Miss Height—'

'It's a possibility, I suppose.'

Lewis grudgingly conceded the point. 'That's still only three, though.'

'Aren't you forgetting Ogleby?'

Lewis stared at him. 'I don't follow you, sir.'

'He's still on my list, Lewis, and I see no earthly or heavenly reason why I should cross him off. Do you?'

Lewis opened his mouth but shut it again. And the phone went.

It was the Dean of the Examinations Syndicate, phoning from Lonsdale. Bartlett had rung him up the previous evening. What a terrible business it all was! Frightening. He just wanted to mention a little thing that had occurred to him. Did Morse remember asking about relationships within the Syndicate? Well, somehow the murders of Quinn and Ogleby had brought it all back. It had been just a *little* odd, he'd thought. It was the night when they'd had the big do at the Sheridan, with the Al-jamara lot. Some of them had stayed very late, long after the others had gone off to bed. Quinn was one of them, and Ogleby another; and the Dean had felt at the time (he could be *totally* wrong, of course) that Ogleby had been waiting for Quinn to go; had been watching him in a rather curious way. And when Quinn had left, Ogleby had followed him out almost immediately. It was only a *very* small thing, and actually putting it into words made it seem even smaller. But there it was. The Dean had now unburdened himself, and he hoped he hadn't wasted the Inspector's time.

Morse thanked him and put the phone down. As the Dean said, it didn't seem to add up to much.

In mid-morning Bell rang from Oxford. The medical evidence suggested that Ogleby had died only minutes before he was found. There were no prints other than Ogleby's on the poker or on the desk where the papers had been strewn around; Morse could re-examine whatever he wanted at any time, of course, but there seemed (in Bell's view) little that was going to help him very much. The blow that had crushed Ogleby's thin skull must have been struck with considerable ferocity, but may have required only minimal strength. It had probably been delivered by a right-handed person, and the central point of impact was roughly five centimetres above the occipital bone, and roughly two centimetres to the right of the parietal foramen. The result of the blow—

'Skip it,' said Morse.

'I know what you mean.'

'Is Miss Height still—?'

'You can't see her till lunchtime. Doc's orders.'

'Still in the Radcliffe?'

'Yep. And you'll be the second person to see her, I promise.'

A young nurse put her head round the screens curtaining the bed on the women's accident ward. 'You've got another visitor.'

Monica appeared drawn and nervous as Morse looked down at her, sitting up against the pillow, her ample hospital nightie softening the contours of her lovely body. 'Tell me about it,' said Morse simply.

Her voice was quiet but firm: 'There's not much to tell, really. I called to see him about half-past eight. He was just lying—'

'You had a key?'

She nodded. 'Yes.' Her eyes seemed suddenly very sad, and Morse pressed the point no further. Whether Philip Ogleby had been to see *The Nymphomaniac* was a question still in doubt; but it was perfectly clear that the nymphomaniac had been to see *him* – at fairly regular intervals.

'He was lying there—?'

She nodded. 'I thought he must have had a heart attack or something. I wasn't frightened, or anything like that. I knelt down and touched his shoulder – and his – his head was – was almost in the fireplace, and I saw the blood—' She shook her head, as though to rid herself of that horrific sight. 'And I got blood and – and stuff, over my hands – and I didn't know what to do. I just couldn't stay in that terrible room. I knew there was

191

a phone there but – but I went out into the street and rang the police from the phone box. I don't remember any more. I must have stepped out of the box and just – fainted. The next thing I remember was being in the ambulance.'

'Why did you go to see him?' (He had to ask it.)

'I – I hadn't really had any chance to talk to him about – about Nick and—' (Lying again!)

'You think he knew something about Quinn's murder?'

She smiled sadly and wearily. 'He was a very clever man, Inspector.'

'You didn't see anyone else?'

She shook her head.

'Could there have been anyone else – in the house?'

'I don't know. I just don't know.'

Should he believe her? She'd told so many lies already. But there must have been *some* cause for the lies; and Morse was convinced that if only he could discover that cause he would make the biggest leap forward in the case so far . . . It was the Studio 2 business that worried him most. Why, he repeated to himself, *why* had Monica and Donald Martin lied so clumsily about it? And as he wrestled with the problem once again, he began to convince himself that all four of them – Monica, Martin, Ogleby, and Quinn – must have had some collective reason for being in Studio 2 that Friday afternoon, for he just could not bring himself to believe that their several paths had converged for purely fortuitous reasons. Even Morse, who accepted the majority of improbable coincidences with a curiously credulous gullibility, was not prepared to swallow that!

Something – *something* must have happened at Studio 2 that afternoon. What? Think of anything, Morse, anything – it wouldn't matter. Quinn had got there early, just after the doors opened. Then Martin had come in, sneaking into the back row and waiting and looking nervously around. Had he seen Quinn? Had Quinn seen *him*? The lights must have been dim; but not so dim as all that, especially as the eyes slowly accustomed themselves to the gloom. *Then*, what? Monica had come in, and Martin saw her, and they sat there together, and Martin told her that he had seen *Quinn*. What would they do? They'd leave. Pronto! Go on, Morse. If Martin had seen Quinn – and Quinn had not seen him – he would have left the cinema immediately, waited outside for Monica, told her that they couldn't stay there, and suggested somewhere else . . . Yes. But where had Ogleby fitted in? The number on his ticket, some forty-odd numbers after Quinn's, suggested (if the manageress had done her sums right) that Ogleby had not appeared in Studio 2 until about four or five o'clock. How did *that* fit into the pattern, though? Augh! It didn't fit. Try again, Morse. Something must have frightened *Monica* off, perhaps. Yes. That was a slightly more promising hypothesis. Had she seen something? Someone? The cause of all the lies? After learning that Quinn had been in Studio 2, she had told another lie, and . . . Oh Christ! What a muddle his mind was in! The pictures flickered fitfully upon the wall, the faces fading and changing, and fading again . . .

'You've been a long way away, Inspector.'

'Mm? Oh, sorry. Just daydreaming.'

'About me?'

'Among others.'

On the table beside the bed was a copy of *The Times*, folded at the crossword page; but only three or four words were written into the diagram, and Morse found himself wondering and wandering off again. Wondering if Monica knew where the Islets of Langerhans were situated . . . Well, if she didn't, the nurse could soon— *Just a minute!* His thinning hair seemed to be standing on end, and his scalp suddenly tingled with a thousand tiny prickles. Oh yes! It was a beautiful idea, and the old questions flooded his brain. In what sea are the Islets of Langerhans? When was George Washington assassinated? Who was Kansas-Nebraska Bill? In what year did R. A. Butler become prime minister? Who composed the Trout Quartet? By what name was the Black Prince known when he became king? *The questions were all non-questions.* George W. wasn't assassinated, and K.-N. Bill wasn't *anybody*; he was a Bill before the Senate. The same with all of them. They were questions which couldn't be answered, because they were questions which couldn't be asked. Morse had become besotted with trying to find out who had been at Studio 2, when they had been there, why they had been there. But what if they were all non-questions. What if *no one* had been in Studio 2? Everything in the case had been designed to mislead him into thinking that they had been there. Some of them – all of them, perhaps – *wanted* him to think so. And he had blindly stumbled along the gangway down the darkened cinema, groping his way like a blind man, and trying to see (O fool of a fool!) who was sitting there. But perhaps there was no one, Morse. No one!

'Who did you see going into Studio 2, Miss Height?'

'Why don't you call me "Monica"?'

The nurse put her head through the curtains, and told Morse that he really ought to leave now; he'd already gone way over his time. He stood up and looked down at her once more, and kissed the top of her head gently.

'You didn't see anyone going in to Studio 2, did you, Monica?'

For a second there was hesitation in her eyes, and then she looked at him earnestly. 'No. I didn't. You must believe that.'

She took Morse's hand and squeezed it gently against her soft breast. 'Come again, won't you? And try to look after me.' Her eyes sought his and he realized once more how desperately desirable she would always be to lonely men – to men like him. But there was something else in her eyes: the look of the hunted fleeing from the hunter; the haunted look of fear. 'I'm frightened, Inspector. I'm so very frightened.'

Morse was thoughtful as he walked the long corridors before finally emerging through the flappy celluloid doors into the entrance road by the side of the Radcliffe, where the Lancia stood parked on an 'Ambulance Only' plot. He started up the engine and was slowly steering through the twisting alleys that led down into Walton Street when he saw a familiar figure striding up towards the hospital. He stopped the car and wound down the window.

'I'm glad to see you, Mr Martin. In fact I was just coming along to see you. Jump in.'

'Sorry. Not now. I'm going to see—'

'You're not.'

'Who says?'

'No one's going in to see her until I say so.'

'But when—?'

'Jump in.'

'Do I have to?'

Morse shrugged his shoulders. 'Not really, no. You please yourself. At least, you please yourself until I decide to take you in.'

'What's that supposed to mean?'

'What it says, sir. Until I decide to take you in and charge you—'

'*Charge* me? What with?'

'Oh, I could think up something pretty quickly, sir.'

The dull eyes stared at Morse in anxious bewilderment. 'You must be joking.'

'Of course I am, sir.' He leaned across and opened the Lancia's nearside door, and Donald Martin sullenly eased his long body into the passenger seat.

The traffic was heavy as they drove up the narrow street, and Morse decided to turn right and cut straight across to Woodstock Road. As he stopped at yet another Pelican crossing, he realized just how close the Syndicate building was to Studio 2. And as the lights turned to flashing amber, he held the car on half-clutch as a late pedestrian galloped his way across: a bearded young man. He was in too much of a rush to recognize Morse; but Morse recognized *him*, and the last words that Monica had spoken re-echoed in his mind. In his rear mirror he could see that the man was walking briskly down the right-hand side of Woodstock Road towards the Radcliffe Infirmary, and he swung the Lancia sharp left at the next turning, furiously cursing the crawling stream of cars. He parked on the double yellow lines at the back of the Radcliffe, told Martin to stay where he was, and ran like a crippled stag to the accident ward. She was still there: still sitting up prettily amid the pillows as he peeped behind the screens. Phew! He rang up HQ from the Sister's office, told Dickson he was to get there immediately, and stood there breathing heavily.

'You all right, Inspector.'

'Just about, thank you, Sister. But listen. I don't want anyone to talk to Miss Height or to get anywhere near her. All right? And if anyone *does* try to visit her, I want to know who it is. One of my men will be here in ten minutes.'

He paced impatiently up and down the corridor waiting for Dickson's arrival. Like Pilgrim he seemed to be making but sluggish progress – up the hill of difficulty and down into the slough of despond. But there was no sign of whatsoever of Richard Bartlett. Perhaps Morse was imagining things.

197

Chapter Twenty-One

THREE-QUARTERS OF an hour later, with the office clock showing half-past two, Morse's irritation with the young philanderer was mounting towards open animosity. What a flabby character Donald Martin was! He admitted most things, albeit with some reluctance. His relationship with Monica had sputtered into sporadic passion, followed by the usual remorse and the futile promises that the affair had got to finish. Certainly it was he who had always tried to force the pace; yet when they were actually making love together (Morse drew the blinds across his imagination) he knew that she was *glad.* She could surrender herself so completely to physical love; it was wonderful, and he had known nothing like it before. But when the passion was spent, she would always retreat into indifference – callousness, almost. Never had she made any pretence about her reasons for letting him take her: it was purely physical. Never had she spoken of love, or even of deep affection . . . His wife (he was sure of it) had no suspicions of his unfaithfulness, although she must have sensed (of course she must!) that the careless rapture of their early married days had gone – perhaps for ever.

How despicable the man was! His dark, lank hair, his horn-rimmed glasses, his long, almost effeminate fingers. Ugh! Nor was Morse's dark displeasure dissipated as Martin repeated what he had already told Lewis about his whereabouts the previous evening. He'd been lucky to find a parking space in the Broad, and he'd gone to the King's Arms first, where he thought the barmaid would probably remember him. Then to the White Horse, where he didn't know anyone. Another pint. Then down to the Turl Bar. Another pint. No he didn't often go out for a binge: very rarely in fact. But the last few days had been a nightmarish time. He'd found he couldn't sleep at all well, and beer had helped a bit; it usually did. But why did Morse keep on and on at him about it? He'd gone nowhere near Ogleby's! Why should he? What, for heaven's sake, could he have had to do with Ogleby's murder? He'd not even known him very well. He doubted if anybody in the office knew him very well.

Morse said nothing to enlighten him. 'Let's come back to last Friday afternoon.'

'Not again, surely! I've told you what happened. All right, I lied for a start, but—'

'You're lying now! And if you're not careful you'll be down in the cells until you *do* tell me the truth.'

'But I'm *not* lying.' He shook his head miserably. 'Why can't you believe me?'

'Why did you say you spent the afternoon at Miss Height's house?'

'I don't know, really. Monica thought . . .' His voice trailed off.

'Yes. She's told me.'

'Has she?' His eyes seemed suddenly relieved.

'Yes,' lied Morse. 'But if you don't want to tell me yourself, we can always wait, sir. I'm in no great rush myself.'

Martin looked down at the carpet. 'I don't know why she didn't want to say we'd been to the pictures. I don't – honestly! But I didn't think it mattered all that much, so I agreed to what she said.'

'It's a bit odd to say you'd been to bed when all you'd done was sit together in the cinema!'

Martin seemed to recognize the obvious truth of the assertion, and he nodded. 'But it's the truth, Inspector. It's the honest truth! We stayed in the cinema till about quarter to four. You've got to believe that! I had nothing at all – nothing! – to do with Nick's death. Nor did Monica. *We were together* – all the afternoon.'

'Tell me something about the film.'

So Martin told him, and Morse knew that he could hardly be fabricating such entirely gratuitous obscenities. Martin *had* seen the film; seen it some time, anyway. Not necessarily that Friday, not necessarily with Monica, but . . .

Martin was convincing him, he knew that. Assume he *was* there that Friday afternoon. With Monica? Yes, assume that too. Sit them down there on the back row of the rear lounge, Morse. Martin had been waiting for her, and she'd come in. Yes, keep going! She'd come in and . . . and they had stayed after all! Who, if anyone, had they seen? No. Go back a bit. Who had Martin seen going in? No. Who had Monica seen? Going in? Or . . . ? Yes. Yes!

Think of it the other way for a minute. Ogleby had gone into the cinema at about quarter to five, say. But he must have known all about Quinn's ticket, mustn't he? In fact he must have *seen* it. When? Where? Why had he made a careful freehand drawing of that ticket? Ogleby must have known, or at least suspected, that the ticket was vitally important. All right. Agree that Monica and Martin had seen the film together. But had *Quinn* gone? Or had someone just wished to make everyone else *think* that he'd gone? Who? Who knew of the ticket? Who had drawn it? Where had he found it, Morse? My God, yes! What a stupid blind fool he'd been!

Martin had stopped talking minutes before, and was looking curiously at the man in the black leather chair, sitting there smiling serenely to himself. It had all happened, as it always seemed to do with Morse, in the twinkling of an eye. Yes, as he sat there, oblivious to everything about him, *Morse felt he knew when Nicholas Quinn had met his death.*

HOW?

CHAPTER TWENTY-TWO

EARLY ON SATURDAY evening Mr Nigel Denniston decided to begin. He found that the majority of his O-level English Language scripts had been delivered, and he began his usual preliminary task of putting the large buff-coloured envelopes into alphabetical order, and of checking them against his allocated schedule. The examiners' meeting was to be held in two days' time, and before then he had to look at about twenty or so scripts, mark them provisionally in pencil, and present them for scrutiny to the senior examiner, who would be interviewing each of his panel after the main meeting. Al-jamara was the first school on his list, and he slit open the carefully sealed envelope and took out the contents. The attendance sheet was placed on top of the scripts, and Denniston's eyes travelled automatically and hope-fully down to the 'Absentee' column. It was always a cause of enormous joy to him if one or two of his candidates had been smitten with some oriental malady; but Al-jamara was a disappointment. According to the attendance sheet there were five candidates entered, and all five were duly registered as 'present' by the distant invigilator. Never mind. There was always the chance of finding one or two of those delightful children who knew nothing and who wrote nothing; children for whom the wells of inspiration ran dry after only a couple of laboured sentences. But no. No luck there, either. None of the five candidates had prematurely given up the ghost. Instead, it was the usual business: page after page of ill-written, unidiomatic, irrelevant twaddle, which it was his assignment to plough through (and almost certainly to plough), marking in red ink the myriad errors of grammar, syntax, construction, spelling and punctuation. It was a tedious chore, and he didn't really know why year after year he took it on. Yet he did know. It was a bit of extra cash; and if he didn't mark, he would only be sitting in front of the TV, forever arguing with the family about which of the channels they should watch . . . He flicked through the first few sheets. Oh dear! These foreigners might be all right at Mathematics or Economics or that sort of thing. But they couldn't write *English* – that was a fact. Still, it wasn't really surprising. English was their second language, poor kids; and he felt a little less jaundiced as he took out his pencil and started.

An hour later he had finished the first four scripts. The candidates had tried – of course they had. But he felt quite unjustified in awarding the sort of marks that could bring them anywhere near the pass range. Tentatively he had written his own provisional percentages at the top right-hand corner of each script: 27%, 34%, 35%, 19%. He decided to finish off the last one before supper.

This was a better script. My goodness, it was! And as he read on he realized that it was very good indeed. He put aside his pencil and read through the essay with genuine interest, bordering on delight. Whoever the boy was, he'd written beautifully. There were a few awkward sentences, and a sprinkling of minor errors;

but Denniston doubted whether he himself could have written a better essay under examination conditions. He had known the same sort of thing before, though. Sometimes a candidate would memorize a whole essay and trot it out: beautiful stuff, lifted lock, stock and paragraph from one of the great English prose stylists; but almost invariably in such cases, the subject matter was so wildly divorced from the strict terms of the question set as to be completely irrelevant. But not here. Either the lad was quite exceptionally able, or else he had been extraordinarily fortunate. That wasn't for Denniston to decide, though; his job was to reward what was on the script. He pencilled in 90%; and then wondered why he hadn't given it 95%, or even 99%. But like almost all examiners, he was always frightened of using the full range of marks. The lad would fly through, anyway. Wonderful lad! Perfunctorily Denniston looked at the name: Dubal. It meant nothing to him at all.

In Al-jamara itself, the last of the autumn examinations, crowded into just the one week, had finished the previous afternoon, and George Bland relaxed with an iced gin and tonic in his air-conditioned flat. It had taken him only a few weeks to regret his move. Better paid, certainly; but only away from Oxford had he begun fully to appreciate the advantages of his strike-ridden, bankrupt, beautiful homeland. He missed, above all, the feeling of belonging somewhere which, however loosely, he could think of as his home: the pub at night; the Cotswold villages with their greens and ancient churches; the concerts, the plays, the lectures, and the general air of learning; the oddities forever padding their faddish, feckless paths around the groves of the Muses. He'd never imagined how much it all meant to him ... The climate of Al-jamara was overwhelming, intolerable, endlessly enervating; the people alien – ostensibly hospitable, but secretly watchful and suspicious ... How he regretted the move now!

The news had worried him; would have worried anyone. It was for information only, really – no more; and it had been thoughtful of the Syndicate to keep him informed. The International Telegram had arrived on Wednesday morning: TRAGIC NEWS STOP QUINN DEAD STOP MURDER SUSPECTED STOP WILL WRITE STOP BARTLETT. But there had been another telegram, received only that morning; and this time it was unsigned. He had burned it immediately, although he realized that no one could have suspected the true import of the brief, bleak lines. Yet it had always been a possibility, and he was prepared. He walked over to his desk and took out his passport once more. All was in order; and tucked safely inside was his ticket on the scheduled flight to Cairo, due to leave at noon the following day.

CHAPTER TWENTY-THREE

THERE WAS A car outside No 1 Pinewood Close as Frank Greenaway pulled into the crescent; but he didn't recognize it and gave it no second thought. He could fully understand Joyce's point of view, of course. He wasn't too keen to go back there himself, and it wasn't right to expect her to be there on her own while he was out at work. She'd have the baby to keep her company, but— No. He agreed with her. They would find somewhere else, and in the meantime his parents were being very kind. Not that he wanted to stay with them *too* long. Like somebody said, fish and visitors began to smell after three days ... They could leave most of their possessions at Pinewood Close for a week or two, but he had to pick up a few things for Joyce (who would be leaving the John Radcliffe the next morning), and the police had said it would be all right.

As he got out of his car, he noticed that the street lamp had been repaired, and the house where he and Joyce had lived, and wherein Quinn had been found murdered, seemed almost ordinary again. The front gate stood open, and he walked up to the front door, selecting the correct key from his ring. The garage doors stood open, propped back by a couple of house bricks. Frank opened the front door very quietly. He was not a nervous man, but he felt a slight involuntary shudder as he stepped into the darkened hallway, the two doors on his right, the stairs almost directly in front of him. He would hurry it up a bit; he didn't much fancy staying there too long on his own. As he put his hand on the banister he noticed the slim line of light under the kitchen door: the police must have forgotten . . . But then he heard it, quite distinctly. Someone was in the kitchen. Someone was quietly moving around in there . . . The demon fear laid its electrifying hand upon his shoulder, and without conscious volition he found himself a few seconds later scurrying hurriedly along the concrete drive towards his car.

Morse heard the click of the front door, and looked out into the passageway. But no one. He was imagining things again. He returned to the kitchen, and bent down once more beside the back door. Yes, he *had* been right. There was no mud on the carpets in the other downstairs rooms, and they had been hoovered only an hour or so before Quinn was due to return. But beside the back door there *were* signs of mud, and Morse knew that someone had taken off his shoes, or her shoes, and left them beside the doormat. And even as he had stood there his own shoes crunched upon the gritty, dried mud with the noise of someone trampling on cornflakes.

He left the house and got into the Lancia. But then he got out again, walked back, closed the garage doors, and finally the garden gate behind him.

Ten minutes later he drew up outside the darkened house in Walton Street, where a City constable stood guard before the door.

'No one's tried to get in, Constable?'

'No, sir. Few sightseers always hanging around, but no one's been in.'

'Good. I'll only be ten minutes.'

Ogleby's bedroom seemed lonely and bleak. No pictures on the walls, no books on the bedside table, no ornaments on the dressing table, no visible signs of heating. The large double bed monopolized the confined space, and Morse turned back the coverlet. Two head pillows lay there, side by side, and a pair of pale yellow pyjamas were tucked just beneath the top sheet. Morse picked up the nearer pillow, and there he found a neatly folded négligé – black, flimsy, almost transparent, with a label proclaiming 'St Michael'.

No one had yet bothered to clean up the other room, and the fire which had blazed merrily the night before was nothing now but cold, fine ash into which some of the detectives had thrown the tipped butts of their cigarettes. It looked almost obscene. Morse turned his attention to the books which lined the high shelves on each side of the fireplace. The vast majority of them were technical treatises on Ogleby's specialisms, and Morse was interested in only one: *Medical Jurisprudence and Toxicology*, by Glaister and Rentoul. It was an old friend. A folded sheet of paper protruded from the top, and Morse opened the book at that point: page 566. In heavy type, a quarter of the way down the page, stood the heading 'Hydrocyanic Acid'.

At the Summertown Health Clinic, Morse was shown immediately into Dr Parker's consulting room.

'Yes, Inspector, I'd looked after Mr Ogleby for – oh, seven or eight years now. Very sad really. Something may have turned up, but I very much doubt it. Extremely rare blood disease – nobody knows much about it.'

'You gave him about a year, you say?'

'Eighteen months, perhaps. No longer.'

'He knew this?'

'Oh yes. He insisted on knowing everything. Anyway, it would have been useless trying to keep it from him. Medically speaking, he was a very well-informed man. Knew more about his illness than I did. Or the specialists at the Radcliffe, come to that.'

'Do you think he told anybody?'

'I doubt it. Might have told one or two close friends, I suppose. But I knew nothing about his private life. For all I know, he didn't have any close friends.'

'Why do you say that?'

'I don't know. He was a – a bit of a loner, I think. Bit uncommunicative.'

'Did he have much pain?'

'I don't think so. He never said so, anyway.'

'He wasn't the suicidal sort, was he?'

'I don't think so. Seemed a pretty balanced sort of chap. If he *were* going to kill himself, he would have done it simply and quickly, I should have thought. He would certainly have been in his right mind.'

'What would you say is the simplest and quickest way?'

Parker shrugged his shoulders. 'I think I'd have a quick swig of cyanide, myself.'

Morse walked thoughtfully to the car: he felt a

sadder, if not a much wiser man. Anyway, one more call to make. He just hoped Margaret Freeman hadn't gone off to a Saturday night hop.

Although earlier in the evening Lewis had been quite unable to fathom the Inspector's purposes, he had quite looked forward to the duties assigned to him.

Joyce Greenaway was pleasantly co-operative, and she tried her best to answer the Sergeant's strange questions. As she had told Inspector Morse, she couldn't be certain that the name *was* Bartlett, and she could see no point whatsoever in trying (although she did try) to remember whether he'd been addressed as Bartlett or Dr Bartlett. She was quite sure, too, that she could never hope to recognize the voice again: her hearing wasn't all that good at the best of times and – well, you couldn't recognize a voice again just like that, could you. What were they talking about? Well, as a matter of fact, she did just have the feeling that they were arranging to meet somewhere. But further than that – when, where, why – no. No ideas at all.

Lewis got it all down in his notebook; and when he'd finished he made the appropriate noises to the little bundle of life that lay beside the bed.

'Have you got any family, Sergeant?'

'Two daughters.'

'We had a name all ready if it had been a girl.'

'There's a lot of nice boys' names.'

'Yeah, I suppose so. But somehow— What's your Christian name, Sergeant?'

Lewis told her. He'd never liked it much.

'What about the Inspector? What's his Christian name?'

Lewis frowned for a few seconds. Funny, really. He'd never thought of Morse as having one. 'I don't know. I've never heard anyone call him by his Christian name.'

From the John Radcliffe Lewis drove down to the railway station. There were four taxi firms, and Lewis received conflicting pieces of advice about the best way to tackle his assignment. It really should have been a comparatively easy job to find out who (if anyone) had taken Roope from the station to the Syndicate building at about 4.20 p.m. on the 21st November. But it wasn't. And when Lewis had finally completed his rounds he doubted whether the answer he'd come up with was the one that Morse had expected or hoped for.

It was after half-eight before Lewis reached Littlemore Hospital.

Dr Addison, who was on night duty, had not himself had a great deal to do with Richard Bartlett's case, although he knew *of* it, of course. He fetched the file, but refused to let Lewis look through it himself. 'There are some very *personal* entries, you know, Officer, and I think that I can give you the information you want without—'

'I don't really want any details about Mr Bartlett's mental troubles. Just a list of the institutions that he's stayed in over the past five years, the clinics he's been to, the specialists he's seen – and the dates, of course.'

Addison looked annoyed. 'You want all that? Well, I suppose, if it's really necessary . . .' The file contained a wadge of papers two inches thick, and Lewis patiently made his notes. It took them almost an hour.

'Well, many thanks, sir. I'm sorry to have taken up so much of your time.'

Addison said nothing.

As Lewis finally got up to leave he asked one last question, although it wasn't on Morse's list.

'What's the trouble with Mr Bartlett, sir?'

'Schizophrenia.'

'Oh.' Lewis thanked him once again, and left.

Morse was not in his office when Lewis arrived back. They'd arranged to meet again at about ten if each could manage it. Had Morse finished his own inquiries yet? Like as not he had, and gone out for a pint. Lewis looked at his watch: it was just after ten past ten, and he might as well wait. Morse must have been looking up something for his crossword, for the *Chambers* lay on the cluttered desk. Lewis opened it. 'Ski-'? No. 'Sci-'? No. He'd never been much of a hand at spelling. 'Sch-'? Ah! There it was: '*ski-zo-freni-a*, or *skid-zo*, n., dementia prae-cox or kindred form of insanity, marked by introversion and loss of connexion between thoughts, feeling and actions.'

Lewis had moved on to 'dementia' when Morse came in, and it was quite clear that for once in a lifetime he had *not* been drinking. He listened with great care to what Lewis had to tell him, but seemed neither surprised nor excited in any way.

It was at a quarter to eleven that he dropped his bombshell. 'Well, Lewis, my old friend. I've got a surprise for you. We're going to make an arrest on Monday morning.'

'That's when the inquest is.'

'And that's when we're going to arrest him.'

'Can you do that sort of thing at an inquest, sir? Is it legal?'

'Legal? I know nothing about the law. But perhaps you're right. We'll make it just *after* the inquest, just as he's—'

'What if he's not there?'

'I think he'll be there all right,' said Morse quietly.

'You're not going to tell me who he is?'

'What? And spoil my little surprise? Now, what do you say we have a pint or two? To celebrate, sort of thing.'

'The pubs'll be shut, sir.'

'Really?' Morse feigned surprise, walked over to a wall cupboard, and fetched out half a dozen pint bottles of beer, two glasses, and an opener.

'You've got to plan for all contingencies in our sort of job, Lewis.'

Margaret Freeman had been tossing and turning since she went to bed at eleven, and she finally got up at 1.30 a.m. She tiptoed past her parents' room, made her way silently to the kitchen, and put the kettle on. It was no longer a matter of being frightened, as it had been earlier in the week, when she had blessed the fact that she didn't live on her own like some of the girls did; it was more a matter of being puzzled now: puzzled about what Morse had asked her. The other girls thought that the Inspector was a bit dishy; but she didn't. Too old – and too vain. Combing his hair when he'd come in, and trying to cover up that balding patch at the back! Men! But she'd like Mr Quinn – liked him rather more than she should have done . . . She poured herself a cup of tea and sat down at the kitchen table. Why had Morse asked her that question? It made it seem as if she held the secret to something important; it *was* important, he'd said. But why did he want to know? She had lain awake thinking and thinking, and asking herself just why he should have asked her *that*. Why was it so important for him to know if Mr Quinn had put her own initials on the little notes he left? Of course he had! She was the one who most needed to know, wasn't she? After all, she *was* his confidential secretary. Had been, rather . . . She poured herself a second cup of tea, took it back to her room, and turned on the bedside reading lamp. Menacing shadows seemed to loom against the far wall as she settled herself into bed. She tried to sit very still, and suddenly felt very frightened again.

CHAPTER TWENTY-FOUR

ON MONDAY MORNING Lewis was waiting outside as the door of Superintendent Strange's office opened, and he caught the tail-end of the conversation.

'... cock-eyed, but—'

'Have I ever let you down, sir?'

'Frequently.'

Morse winked at Lewis and closed the door behind him. It was 10.30 a.m. and the inquest was due to start at eleven. Dickson was waiting outside with the car, and together the three policemen drove down into Oxford.

The inquest was to be held in the courtroom behind the main Oxford City Police HQ in St Aldates, and a small knot of people was standing outside, waiting for the preceding hearing to finish. Lewis looked at them. He had written (as Morse had carefully briefed him) to all those concerned in any way with Quinn's murder: some would have to take the stand anyway; others ('but your presence will be appreciated') would not. The Dean of the Syndicate stood there, his hands in his expensive dark overcoat, academically impatient; the Secretary, looking duly grave; Monica Height looking palely attractive; Martin prowling around the paved yard like a nervous hyaena; Roope, smoking a cigarette and staring thoughtfully at the ground; Mr Quinn senior, lonely, apart, staring into the pit of despair; and Mrs Evans and Mrs Jardine, leagues apart in the social hierarchy, yet managing to chat away quite merrily about the tragic events which had brought them together.

It was ten minutes past eleven before they all filed into the court, where the coroner's sergeant, acting as chief usher, quietly but firmly organized the seating to his liking, before disappearing through a door at the back of the court, and almost immediately reappearing with the coroner himself. All rose to their feet as the sergeant intoned the judicial ritual. The proceedings had begun.

First the identification of the deceased was established by Mr Quinn senior; then Mrs Jardine took the box; then Martin; then Bartlett; then Sergeant Lewis; then Constable Dickson. Nothing was added to, nothing subtracted from, the statements the coroner had before him. Next the thin humpbacked surgeon gave evidence of the autopsy, reading from a prepared script at such a breakneck speed and with such a wealth of physiological detail that he might just as well have been reciting the Russian creed to a class of the educationally subnormal. When he had reached the last full stop, he handed the document perfunctorily to the coroner, stepped carefully down, and walked briskly out of the courtroom and out of the case. Lewis wondered idly what his fee would be . . .

'Chief Inspector Morse, please.'

Morse walked to the witness box and took the oath in a mumbled gabble.

'You are in charge of the investigation into the death of Mr Nicholas Quinn.'

Morse nodded. 'Yes, sir.'

Before the coroner could proceed, however, there was a slight commotion at the entrance door; and a series of whispered exchanges, which resulted in a bearded young man being admitted and taking his place next to Constable Dickson on one of the low benches. Lewis was glad to see him: he had begun to wonder if his letter to Mr Richard Bartlett had gone astray.

The coroner resumed: 'Are you prepared to indicate to the court the present state of your investigations into this matter?'

'Not yet, sir. And with your honour's permission, I wish to make formal application for the inquest to be adjourned for a fortnight.'

'Am I to understand, Chief Inspector, that your inquiries are likely to be completed within that time?'

'Yes, sir. Quite shortly, I hope.'

'I see. Am I right in saying that you have as yet made no arrest in this case?'

'An arrest is imminent.'

'Indeed?'

Morse took a warrant from his inside pocket and held it up before the court. 'It may be somewhat unusual to introduce such a note of melodrama into your court, your honour; but immediately after the adjournment of this inquest – should, of course, your honour allow the adjournment – it will be my duty to make an arrest.' Morse turned his head slightly and ran his eyes along the front bench: Dickson, Richard Bartlett, Mrs Evans, Mrs Jardine, Martin, Dr Bartlett, Monica

Height, Roope, and Lewis. Yes, they were all there, with the murderer seated right amongst them! Things were going according to plan.

The coroner formally adjourned the inquest for two weeks and the court stood as the august personage reluctantly departed. Now there was a hush over the assembly; no one seemed to breathe or to blink as Morse slowly stepped down from the witness box, and stood momentarily before Richard Bartlett, and then walked on; past Mrs Evans; past Mrs Jardine; past Martin; past Bartlett; past Monica Height; and then stood in front of Roope. And stayed there.

'Christopher Algernon Roope, I have here a warrant for your arrest in connection with the murder of Nicholas Quinn.' The words echoed vaguely around the hushed court, and still nobody seemed to breathe. 'It is my duty to tell you—'

Roope stared at Morse in disbelief. 'What the *hell* are you talking about?' His eyes darted first to the left and then to the right, as if calculating his chances of making a quick dash for it. But to his right stood the bulky figure of Constable Dickson; and immediately to his left Lewis laid a heavy hand upon his shoulder.

'I hope you'll be sensible and come quietly, sir.'

Roope spoke in a harsh whisper. 'I hope you realize what a dreadful mistake you're making. I just don't know—'

'Leave it for later,' snapped Morse.

All eyes were on Roope as he walked out, Dickson on his right and Lewis on his left; but still no one said a word. It was as if they had all been struck dumb, or just witnessed a miracle, or stared into the face of the Gorgon.

Bartlett was the first to move. He looked utterly dumbfounded and walked like an automaton towards his son. Monica's eyes crossed the gap that Bartlett had left, and found Donald Martin's looking directly into her own. It was the merest imperceptibility, perhaps; but it was there. The slightest shaking of her head; the profound, dead stillness of her eyes: 'Shut up, you fool!' they seemed to say. 'Shut up, you stupid fool!'

CHAPTER TWENTY-FIVE

'YOU HAD MIXED luck with this wicked business, Roope. You had a bit of good luck, I know; and you made the most of it. But you also had some bad luck: things happened that no one, not even you, could have foreseen. And although you tried to cope as best you could – in fact, you almost succeeded in turning it to your own advantage – you had to be just that little bit *too* clever. I realized that I was up against an exceptionally cunning and resourceful murderer, but in the end it was your very cleverness that gave you away.'

The three of them, Morse, Lewis, Roope, sat together in Interview Room No 1. Lewis (who had been firmly cautioned by Morse to keep his mouth shut, whatever the provocation) was seated by the door, whilst Morse and Roope sat opposite each other at the small table. Morse, the hunter, seemed supremely confident as he sat back on the wooden chair, his voice calm, almost pleasant. 'Shall I go on?'

'If you must. I've already told you what a fool you're making of yourself, but you seemed determined to listen to no one.'

Morse nodded. 'All right. We'll start in the middle, I think. We'll start at the point where you walked into the Syndicate building at about 4.25 p.m. a week last Friday. The first person you saw was the caretaker, Noakes, mending a broken light-tube in the corridor. But it was soon clear to you that there was no one else in the downstairs offices at all. No one! You concocted some appropriate tale about having to leave some papers with Dr Bartlett, and since he was out you had the best reason in the world for trying to find one of the others and for looking into their offices. You looked into Quinn's, of course, and everything was just as you'd known it would be – as you'd *planned* it would be. Everything was cleverly arranged to give the clear impression to anyone going into his room that Quinn was *there* – in the office; or, at least, would be there again very soon. It was raining heavily all day Friday – a piece of good luck! – and there, on the back of Quinn's chair, was his green anorak. Who would leave the office on a day like that without taking his coat? And the cabinets were left *open*. Now cabinets contain question papers, and the Secretary would have been down like a hawk on any of his colleagues who showed the slightest carelessness over security. But what are we asked to believe in Quinn's case? Quinn? Recently appointed; briefed, doubtless *ad nauseam*, about the need for the strictest security at every second of every day. And what does he do, Roope? He goes out and leaves his cabinets open! Yet, at the very same time, we find evidence of Quinn's punctilious adherence to the Secretary's instructions. Since he took up his job a few months previously, he has been told, very pointedly told, that it doesn't matter in the slightest if he takes time off during the day. *But* – if he does go out, he's to leave a note informing anyone who might want him exactly where he is or what he's doing. In other words, what Bartlett says is all the law and the commandments. Now, I find the combination of these two sets of circumstances extremely suggestive, Roope. Some of us are idle and careless, and some of us are fussy and conscientious. But very few of us manage to be both at the same time. Wouldn't you agree?'

Roope was staring through the window on to the concrete yard. He was watchful and tensed, but he said nothing.

'The caretaker told you that he was going off for tea, and before long you were alone – *or so you thought* – on the ground floor of the Syndicate building. It was still only about half past four, and although I suspect you'd originally planned to wait until the whole office was empty, this was too good a chance to miss. Noakes, quite unwittingly, had given you some very interesting information, though you could very easily have found it out for yourself. The only car left in the rear car park was *Quinn's*. Well, what happened then was this, or something very like it. You went into Quinn's room once more. You took his anorak, and you put it on. You kept your gloves on, of course, and you folded up the plastic mac you'd been wearing. Then you saw that note once more, and you decided that you might as well pocket it. Certainly Quinn wouldn't have left it on the desk if he'd returned, and from this point on you had to think and act exactly as Quinn would have done. You walked out of the back door and found – as you knew you would – that Quinn's car keys were in his anorak pocket. No one was around, of course: the weather was still foul – though ideal for you. You got into the car and you drove away from the building. Noakes in fact saw you leave as he sat upstairs having a cup of tea. But he thought – why shouldn't he? – that it was Quinn. After all, he could only see the top of the car. So? That was that. The luck was on your side at this stage, and you made the most of it. The first part of the great deception was over, and you'd come through it with flying colours!'

Roope shuffled uneasily on his hard wooden chair, and his eyes looked dangerous; but again he said nothing.

'You drove the car to Kidlington and you parked it safely in Quinn's own garage in Pinewood Close, and here again you had a curious combination of good and bad luck. First the good luck. The rain was still pouring down and no one was likely to look too carefully at the man who got out of Quinn's car to unlock his own garage doors. It was dark, too, and the corner of Pinewood Close was even darker than usual because someone – *someone*, Roope, had seen to it that the street lamp outside the house had been recently and conveniently smashed. I make no specific charges on that point, but you must allow me to harbour my little suspicions. So, even if anyone *did* see you, hunched up in Quinn's green anorak, head down in the rain, I doubt whether any suspicions would have been aroused. You were very much the same build as Quinn, and like him you had a beard. But in another way the luck was very much against you. It so happened, and you couldn't help noticing the fact, that a woman was standing at the upstairs front window. She'd been waiting a long time, frightened that her baby was going to be born prematurely; she had rung her husband at Cowley several times, and she was impatiently expecting him at any minute. Now, as I say, this was not in itself a fatal occurrence. She'd seen you, of course, but it never occurred to her for a second that the person she saw was anyone but Quinn; and you yourself must have totted up the odds and worked on exactly that assumption. Nevertheless, she'd seen you go *into the house* where you immediately discovered that Mrs Evans – you must have had a complete dossier on all the domestic arrangements – as I say, Mrs Evans, by a sheer fluke, had not finished the cleaning. What's more, she'd left a note to say she would be coming back! That was bad luck, all right, and yet you suddenly saw the chance of turning the tables completely. You read the note from Mrs Evans, and you screwed it up and threw it into the wastepaper basket. You lit the gas fire, putting the match you used carefully back into your matchbox. You shouldn't have done that, Roope! But we all make mistakes, don't we? And then – the masterstroke! You had a note in your pocket – a note written by Quinn himself, a note which not only looked genuine; it *was* genuine. Any handwriting expert was going to confirm, almost at a glance, that the writing was Quinn's. Of course he'd confirm it. The writing *was* Quinn's. You were hellishly lucky, though, weren't you? The note was addressed to Margaret Freeman, Quinn's confidential secretary. But not by name. By initials. MF. You found a black thin-point biro in Quinn's anorak, and very carefully you changed the initials. Not too difficult, was it? A bit of a squiggle for "rs" after the M, and an additional bar at the bottom of the F, converting it into an E. The message was good enough – vague enough, anyway – to cover the deception. How you must have smiled as you placed the note carefully on the top of the cupboard. Yes, indeed! And then you went out again. You didn't want to take any risks, though; so you went via the back door, out into the back garden, through the gap in the fence and over the path across the field to the Quality supermarket. You had to get out of the house anyway, so why not carry through with the bluff? You bought some provisions, and even as you walked round the shelves your brain was working non-stop. Buy something that made it look as though Quinn was having someone in for a meal that evening! Why not? Another clever touch. Two steaks and all the rest of it. But you shouldn't have bought the butter, Roope! You got the wrong brand, and he had plenty in the fridge, anyway. As I say, it was clever. But you were getting a bit *too* clever.'

'Like you are, Inspector.' Roope bestirred himself at last. He took out a cigarette and lit it, putting the match carefully into the ashtray. 'I can't honestly think that you expect me to believe such convoluted nonsense.' He spoke carefully and rationally, and appeared much more at ease with himself. 'If you've nothing better to talk about than such boy-scout fancy-dress twaddle, I suggest you release me immediately. But if you want to persist with it, I shall have to call in my lawyer. I refused to do this when you told me of my rights earlier – I knew my rights, anyway, Inspector – but I thought I'd rather have my own innocence at my side than any pettifogging lawyer. But you're driving me a bit too far, you know. You've not the slightest shred of evidence for any of these fantastic allegations you've made against me. Not the slightest! And if you can't do any better than this I suggest that it may be in your own interests, not just mine, to pack in this ridiculous charade immediately.'

'You deny the charges then?'

'Charges? *What* charges? I'm not aware that you've made any charges.'

'You deny that the sequence of events—'

'Of *course*, I deny it! Why the hell should anyone go to all that trouble— ?'

'Whoever murdered Quinn had to try to establish an alibi. And he did. A very clever alibi. You see all the indications in this case seemed to point to Quinn being alive on Friday evening, certainly until the early evening, and it was vital—'

'You mean Quinn *wasn't* alive on Friday evening?'

'Oh no,' said Morse slowly. '*Quinn had been dead for several hours.*'

There was a long silence in the small room, broken finally by Roope. 'Several hours, you say?'

Morse nodded. 'But I'm not *quite* sure exactly when Quinn was murdered. I rather hoped you might be able to tell me.'

Roope laughed aloud, and shook his head in bewilderment. 'And you think *I* killed Quinn?'

'That's why you're here, and that's why you're going to stay here – until you decide to tell me the truth.'

Roope's voice suddenly became high-pitched and exasperated. 'But – but I was in London that Friday. I *told* you that. I got back to Oxford at four-fifteen. Four-fifteen! Can't you believe that?'

'No, I can't,' said Morse flatly.

'Well, look, Inspector. Let's just get one thing straight. I don't suppose I could account for my movements – at least not to your satisfaction – from, let's say, five o'clock to about eight o'clock that night. And you wouldn't believe me, anyway. But if you're determined to keep me in this miserable place much longer, at least charge me with something I *could* have done. All right! I drove Quinn's car and did his shopping and God knows what else. Let's accept all that bloody nonsense, if it'll please you. *But charge me with murdering Quinn as well.* At twenty past four – whenever you like, I don't care! Five o'clock. Six o'clock. Seven o'clock. Take your pick. But for Christ's sake show *some* sense. *I was in London until three o'clock or so, and I was on the train until it reached Oxford.* Don't you understand that? Make something up, if you like. But please, *please* tell me when and how I'm supposed to have murdered the man. That's all I ask.'

As Lewis looked at him, Morse seemed to be growing a little less confident. He picked up the papers in front of him and shuffled them around meaninglessly. Something seemed to have misfired somewhere – that was for sure.

'I've only got your word, Mr Roope' (it was *Mr* Roope now) 'that you caught that particular train from London. You were at your publishers', I know that. We've checked. But you could—'

'May I use your phone, Inspector?'

Morse shrugged and looked vaguely disconsolate. 'It's a bit unusual, I suppose, but—'

Roope looked through the directory, rang a number, and spoke rapidly for a few minutes before handing the receiver to Morse. It was the Cabriolet Taxis Services, and Morse listened and nodded and asked no questions. 'I see. Thank you.' He put down the phone and looked across at Roope. 'You had more success than we did, Mr Roope. Did you find the ticket collector, too?'

'No. He's had flu, but he'll be back at work this week sometime.'

'You've been very busy.'

'I was worried – who wouldn't be? You kept asking me where I was, and I thought you'd got it in for me, and I knew it would be sensible to try to check. We've all got an instinct for self-preservation, you know.'

'Ye-es.' Morse ran the index finger of his left hand along his nose – many, many times; and finally came to a decision. He dialled a number and asked for the editor of the *Oxford Mail.* 'I see. We're too late, then. Page one, you say? Oh dear. Well it can't be helped. What about Stop Press? Could we get anything in there? . . . Good. Let's say er "Murder Suspect Released. Mr C. A. Roope (see page 1), arrested earlier today in connection with the murder of Nicholas Quinn, was released this afternoon. Chief Inspector—" What? No more room? I see. Well, it'll be better than nothing. Sorry to muck you about . . . Yes, I'm afraid these things do happen sometimes. Cheers.'

Morse cradled the phone and turned towards Roope. 'Look, sir. As I say, things like this do—'

Roope got to his feet. 'Forget it! You've said enough for one day. Can I assume I'm free to go now?' There was a sharp edge on his voice.

'Yes, sir. And, as I say . . .' Roope looked at him with deep contempt as the feeble sentence whimpered away. 'Have you a car here, sir?'

'No. I don't have a car.'

'Oh no, I remember. If you like, Sergeant Lewis here will—'

'No, he won't! I've had quite enough of your sickening hospitality for one day. I'll bus it, thank you very much!'

Before Morse could say more, he had left the room and was walking briskly across the courtyard in the bright and chilly afternoon.

During the last ten minutes of the interview Lewis had felt himself becoming progressively more perplexed, and at one stage he had stared at Morse like a street-idler gaping at the village idiot. What *did* Morse think he was doing? He looked again at him now, his head down over the sheets of paper on the table. But even as Lewis looked, Morse lifted his head, and a strangely self-satisfied smile was spreading over his face. He saw that Lewis was watching him, and he winked happily.

Chapter Twenty-Six

THE MAN INSIDE the house is anxious, but reasonably calm. The phone rings stridently, imperiously, several times during the late afternoon and early evening. But he does not answer it, for he has seen the post-office van repairing (repairing!) the telephone wires just along the road. Clumsy and obvious. They must think him stupid. Yet all the time he knows that *they* are not stupid, either, and the knowledge nags away in his mind. Over and over again he tells himself that they cannot *know*; can only guess; can never prove. The maze would defeat an indefatigable Ariadne, and the ball of thread leads only to blind and bricked-up alleyways. Infernal phone! He waits until the importunate caller has exhausted a seemingly limitless patience, and takes the receiver off its stand. But it purrs – intolerably. He turns on the transistor radio at ten minutes to six and listens, yet with only a fraction of his conscious faculties, to the BBC's City correspondent discussing the fluctuations in the *Financial Times* index, and the fortunes of the floating pound. He himself has no worries about money. No worries at all.

The man outside the house continues to watch. Already he has been watching for over three and a half hours, and his feet are damp and cold. He looks at his luminous watch: 5.40 p.m. Only another twenty minutes

233

before his relief arrives. Still no movement, save for the shadow that repeatedly passes back and forth across the curtained window.

If sleep be defined as the relaxation of consciousness, the man inside the house does not sleep that night. He is dressed again at 6 a.m. and he waits. At 6.45 a.m. he hears the clatter of milk bottles in the darkened road outside. But still he waits. It is not until 7.45 a.m. that the paper boy arrives with *The Times*. It is still dark, and the little business is speedily transacted. Uncomplicated; unobserved.

The man outside the house has almost given up hope when at 1.15 p.m. the door opens and a man emerges and walks unhurriedly down towards Oxford. The man outside switches to 'transmission' and speaks into his mobile radio. Then he switches to 'reception', and the message is brief and curt: 'Follow him, Dickson! And don't let him see you!'

The man who had been inside the house walks to the railway station, where he looks around him and then walks into the buffet, orders a cup of coffee, sits by the window, and looks out onto the car park. At 1.35 a car drives slowly past – a familiar car, which turns down the incline into the car park. The automatic arm is raised and the car makes for the furthest corner of the area.

The car park is almost full. The man in the buffet puts down his half-finished coffee, lights a cigarette, puts the spent match neatly back into the box, and walks out.

At 2.00 p.m. the young girl in the maroon dress can stand it no longer. The customers, too, though they are only few, have been looking at him queerly. She walks from behind the counter and taps him on the shoulder. He is not much above medium height. 'Excuse me, sir. Bu' have you come in for a coffee, or somethin'?'

'No. I'll have a cup o'tea, please.' He speaks pleasantly, and as he puts down his powerful binoculars she sees that his eyes are a palish shade of grey.

It is just after five when Lewis gets home. He is tired and his feet are like ice.

'Are you home for the night?'

'Yes, luv, thank goodness! I'm freezing cold.'

'Is that bloody man, Morse, tryin' to give you pneumonia, or somethin'?'

Lewis hears his wife all right, but he is thinking of something else. 'He's a clever bugger, Morse is. Christ, he's clever! Though whether he's *right* or not . . .' But his wife is no longer listening, and Lewis hears the thrice-blessed clatter of the chip pan in the kitchen.

CHAPTER TWENTY-SEVEN

IN THE SYNDICATE building on Wednesday morning, Morse told Bartlett frankly about the virtual certainty of some criminal malpractice in the administration of the examinations. He mentioned specifically his suspicions about the leakage of question papers to Al-jamara, and passed exhibit No 1 across the table.

3rd March

Dear George,
Greetings to all at Oxford. Many thanks for your
letter and for the summer examination package.
All Entry Forms and Fees Forms should be ready
for final dispatch to the Syndicate by Friday
20th or at the very latest, I'm told, by the 21st.
Admin has improved here, though there's room
for improvement still; just give us all two or three
more years and we'll really show you! Please
don't let these wretched 16+ proposals destroy
your basic O- and A-pattern. Certainly this
sort of change, if implemented immediately,
would bring chaos.
Sincerely yours,

Bartlett frowned deeply as he read the letter, then opened his desk diary and consulted a few entries. 'This is, er, a load of nonsense – you realize that, don't you? All entry forms had to be in by the first of March this year. We've installed a mini-computer and anything arriving after—'

Morse interrupted him. 'You mean the entry forms from Al-jamara were already in when that letter was written?'

'Oh yes. Otherwise we couldn't have examined their candidates.'

'And you did examine them?'

'Certainly. Then there's this business of the summer examination package. They couldn't possibly have received that before early April. Half the question papers weren't printed until then. And there's something else wrong, isn't there, Inspector? The 20th March isn't a Friday. Not in my diary, anyway. No, no. I don't think I'd build too much on this letter. I'm sure it can't be from one of our—'

'You don't recognize the signature?'

'Would anybody? It looks more like a coil of barbed wire—'

'Just read down the right-hand side of the letter, sir. The last word on each line, if you see what I mean.'

In a flat voice the Secretary read the words aloud: 'your – package – ready – Friday – 21st – room – three – Please – destroy – this – immediately.' He nodded slowly to himself. 'I see what you mean, Inspector, though I must say I'd never have spotted it myself . . . You mean you think that George Bland was—'

' – was on the fiddle, yes. I'm convinced that this letter told him exactly where and when he could collect the latest instalment of his money.'

Bartlett took a deep breath and consulted his diary

once more. 'You may just be onto something, I suppose. He wasn't in the office on Friday 21st.'

'Do you know where he was?'

Bartlett shook his head and passed over the diary, where among the dozen or so brief, neatly written entries under 21st March Morse read the laconic reminder: 'GB not in office.'

'Can you get in touch with him, sir?'

'Of course. I sent him a telegram only last Wednesday – about Quinn. They'd met when—'

'Did he reply?'

'Hasn't done yet.'

Morse took the plunge. 'Naturally I can't tell you everything, sir, but I think you ought to know that in my view the deaths of both Quinn and Ogleby are directly linked with Bland. I think that Bland was corrupt enough to compromise the integrity of this Syndicate at every point – if there was money in it for him. But I think there's someone *here*, too, not necessarily on the staff, but someone very closely associated with the work of the Syndicate, who's in collaboration with Bland. And I've little doubt that Quinn found out who it was, and got himself murdered for his trouble.'

Bartlett had been listening intently to Morse's words, but he evinced little surprise. 'I thought you might be going to say something like that, Inspector, and I suppose you think that Ogleby found out as well, and was murdered for the same reason.'

'Could be, sir. Though you may be making a false assumption. You see, it may be the murderer of Nicholas Quinn has already been punished for his crime.'

The little Secretary was genuinely shocked now. His eyebrows shot up an inch, and his frameless lenses settled even lower on his nose, as Morse slowly continued.

'I'm afraid you must face the real possibility, sir, that Quinn's murderer worked here under your very nose; the possibility that he was in fact your own deputy-secretary – *Philip Ogleby*.'

Lewis came in ten minutes later as Morse and Bartlett were arranging the meeting. Bartlett was to phone or write to all the Syndicate members and ask them to attend an extraordinary general meeting on Friday morning at 10 a.m.; he was to insist that it was of the utmost importance that they should cancel all other commitments and attend; after all, two members of the Syndicate had been murdered, hadn't they?

In the corridor outside Lewis whispered briefly to Morse. 'You were right, sir. It rang for two minutes. Noakes confirms it.'

'Excellent. I think it's time to make a move then, Lewis. Car outside?'

'Yes, sir. Do you want me with you?'

'No. You get to the car; we'll be along in a minute.' He walked along the corridor, knocked quietly on the door, and entered. She was sitting at her desk signing letters, but promptly took off her reading glasses, stood up, and smiled sweetly. 'Bit early to take me for a drink, isn't it?'

'No chance, I'm afraid. The car's outside – I think you'd better get your coat.'

The man inside does not go out this same Wednesday morning. The paper boy lingers for a few seconds as he puts *The Times* through the letter box, but no lucrative errand is commissioned this morning; the milkman delivers one pint of milk; the postman brings no letters; there are no visitors. The phone has gone several times earlier, and at twelve o'clock it goes again. Four rings; then, almost immediately it resumes, and mechanically the man counts the number of rings again – twenty-eight, twenty-nine, thirty. The phone stops, and the man smiles to himself. It is a clever system. They have used it several times before.

The man outside is still waiting; but expectantly now, for he thinks that the time of reckoning may be drawing near. At 4.20 p.m. he is conscious of some activity at the back of the house, and a minute later the man inside emerges with a bicycle, rides quickly away up a side turning, and in less than five seconds has completely disappeared. It has been too quick, too unexpected. Constable Dickson swears softly to himself and calls up HQ, where Sergeant Lewis is distinctly unamused.

The car park is again very full today, and Morse is standing by the window in the buffet bar. He wonders what would happen if a heavy snow shower were to smother each of the cars in a thick white blanket; then each of the baffled motorists would need to remember exactly where he had left his car, and go straight to that spot – and find it. Just as Morse finds the spot again through his binoculars. But he can see nothing, and half an hour later, at 5.15 p.m., he can still see nothing. He gives it up, talks to the ticket collector, and learns beyond all reasonable doubt that Roope was not lying when he said he'd passed through the ticket barrier, as if from the 3.05 train from Paddington, on Friday, 21st November.

As he steps out of his front door at 9.30 a.m. the next day, Thursday, 4th December, the man who has been inside is arrested by Sergeant Lewis and Constable Dickson of the Thames Valley Constabulary, CID Branch. He is charged with complicity in the murders of Nicholas Quinn and Philip Ogleby.

Chapter Twenty-Eight

The case was over now, or virtually so, and Morse had his feet up on his desk, feeling slightly over-beered and more than slightly self-satisfied, when Lewis came in at 2.30 on Thursday afternoon. 'I found him, sir. Had to drag him out of a class at Cherwell School – but I found him. It was just what you said.'

'Well that's the final nail in the coffin and—' He suddenly broke off. 'You don't look too happy, Lewis. What's the trouble?'

'I still don't understand what's happening.'

'Lewis! You don't want to ruin my little party-piece in the morning, do you?'

Lewis shrugged a reluctant consent, but he felt like an examinee who has just emerged from the examination room, conscious that he should have done very much better. 'I suppose you think I'm not very bright, sir.'

'Nothing of the sort! It was a very clever crime, Lewis. I was just a bit lucky here and there, that's all.'

'I suppose I missed the obvious clues – as usual.'

'But they *weren't* obvious, my dear old friend. Well, perhaps . . .' He put his feet down and lit a cigarette. 'Let me tell you what put me on to the track, shall I? Let's see now. First of all, I think, the single most important fact in the whole case was Quinn's deafness. You see Quinn was not only hard of hearing; he was very very deaf. But we learned that he was quite exceptionally proficient in the art of lip-reading; and I'm quite sure that because he could lip-read so brilliantly Quinn discovered the staggering fact that one of his colleagues was crooked. You see the real sin against the Holy Ghost for anyone in charge of public examinations is to divulge the contents of question papers beforehand; and Quinn discovered that one of his colleagues was doing precisely that. *But*, Lewis, I failed to take into account a much more obvious and much more import-ant implication of Quinn's being deaf. It sounds almost childishly simple when you think of it – in fact an idiot would have spotted it before I did. It's this. Quinn was a marvel at reading from the lips of others – agreed? He might just as well have had ears, really. But he could only, let's say, *hear* what others were saying when he could *see* them. Lip-reading's absolutely useless when you can't see the person who's talking; when someone stands behind you, say, or when someone in the corri-dor outside shouts that there's a bomb in the building. Do you see what I mean, Lewis? If someone knocked on Quinn's office door, he couldn't hear anything. But as soon as someone opened the door and *said* something – he was fine. All right? Remember this, then: *Quinn couldn't hear what he didn't see.*'

'Am I supposed to see why all that's important, sir?'

'Oh yes. And you *will* do, Lewis, if only you think back to the Friday when Quinn was murdered.'

'He was definitely murdered on the Friday, then?'

'I think if you pushed me I could tell you to within sixty seconds!' He looked very smug about the whole thing, and Lewis felt torn between the wish to satisfy his own curiosity and a reluctance to gratify the chief's inflated ego even further. Yet he thought he caught a glimpse of the truth at last ... Yes, of course. Noakes had said ... He nodded several times, and his curiosity won.

'What about all this business at the cinema, though? Was that all a red herring?'

'Certainly not. It was *meant* to be a red herring, but as things turned out – not too luckily from the murderer's point of view – it presented a series of vital clues. Just think a minute. Everything we began to learn about Quinn's death seemed to take it further and further forward in time: he rang up a school in Bradford at about 12.20; he went to Studio 2 at about half-past one, after leaving a note in his office for his secretary; he came back to the office about a quarter to five, and drove home; he left a note for his cleaning woman and got some shopping in; he's heard on the phone about ten past five; certainly no one except Mrs Evans comes to see him before six-thirty or so, because Mrs Greenaway is keeping an eagle eye on the drive. So? So Quinn must have been murdered later that evening, or even on the following morning. The medical report didn't help us much either way, and we had little option but to follow our noses – which we did. But when you come to add all the evidence up, no one actually *saw* Quinn after midday on Friday. Take the phone call to Bradford. If you're a schoolmaster – and all of the staff at the Syndicate had taught at one point – you know that 12.20 is just about the worst time in the whole day to try to get a member of staff. School lessons may finish earlier in a few schools but the vast majority don't. In other words that call was made with not the least expectation that its purpose would be successful. That is, unless the purpose was to mislead *me* – in which case I'm afraid it was highly successful. Now, take the note Quinn left. We know that Bartlett is a bit of a tartar about most aspects of office routine; and one of his rules is that his assistant secretaries must leave a note when they go out. Now, Quinn had been with the Syndicate for three months, and being a keen young fellow and anxious to please his boss, he must have left dozens of little notes during that time; and anyone, if he or she was so minded, could have taken one, especially if that someone needed one of the notes to further an alibi. And someone did. Then there's the phone call Mrs Greenaway heard. But note once again that she didn't actually *see* him making it. She's nervous and anxious: she thinks the baby's due, and the very last thing she wants to indulge in is a bit of eavesdropping. All she wants is the line to be free! When she hears voices she doesn't want to listen to them – she wants them to *finish*. And if the other person – the one she thinks Quinn is ringing – is doing most of the talking at that point . . . You see what I was getting at with Roope, Lewis? If *Roope* were talking – putting in just the occasional "yes" and "no" and so on – Mrs Greenaway, who says she doesn't hear too well anyway, would automatically assume it was *Quinn*. Both Quinn and Roope came from Bradford, and both spoke with a pretty broad northern accent, and all Mrs Greenaway remembers clearly is that *one* of the voices was a bit cultured and donnish. Now, that doesn't take us much further, I agree. At the most it tells us that the telephone conversation wasn't between Quinn and Roope. But I knew that, Lewis, because I knew that Quinn must have been dead for several hours when someone spoke from Quinn's front room.'

'It was a bit of luck for him that Mrs Greenaway didn't—'

Morse was nodding. 'Yes. But the luck wasn't all on his side. Remember that Mrs Evans—'

'You've explained how that could have happened, sir. It's just this Studio 2 business I can't follow.'

'I'm not surprised. We had everybody telling us lies about it. But let me give you one or two clues. Martin and Monica Height had decided to go to the pictures on Friday afternoon, and yet they stupidly tried to change their alibi – change a good alibi for a lousy alibi. Just ask yourself *why*, Lewis. The only sensible answer that I could think of was that they had *seen* something – or one of them had seen something – which they weren't prepared to talk about. Now, I think that Monica, at least on this point, was prepared to tell me the truth – the literal truth. I asked her whether she had seen someone else going *in*; and she said no.' Morse smiled slowly: 'Do you see what I mean now?'

'No, sir.'

'Keep at it, Lewis! You see, whatever happened in the early afternoon of that Friday, *Martin and Monica stayed to see the film*. Do you understand that? Whatever upset them – or, as I say, upset one of them – it didn't result in their leaving the cinema. Need I go on?'

Need he go on! Huh! Lewis was more lost than ever, but his curiosity would give him no peace. 'What about Ogleby, then?'

'Ah. Now we're coming to it. Ogleby lied to me, Lewis. He told me one or two lies of the first water. *But the great majority of the things Ogleby said were true.* You were there when I questioned him, Lewis, and if you want *some* of the truth, just look back to your notes. You'll find he said some very interesting things. You'll find, for example, that he said he was in the office that Friday afternoon.'

'And you think he was?'

'I know he was. He just *had* to be, you see.'

'Oh,' said Lewis, unseeing. 'And he went to Studio 2 as well, I suppose?'

Morse nodded. 'Later on, yes. And remember that he'd made a careful sketch of another ticket – the ticket that was found in Quinn's pocket. Now. There's a nice little poser for you, Lewis: when and why did Ogleby do that? Well?'

'I don't know, sir. I just get more confused the more I think about it.'

Morse got up and walked across the room. 'It's easy when you think about it, Lewis. Ask yourself just one question: Why didn't he just *take* the ticket? He must have seen it; must have had it in his hands. There's only one answer, isn't there?'

Lewis nodded hopefully and Morse (praise be!) continued.

'Yes. Ogleby wasn't meant to find the ticket. But he did; and he knew that it had been placed wherever it was for a vital purpose, Lewis, *and he knew that he had to leave it exactly where he'd found it.*'

The phone rang and Morse answered it, saying he'd be there straightaway. 'You'd better come along, Lewis. His lawyer's arrived.' As they walked together down to the cellblock, Morse asked Lewis if he had any idea where the Islets of Langerhans were.

'Sounds vaguely familiar, sir. Baltic Sea, is it?'

'No, it's not. It's in the pancreas – if you know where that is.'

'As a matter of fact, I do, sir. It's a large gland discharging into the duodenum.'

Morse raised his eyebrows in admiration. One up to Lewis.

CHAPTER TWENTY-NINE

As Morse looked at the Thursday evening class with their hearing aids, private or NHS, plugged into their ears, he reminded himself that during the previous weeks of the term Quinn had sat there amongst his fellow students, sharing the mysteries and the silent manifestations. There were eight of them, sitting in a single row in front of their teacher, and at the back of the room Morse felt that he was watching a TV screen with the sound turned off. The teacher was talking, for her lips moved and she made the natural gestures of speech. But no sound. When Morse had managed to rid himself of the suspicion that *he* had suddenly been struck deaf, he watched the teacher's lips more closely, and tried as hard as he could to read the words. Occasionally one or other of the class would raise a hand and voice a silent question, and then the teacher would write up a word on the blackboard. Frequently, it appeared, the difficult words – the words that the class were puzzled by – began with 'p', or 'b', or 'm'; and to a lesser extent with 't', 'd', or 'n'. Lip-reading was clearly a most sophisticated skill.

At the end of the class, Morse thanked the teacher for allowing him to observe, and spoke to her about Quinn. Here, too, he had been the star pupil, it seemed, and all the class had been deeply upset at the news of his death. Yes, he really had been very deaf indeed – but one wouldn't have guessed; unless, that is, one had experience of these things.

A bell sounded throughout the building. It was 9 p.m. and time for everyone to leave the premises.

'Would he have been able to hear that?' asked Morse.

But the teacher had temporarily turned away to mark the register. The bell was still ringing. 'Would Quinn have been able to hear that?' repeated Morse.

But she still didn't hear him and, belatedly, Morse guessed the truth. When finally she looked up again, he repeated his question once more. 'Could Quinn hear the bell?'

'Could Quinn hear them all, did you say? I'm sorry, I didn't quite catch—'

'H-ear th-e b-e-ll,' mouthed Morse, with ridiculous exaggeration.

'Oh, the *bell*. Is it ringing? I'm afraid that none of us could ever hear that.'

Thursday was guest night at Lonsdale College, but after a couple of post-prandial ports the Dean of the Syndicate decided he'd better get back to his rooms. He was decidedly displeased at having to rearrange his Friday morning programme, since one of the few duties he positively enjoyed was that of interviewing prospective entrants. As he walked along the quad he wondered morosely how long the Syndicate meeting would last, and why exactly Tom Bartlett had been so insistent. It was all getting out of hand, anyway. He was getting too old for the post, and he looked forward to his retirement in a year's time. One thing was certain: he just couldn't cope with events like those of the past fortnight.

He looked through the pile of UCCA forms on his desk and read the fulsome praises heaped upon the heads of their pupils by headmasters and headmistresses, so desperately anxious to lift their schools a few paces up the table in the Oxbridge League. If only such heads would realize that all their blabber was, if anything, counter-productive! On the first form he read some headmistress's report on a young girl anxious to take up one of the few places at Lonsdale reserved for women. The girl was (naturally!) the most brilliant scholar of her year and had won a whole cupboardful of prizes; and the Dean read the headmistress's comments in the 'Personality' column: 'Not unattractive and certainly a very vivacious girl, with a puckish sense of humour and a piquant wit.' The Dean smiled slowly. What a sentence! Over the years he had compiled his own little book of synonyms:

'not unattractive'	=	'hideous to behold'
'vivacious'	=	'usually drunk'
'puckish'	=	'batty'
'piquant'	=	'plain rude'

Ah well. Perhaps she wasn't such a bad prospect after all! But he wouldn't be interviewing her himself. Blast the Syndicate! It would have been interesting to test his little theory once more. So often people tried to create the impression of being completely different from their true selves, and it wasn't all that difficult. A smiling face, and a heart as hard as a flintstone! The opposite, too: a face set as hard as a flint and ... A vague memory stirred in the Dean's mind. Chief Inspector Morse had mentioned something similar, hadn't he? But the Dean couldn't quite get hold of it. Never mind. It couldn't be very important.

Bartlett had received the call from Mrs Martin at eight o'clock. Did he know where Donald was? Had he got a meeting? She knew he had to work late some nights, but he had never been away as long as this. Bartlett tried to make the right noises; said not to worry; said he would ring her back; said there must be some easy explanation.

'Oh Christ!' he said, after putting the receiver down.

'What's the matter, Tom?' Mrs Bartlett had come through into the hall and was looking at him anxiously.

He put his hand gently on hers, and smiled wearily. 'How many times have I told you? You mustn't listen in to my telephone calls. You've got enough—'

'I never do. You know that, Tom. But—'

'It's all right. It's not your problem; it's mine. That's what they pay me for, isn't it? I can't expect a fat salary for nothing, can I?'

Mrs Bartlett put her arm lovingly on his shoulder. 'I don't know what they pay you, and I don't want to know. If they paid you a million it wouldn't be too much! But—' She was worried, and the little Secretary knew it.

'I know. The world suddenly seems to have gone crazy, doesn't it? That was Martin's wife. He's not home yet.'

'Oh no!'

'Now, now. Don't start jumping to silly conclusions.'

'You don't think—?'

'You go and sit down and pour yourself a gin. And pour one for me. I shan't be a minute.' He found Monica's number and dialled. And like someone else the day before, he found himself mechanically counting the dialling tones. Ten, twenty, twenty-five. Sally must be out, too. He let it ring a few more times, and then slowly replaced the receiver. The Syndicate seemed to be on the verge of total collapse.

He thought back on the years during which he had worked so hard to build it all up. And somehow, at some point, the foundation had begun to shift and cracks to appear in the edifice above. He could almost put the exact time to it: the time when Roope had been elected on to the Board of the Syndics. Yes. That was when things had started crumbling. Roope! For a few minutes the little Secretary stood indecisively by the phone, and knew that he could willingly murder the man. Instead he rang Morse's number at the Thames Valley HQ, but Morse was out, too. Not that it mattered much. He'd mention it to him in the morning.

CHAPTER THIRTY

MRS SETH ARRIVED at a quarter to ten and made her way upstairs to the Board Room. She was the first of the Syndics to arrive, and as she sat down her thoughts drifted back ... back to the last time she had sat there, when she had recalled her father ... when Roope had spoken ... when Quinn had been appointed ... The room was gradually filling up, and she acknowledged a few muted 'good mornings'; but the atmosphere was one of gloom, and the other Syndics sat down silently and let their own thoughts drift back, as she had done. Sometimes one or two of the graduate staff attended Syndics' meetings, but only by invitation; and none was there this morning except Bartlett, whose tired, drawn face did little more than reflect the communal mood. A man was sitting next to Bartlett, but she didn't know him. Must be from the police. Pleasant-looking man: about her own age – mid-, late-forties, going a bit thin on top; nice eyes, though they seemed to look at you and through you at the same time. There was another man, too – probably another policeman; but he was standing diffidently outside the magic circle, with a notebook in his hands.

At two minutes past ten, when all except one of the chairs were occupied, Bartlett stood up and in a sad and disillusioned little speech informed the assembly of the police suspicions – his own, too – that the integrity of their own foreign examinations had been irreparably impaired by the criminal behaviour of one or two people, people in whom the Syndicate had placed complete trust; that it was the view of Chief Inspector Morse ('on my right') that the deaths of Quinn and Ogleby were directly connected with this matter; that, after the clearing-up of the comparatively small autumn examination, the activities of the Syndicate would necessarily be in abeyance until a complete investigation had been made; that the implications of a possible shut-down were far-reaching, and that the full co-operation of each and every member of the Syndicate would be absolutely essential. But such matters would have to wait; the purpose of their meeting this morning was quite different, as they would see.

The Dean thanked the Secretary and proceeded to add his own lugubrious thoughts on the future of the Syndicate; and as he tediously ummed and ahed his way along, it became clear that the Syndics were getting rather restless. Words were whispered along the tables: 'One or *two*, didn't Bartlett say?' 'Who do you think?' 'Why have we got the police *here*?' 'They *are* the police, aren't they?'

The Dean finished at last, and the whispering finished, too. It was a strange reversal of the natural order, and Mrs Seth thought it had everything to do with the man seated on Bartlett's right, who thus far had sat impassively in his chair, occasionally running the index finger of his left hand along the side of his nose. She saw Bartlett turn towards Morse and look at him quizzically; and in turn she saw Morse nod slightly, before slowly rising to his feet.

'Ladies and gentlemen. I asked the Secretary to call this meeting because I thought it only proper that you should all know something of what we've discovered about the leakage of question papers from this office. Well, you've heard something about that and I think' (he looked vaguely at the Dean and then at Bartlett) 'I think that we may say that officially the meeting is over, and if any of you have commitments that can't wait, you should feel free to go.' He looked around the tables with cold, grey eyes, and the tension in the room perceptibly tautened. No one moved a muscle, and the stillness was profound. 'But perhaps it's proper, too,' resumed Morse, 'that you should know something about the police investigations into the deaths of Mr Quinn and Mr Ogleby, and I'm sure you will all be very glad to know that the case is now complete – or almost complete. Let's put it in the official jargon, ladies and gentlemen, and say that a man has been arrested and is being held for questioning in connection with the murders of Quinn and Ogleby.'

The silence of the room was broken only by the rustle of paper as Lewis turned over a page in his notebook: Morse held the ring and the assembled Syndics hung on his every word. 'You will know, or most of you will, that last Monday one of your own colleagues, Mr Christopher Roope, was detained in connection with Quinn's murder. You will know, too, I think, that he was released shortly afterwards. The evidence against him appeared to us insufficient to warrant further detention, and everything seemed to point to the fact that he had a perfectly valid alibi for the period of time on Friday, 21st November, when in the view of the police Quinn must have been murdered. Yet I must tell you all here and now that without a shadow of doubt, Roope was the person responsible for selling the soul of the Syndicate – certainly in Al-jamara, and for all I know in several of your other overseas centres as well.' Some of the Syndics drew in their breaths, some opened their mouths slightly, but never for a second did their eyes leave Morse. '*And*, ladies and gentlemen, in all this his principal lieutenant was your former colleague, Mr George Bland.' Again the mingled surprise and shock around the table; but again the underlying hush and expectation. 'The whole thing was brought to light by the vigilance and integrity of one man – Nicholas Quinn. Now, precisely when Quinn made his discovery we shall perhaps never know for certain; but I should guess it may well have been at the reception given by the Al-jamara officials, when the drink was flowing freely, when some of the guilty were less than discreet, and when Quinn read things on the lips of others so clearly that they might just as well have been shouted through a megaphone. And it was, I believe, as a direct result of Quinn's deeply disturbing discovery that he was murdered – to stop him talking, and so ensure that those guilty of betraying public confidence should continue to draw their rewards – very considerable rewards, no doubt – from their partners in crime abroad. Furthermore, I think that in addition to telling the guilty party of what he knew, or at least of what he strongly suspected, Quinn told someone else: someone he firmly believed had absolutely nothing to do with the crooked practices that were going on. That someone was Philip Ogleby. There is evidence that Quinn had far too much to drink at the reception, and that Ogleby followed him out as he left. Again I am guessing. But I think it more than likely that Ogleby caught up with Quinn, and told him that he would be a fool to drive himself home in such a drunken condition. He may have offered to drive him home, I don't know. But what is almost certain is that Quinn told Ogleby what he knew. Now, if Ogleby were in the racket himself, many of the things which were so puzzling about Quinn's murder would begin to sort themselves out. Of all Quinn's colleagues, Ogleby was the one person who had no alibi for the key period of Friday afternoon. He went back to the office after lunch, and he was there – or so he said – the rest of the afternoon. Now whoever killed Quinn had to be in the office both in the latter part of the morning, and again between half past-four and five; and if any single person from the office was guilty of murdering Quinn, there was only one genuine suspect – *Ogleby*, the very man in whom Quinn had confided.'

There was a slight murmur around the table and one or two of the Syndics stirred uneasily in their chairs; but Morse resumed, and the effect was that of a conductor tapping his baton on the rostrum.

'Ogleby lied to me when I questioned him about his exact whereabouts that Friday afternoon. I've been able to look back on the evidence he gave, since my Sergeant here' – a few heads turned and Lewis sheepishly acknowledged his moment of glory – 'took full notes at the time, and I can now see where Ogleby lied – where he *had* to lie. For example, he insisted that he was in the office at about 4.30 p.m., when not only Mr Roope but also Mr Noakes, the caretaker, could swear quite categorically that he *wasn't*. Now, this I find very strange. Ogleby lied to me on the one point which seemed to prove his guilt. Why? Why did he say he was here all that afternoon? Why did he begin to tie the noose round his own neck? It's not an easy question to answer, I agree. But there *is* an answer; a very simple answer: *Ogleby was not lying*. On that point, at least, he was telling the truth. He *was* here, although neither Roope nor Noakes saw him. And when I looked back on his evidence, I began to ask myself whether one or two other things, which on the face of it seemed obvious lies, were in fact nothing of the sort. So it was that I gradually began to understand exactly what had happened that Friday afternoon, and to realize that Ogleby was entirely innocent of the murder of Nicholas Quinn. The fact of the matter is that precisely because Ogleby was in the office on the afternoon of Friday, 21st November, *he knew who had murdered Quinn*; and because of this knowledge, he was himself murdered. Why Ogleby didn't confide his virtually certain suspicions to me, I shall never really know. I think I can guess, but ... Anyway, we can only be grateful that the murderer has been arrested and is now in custody at Police Headquarters. He has made a full statement.' Morse pointed dramatically to the empty chair. 'That's where he usually sits, I believe. Yes, ladies and gentlemen, your own colleague, *Christopher Roope*.'

A babel of chatter now broke out in the room, and

Mrs Seth was weeping silently. Yet even before the general hubbub had subsided there was a further moment of high drama. After several whispered conversations along the top table, the Vice-Dean requested permission to make a brief statement, and Morse sat down and began doodling aimlessly on the blotter in front of him.

'I hope the Chief Inspector will forgive me, but I wish to clear up one point, if I may. Did I understand him to say that whoever killed Quinn had to be in the Syndicate building both in the morning and also at the end of the afternoon?'

Morse replied at once. 'You understood correctly, sir. I don't wish to go into all the details of the case now; but Quinn was murdered at about twelve noon on Friday – no, let me be more honest with you – at *precisely* twelve noon on Friday 21st, and his dead body was taken from this building, in the boot of his own car, at approximately 4.45 p.m. Does that satisfy you, sir?'

The Vice-Dean coughed awkwardly and managed to look extraordinarily uncomfortable. 'Er, no, Chief Inspector. I'm afraid it doesn't. You see I myself went to London that Friday morning and I caught the 3.05 back to Oxford, arriving here about a quarter, twenty past four; and the plain truth is that *Roope was on the same train.*'

In the stunned silence which greeted this new evidence, Morse spoke quietly and slowly. 'You travelled back with him, you mean?'

'Er, no, not exactly. I, er, I was walking along the platform and I saw Roope getting into a first-class carriage. I didn't join him because I was travelling second.' The Vice-Dean was glad not to have to elaborate on the truth. Even if he'd had a first-class ticket he would rather have sat in a second-class carriage than share a journey with Roope. He'd always hated Roope. What an ironic twist of fortune that he, the Vice-Dean, should be instrumental in clearing him of murder!

'I wish,' said Morse, 'that you could have told me that earlier, sir – not, of course' (he held up a hand to forestall any misunderstanding) 'that you could have known. But what you say is no surprise, sir. You see, *I knew that Roope caught the 3.05 from Paddington.*'

Several of the Syndics looked at each other; and there was a general air of bewilderment in the room. It was Bartlett himself who tried to put their unspoken questions into words. 'But only a few minutes ago you said—'

'No, sir,' interrupted Morse. 'I know what you're going to say, and you'd be wrong. I said that no one could have murdered Quinn without being in this building at two key periods; and that fact is quite unchallengeable. I repeat, *no single person* could have carried out the devilish and ingenious plan which was put into operation.' He looked slowly round the room and the full implication of his words slowly sunk into the minds of the Syndics. To Mrs Seth his voice seemed very quiet and far away now; yet at the same time heightened and tense as if the final disclosure were imminent at last. She saw Morse nod across and over her head, and she turned slightly to see Sergeant Lewis walk quietly to the door and leave the Board Room. What—? But Morse was talking again, in the same quiet, steely voice.

'As I say, we must accept the undoubted fact that one person, on his or her own, could not have carried through the murder of Quinn. And so, ladies and gentlemen, the inference is inevitable: *we are looking for two people.* Two people who must share the same motives; two people for whom the death of Quinn is a vital necessity; two people who have a strangely close relationship; two people who can work and plot together; two people who are well known to you – *very* well known . . . And before Sergeant Lewis comes back, let me just emphasize one further point, because I don't think some of you listened very carefully to what I said. I said that Roope had been arrested and charged with murder. But I did not say *whose* murder. In fact I am absolutely convinced of one thing – *Christopher Roope did not murder Nicholas Quinn.*'

In Quinn's former office Monica Height and Donald Martin had not spoken to each other, although it was now more than half an hour since the two constables had fetched them. Monica felt herself moving through a barren, arid landscape, her thoughts, her emotions, even her fears, now squeezed dry – passionless and empty. During the first few minutes she had noticed one of the constables eyeing her figure; but, for once, she experienced complete indifference. What a fool she'd been to think that Morse wouldn't guess! Little or nothing seemed to escape that beautifully lucid mind . . . Yes, he had guessed the truth, though quite how he had seen through her story she couldn't begin to understand. Funny, really. It hadn't been a big lie, at all. Not like the stupid, stupid lies that she and Donald had told at the beginning. Donald! What a non-man he now seemed, sitting there next to her: sullen, silent, contemptible; as hopeless as she, for there was little chance for him, either. The truth would have to come out – all of it. The courts, the newspapers ... For a moment she managed to feel a fraction of sympathy for him, for it was her fault really, not his. From the day of his appointment she had known, known instinctively, that she could do with him exactly as she wished ...

The door opened and Lewis came in. 'Will you please come with me, Miss Height?'

She got to her feet slowly and walked up the wooden stairs. The door of the Board Room was closed and she hesitated a few seconds as Lewis opened it and stood aside for her. The burden on her conscience had become intolerable. Yes, it would be relief at last.

Mrs Seth turned her head as the door behind her opened. The Inspector had just been talking about Studio 2 in Walton Street; but her mind was growing numb and she had hardly been able to follow him. She heard a man's voice say quietly, 'After you, Miss Height.' Monica Height! Dear God, no! It couldn't be. Monica Height and Martin! She'd heard rumours, of course. Everyone must have heard rumours but ... Monica was sitting in Roope's seat now. Roope's! Had Morse meant Roope and Monica? *Two* people, he'd said ... But Morse was speaking again.

'Miss Height. I interviewed you early on in the case, and you claimed you had spent the afternoon of Friday, 21st November, with Mr Martin. Is that correct?'

'Yes.' Her voice was almost inaudible.

'And you said that you had spent the afternoon at your own house?'

'Yes.'

'And subsequently you agreed that this was not the truth?'

'Yes.'

'You said that in fact you had spent the afternoon with Mr Martin at Studio 2 in Walton Street?'

'Yes.'

'When I originally questioned you about this, I asked whether, apart from Mr Martin, you had seen anyone you knew in the cinema. Do you remember?'

'Yes, I remember.'

'And your answer was that you had not?'

'Yes; I told you the truth.'

'I then asked you whether you had seen anyone you knew going into the cinema, did I not?'

'Yes.'

'And you said "no".'

'Yes.'

'And you still stick by what you said?'

'Yes.'

'You saw a film called *The Nymphomaniac*?'

'Yes.'

'And you stayed with Mr Martin until the film was finished?'

'We left just a few minutes before it was due to finish.'

'Am I right, Miss Height, in saying that I could have asked you a different question? A question which might have had a vital bearing on the murder of Nicholas Quinn?'

'Yes.'

'And that question would not have been "Who did you see going *into* the cinema?" but "Who did you see coming *out*?"'

'Yes.'

'And you did see somebody?'

'Yes.'

'Could you recognize the person you saw coming out of Studio 2 that day?'

'Yes.'

'And is that person someone known to you?'

'Yes.'

'Is that someone here, in this room, now?'

'Yes.'

'Will you please indicate to us who that person is?'

Monica Height lifted her arm and pointed. It seemed almost like a magnetic needle pointing to the pole, gradually settling on to its true bearing. At first Mrs Seth thought that the arm was pointing directly at Morse himself. But that couldn't be. And then she followed that accusing finger once more, and she couldn't believe what she saw. Again she traced the line. Again she found the same direction. Oh no. It *couldn't* be, surely? For Monica's finger was pointing directly at one man – *the Secretary of the Syndicate.*

CHAPTER THIRTY-ONE

LEWIS (*mirabile dictu*) had not been kept completely in the dark. It was Lewis who had taken his turn of guard-duty in watching Roope's house. It was Lewis who had seen Roope leave that house and walk slowly to the car park at the railway station. It was Lewis who had traced the paperboy and who had discovered the address of the person to whom Roope had written his brief and urgent note. It was Lewis who had summoned Morse to the station buffet, and who had shared with him the magnificent view of two men seated in the front of a dark brown Vanden Plas at the furthest reach of the railway car park. It was Lewis who had arrested Roope as he had ventured forth, for the last time, the previous morning.

But if Lewis had not been kept in the dark, neither had he exactly been thrown up on to the shores of light; and later the same afternoon he was glad of the opportunity to get a few things clear.

'What really put you on to Bartlett, sir?'

Morse sat back expansively in the black leather chair and told him. 'We learned fairly early on in the case, Lewis, that there was some animosity between Bartlett and Roope; and I kept asking myself why. And very gradually the light dawned: I'd been asking myself the wrong question – a non-question, in fact. There was *no* antagonism between the two at all, although there had to *appear* to be. The two of them were hand in glove

266

over the Al-jamara business, and whatever happened they were anxious for the outside world never to have the slightest suspicion of any collusion between them. It wasn't too difficult, either. Just a bit of feigned needle here and there; sometimes a bit of a row in front of the other Syndics; and above all they had their superb opportunity when the appointment of a successor to Bland cropped up. They had the whole thing planned. It didn't matter much to either of them *who* was appointed; what mattered was that they should disagree, and disagree publicly and vehemently, about the new appointment. So when Bartlett went one way, Roope went the other. It was as simple as that. If Bartlett had been pro-Quinn, Roope would have been anti-Quinn.' A slight frown furrowed Morse's forehead, but was gone almost immediately. 'And it worked beautifully. The rest of the Syndics were openly embarrassed about the hostility between their young colleague, Roope, and their respected Secretary, Bartlett. But that was just as it was meant to be. No one was going to believe that either of them had the slightest thing in common. No one. At first their carefully nurtured antagonism was merely meant to serve as a cover for the crooked arrangements they made with the emirate; but later on, when Quinn discovered the truth about them, the arrangement was ideal for the removal of Quinn. You see what I mean?'

'Yes, I do,' said Lewis slowly. 'But why on earth did Bartlett, of all people, agree to—'

'I know what you mean. I'm sure that in the normal course of events he would never have been tempted in the slightest to line his own pockets at the expense of the Syndicate. But he had an only child, Richard; a young man who had started off life with quite brilliant promise; who carried the high hopes of a proud mum and a proud dad. And suddenly the whole world collapses round the Bartletts' ears. Richard's been working too hard, expectations are too high, and everything goes wrong. He has a nervous breakdown, and goes into hospital. And when he comes out it is clear to the Bartletts that they've got a terrible problem on their hands. He's sent to specialist after specialist, consultant after consultant – and always the same answer: with a prolonged period of treatment he *might* get well again. You discovered yourself, Lewis, that within the past five years Richard Bartlett has spent some time in the most advanced and expensive psychiatric clinics in Europe: Geneva, Vienna, London, and God knows where else. And this isn't for *free*, remember. It must have cost Bartlett thousands of pounds, and I don't think he'd got that sort of money. His salary's more than adequate, but – Well, Roope must have known all about this and, however it came about, the two of them struck a pact. Originally it had been Bland and Roope, I should think. But Bland decided to go for even richer pickings, and Roope had to have someone *inside* the Syndicate if the goose was still to lay the golden eggs. I don't know exactly how they worked it between them, but—'

'Do you know exactly how Bartlett murdered Quinn, sir?'

'Well, not exactly. But I've a pretty good idea, because it was the *only* way the deception could have been worked. Just think a minute. You get your dose, a pretty hefty dose, of cyanide. Roope sees to that side of things. Now, from an indecently large dose of cyanide death follows almost immediately, so there's little problem about actually *killing* Quinn. I should think that Bartlett called him into his office and suggested a drink together. He knew that Quinn was very fond of sherry and told him to pour himself one – and probably one for Bartlett at the same time. He must have wiped the sherry bottle and the glasses beforehand so that—'

'But wouldn't Quinn have smelled the cyanide?'

'He might have done, in normal circumstances; but Bartlett had timed his actions almost to the second. Everything that morning had been geared with devilish ingenuity to the next few minutes.'

'The fire drill you mean.'

'Yes. Noakes had been instructed to set off the alarm at twelve noon precisely and he'd been told to wait for the word from the boss. So? What happens? As soon as Quinn is pouring the sherries, Bartlett picks up the phone, probably turning his back on Quinn, and says "OK, Noakes". And a second or two later the alarm goes. But this is the point, Lewis. *Quinn can't hear the alarm.* The bell is just inside the entrance hall, and although everybody else can hear it perfectly clearly, Quinn can't; and it gives Bartlett just the little leeway he needs. As soon as Quinn has poured the sherries, and only when the time is *exactly* ripe, does he say something like: "The fire alarm! I'd forgotten about that. Toss that back quickly; we can talk afterwards." Quinn must have drained at least half the small glass at a gulp, and almost immediately he must have known that something was desperately wrong. His respiration becomes jerky and he suffers from violently convulsive seizures. In a minute, or at the outside a couple of minutes, he's dead.'

'Why didn't he shout for help, though. Surely—?'

'Ah! I see you still don't appreciate the infinite subtlety of Bartlett's plan. What's happening outside? A fire drill! As you yourself found out, Noakes had been instructed to let the alarm ring for two minutes. Two minutes! That's a long, long time, Lewis, and during it everybody is chattering and clattering down the stairs and along the corridors. Perhaps Bartlett made quite sure that Quinn didn't shout for help; but even if he had managed to shout, I doubt if anyone would have heard him. And remember! *No one is going into Bartlett's office.* The red light has been turned on outside, and none of the staff is going to disobey the golden rule. And even if *everything* had gone wrong, Lewis, even if someone had come in – though I expect Bartlett had locked the door anyway – Quinn's prints are on the bottle and on the glasses, and police inquiries are going to centre on the fundamental question of who had poisoned Bartlett's sherry – presumably with the intention of poisoning *Bartlett,* not Quinn. Anyway, Quinn is dead and *the building is now completely deserted.* Bartlett puts on a pair of gloves, pours his own sherry and whatever is left of Quinn's down the sink in his private little cloakroom – remember it, Lewis? – and locks away the sherry bottle and Quinn's glass in a briefcase. So far so good. Quinn was a fairly slight man and Bartlett may have carried him over his shoulder, or put him into one of the large plastic containers they use there for rubbish, and then dragged him along the polished floor. Probably he carried him, since no scratches or abrasions were found on Quinn's body. But whatever he did, it was only a few yards to the rear entrance, and Quinn's parking place was immediately outside the door. Bartlett, who has already taken Quinn's car key and house key from his pocket – or from his anorak – dumps the body and the briefcase in the boot, locks it, and the deed is done.'

'We should have examined the boot, I suppose, sir.'

'But I did. There were no traces of Quinn at all. That's why I think Bartlett may have used a container of some sort.'

'Then he goes out to join the rest of the staff—'

Morse nodded. 'Standing meekly outside in the cold, yes. He takes over the list, which by this time has been handed round the thirty or so permanent staff, ticks in himself and Quinn as present, and finally decides that all are accounted for.'

'And it was Bartlett who rang the school in Bradford?'

'Certainly. Doubtless he'd been looking out for anything that could be used to help mislead the inevitable investigation, and he must have seen that particular letter in Quinn's tray in the registry earlier that week. If you remember, it was postmarked Monday, 17th November.'

'Then he went home and had a hearty lunch.'

'I doubt it,' said Morse. 'Bartlett's a very clever man, but basically he's not as ruthless as someone like Roope. Anyway, he's still got a lot on his mind. Certainly the trickier half of the plan is over, but he hasn't finished yet. He must have left home at about ten past one, telling his wife – perfectly correctly – that he had to call in at the office before going off to his meeting in Banbury. But before he did that—'

'He called in at Studio 2.'

'Yes. Bartlett bought a ticket, had it torn through, asked the usherette where the "Gents" was, waited there a few minutes, and then nipped out when the girl in the ticket office was busy with one or two more clients. But after that things began to go awry. Not that Bartlett saw Monica Height – I'm pretty sure of that. But she saw him, coming *out* of Studio 2. Monica and Donald Martin, remember want to spend the afternoon together. They can't go to her place, because her daughter's home from school; they can't go to his, because his wife's there all the time; they can go somewhere in the car, but that's hardly a romantic proposition on a rainy November afternoon. So they decide to go to the pictures. But they mustn't be seen going in together; so Martin gets there fairly early, soon after the doors open, and buys a ticket for the rear lounge and sits there waiting. Monica's due to come a few minutes later, and he's straining his eyes and watching *everybody* who comes in. Now get this clear in your mind, Lewis. If Quinn had gone into Studio 2 that afternoon, Martin would certainly have seen him. He'd have seen Bartlett, too. And if he'd seen either of them, *he wouldn't have stayed.* He'd have left immediately, waited discreetly outside for Monica, and told her the bad news. But he did no such thing! Now, put yourself in Monica's shoes. When we questioned her – and Martin – one thing became quite clear: *they'd seen the film;* and they certainly wouldn't have done that if any other member of the Syndicate had come *in.* There was only one explanation: Monica had seen something that, in the light of what she learned later, troubled her sorely. Yet whatever it was, it had not prevented her from joining Martin inside the cinema, all right? We can only draw one conclusion: she saw someone coming *out.* And that someone was Bartlett! He goes back to the Syndicate and he's got a ticket. But where is he to leave it? He could leave it in Quinn's room, because he's got to go in there anyway to leave the note for Margaret Freeman, and to open the cabinets. Bit careless of Bartlett that, when you come to think of it . . .' Morse shook his head as if a fly had alighted on his balding patch. But whatever was troubling him, he let it go. 'Just remember that all this had to be planned meticulously in advance, and from this point onwards things had to be arranged to meet Roope's convenience, not Bartlett's. Roope has dutifully fixed himself up with a watertight alibi until late afternoon, but now he needs some plausible reason for visiting the Syndicate. He couldn't know – nor could Bartlett – that not one of the graduate staff would be there; so it's arranged that he will leave some papers in Bartlett's office. You see, if anyone else is around, he hasn't got much excuse poking around in *Quinn's* office. He'll have to go there later, of course, to get the anorak; but by then he'll have been able to see the lie of the land and he can play things by ear. So they've decided between them that the cinema ticket and Quinn's keys are to be left somewhere carefully concealed on Bartlett's desk or in one of his drawers. Well? What happened then? Roope knocks on Bartlett's door, gets no answer, goes in quickly, leaves his papers, and picks up the ticket and the keys. Easy. Originally the plan must have been for him to hang around somewhere, probably by the trees at the back, until the rest of the graduate staff went home. Then he would only have to nip in the back entrance, pick up the anorak from Quinn's office, and drive off in Quinn's car. But in fact it was easier than he could have hoped. Noakes, it's true, was an unforeseen problem, but as things turned out this helped him enormously. Noakes was able to confirm that *none of the graduate staff was in his office that afternoon.* And when he told Roope that he was off upstairs for a cup of tea, the coast was clear – half an hour or so earlier than he'd expected it to be.'

'And from then onwards it must have gone very much as you said before.'

'Except for one thing. I suggested to Roope when we first brought him in that he'd pocketed the note from Quinn's desk; but I don't think he could have done. Otherwise I can think of no earthly reason why he had to phone Bartlett when he discovered the shattering information that Mrs Evans was going to return. It was the worst moment of the lot, I should think, and Roope almost panicked. The rain was sluicing down outside, and he couldn't just dump the body and run for it. Mrs Greenaway – he must have seen her – was sitting in full view in the room upstairs with the curtains open, and there was only one way for Quinn's body to be carted out, and that was by the front door of the garage. There was nothing to do but to wait; but he couldn't wait *there*. He must have been feeling desperate when he rang up Bartlett; but Bartlett came up with the masterstroke – the note on Quinn's desk! It was a wonderful piece of luck but, my God!, they needed some luck at that stage. Bartlett had only just got back from Banbury, but he drove off again almost immediately, called in at the Syndicate for the note, and met Roope as arranged at the shopping area behind Pinewood Close, where Roope had already bought the groceries. I suppose it must have taken Bartlett at least twenty minutes, but time was still on their side – just. Roope got back to Quinn's, took off his muddy boots, left the note – and went out again. He must have got wet through; but imagine his immense relief, as he watched and waited, first to see Mrs Evans come and go, and then, almost miraculously, an ambulance draw up and take Mrs Greenaway off to the maternity hospital. The house was in darkness then; no one was about; the street lamp was broken; the curtain could go up on the last act. He carries Quinn's body to the back door and into the house, puts it on the carpet by the chair in the living-room, arranges the sherry bottle and the glass on the coffee table, lights the fire – and Bob's your uncle. He walks over the back field again, and catches a bus down to Oxford.'

Lewis reflected. Yes, that's how it must have happened all right, but one thing still puzzled him mightily: 'What about Ogleby? Where does he fit in?'

'As I've told you, Lewis, a good deal of what Ogleby

told us was true, and I think he was virtually certain that Bartlett had killed Quinn long before I ever—'

'Why did he keep it all to himself, though?'

'I dunno. I suppose he must have been trying to prove something to himself before—'

'It doesn't sound very convincing, sir.'

'No, perhaps not.' Morse stared out onto the yard and once again wondered why on earth Ogleby . . . Mm. There were still one or two loose ends that wouldn't quite tie in. Nothing vital, though – and Lewis interrupted his thoughts.

'Ogleby must have been a clever fellow, sir.'

'Oh, I don't know. Remember he had a couple of leagues' start on me.'

'How do you mean, sir?'

'How many times do I have to tell you? *He was in the office that afternoon.*'

'Must have been upstairs, then, because—'

'No. That's where you're wrong. He must have been *downstairs.* And what's more we know exactly where he was and when he was there. He must have realized when he finally got back from lunch that he was the only one of the graduates in the office, and that this was as good a chance as he was going to get to poke around in Bartlett's room. Whether Quinn had told him that he suspected Bartlett *and* Roope, or just Bartlett – we can't know for certain. But he's got cause to suspect Bartlett, and he decides to do a bit of investigation. No one is going to come in, because no one's there. At about 4.30 he hears voices outside – Roope's and Noake's – and he doesn't want to get caught. Where's the obvious place for him to hide, Lewis? In the small cloakroom just behind Bartlett's desk, where I went the first afternoon we went to the office. Ideal! He just stands inside and waits; and he doesn't have to wait long. But what does Ogleby find when he emerges from the cloakroom? He discovers that the cinema ticket and the keys which he'd found earlier have gone! His thoughts must have been in a complete whirl, and he daren't leave Bartlett's office. He hears Noakes in the corridor outside, and later he hears someone walking about, and a few doors opening and slamming to. And still he has to stay where he is. Anyway, he finally satisfies himself that it's safe to come out, and the first thing he notices is that Quinn's car has gone! Perhaps he looks into Quinn's room, I don't know. Has Quinn come in? And gone out again? I don't know how much of the truth he suspected at that point – not much, perhaps; but he knows that Roope has taken some keys and a mysterious cinema ticket, a ticket which he has carefully copied into his diary. It's his one piece of real evidence, and he does what I did. He rang Studio 2, and tried to find out—'

'But he couldn't. So he went along himself.'

Morse nodded. 'And found nothing, poor blighter, except one thing: that in all probability the ticket he'd found must have been bought *that very afternoon*.'

'Funny, isn't it, sir? They were *all* there that afternoon.'

'All except Quinn,' corrected Morse sombrely. 'Have you got your car here?'

'Where are we going, sir?'

'I think we'd better follow in Ogleby's footsteps, and have a look around in Bartlett's office.'

As Lewis drove him for the last time to the Syndicate building, Morse allowed his mind to come to tentative grips with the one or two slight inconsistencies (very slight, he told himself) that still remained. People did odd things on occasions; you could hardly expect a smoothly logical motive behind *every* action, could you? The machine was in good working order now, there was no doubt of that, the cogs fitting neatly and biting powerfully. Just a bit of grit in the works somewhere. Only a little bit, though . . .

In Cell No 2, the little Secretary sat on the bare bed, his mind, like Yeats's long-legged fly, floating on silence.

WHO?

CHAPTER THIRTY-TWO

THE SYNDICATE BUILDING had been locked up, and all the staff informed to stay away until further notice. Only Noakes was performing his wonted duties, and was on hand to let the two policemen in.

Seated at Bartlett's desk, Morse amused himself by switching the red and green lights on and off. He seemed like a little lad with a new toy, and it was clear to Lewis that as usual he would have to do the donkey-work himself.

It was over half an hour later, after Lewis had methodically gone through the safe (and found nothing of interest) that Morse, who had hitherto been staring vacantly round the room, finally condescended to bestir himself. The top right-hand drawer of Bartlett's desk had little to offer but neatly stacked piles of office notepaper, and Morse idly abstracted a sheet and surveyed the decimated graduate team:

T. G. Bartlett, PhD, MA Secretary
P. Ogleby, MA Deputy Secretary
G. Bland, MA
Miss M. M. Height, MA
D. J. Martin, BA

Mm. The typists had been instructed to strike through Bland's name, and print in Quinn's at the bottom. But that wouldn't be necessary any longer. Just strike through the top three; much quicker ... And then there were two ... Would Miss Height be asked to take over? Advertise for new personnel? Or would the Syndicate just fold up? God knew that Donald Martin wasn't going to make much of a Deputy if it were to carry on. What a wet he was! And God help the young men they might appoint if Monica twitched her bewitching backside at 'em! Morse took out his Parker pen and slowly crossed through the names: Dr Bartlett; Philip Ogleby; George Bland. Yes, just the two of them left – and now they could fornicate for a few months to their hearts' content. A few months! Huh! That's all Quinn had been there; not even long enough to get his name printed on the notepaper. Nicholas Quinn ... Morse thought back for a few moments to the lip-reading class he'd attended. Would Quinn have been able to cope at the office if his hearing had failed him completely? No, perhaps not. Lip-reading might be a wonderful thing, but even the teacher of the class had made a mistake, hadn't she? When he'd asked her ...

Morse froze where he sat, and the blood seemed to surge away from his arms and from his shoulders, leaving the top of his body numbed and tingling. Oh God – no! No! Surely not! Oh Christ, oh Blessed Virgin Mary, oh all the Saints and all the Angels – no! His hand was shaking as he wrote out the two names on the notepaper, and he found it impossible to keep his voice steady.

'Lewis! Drop whatever you're doing. Go and stand over by the door and take this notepaper with you.'

A puzzled Lewis did as he was told. 'What now, sir?'

'I want you to read those two names to me – just using your lips. Don't whisper them. Just mouth them, if you know what I mean.'

Lewis did his best.

'Again,' said Morse, and Lewis complied.

'And again ... and again ... and again ... and again.' Morse nodded and nodded and nodded and nodded, and there was a vibrant excitement in his voice as he spoke again. 'Get your coat, Lewis. We've finished here.'

She would say nothing at all for a start, but Morse was merciless. 'Did *you* clean the blood off?' (He'd asked the question a dozen times already.) 'My God, you must be blind if you can't see what's been happening. How many other women has he had? Who was he with last night? Don't you know? Have you never suspected? Did *you* clean the blood off? Did you? Or did he? Don't you understand? – I've got to know. Did *you* clean it off? *I've got to know.*'

Suddenly she broke down completely and burst into bitter, hysterical tears. 'He said – there'd been – an accident. And he – he said he'd – tried – tried to help – until – the ambulance came. It was – it was in – in the Broad – just opposite – opposite Blackwells – and—'

The door opened and a man came in. 'What the *hell?*' His voice had the lash of a whip, and his eyes shone with a primitive, blazing madness. 'What's that fucking man Roope been telling you, you snooping bastard?' He advanced on Morse, and lashed out wildly,

whilst Mrs Martin rushed from the room with a piercing
scream.

'You should get yourself into better shape, Morse.
You're pretty flabby, you know.'

'It's the beer,' mumbled Morse. 'Ouch!'

'That's the last one. See me in a week's time, and
we'll take 'em out. You're all right.'

'Bloody good job I had Lewis with me! Otherwise
you'd have had another corpse.'

'Good, was he?'

Morse smiled crookedly and nodded. 'Christ, you
should have seen him, doc!'

In Morse's office the next morning it was Lewis's turn
to grin. 'Must be a bit tricky talking, sir – with all those
stitches round your mouth.'

'Mm.'

'Well? Tell me, then.'

'What do you want to know?'

'What finally put you on to Martin?'

'Well, it's what I said before, though I didn't really
have a clue what I was talking about. I told you the key
to this case lay in the fact that Quinn was deaf. And so
it was. But I kept on thinking what a marvel he must
have become at lip-reading, and I overlooked the most
obvious thing of all: that even the best lip-reader in the
world is sometimes going to make a few mistakes; and
Quinn did just that. He saw Roope talking to the sheik,

and *he read a name wrongly on his lips.* I learned from the lip-reading class that the commonest difficulty for the deaf is between the consonants "p", "b" and "m", and if you mouth the words "Bartlett" and "Martin", there's very little difference on the lips. The "B" and the "M" are absolutely identical, and the second part of each of the names gets swallowed up in the mouth somewhere. But that's not all. It was *Doctor* Bartlett, and *Donald* Martin. Just try them again. *Very* little difference to see; and if you put the two names together, there's every excuse for a deaf person mixing them up. You see, Roope would never have called the Secretary "Tom", would he? He'd never been on Christian name terms with him, and he never would be. He'd have called him "Bartlett" or "*Doctor* Bartlett". And the sheik would almost certainly have given him his full title. But Martin – well, he was one of them; one of the boys. He was *Donald* Martin.'

'Bit of a jump in the dark, if you ask me.'

'No, it wasn't. Not really. There were one or two loose ends that somehow refused to tuck themselves away, and I had an uneasy feeling that I might have got it all wrong. As you yourself said, it was so much out of character. Bartlett's spent so much of his life building up the work of the Syndicate that it's very difficult to see him stooping to the sort of corruption we've got in this case – let alone murder. But I still couldn't see in what other direction the facts were pointing. Not, that is, until I suddenly saw the light as we sat in Bartlett's office, and then all the loose ends seemed to tidy themselves up automatically. Just think. Quinn discovered – or so he believed – that Bartlett was crooked, and he rang him up. Rang him up, Lewis! You can guess how Quinn dreaded ringing *anyone* up. The fact of the matter was that he couldn't face Bartlett with it any other way, because *he just couldn't believe that he was guilty.*'

'Did Quinn tell Bartlett that he suspected Roope as well?'

'I should think so. Quinn must have been a man remarkably free from any deception, and he probably told both Bartlett and Roope everything he suspected.'

'But why didn't Bartlett do something about it?'

'He must have thought that Quinn had got everything cock-eyed, mustn't he? Quinn was accusing him – the Secretary! – of swindling the Syndicate; and if Quinn was totally wrong about himself, why should he think that Quinn was right about Roope?'

Lewis shook his head slowly. 'All a bit thin, if you ask me, sir.'

'In itself, yes. But let's turn to Monica Height. How on earth are we to account for the bundle of lies she was prepared to tell? It's fairly easy now to see why Martin must have been happy to agree to the lies they cooked up together after Monica told him she'd seen Bartlett coming out of the cinema. In fact I should think that he almost certainly instigated them himself, because it was going to suit his book very well not to have himself associated with Studio 2 in any way. And later, after Monica learned that Quinn himself might have been in Studio 2 that same afternoon she immediately realized that things would look pretty black for

Bartlett if she said anything about seeing him there. And so she continued to conceal the truth. Why, Lewis? For the very same reason that Quinn couldn't face Bartlett: *because she just couldn't believe that he was guilty.*'

Lewis nodded. Perhaps it was all adding up slightly better now.

'And above all,' continued Morse, 'there was Ogleby. He worried me the most, Lewis, and you made the key point yourself: why didn't he tell me what he knew? I think there are two possible reasons. First, that Ogleby was quite prepared to go it alone – he was always a loner, it seems. He knew he hadn't long to live anyway, and it may have added that extra bit of mustard to his life to carry out a single-handed investigation into the quite extraordinary situation he'd stumbled across. It couldn't have mattered much to him that he might be living dangerously – he was living dangerously in any case. But that's as may be. I feel sure there was a second reason, and a much more compelling one. He'd discovered what looked like extremely damning evidence against Bartlett – a man he'd known and worked with for fourteen years – *and he just couldn't believe that he was guilty.* And he was determined to say nothing which could lead us to suspect him – not until he could prove it, anyway.'

'But he didn't get a chance—'

'No,' said Morse quietly. He leaned back in his chair and gently rubbed his swollen lip. 'Anything else while we're at it, my son?'

Lewis thought back over the whole complex case and realized that he hadn't quite got it straight in his mind, even now. 'It was Martin, then, who did all of the things you accused Bartlett of?'

'Indeed it was. And *more*. Martin killed Quinn at exactly the same time and in almost exactly the same way. The deed was done in Martin's office, and Martin had exactly the same opportunity as Bartlett would have had. Admittedly, he was taking a slightly bigger risk, but he'd planned the whole thing – at least up to this point – with meticulous care. You see, the main plot must have been hatched up immediately after Bartlett had announced the fire drill for Friday. But the Syndicate staff only received that notice on the Monday, and there wasn't *all* that much time; and in the event they had to improvise a bit as the situation developed. On the whole I suppose they made the best of the opportunities that arose, but they tried to be a bit too clever – especially about the Studio 2 business, which landed them both in a hell of a lot of unnecessary trouble.'

'Don't get cross with me, sir, but can you just go over that again. I still—'

'I don't think Studio 2 figured in the original plan at all – though I may be wrong, of course. The original idea must have been to try to persuade any caller at Quinn's office that he was there or thereabouts during that Friday afternoon. It was all a bit clumsy, but just about passable – the note to his typist, the anorak, the filing cabinet, and so on. Now, I'd guess that Martin's nerves must have been pretty near breaking-point after he'd killed Quinn, and he must have breathed a huge sigh of relief when he managed to persuade Monica to spend the afternoon with him: the fewer people in the office that afternoon the better, and being with Monica gave him a reasonable alibi if things didn't go according to plan. As I say, I don't think that at this state there was the remotest intention of planting the torn half of a cinema ticket on Quinn's body. But remember what happened. Martin and Monica decided to lie about going to the cinema; and Martin himself gradually began to take stock of the situation. He must have realized that the elaborate attempt to convince everyone that Quinn was alive and well at the Syndicate was pretty futile. No one's there to be convinced. Bartlett's not there – he knows that; he himself and Monica are not there, either; Quinn is dead; and Ogleby is out lunching with the OUP people and may not go back to the office at all. So. He gets his brainwave: he'll get Roope to put the cinema ticket in one of Quinn's pockets.'

'But when—?'

'Just a minute. After leaving the cinema – by the way, Martin lied to me there, and I ought to have noticed it earlier. He tried to stretch his alibi by saying he left at a quarter to four; but as we know from Monica they both left just before the film was due to end – at about a quarter past three. Obviously they'd want to get out before the general exodus – less risk of being seen. Anyway, after leaving the cinema, they went their separate ways: Monica went home; and so did Martin, except that on his way he called in at the Syndicate, at about 3.20, found no one about – not even Ogleby – and left his own cinema ticket in Bartlett's room for Roope to pick up.'

'But Roope wouldn't have known—?'

'Give me a chance, Lewis. Martin must have written a very brief note – "Stick this in his pocket", or something like that – and put it with the ticket and the keys. Then, about ten minutes later, Ogleby got back, found everyone else out, and decided that this was as good an opportunity as he'd get of poking around in Bartlett's room; and he was so puzzled by what he found there that he copied out the cinema ticket into his diary.'

'And then Martin went home, I suppose.'

Morse nodded. 'And made sure, I should think, that somebody saw him, especially during the vital period between 4.30 and five o'clock, when he knew that Roope was performing *his* part in the crime. He must have thought he could relax a bit; but then Roope rang him up from Quinn's house at just after five o'clock with the shattering news that Quinn's charlady – Well, you know the rest.'

Lewis let it all sink it, and he finally seemed to see the whole pattern clearly. Almost the whole pattern. 'What about the paperboy? Did Roope send him with a letter to Bartlett just—'

' – just to make things difficult for Bartlett, yes. Roope must have said he wanted to have an urgent talk with him about police suspicions – or something like that. Roope knew, of course, that we were watching him like a hawk, and so he walked slowly down to the railway station and let us follow him.'

'You haven't talk to Bartlett about that?'

'Not yet. After we'd let him go, I thought we ought to give him a bit of a breather, poor fellow. He'd had a rough time.'

Lewis hesitated. 'There *is* just one more thing, sir.'

'Yes?'

'Bartlett will have *something* to explain away, won't he? I mean he *did* go to Studio 2.'

Morse smiled as widely as his swollen mouth would allow him. 'I reckon I can answer that one for you. Bartlett's as human as the rest of us, and perhaps it's a long time since he's seen the likes of Inga Nielsson unbuttoning her blouse. The film started at 1.30, and since he didn't need to leave for Banbury until about 2.30, he decided to be a dirty old man for an hour or so. But don't blame him, Lewis! Do you hear me? Don't blame him. He must have gone in immediately the doors opened, sat there in the rear lounge, and then, as his eyes accustomed themselves to the darkness, *he saw Martin come in.* But Martin didn't see *him*; and Bartlett did what anyone in his position would do – he got out, quick.'

'And that's when Monica saw him?'

'That's it.'

'So he didn't see the film after all?'

Morse shook his head sadly. 'And if you've got any more questions, leave 'em till tomorrow. I've got a treat for you tonight.'

'But I promised the wife—'

Morse pushed the phone over. 'Tell her you'll be a bit late.'

They sat side by side in a fairly crowded gathering, with only the green 'Exit' lights shining up brightly in the gloom. Morse had bought the tickets himself – rear lounge: after all, it was something of a celebration.

'Christ, look at those!' whispered Morse, as the camera moved in on the buxom blonde beauty, her breasts almost toppling out over the low-cut closely-clinging gown.

'Take it off!' shouted a voice from somewhere near the front, and the predominantly male audience sniggered sympathetically, whilst Morse settled himself comfortably in his seat and prepared to gratify his baser instincts. And with only token reluctance, Lewis prepared to do the same.

EPILOGUE

THE SYNDICATE WAS forced to close down as soon as the autumn examination results had been issued, and its overseas centres were parcelled out amongst the other GCE Boards. The building itself has been taken over by a department of HM Inspectorate of Taxes, and today female clerks clack up and down its polished corridors, and talk of girlish things in the rooms where once the little Secretary and his graduate staff administered their examinations.

From her considerable private income, Mrs Bartlett bought a farm in Hampshire, where Richard at last found a life which served to soothe his troubled mind, and where his father's eyes were occasionally seen to blink almost boyishly again behind the rimless spectacles.

Until Sally had completed her undistinguished school career, Miss Height stayed in Oxford, taking on some part-time teaching. Several times in the months that followed the conviction of the Syndicate murderers, she had found her way to the Horse and Trumpet – just for old time's sake, she told herself. How dearly she would have loved to see him again! She owed him a drink, anyway, and she wanted to square the account; to make up for things, as it were. But much as she had willed it, she had never found him there.

More than sufficient evidence was found to justify the immediate disqualification of Master Muhammad

Dubal from all his autumn O-level examinations; and six weeks later his father, the sheik, was listed among the 'missing' after a 'bloodless' coup within the emirate.

George Bland, though reported to have been seen in various eastern capitals, remains unpunished still; yet perhaps no criminal can live without some little share of justice.

No 1 Pinewood Close is tenanted again, both upstairs and down; and Mrs Jardine is thinking of buying herself a new outfit. As she'd expected, it had been no more than a few weeks before the notoriety had died down. Life was like that, as she had known.

Just after Christmas, at a christening in East Oxford, the minister dipped a delicate finger into the font, and in the name of the Holy Trinity enlisted his little charge in the myriad of ranks of the great Church Militant. But the water was icy cold and Master Nicholas John Green-away squawked stentoriously. In the end, the name had been Frank's choice: it had sort of grown on him, he said. But as Joyce took the baby in her arms and lovingly there-thered his raucous cries, her mind ranged back to the day when Nicholas, her son, was born, and when another man called Nicholas had died.

SERVICE OF ALL THE DEAD

For John Poole

I had rather be a doorkeeper in the house of
my God: than to dwell in the tents of ungodliness

(Psalm 84:10)

The First Book
of Chronicles

elderly gentlemen, screened off from the public gaze

CHAPTER ONE

LIMPLY THE REVEREND Lionel Lawson shook the last smoothly gloved hand, the slim hand of Mrs Emily Walsh-Atkins, and he knew that the pews in the old church behind him were now empty. It was always the same: whilst the other well-laundered ladies were turning their heads to chat of fêtes and summer hats, whilst the organist played his exit voluntary, and whilst the now discassocked choirboys tucked their T-shirts into flare-line jeans, Mrs Walsh-Atkins invariably spent a few further minutes on her knees in what had sometimes seemed to Lawson a slightly exaggerated obeisance to the Almighty. Yet, as Lawson knew full well, she had plenty to be thankful for. She was eighty-one years old, but managed still to retain an enviable agility in both mind and body; only her eyesight was at last beginning to fail. She lived in north Oxford, in a home for elderly gentlewomen, screened off from the public gaze by a high fence and a belt of fir-trees. Here, from the front window of her living-room, redolent of faded lavender and silver-polish, she could look out on to the well-tended paths and lawns where each morning the resident caretaker unobtrusively collected up the Coca Cola tins, the odd milk bottle and the crisp packets

3

thrown over by those strange, unfathomably depraved young people who, in Mrs Walsh-Atkins' view, had little right to walk the streets at all – let alone the streets of her own beloved north Oxford. The home was wildly expensive; but Mrs W.-A. was a wealthy woman, and each Sunday morning her neatly sealed brown envelope, lightly laid on the collection-plate, contained a folded five-pound note.

'Thank you for the message, Vicar.'

'God bless you!'

This brief dialogue, which had never varied by a single word in the ten years since Lawson had been appointed to the parish of St Frideswide's, was the ultimate stage in non-communication between a priest and his parishioner. In the early days of his ministry, Lawson had felt vaguely uneasy about 'the message' since he was conscious that no passage from his sermons had ever been declaimed with particularly evangelistic fervour; and in any case the rôle of some divinely appointed telegram boy was quite inappropriate – indeed, quite distasteful – to a man of Lawson's moderately high-church leanings. Yet Mrs Walsh-Atkins appeared to hear the humming of the heavenly wires whatever his text might be; and each Sunday morning she reiterated her gratitude to the unsuspecting harbinger of goodly tidings. It was purely by chance that after his very first service Lawson had hit upon those three simple monosyllables – magical words which, again this Sunday morning, Mrs Walsh-Atkins happily clutched to her bosom, along with her Book of Common Prayer, as she walked off with her usual sprightly gait towards St Giles, where her regular taxi-driver would be waiting in the shallow lay-by beside the Martyrs' Memorial.

The vicar of St Frideswide's looked up and down the hot street. There was nothing to detain him longer, but he appeared curiously reluctant to re-enter the shady church. A dozen or so Japanese tourists made their way along the pavement opposite, their small, bespectacled cicerone reciting in a whining, staccato voice the city's ancient charms, his sing-song syllables still audible as the little group sauntered up the street past the cinema, where the management proudly presented to its patrons the opportunity of witnessing the intimacies of Continental-style wife-swapping. But for Lawson there were no stirrings of sensuality: his mind was on other things. Carefully he lifted from his shoulders the white silk-lined hood (M.A. Cantab.) and turned his gaze towards Carfax, where already the lounge-bar door of the Ox stood open. But public houses had never held much appeal for him. He sipped, it is true, the occasional glass of sweet sherry at some of the diocesan functions; but if Lawson's soul should have anything to answer for when the archangel bugled the final trumpet it would certainly not be the charge of drunkenness. Without disturbing his carefully parted hair, he drew the long white surplice over his head and turned slowly into the church.

Apart from the organist, Mr Paul Morris, who had now reached the last few bars of what Lawson recognized as some Mozart, Mrs Brenda Josephs was the only person left in the main body of the building. Dressed

in a sleeveless, green summer frock, she sat at the back
of the church, a soberly attractive woman in her mid-
or late thirties, one bare browned arm resting along
the back of the pew, her finger-tips caressing its smooth
surface. She smiled dutifully as Lawson walked past;
and Lawson, in his turn, inclined his sleek head in
a casual benediction. Formal greetings had been
exchanged before the service, and neither party now
seemed anxious to resume that earlier perfunctory
conversation. On his way to the vestry Lawson stopped
briefly in order to hook a loose hassock into place at
the foot of a pew, and as he did so he heard the door
at the side of the organ bang shut. A little too noisily,
perhaps? A little too hurriedly?

The curtains parted as he reached the vestry and a
gingery-headed, freckle-faced youth almost launched
himself into Lawson's arms.

'Steady, boy. Steady! What's all the rush?'

'Sorry, sir. I just forgot ...' His breathless voice
trailed off, his right hand, clutching a half-consumed
tube of fruit gums, drawn furtively behind his back.

'I hope you weren't eating those during the sermon?'

'No, sir.'

'Not that I ought to blame you if you were. I can get
a bit boring sometimes, don't you think?' The peda-
gogic tone of Lawson's earlier words had softened now,
and he laid his hand on the boy's head and ruffled his
hair lightly.

Peter Morris, the organist's only son, looked up at
Lawson with a quietly cautious grin. Any subtlety of
tone was completely lost upon him; yet he realized that

everything was all right, and he darted away along the back of the pews.

'Peter!' The boy stopped in his tracks and looked round. 'How many times must I tell you? You're not to run in church!'

'Yes, sir. Er – I mean, no, sir.'

'And don't forget the choir outing next Saturday.'

''Course not, sir.'

Lawson had not failed to notice Peter's father and Brenda Josephs talking together in animated whispers in the north porch; but Paul Morris had now slipped quietly out of the door after his son, and Brenda, it seemed, had turned her solemn attention to the font: dating from 1345, it was, according to the laconic guide-book, number one of the 'Things to Note'. Lawson turned on his heel and entered the vestry.

Harry Josephs, the vicar's warden, had almost finished now. After each service he entered, against the appropriate date, two sets of figures in the church register: first, the number of persons in the congregation, rounded up or down to the nearest five; second, the sum taken in the offertory, meticulously calculated to the last half-penny. By most reckonings, the church of St Frideswide's was a fairly thriving establishment. Its clientèle was chiefly drawn from the more affluent sectors of the community, and even during the University vacations the church was often half-full. It was to be expected, therefore, that the monies to be totalled by the vicar's warden, then checked by the vicar himself, and thereafter transferred to the church's number-one account with Barclays Bank in the High, were not inconsiderable. This morning's takings, sorted by denominations, lay on Lawson's desk in the vestry: one five-pound note; about fifteen one-pound notes; a score or so of fifty-pence pieces and further sundry piles of smaller coinage, neatly stacked in readily identifiable amounts.

'Another goodly congregation, Harry.' 'Goodly' was a favourite word in Lawson's vocabulary. Although it had always been a matter of some contention in theological circles whether the Almighty took any great interest in the counting of mere heads, it was encouraging, on a secular assessment, to minister to a flock that was at least numerically fairly strong; and the word 'goodly' seemed a happily neutral word to blur the distinction between the 'good', by purely arithmetical reckoning, and the 'godly', as assessed on a more spiritual computation.

Harry nodded and made his entries. 'Just check the money quickly if you will, sir. I made it a hundred and thirty-five in the congregation, and I make it fifty-seven pounds twelve pence in the collection.'

'No ha'pennies today, Harry? I think some of the choirboys must have taken my little talk to heart.' With the dexterity of a practised bank clerk he riffled through the pound notes, and then passed his fingers over the piles of coins, like a bishop blessing heads at a confirmation service. The addition of monies was correct.

'One of these days, Harry, you're going to surprise me and make a mistake.'

Josephs' eyes darted sharply to Lawson's face, but

the expression there, as the minister put his signature to the right-hand column of the church register, was one of bland benignity.

Together vicar and warden placed the money in an ancient Huntley & Palmer biscuit tin. It looked an unlikely repository for any great store of wealth; but when at one of its recent meetings the church council had discussed the problem of security no one had come up with any brighter suggestion, except for the possibility that a slightly later vintage of a similar tin might perhaps more firmly corroborate the notion that the receptacle open to view on the back seat of Josephs' Allegro contained nothing more precious than a few ginger-snaps and arrowroots left over from a recent social.

'I'll be off, then, Vicar. The wife'll be waiting.'

Lawson nodded and watched his warden go. Yes, Brenda Josephs would be waiting; she had to be. Six months previously Harry had been found guilty on a charge of drunken driving, and it was largely through Lawson's plea for mitigation that the magistrate's sentence of a fifty-pound fine and one year's suspension had seemed so comparatively lenient. The Josephs' home was in the village of Wolvercote, some three miles north of the city centre, and buses on Sundays were a rarer sight than five-pound notes on a collection-plate.

The small vestry window looked out on the south side of the church, and Lawson sat down at the desk and stared blankly into the graveyard where the grey, weathered tombstones tilted at their varied angles from the vertical, their crumbling legends long since overgrown with moss or smoothed away by centuries of wind and rain. He both looked and felt a worried man, for the simple truth was that there should have been *two* five-pound notes in the collection that morning. Was there just a possibility, though, that Mrs Walsh-Atkins had at last exhausted her store of five-pound notes and put five separate one-pound notes into the collection? If she had, though, it would have been the first time for – oh, years and years. No. There was a much more probable explanation, an explanation that disturbed Lawson greatly. Yet there was still the slimmest chance that he was mistaken. 'Judge not that ye be not judged.' Judge not – at least until the evidence is unequivocal. He took out his wallet and from it drew a piece of paper on which earlier that same morning he had written down the serial number of the five-pound note which he himself had sealed in a small brown envelope and placed in the morning collection. And only two or three minutes ago he had checked the last three numbers of the five-pound note which Harry Josephs had placed in the biscuit tin: they were not the numbers he had written down.

Something of this sort Lawson had suspected for several weeks, and now he had proof of it. He should, he knew, have asked Josephs to turn out his pockets on the spot: that was his duty, both as a priest and as a friend (friend?), for somewhere on Josephs' person would have been found the five-pound note he had just stolen from the offertory. At last Lawson looked down at the piece of paper he had been holding and read the serial number printed on it: AN 50 405546. Slowly he lifted his eyes and stared across the churchyard once more. The sky had grown suddenly overcast, and when half an hour later he walked down to the vicarage in St Ebbe's the air was heavy with the threat of rain. It was as if someone had switched off the sun.

CHAPTER TWO

ALTHOUGH HE PRETENDED still to be asleep, Harry
Josephs had heard his wife get up just before seven,
and he was able to guess her movements exactly. She
had put on her dressing-gown over her nightdress,
walked down to the kitchen, filled the nettle, and then
sat at the table smoking her first cigarette. It was only
during the past two or three months that Brenda had
started smoking again, and he was far from happy
about it. Her breath smelt stale, and the sight of an ashtray full of stubs he found quite nauseating. People
smoked a lot when they were worried and tense, didn't
they? It was just a drug really, like a slug of aspirin, or a
bottle of booze, or a flutter on the horses . . . He turned
his head into the pillow, and his own anxieties once
more flooded through his mind.

'Tea.' She nudged his shoulder gently and put the
mug down on the small table that separated their twin
beds.

Josephs nodded, grunted, and turned on to his back,
watching his wife as she stood in front of the dressing-
table and slipped the nightdress over her head. She was
thickening a little round the hips now, but she was still
leggily elegant and her breasts were full and firm. Yet

Josephs did not look at her directly as she stood momentarily naked before the mirror. Over the past few months he had felt increasingly embarrassed about gazing at her body, as if somehow he were intruding into a privacy he was no longer openly invited to share.

He sat up and sipped his tea as she drew up the zip at the side of her nigger-brown skirt. 'Paper come?'

'I'd have brought it up.' She bent forward from the waist and applied a series of cosmetic preparations to her face. Josephs himself had never followed the sequence with any real interest.

'Lot of rain in the night.'

'Still raining,' she said.

'Do the garden good.'

'Mm.'

'Had any breakfast?'

She shook her head. 'There's plenty of bacon, though, if you – ' (she applied a thin film of light pink to her pouting lips) ' – and there's a few mushrooms left.'

Josephs finished his tea and lay back on the bed. It was twenty-five past seven and Brenda would be off in five minutes. She worked mornings only at the Radcliffe Infirmary, at the bottom of the Woodstock Road, where two years ago she had taken up her nursing career once again. Two years ago! That was just after . . .

She came across to his bedside, lightly touched her lips to his forehead, picked up his mug, and walked out of the room. But almost immediately she was back again. 'Oh, Harry. I nearly forgot. I shan't be back for lunch today. Can you get yourself something all right?

13

I really must go and do some shopping in town. Not that I'll be late – three-ish at the latest, I should think. I'll try to get something nice for tea.'

Josephs nodded and said nothing, but she was lingering by the door. 'Anything you want – from town, I mean?'

'No.' For a few minutes he lay quite still listening to her movements below.

'By-ee!'

'Goodbye.' The front door clicked to behind her. 'Goodbye, Brenda.'

He turned the bedclothes diagonally back, got up, and peered round the side of the curtained window. The Allegro was being backed out carefully into the quiet, wet street and then, with a sudden puff of blue exhaust smoke, was gone. To the Radcliffe was exactly 2.8 miles: Josephs knew that. For three years he had made the identical journey himself, to the block of offices just below the Radcliffe where he had worked as a civil servant after his twenty years' service in the forces. But two years ago the staff had been axed following the latest public-expenditure cuts, and three of the seven of them had been declared redundant, including himself. And how it still rankled! He wasn't the oldest and he wasn't the least experienced. But he was the least experienced of the older men and the oldest of the less experienced. A little silver handshake, a little farewell party, and just a little hope of finding another job. No, that was wrong: almost no hope of finding another job. He had been forty-eight then. Young enough, perhaps, by some standards. But the sad truth had slowly seeped into his soul: no one really wanted him any longer. After more than a year of dispiriting idleness, he had, in fact, worked in a chemist's shop in Summertown, but the branch had recently closed down and he had almost welcomed the inevitable termination of his contract. He – a man who had risen to the rank of captain in the Royal Marine Commandos, a man who had seen active service against the terrorists in the Malayan jungles – standing politely behind the counter handing over prescriptions to some skinny, pale-faced youth or other who wouldn't have lasted five seconds on one of the commando assault-courses! And, as the manager had insisted, saying 'Thank you, sir,' into the bargain!

He shut the thought away, and drew the curtains open.

Just up the road a line of people queued at the bus-stop, their umbrellas raised against the steady rain which filtered down on the straw-coloured fields and lawns. Lines he had learned at school drifted back into his mind, serving his mood and seeming to fit the dismal prospect before him:

> And ghastly thro' the drizzling rain
> On the bald street breaks the blank day.

He caught the 10.30 a.m. bus into Summertown, where he walked into the licensed betting-office and studied the card at Lingfield Park. He noticed that by some strange coincidence The Organist was running in the two-thirty, and Poor Old Harry in the four o'clock. He wasn't usually over-influenced by names, but when he recalled his lack of success through undue reliance on the form-book he suspected that it might have been more profitable if he had been. In the ante-post betting odds, The Organist was one of the co-favourites, and Poor Old Harry wasn't even quoted. Josephs walked along the series of daily newspapers affixed to the walls of the office: The Organist was napped in a couple of them; Poor Old Harry seemed to have no support whatsoever. Josephs allowed himself a rueful grin: probably neither of them was destined to be first past the post, but ... why not? Take a chance, Harry boy! He filled in a square white betting-slip and pushed it over the counter with his money:

Lingfield Park: 4 p.m.
£2 win: Poor Old Harry.

A year or so previously, after purchasing two tins of baked beans from a supermarket, he had been given change for one pound instead of for the five-pound note he knew he had handed over. His protestations on that occasion had necessitated a full till-check and a nervy half-hour wait before the final justification of his claim; and since that time he had been more careful, always memorizing the last three numbers of any five-pound note he tendered. He did so now, and repeated them to himself as he waited for his change: 546 ... 546 ... 546 ...

The drizzle had virtually stopped when at 11.20 a.m. he walked unhurriedly down the Woodstock Road.

Twenty-five minutes later he was standing in one of the private car parks at the Radcliffe where he spotted the car almost immediately. Threading his way through the closely parked vehicles, he soon stood beside it and looked through the offside window. The milometer read 25,622. That tallied: it had read 619 before she left. And if she now followed the normal routine of any sensible person she would walk down into Oxford from here, and when she got home the milometer would read 625 – 626 at the most. Finding a suitable vantage-point behind a moribund elm tree he looked at his watch. And waited.

At two minutes past twelve the celluloid doors leading to E.N.T. Outpatients flapped open and Brenda Josephs appeared and walked briskly to the car. He could see her very clearly. She unlocked the door and sat for a few seconds leaning forward and viewing herself in the driving-mirror, before taking a small scent-bottle from her handbag and applying it to her neck, first to one side, then to the other. Her safety-belt remained unfastened as she backed none too expertly out of the narrow space; then the right blinker on as she drove out of the car park and up to the Woodstock Road; then the orange blinker flashing left (left!) as she edged into the traffic departing north and away from the city centre.

He knew her next moves. Up to the Northern Ring Road roundabout, there cutting through Five Mile Drive, and then out on to the Kidlington Road. He knew his own move, too.

The telephone kiosk was free and, although the local

17

directory had long since been stolen, he knew the number and dialled it.

'Hello?' (A woman's voice.) 'Roger Bacon School, Kidlington. Can I help you?'

'I was wondering if I could speak to Mr Morris, Mr Paul Morris, please. I believe he's one of your music teachers.'

'Yes, he is. Just a minute. I'll just have a look at the timetable to see if . . . just a minute . . . No. He's got a free period. I'll just see if he's in the staff-room. Who shall I say?'

'Er, Mr Jones.'

She was back on the line within half a minute. 'No, I'm afraid he doesn't seem to be on the school premises, Mr Jones. Can I take a message?'

'No, it doesn't really matter. Can you tell me whether he's likely to be at school during the lunch-hour?'

'Just a minute.' (Josephs heard the rustling of some papers. She needn't have bothered, though, he knew that.) 'No. He's not on the list for lunches today. He usually stays but—'

'Don't worry. Sorry to have been a nuisance.'

He felt his heart pounding as he rang another number – another Kidlington number. He'd give the bloody pair a fright! If only he could drive a car! The phone rang and rang and he was just beginning to wonder . . . when it was answered.

'Hello?' (Just that. No more. Was the voice a little strained?)

'Mr Morris?' (It was no difficulty for him to lapse into the broad Yorkshire dialect of his youth.)

'Ye-es?'

'Electricity Board 'ere, sir. Is it cónvénient for us to come along, sir? We've—'

'Today, you mean?'

'Aye. This lunch-taime, sir.'

'Er – er – no, I'm afraid not. I've just called in home for a second to get a – er – book. It's lucky you caught me, really. But I'm due back at school – er – straight away. What's the trouble, anyway?'

Josephs slowly cradled the phone. That would give the sod something to think about!

When Brenda arrived home at ten minutes to three, he was clipping the privet hedge with dedicated precision. 'Hello, love. Have a good day?'

'Oh. Usual, you know. I've bought something nice for tea, though.'

'That's good news.'

'Have any lunch?'

'Mouthful of bread and cheese.'

She knew he was telling a lie, for there was no cheese in the house. Unless, of course, he'd been out again . . .? She felt a sudden surge of panic as she hurried inside with her shopping bags.

Josephs continued his meticulous clippings along the tall hedge that separated them from next door. He was in no hurry, and only when he was immediately alongside the offside front door of the car did he casually glance at the fascia dials. The milometer read 25,633.

As he always did, he washed up after their evening meal by himself, but he postponed one small piece of investigation until later, for he knew that as surely as night follows day his wife would make some excuse for retiring early to bed. Yet, strange as it seemed, he felt almost glad: it was he who was now in control of things. (Or, at least, that is what he thought.)

She was on cue, all right – just after the news headlines on BBC 1: 'I think I'll have a bath and an early night, Harry. I – I feel a bit tired.'

He nodded understandingly. 'Like me to bring you a cup of Ovaltine?'

'No, thanks. I shall be asleep as soon as I hit the pillow. But thanks anyway.' She put her hand on his shoulder and gave it the slightest squeeze, and for a few seconds her face was haunted by the twin spectres of self-recrimination and regret.

When the water had finished running in the bathroom, Josephs went back into the kitchen and looked in the waste bin. There, screwed up into small balls and pushed right to the bottom of the débris, he found four white paper bags. Careless, Brenda! Careless! He had checked the bin himself that same morning, and now there were four newcomers, four white paper bags, all of them carrying the name of the Quality supermarket at Kidlington.

After Brenda had left the next morning, he made himself some coffee and toast, and sat down with the *Daily Express*. Heavy overnight rain at Lingfield Park had upset a good many of the favourites, and there were no congratulatory columns to the wildly inaccurate prognostications of the racing tipsters. With malicious glee he noticed that The Organist had come seventh out of eight runners; and Poor Old Harry – had won! At sixteen to one! Whew! It hadn't been such a blank day after all.

CHAPTER THREE

THE LAST LESSON of the week could hardly have provided a more satisfactory envoi. There were only five of them in the O Level music group, all reasonably anxious to work hard and to succeed, all girls; and as they sat forward awkwardly and earnestly, their musical scores of Piano Sonata Opus 90 on their knees, Paul Morris vaguely reminded himself how exquisitely Gilels could play Beethoven. But his aesthetic sense was only minimally engaged, and not for the first time during the past few weeks he found himself wondering whether he was really cut out for teaching. Doubtless, these particular pupils would all get decent O Level grades, for he had sedulously drilled the set works into them – their themes, their developments and recapitulations. But there was, he knew, little real radiance either in his own exposition of the works or in his pupil's appreciation of them; and the sad truth was that what until so recently had been an all-consuming passion was now becoming little more than pleasurable background listening. From Music to Muzak – in three short months.

Morris had moved from his previous post (it was almost three years ago now) primarily to try to forget that terrible day when the young police constable had come to tell him that his wife had been killed in a car accident; when he had gone along to the primary school to collect Peter and watched the silent, tragic tears that sprang from the boy's eyes; and when he had wrestled with that helpless, baffled anger against the perversity and cruelty of the Fates which had taken his young wife from him – an anger which over those next few dazed and despairing weeks had finally settled into a firm resolve at all costs to protect his only child whenever and wherever he could. The boy was something – the only thing – that he could cling to. Gradually, too, Morris had become convinced that he had to get away, and his determination to move – to move anywhere – had grown into an obsession as weekly the Posts Vacant columns in *The Times Educational Supplement* reminded him of new streets, new colleagues, a new school – perhaps even a new life. And so finally he had moved to the Roger Bacon Comprehensive School on the outskirts of Oxford, where his breezy interview had lasted but fifteen minutes, where he'd immediately found a quiet little semi-detached to rent, where everyone was very kind to him – but where his life proved very much the same as before. At least, until he met Brenda Josephs.

It was through Peter that he had established contact with St Frideswide's. One of Peter's friends was a keen member of the choir, and before long Peter had joined, too. And when the aged choirmaster had finally retired it was common knowledge that Peter's father was an organist, and the invitation asking him to take over was accepted without hesitation.

Gilels was lingering *pianissimo* over the last few bars when the bell sounded the end of the week's schooling. One of the class, a leggy, large-boned, dark-haired girl, remained behind to ask if she could borrow the record for the weekend. She was slightly taller than Morris, and as he looked into her black-pencilled, languidly amorous eyes he once more sensed a power within himself which until a few months previously he could never have suspected. Carefully he lifted the record from the turntable and slipped it smoothly into its sleeve.

'Thank you,' she said softly.

'Have a nice weekend, Carole.'

'You, too, sir.'

He watched her as she walked down the steps from the stage and clattered her way across the main hall in her high wedge-heeled shoes. How would the melancholy Carol be spending her weekend? he wondered. He wondered, too, about his own.

Brenda had happened just three months ago. He had seen her on many occasions before, of course, for she always stayed behind after the Sunday morning service to take her husband home. But that particular morning had not been just another occasion. She had seated herself, not as usual in one of the pews at the back of the church, but directly behind him in the choir-stalls; and as he played he'd watched her with interest in the organ-mirror, her head slightly to one side, her face set in a wistful, half-contented smile. As the deep notes died away around the empty church, he had turned towards her.

'Did you like it?'

She had nodded quietly and lifted her eyes towards him.

'Would you like me to play it again?'

'Have you got time?'

'For you I have.' Their eyes had held then, and for that moment they were the only two beings alive in the world.

'Thank you,' she whispered.

Remembrance of that first brief time together was even now a source of radiant light that shone in Morris's heart. Standing by his side she had turned over the sheet-music for him, and more than once her arm had lightly brushed his own . . .

That was how it had begun, and how, he told himself, it had to end. But that couldn't be. Her face haunted his dreams that Sunday night, and again through the following nights she would give his sleeping thoughts no rest. On the Friday of the same week he had rung her at the hospital. A bold, irrevocable move. Quite simply he had asked her if he could see her some time – that was all; and just as simply she had answered 'Yes, of course you can' – words that re-echoed round his brain like the joyous refrain of the Seraphim.

In the weeks that followed, the frightening truth had gradually dawned on him: he would do almost anything to have this woman for his own. It was not that he bore any malice against Harry Josephs. How could he? Just a burning, irrational jealousy, which no words from Brenda, none of her pathetic pleas of reassurance could assuage. He wished Josephs out of the way – of course he did! But only recently had his conscious mind accepted the stark reality of his position. Not only did he wish Josephs out of the way: he would be positively happy to see him dead.

'You stayin' much longer, sir?'

It was the caretaker, and Morris knew better than to argue. It was a quarter past four, and Peter would be home.

The regular Friday evening fish and chips, liberally vinegared and blotched with tomato sauce, were finished, and they stood together at the kitchen sink, father washing, son drying. Although Morris had thought long and hard about what he would say, it was not going to be easy. He had never before had occasion to speak to his son about matters connected with sex; but one thing was quite certain: he had to do so now. He remembered with devastating clarity (he had only been eight at the time) when the two boys next door had been visited by the police, and when one of the local ministers had been taken to court, and there convicted and sentenced to prison. And he remembered the new words he had then learned, words that his school-fellows had learned, too, and laughed about in lavatory corners: slimy words that surfaced ever after in his young mind as if from some loathsome, reptilian pool.

'I think we may be able to get you that racing bike in a couple of months.'

'*Really*, Dad?'

'You have to promise me to be jolly careful . . .'

But Peter was hardly listening. His mind was racing as fast as the bike was going to race, his face shining with joy . . .

'Pardon, Dad?'

'I said, are you looking forward to the outing to-morrow?'

Peter nodded, honestly if comparatively unenthusi-astically. ''Spect I'll get a bit fed up on the way back. Like last year.'

'I want you to promise me something.'

Another promise? The boy frowned uncertainly at the serious tone in his father's voice, and rubbed the tea-towel quite unnecessarily round and round the next plate, anticipating some adult information, confiden-tial, and perhaps unwelcome.

'You're still a young lad, you know. You may think you're getting a bit grown-up, but you've still got a lot to learn. You see, some people you'll meet in life are very nice, and some aren't. They may seem nice, but – but they're not nice at all.' It sounded pathetically inadequate.

'Crooks, you mean?'

'In a way they're crooks, yes, but I'm talking about people who are bad inside. They want – strange sorts of things to satisfy them. They're not normal – not like most people.' He took a deep breath. 'When I was about your age, younger in fact . . .'

Peter listened to the little story with apparent uncon-cern. 'You mean, he was a queer, Dad?'

'He was a homosexual. Do you know what that means?'

27

''Course I do.'

'Listen, Peter, if any man ever tries anything like that – anything! – you have nothing at all to do with it. Is that clear? And, what's more, you'll tell me. All right?'

Peter tried so very hard to understand, but the warning seemed remote, dissociated as yet from his own small experience of life.

'You see, Peter, it's not just a question of a man – touching' (the very word was shudderingly repulsive) 'or that sort of thing. It's what people start talking about or – or photographs that kind of—'

Peter's mouth dropped open and the blood froze in his freckled cheeks. So *that* was what his father was talking about! The last time had been two weeks ago when three of them from the youth club had gone along to the vicarage and sat together on that long, black, shiny settee. It was all a bit strange and exciting, and there had been those photographs – big, black and white, glossy prints that seemed almost clearer than real life. But they weren't just pictures of *men*, and Mr Lawson had talked about them so – so naturally, somehow. Anyway, he'd often seen pictures like that on the racks in the newsagent's. He felt a growing sense of bewilderment as he stood there by the sink, his hands still clutching the drying-cloth. Then he heard his father's voice, raucous and ugly, in his ears, and felt his father's hand upon his shoulder, shaking him angrily.

'Do you hear me? Tell me about it!'

But the boy didn't tell his father. He just couldn't. What was there to tell anyway?

CHAPTER FOUR

THE COACH, A wide luxury hulk of a thing, was due to leave Cornmarket at 7.30 a.m., and Morris joined the group of fussy parents counterchecking on lunch bags, swimming gear and pocket money. Peter was already ensconced between a pair of healthily excited pals on the back seat, and Lawson once more counted heads to satisfy himself that the expedition was fully manned and could at last proceed. As the driver heaved round and round at the huge horizontal steering-wheel, slowly manœuvring the giant vehicle into Beaumont Street, Morris had his last view of Harry and Brenda Josephs sitting silently together on one of the front seats, of Lawson folding his plastic raincoat and packing it into the overhead rack, and of Peter chatting happily away and like most of the other boys disdaining, or forgetting, to wave farewell. All *en route* for Bournemouth.

It was 7.45 a.m. by the clock on the south face of St Frideswide's as Morris walked up to Carfax and then through Queen Street and down to the bottom of St Ebbe's, where he stopped in front of a rangy three-storeyed stuccoed building set back from the street behind bright yellow railings. Nailed on to the high wooden gate which guarded the narrow path to the

29

front door was a flaking notice-board announcing in faded capitals ST FRIDESWIDE'S CHURCH AND OXFORD PASTORATE. The gate itself was half-open; and as Morris stood self-consciously and indecisively in the deserted street a whistling paper boy rode up on his bicycle and inserted a copy of *The Times* through the front door. No inside hand withdrew the newspaper, and Morris walked slowly away from the house and just as slowly back. On the top floor a pale yellow strip of neon lighting suggested the presence of someone on the premises, and he walked cautiously up to the front door where he rapped gently on the ugly black knocker. With no sound of movement from within, he tried again, a little louder. There must be someone, surely, in the rambling old vicarage. Students up on the top floor, probably? A housekeeper, perhaps? But again as he held his ear close to the door he could hear no movement; and conscious that his heart was beating fast against his ribs he tried the door. It was locked.

The back of the house was enclosed by a wall some eight or nine feet high; but a pair of gates, with NO PARKING amateurishly painted in white across them, promised access to somewhere, and turning the metal ring Morris found the gate unlocked. He stepped inside. A path led alongside the high stone wall beside an ill-tended stretch of patchy lawn, and quietly closing the gates behind him Morris walked up to the back door, and knocked with a quiet cowardice. No answer. No sound. He turned the door-knob. The door was unlocked. He opened it and went inside. For several seconds he stood stock-still in the wide hallway, his eyes unmoving as an alligator's. Across the hall *The Times* protruded downwards through the front-door letter-box like the tongue of some leering gargoyle, the whole house as still as death. He forced himself to breathe more naturally and looked around him. A door on his left was standing ajar, and he tiptoed across to look inside. 'Anyone there?' The words were spoken very softly, but they gave him an odd surge of confidence as though, should anyone be there, he was obviously trying to be noticed. And someone was there; or had been, until very recently. On a formica-topped table lay a knife, stickily smeared with butter and marmalade, a solitary plate strewn with toast crumbs, and a large mug containing the dregs of cold tea. The remains, no doubt, of Lawson's breakfast. But a sudden shudder of fear climbed up Morris's spine as he noticed that the grill on the electric cooker was turned on full, its bars burning a fierce orange-red. Yet there was the same eerie stillness as before, with only the mechanical tick-tock of the kitchen clock to underline the pervasive silence.

Back in the hallway, he walked quietly across to the broad staircase, and as lightly as he could climbed up to the landing. Only one of the doors was open; but one was enough. A black-leather settee was ranged along one side of the room, and the floor was fully carpeted. He walked noiselessly across to the roll-top desk beside the window. It was locked, but the key lay on the top. Inside, two neatly written sheets of paper – on which he read the text and notes for some forth-coming sermon – lay beneath a paper-knife, curiously fashioned in the shape of a crucifix, the slitting-edge, as it seemed to Morris, wickedly (and quite needlessly?) sharp. He tried first the drawers on the left – all of them gliding smoothly open and all of them apparently fulfilling some innocent function; and the same with the top three drawers on the right. But the bottom one was locked, and the key to it was nowhere to be seen.

As a prospective burglar Morris had anticipated the stubbornness of locks and bolts only to the extent of a small chisel which he now took from his pocket. It took him more than ten minutes, and when finally the bottom drawer lay open the surrounding oblong frame was irreparably chipped and bruised. Inside lay an old chocolate-box, and Morris was slipping off the criss-cross of elastic bands when a slight sound caused him to whip round, his eyes wide with terror.

Standing in the doorway was a man with a lathered face, his right hand holding a shaving-brush, his left clutching a dirty pink towel about his neck. For a second Morris felt a shock that partly paralysed his terror, for his immediate impression was that the man was Lawson himself. Yet he knew he must be mistaken, and the logic that for a moment had threatened to disintegrate was swiftly reasserting itself. The man was about the same height and build as Lawson, yes. But the face was thinner and the hair was greyer; nor was the man's voice, when finally he spoke, in any way like Lawson's own, but a voice and a mode of expression that seemed to mask a curious combination of the cultured and the coarse:

'May I ask what the 'ell you're doing 'ere, mate?'

Morris recognized him then. He was one of the drop-outs who sometimes congregated in Bonn Square or Brasenose Lane. Indeed, Lawson had brought him to church a few times, and there was a whisper of rumour that the two men were related. Some had even suspected that the man was Lawson's brother.

At Bournemouth the sun shone brightly out of a clear sky, but the wind was chill and blustery, and Brenda Josephs, seated in an open deck-chair, envied the other holiday-makers who sat so snugly, it seemed, behind their striped wind-breaks. She felt cold and bored – and more than a little disturbed by that little remark of Harry's on the coach: 'Pity Morris couldn't make it.' That was all. That was all . . .

The boys had thrown themselves around with phenomenal energy: playing beach football (Harry had organized that), running into the sea, clambering up and down the rocks, guzzling Coke, guttling sandwiches, crunching crisps, then back into the sea. But for her – what an empty, fruitless day! She was officially the 'nurse' of the party, for invariably someone would feel sick or cut his knee. But she could have been with Paul all day. All day! No risk, either. Oh God! She couldn't bear to think of it . . .

The farther stretches of the sea twinkled invitingly in the sun, but along the shore-line the crashing breakers somersaulted into heavy spray. It was no day for tentative paddlers, but huge fun for the boys who were still leaping tirelessly against the waves, Lawson with them, white-skinned as a fish's underbelly, laughing, splashing, happy. It all seemed innocent enough to Brenda, and she couldn't really believe all that petty church gossip. Not that she liked Lawson much; but she didn't dislike him, either. In fact she'd thought more than once that Lawson must suspect something about herself and Paul; but he'd said nothing . . . so far.

Harry had gone for a walk along the esplanade, and she was glad to be left to herself. She tried to read the newspaper, but the sheets flapped and billowed in the breeze, and she put it back into the carrier bag, alongside the flask of coffee, the salmon sandwiches, and her white bikini. Yes. Pity about the bikini . . . She had become increasingly conscious of her body these past few months, and she would have enjoyed seeing the young lads gawping up at her bulging breasts. What was happening to her . . .?

When Harry returned an hour or so later it was quite clear that he had been drinking, but she made no comment. As a concession to the English summer he had changed into a pair of old shorts – long, baggy service-issue in which (according to Harry) he and his men had flushed the Malaysian jungles of all the terrorists. His legs had grown thinner, especially round the thighs, but they were still muscular and strong. Stronger than Paul's, but . . . She stemmed the gathering flood of thoughts, and unfolded the tin-foil round the sandwiches.

She averted her eyes from her husband as he slowly masticated the tinned salmon. What *was* happening to her? The poor fellow couldn't even eat now without her experiencing a mild disgust. She would have to do something, she knew that. And soon. But what *could* she do?

It was not on that joyless day at Bournemouth (although it was very soon after) that Brenda Josephs recognized the ugly fact that had been standing at the threshold of her mind: she now hated the man she had married.

'Have you heard that somebody might be helping himself from the collection? It's only a rumour but . . .' It was the following morning when Morris heard the first whisperings; but in his mind – as in many others' – the alleged hebdomadal thefts were already firmly substantiated in the higher courts of heaven and now stood only in need of a little terrestrial corroboration. There were – surely – only two obvious opportunities, and two possible suspects: Lawson at the altar and Josephs in the vestry. And during the penultimate verse of the offertory hymn Morris turned the organ-mirror slightly to the right and adjusted the elevation so that he had a good view of the large, gilt crucifix standing on the heavily brocaded altar cloth; and of Lawson holding high the collection-plate, then lowering it and leaning forward in a tilted benediction before handing it back to the vicar's warden. It had been impossible to see Lawson's hands clearly, but nothing had been taken – Morris could have sworn to it. So it must be that contemptible worm Josephs! Much more likely – counting the cash all alone in the vestry. Yes. And yet . . . And yet, if the church funds *were* being pilfered, wasn't there a much likelier culprit than either? The scruffy-looking man from the Church Army hostel, the man who had been there again this morning, sitting next to Josephs at the back of the church, the man Lawson had befriended – and the man whom Morris himself had encountered the previous morning in the vicarage.

A few minutes later he closed the organ-door quietly behind him and managed a cheerful 'Good morning' to Mrs Walsh-Atkins as she finally rose from her knees. But in truth he was far from cheerful; and as he walked slowly up the central aisle his mind for once was not wholly preoccupied with thoughts of Brenda Josephs, whom he could now see waiting for him by the font. Like Lawson at this time a week ago, he felt a very worried man.

CHAPTER FIVE

ON WEDNESDAY OF the same week, no one seemed to mind the woman as she stood by the shop window examining with slow deliberation one bulky sample-book after another. 'Just looking,' she told the assistant. She'd known what would happen, of course: from the bus-stop in Woodstock Road he would walk down South Parade (where Cromwell had once arranged his Roundheads), turn right into Banbury Road, and then go into the licensed betting-office just opposite the carpet-shop. And he had already done so. She knew, too, that he would have to come out sooner rather than later, since he was due home for lunch – lunch with *her* – at about one o'clock; and he had another call to pay before then, had he not?

It was 11.20 a.m. when Harry Josephs at last emerged, and his wife drifted quietly behind a line of vertically stacked linoleum rolls, watching him. Back up to South Parade, where he pushed the button at the pelican crossing and waited to cross the Banbury Road. Just as she'd thought. She left the shop with a guilty 'Thank you', and kept well behind him as he walked with his slightly splay-footed gait up towards north Oxford, his brown suit clearly visible beyond the other pedestrians.

He would turn right very soon now (how much she knew!) into Manning Terrace; and she skipped and waltzed her way in and out of the prams as soon as he disappeared. He was on the right-hand side of the terrace, about seven or eight houses along, and he would be stopping just about there (yes!) and walking up the short path to one of the front doors. She knew not only the number of the house but also the woman who lived there; knew the style and colour of her hair even – long and prematurely grey, like the strand she'd found on Harry's suit one day the previous week. Ruth Rawlinson! That was the name of the woman who lived at number 14, the woman whom her husband had been seeing; and it was all just as Lionel Lawson had told her it was. She hurried back to the Summertown car park. She would just have time to put in a brief appearance at the Radcliffe Infirmary, and to tell the nursing officer that her dental appointment had taken much longer than expected and that she'd make up the time tomorrow.

As she drove down into Oxford her lips were curled in a cruelly contented smile.

At 8 p.m. on the Wednesday of the following week, Ruth Rawlinson took little notice when she heard the click and the creak of the north door opening. People often came in to look around, to admire the font, to light a candle, to pray even; and she silently wiped her wet cloth over the wooden floor of the pew behind one of the pillars in the south aisle. The stranger, whoever he might be, was now standing still, for the echo of his footsteps had died away in the empty, darkening church. This was just about the time when the place could get almost eerie – and time for Ruth to go home. Of indeterminate age, anywhere between mid-thirties and late forties, she wiped her pale forehead with the back of her wrist and brushed back a wisp of straggling hair. She'd done enough. Twice a week, on Mondays and Wednesdays, she spent about two hours in St Frideswide's (usually in the mornings), cleaning the floors, dusting the pews, polishing the candlesticks, turning out the dying flowers; and once every three months washing and ironing all the surplices. For these good works her motives were obscure, not least to Ruth herself: sometimes she suspected they sprang from an almost pathological need to escape for a brief while her demanding, discontented, self-centred invalid of a mother, with whom she shared her house; at other times, especially on Sundays, she felt her motives sprang from a deeper source, for she found herself profoundly moved in spirit by the choral mass, especially by Palestrina, and then she would approach the altar of the Lord to partake the host with an almost mystical sense of wonder and adoration.

The footsteps had started again, and as they moved slowly up the central aisle she peered over the top of the pew. He looked somehow familiar, but he was half turned away from her and for a while she failed to recognize him: his subfusc suit seemed of good quality cloth, though loose-fitting and shabby; and his face (so far as she could see it) was matted with greyish stubble.

He peered vaguely across the pews, first to the left, then to the right, before stopping at the chancel steps. Was he looking for something – or someone? Instinctively Ruth felt it better if he remained unaware of her presence, and very very quietly she wiped the cloth over the winking suds.

The north door clicked and groaned again, and she dipped the soapy cloth more boldly into the dirty water; but almost immediately her body froze over the bucket.

'You came, then?'

'Keep your voice down!'

'There's nobody here.'

The newcomer walked down the central aisle and the two men met half-way. They spoke in hushed voices, but the few snatches of their conversation that carried to Ruth's ears were readily and frighteningly comprehensible.

'. . . given you more than enough already and you're not getting a penny more . . .'

'. . . *told* you, Mister Morris. It's just to tide me over, that's all. And I'm sure you wouldn't want me to tell my brother . . .' The voice seemed a curious combination of the cultured and the coarse.

The ugly word 'blackmail' rose to the surface of Ruth's mind; but before she could learn more the door had opened again to admit a small group of tourists, one of whom in a nasal twang was soon admiring 'that cute lil farnt'.

*

Half of the long school holiday had now passed and the
August sun shone gloriously. Brenda and Harry Josephs
were in Tenby for a week; Lawson had just come back
from a brief holiday in Scotland; Peter Morris was away
at scout camp; and his father was decorating the
staircase – amongst other things.

It was at 1.30 p.m. that he was sitting in the Old Bull
at Deddington and deciding that he oughtn't to drink
any more. After all, he had to drive home. And he had
the additional responsibility of a passenger.

'I think we ought to go now,' he said.

Carole nodded, and drained her third Babycham.
From the start she had felt embarrassment at being
with him, and things hadn't been helped much by the
way he'd been speaking to her – so naturally! So
unendearingly! It wasn't at all what she'd expected. Or
hoped. She'd been in a pub before, of course – quite a
few times; but only for a giggle round the juke-box with
some of the others from school. But this? The whole
thing had been a ghastly mistake, somehow; and yet it
could have been so very different . . .

The car was parked at the far end of the tarmac
behind the pub, and Morris politely unlocked and
opened the door for his passenger before getting into
the driver's seat and fitting the key into the ignition.

'You won't say anything at all about this, will you?'

''Course I won't.'

'You mustn't tell anyone.'

'I shan't tell a soul,' she said. Her eyes, the lids
shaded in a lurid blue, were dull with disappointment.

Morris took a deep breath. 'Put your safety belt on, my girl. Better safe—'

He leaned over to help fix the awkward thing, and was aware of the softness of her breast against his arm. With what seemed almost paternal affection he took her hand in his; and as she turned her head towards him he put his mouth lightly to hers and felt her full lips softly cushioning his own. He had meant no more than that; but he lingered there as the girl's lips gently – yet so perceptibly! – pushed forward against his own. And still he lingered, savouring long the sensual delight. He put his arm along the seat, easing her more closely towards him; and then the tip of her tongue tentatively tried the entrance to his mouth, and the smouldering smoke burst forth in a blazing flame ... Eagerly she pulled down his hand to her naked thigh, and her legs opened slowly and invitingly, like the arms of a saint in a holy benediction.

They broke away from each other guiltily as a car backed into the space beside them, and Morris drove off to Kidlington, dropping her (where he had picked her up) on the north side of the village.

'Would you like to come to see me sometime?' They were the first words that either of them had spoken on the way back.

'When do you mean?'

'I dunno.' His throat was very dry. 'Now?'

'All right.'

'How long will it take you from here?'

'Ten minutes.'

'You'd better come in the back way.'

'All right.'

'I want you, Carole!'

'I want you, sir.' ('Sir'! My God! What was he doing?)

'Be as quick as you can.'

'I will, don't worry.'

In the kitchen he opened a bottle of Beaujolais, fetched two glasses from the living-room, and looked yet again at his watch. Just another five minutes. Come on, Carole! . . . Already in his mind he was unfastening the buttons down the front of her white blouse, and his hands were slipping inside to fondle her breasts . . . He breathed deeply and waited with an almost desperate impatience.

When finally he heard the timid knock, he walked to the back door like a man newly ushered through the gates of Paradise.

'Good afternoon,' said Lawson. 'I hope I've not called at an inconvenient time? I wonder if I can come in and talk to you. It's – er – it's rather important.'

The Second Book
of Chronicles

CHAPTER SIX

BUT FOR HIS dilatoriness and indecisiveness Detective Chief Inspector Morse would have been cruising among the Greek islands. Three months earlier, in January, he had discussed Easter bookings with the Town and Gown travel agency, taken home a Technicolor brochure, rung up his bank manager to discover the going rate for the drachma, bought a slim Modern Greek phrase-book, and even managed to find his passport again. He had never been to Greece; and now, a bachelor still, forty-seven years old, he retained enough romance in his soul to imagine a lazy liaison with some fading film star beside the wine-dark waves of the Aegean. But it was not to be. Instead, on this chilly Monday mid-morning in early April, he stood at a bus-stop in north Oxford, with a fortnight's furlough before him, wondering exactly how other people could organize their lives, make decisions, write a letter even.

Still no bus in sight.

A heavily pregnant mother pushed a rickety, collapsible pram into the shelter, unstrapped the infant within it, and then stuck her head out to admonish her slightly older offspring, already exhibiting, as it

47

seemed to Morse, the lively potential of a fully fledged criminal. 'Stop frowin' dem bricks, Jason!'

Jason! Jason and the Argonauts sailing up to the Hellespont . . . Morse felt he could have done without the reminder – the second reminder, in fact, that morning; for Radio Oxford had just broadcast an interview with the new vicar of St Frideswide's, recently returned from a fortnight in a monastery on the island of Patmos.

Morse stood aside to allow Jason's formidable mother to enter the bus first. She asked for 'St Frideswide's', and as she fiddled one-handedly in her purse the other passengers watched in helpless silence as the hero of the *Argosy* wiped his filthy shoes over the nearest seat-cover.

Morse knew where St Frideswide's was, of course: one of the string of ecclesiastical edifices along Cornmarket . . . where there had been some rather curious occurrences the previous Autumn . . . when he himself had been away on an eight-week secondment in west Africa . . .

'Where to, mate?'

'Er' (it was more than a year since Morse had been on a bus) 'St Frideswide's, please.' It was as good a stop as any for the Ashmolean, and Morse had promised himself an hour or so in the galleries: it would be good to see the Tiepolo again; and the Giorgione.

But he saw neither that morning.

Whilst Mrs Jason was extricating his pram from the luggage-rack, the triumphant young vandal himself was already at large in the street, and very soon the bottom half of a notice affixed to the church railings was torn from its moorings.

''Ow many times 'ave I _told_ you, Jason?' This rhetorical question was accompanied by a clumping clout across the youngster's ears, and the bawling brat was finally dragged away.

The notice now read: ST FRIDESWIDE'S EASTER JUMBLE SALE. That was all. Any details of date, time and place had vanished with the passing of Jason.

Morse was a believer neither in the existence of God nor in the fixity of the Fates. About such things he never quite knew what he should think; and, like Hardy's, his philosophy of life amounted to little more than a heap of confused impressions, akin to those of a bewildered young boy at a conjuring show. Yet, as he looked back, it seemed somehow pre-ordained that his steps should take him on only one course that morning; and he took that course now as, in obedience to some strangely compelling impulse, he walked the few steps across the pavement and unlatched the door at the north porch of St Frideswide's.

CHAPTER SEVEN

As a schoolboy, Morse had once paid a few shillings for a book on architecture and had traipsed around a good many churches, earnestly tracing the development of Early English into Gothic. But the enthusiasm, like so many, had been short-lived. And as he stood in the vaulted silence, looking down the central aisle towards the altar, with the heavily curtained vestry to the right behind him, few of the architectural features were familiar any longer; and his mind, whilst not uninformed, remained maddeningly blank – like that of an amnesic ornithologist at a duck-pond. A ring of candles burned around the effigy of some saint or other, and an occasional elongated asterisk of light was reflected in a gleaming flash from an adjacent crucifix. The air was heavy with incense.

As he walked slowly towards the chancel, Morse realized that he'd been wrong about the silence, though. Somewhere he could hear a quiet, rhythmic scratching noise, like that of a church mouse scampering about in the wainscoting. But the noise was too regular for that; and suddenly Morse knew that he was not alone. A grey head rose above the level of the front pew and nodded neutrally as the visitor stopped alongside. She wiped her pale forehead with the back of her wrist and blew a stray hair from her vision before bending over her work once more, the concentric rings of soap on the wooden floor dissolving beneath her wiping-cloth, the bucket rattling as she moved to the next rectangle.

'Good morning.' Morse smiled amiably as he looked down at her. 'You don't seem to have got any of those brochure things – you know, telling people what to look at.'

'No. We ran out last week, but the Vicar's having some more printed.'

'The Vicar? That's Mr Lawson, isn't it?'

'No, it isn't.' Her large brown eyes looked up at him cautiously, and she suddenly seemed a good deal younger than he'd thought. 'It's Mr Meiklejohn. He's been here since last November.'

'I must have been thinking of one of the other churches.'

'No. Mr Lawson *was* here.' She hesitated. 'He – he died last October.'

'Oh dear. I'm sorry about that.'

For a few seconds there was silence between them.

'I think you knew he was dead,' said the woman quietly.

Morse blinked at her happily. 'Did I?'

'You're another one of those reporters, aren't you?'

Morse shook his head and told her. He was a police officer attached to the Thames Valley Police H.Q. in Kidlington – not to the City Police in St Aldates; he'd heard vaguely about the case but had never been on it himself; in fact, he'd been out of the country at the time.

'Were you involved in any way?' he asked.

'As a matter of fact I was, yes.'

'Pardon?' She spoke so very quietly now that Morse took a step nearer to her.

'I was here in the church on the night of the murder.'

'I see. Do you mind telling me something about it?'

She dried her hands along her faded blue jeans, worn almost threadbare at the knees, and stood up. 'Wait a minute.'

There was a natural elegance about her walk, and Morse's eyes followed her with a slightly quickened interest as she disappeared somewhere at the back of the church, and re-emerged a minute later carrying a brown handbag. She had taken the opportunity to arrange her straggling hair, and Morse began to realize that she must once have been an attractive woman.

'Here you are.' She handed him a cheap brown envelope containing several cuttings from the *Oxford Mail*, and Morse sat down in the pew opposite her and carefully unfolded the thin sheets. The first cutting was dated Tuesday, 27 September of the previous year:

CHURCHWARDEN MURDERED DURING SERVICE

WHILST the congregation was singing the last hymn, Mr H. A. Josephs was last night stabbed to death in the vestry of St Frideswide's Church, Cornmarket.

Chief Inspector Bell of the Oxford City Police, who is in charge of the murder enquiries, told our reporter that Mr Josephs, one of the two churchwardens at St Frideswide's, had just taken the collection and was almost certainly counting it as he was attacked.

When the police arrived there was no sign of the collection-plate itself or of the money. Inspector Bell said that if robbery had been the sole motive the murder was doubly tragic, since only a dozen or so people had attended the evening service, and the offertory could have amounted at most only to about two or three pounds.

Several members of the congregation had heard sounds of some disturbance at the back of the church, but no one suspected that anything was seriously wrong until Mr Josephs had shouted for help. The vicar, the Reverend L. Lawson, immediately suspended the service and summoned the police and the ambulance, but Mr Josephs died before either could arrive.

The knife used by the murderer was of a dull, golden colour, cast in the shape of a crucifix, with the blade honed to a razor sharpness. Police are anxious to hear from anyone who has knowledge of such a knife.

Mr Josephs, aged 50, was married and lived in Port-Meadow Drive, Wolvercote. He came to Oxford after the bar
brilliantly pushed over
left-foot shot was
serving as a regular officer in the Royal Marine Commandos and saw active service in Malaya. Until two years ago he worked for the Inland Revenue Department. There are no children. The inquest is to be held next Monday.

Morse quickly read through the article again, for there were a couple of things, quite apart from the extraordinary typography of the last paragraph, that puzzled him slightly.

'Did you know him very well?'

'Pardon?' The woman stopped her scrubbing and looked across at him.

'I said did you know Josephs well.'

A flicker of unease in those brown eyes? Had she heard him the first time?

'Yes, I knew him quite well. He was a churchwarden here. It says so, doesn't it?'

Morse let it go and turned his attention to the second cutting, dated Tuesday, 4 October:

INQUEST RIDDLE

THE inquest on Mr H. A. Josephs, who was stabbed to death last week at St Frideswide's Church, was adjourned yesterday after a twenty-minute hearing, but not before the court had heard some startling new evidence. The post-mortem report on Mr Josephs showed that a lethal quantity of morphine was present in the stomach, but it seemed clear that it was the stab-wound which was the immediate cause of death.

Earlier, Mr Paul Morris, of 3 Home Close, Kidlington, had given evidence of formal identification. He had been the organist during the service and was in fact playing the last hymn when Mr Josephs was murdered.

Another witness, Miss Ruth Rawlinson, of 14 Manning Terrace, Summertown, said that she heard noises coming from the vestry during the singing of the last hymn, and had turned to see Mr Josephs call out and slump beside the vestry curtains.

Chief Inspector Bell, of the Oxford City Police, informed the Coroner that he was as yet unable to re-

port on any firm develop-
ments in the case but that
enquiries were proceeding.
The Coroner extended his
deepest sympathy to Mrs
Brenda Josephs, the de-
ceased's wife.

The funeral service will be
held at St Frideswide's on
Thursday at 2.30 p.m.

The narrative was bald, but interesting enough,
wasn't it? What was morphine doing in the poor
beggar's innards? Somebody must have wanted him out
of the way pretty badly, and that somebody had so far
got away with it and was still walking around – probably
walking around the streets of Oxford – a free man. Or
a free woman perhaps, he reminded himself, as he
glanced across the aisle.

Morse looked about him with renewed interest. He
was actually sitting a few yards from the scene of the
crime, and he tried to imagine it all: the organ playing,
the few members of the congregation standing, heads
bowed over their hymn books – one minute, though!
Where was the organ? He got to his feet and walked up
the broad, shallow steps of the chancel. Yes. There it
was, on the left-hand side behind two rows of choir-
stalls, with a blue curtain stretched across in front of it
to hide the body of the organist; and a mirror, too, fixed
just above the high top manual, so that, however much
he was concealed from the view of all others, the organist himself could keep an observant eye on the minister
and the choir – and on the congregation as well, if he
wanted to. If you swung the mirror round a bit ...
Morse sat himself behind the curtain on the organ-seat
and looked into it. He could see the choir-stalls behind

him and the main body of the chancel. Mm. Then, like a nervous learner before starting off on a driving test, he began adjusting the mirror, finding that it moved easily and noiselessly: up and down, right and left – wherever he wanted it. First, to the right and slightly down, and he found himself looking straight at the intricately woven gold design on the front of the green altar-cloth; then to the left and down, and he could see the head and shoulders of the cleaning woman, her elbows circling sedulously over the soapy suds; then further still to the left and up slightly, almost as far as the mirror would go – and Morse suddenly stopped, a needle-sharp sensation momentarily flashing across his temples. So very clearly he could now see the front curtains of the vestry, could even see the fold where they would swing back to let the choir on its way; the fold where they had once opened – perhaps only slightly? – to reveal the figure of a man shouting desperately above the swell of the organ notes, a man with a knife stuck firm and deep through his back, a man with only a moment or two to live ... What if the organist – Morris, wasn't it? – had actually been looking at the vestry curtains during those fateful, fatal seconds? What if he'd seen something? Something like ...

The rattle of the pail brought his airborne fancies down to earth. What possible reason could Morris have had for turning the mirror to such an improbable angle as he played the last hymn? Forget it! He turned on the smooth bench and looked over the curtain. The cleaner was packing up by the look of things, and he hadn't read the other cuttings yet. But before he got off the bench his mind again took wing and was floating as effortlessly as a kittiwake keeling over the cliffs. It was the organ-curtain ... He was himself a man of just over medium height, but even someone three or four inches taller would be fairly well concealed behind that curtain. The back of the head would be showing, but little else; and if Morris was a small man he would have been almost completely concealed. Indeed, as far as the choir and congregation were concerned, the organist might ... might not have been Morris at all!

He walked down the chancel steps. 'Mind if I keep these cuttings? I'll post them back to you, of course.'

The woman shrugged. 'All right.' It seemed a matter of little concern to her.

'I don't know your name, I'm afraid,' began Morse, but a small middle-aged man had entered the church and was walking briskly towards them.

'Morning, Miss Rawlinson.'

Miss Rawlinson! One of the witnesses at the inquest. Well, well! And the man who had just come in was doubtless Morris, the other witness, for he had already seated himself at the organ, where a few switches were clicked on and where a whirr of some hidden power was followed by a series of gruff bass blasts, as if the instrument were breaking wind.

'As I say, I can post 'em,' said Morse, 'or pop 'em through your letter-box. 14 Manning Road, isn't it?'

'Manning *Terrace*.'

'Oh yes.' Morse smiled at her good-naturedly. 'Memory's not what it was, I'm afraid. They tell me we lose about 30,000 brain cells a day once we're past thirty.'

'Just as well we all have plenty to start with, Inspector.' There was perhaps just a hint of mockery in her steady eyes, but Morse's lightheartedness had evoked no reciprocal response.

'I'll just have a quick word with Mr Morris before—'

'That's not Mr Morris.'

'Pardon?'

'That's Mr Sharpe. He was deputy organist when Mr Morris was here.'

'And Mr Morris isn't here any longer?' said Morse slowly.

She shook her head.

'Do you know where he's gone?'

Did she? Again there seemed some hesitation in the eyes. 'N-no, I don't. He's left the district. He left last October.'

'Surely he must have—'

'He left his post at the school and, well, he just went.'

'But he must have—'

She picked up the bucket and prepared to leave. 'Nobody knows where he went.'

But Morse sensed she was lying. 'It's your duty to tell me, you know, if you've any idea at all where he went.' He spoke now with a quiet authority, and a flush arose in the woman's cheeks.

'It's nothing really. Just that he – he left at the same time as someone else. That's all.'

'And it was fairly easy to put two and two together?'

She nodded. 'Yes. You see, he left Oxford the same week as Mrs Josephs.'

CHAPTER EIGHT

MORSE LEFT THE church and strolled over to the snack bar.

'One coffee, please,' he said to the girl lounging by the pay-desk.

'If you go an' si' down, one of the girls'll come.'

'Oh.' It all seemed a roundabout business.

He sat and stared abstractedly through the large window, flecked now with drizzle, and watched the people walking to and fro along Cornmarket. Immediately opposite him, fencing in the church and the churchyard, were the sharply pointed, black-painted railings of St Frideswide's, against which a bearded, damp-looking tramp was leaning uncertainly, a bottle of something hanging loosely in his lefthand.

'Order, please?' It was the same waitress.

'You just had it,' snapped Morse.

'I'm sorry, sir, bu'—'

'Forget it, luv.'

He left and walked back across the street.

'How goes it, brother?'

The tramp looked at Morse warily through an incongruous pair of dark sunglasses: unsolicited interest in his well-being was quite clearly no everyday occurrence. 'Could do wiv a cup o' tea, guv.'

Morse pushed a couple of ten-pence pieces into a surprisingly clean hand. 'Do you usually stand here?'

'Nah. Usually be'ind Brasenose College. Makes a change, though, don't it?'

'Some nice kind people come out of the church, do they?'

'Sometimes.'

'You know the minister here?'

'Nah. Tell yer to push off, like as not, this one. Knew the other one, though. Real gent he was, guv. Sometimes 'e'd take yer down to the vicarage an' give yer a real square meal, 'e would.'

'Is he the one who died?'

The tramp looked at Morse with what could have been a glint of suspicion behind the dark lenses, and took a swig on the bottle. 'Christ, you can say that again, mister.' He shuffled along the railings towards Carfax, and was gone.

Morse crossed the road yet again, and walked past the snack bar, past a well-stocked bicycle-shop, past the cinema, and then turned left into the curving sweep of Beaumont Street. Momentarily he debated between the Ashmolean, just opposite on his right, and the Randolph, immediately on his left. It wasn't a fair contest.

The cocktail-bar was already quite full as Morse waited rather impatiently for a group of Americans to sort out their gins and tarnics. The barmaid wore a low-cut dress and Morse watched with what he told himself was a fascinated indifference as she finally leaned forward over the beer pump to pull his order. She was too young, though – no more than twenty-odd – and Morse was beginning to formulate the philosophy that men were attracted to women of roughly their own age – well, give or take ten years or so either way.

He sat down, savoured his beer, and took out cutting number three from his pocket. It was dated Wednesday, 19 October.

TRAGIC FALL FROM CHURCH TOWER

YESTERDAY morning the Reverend Lionel Lawson fell to his death from the tower of St Frideswide's Church in Cornmarket. Only ten minutes earlier he had conducted the regular 7.30 a.m. Communion Service, and two members of the congregation were among the first to discover the tragedy.

The church tower, formerly a favourite viewing-point for tourists, has been closed to the public for the last two years as signs of crumbling have become evident in the stone fabric on the north side. But the tower was not considered unsafe, and only a year ago workmen had been up to check the leads.

Mr Lawson, a bachelor, aged 41, had been vicar of St Frideswide's for almost eleven years. He will be remembered above all, perhaps, for his social work, since in addition to his deep involvement with the church's flourishing youth activities he invariably took a compassionate interest in the plight of the homeless, and there can be few regular down-and-outs in Oxford who have not at some time or another enjoyed his hospitality.

As a churchman he made no apologies for his High Anglican views, and although his strongly voiced hostility towards the ordination of women was not universally popular his large and loyal congregation will mourn the death of a dear friend and pastor. He studied theology at Christ's College, Cambridge, and later at St Stephen's House, Oxford.

Only last month Mr H. A. Josephs, churchwarden of St Frideswide's, was found stabbed to death in the church vestry.

Mm. Morse looked at the last sentence again and wondered why the reporter had deemed it his duty to stick it in. Wasn't there a bit too much of that *post hoc, propter hoc* suspicion about it? Yet a murder followed very shortly afterwards by a suicide was by no means uncommon, and the reporter would hardly have been the only one to suspect some causal connection. For if Lawson had somehow managed to murder Josephs, then it was surely only honourable and proper for a servant of the Lord to be stricken so sorely in conscience as to chuck himself off the nearest or most convenient pinnacle, was it not?

Morse drained his beer, fiddled in his pockets for some more change, and looked vaguely around him. A woman had just walked up to the bar and he studied her back view with growing interest. A good deal nearer his own age than the barmaid, certainly: black-leather, knee-length boots; slim figure; tight-belted, light-fawn raincoat; spotted red headscarf. Nice. On her own, too.

Morse sauntered up beside her and heard her order a dry Martini; and the thought crossed his mind that all he had to do was to pay for her drink, ask her over to his lonely corner, and talk of this and that in a quiet, unassuming, intelligent, fascinating, masterly way. And then – who knows? But a middle-aged customer had risen from his seat and clapped a hand on her shoulder.

'I'll get that Ruth, love. You sit down.'

Miss Rawlinson unfastened her headscarf and smiled. Then, as she appeared to notice Morse for the first time, the smile was gone. She nodded – almost curtly, it seemed – and turned away.

After his third pint, Morse left the cocktail-bar and from the foyer rang through to the City Police Station. But Chief Inspector Bell was on holiday, he was told – in Spain.

It was a long time since Morse had undertaken any extended exercise, and he decided on impulse to walk up to north Oxford. Only half an hour, if he stepped it out. As if to deride his decision, bus after bus passed him: Cutteslowe buses, Kidlington buses, and the eternally empty Park and Ride buses, subsidized at huge cost by the City Fathers in the vain hope of persuading shoppers to leave their cars on the outskirts. But Morse kept walking.

As he came up to the Marston Ferry crossroads he watched, almost mesmerized, as a north-bound car pulled out of the inside lane into the path of an overtaking motor-cycle. The rider was thrown slithering to the other side of the road where his white helmet hit the kerb with a sickening thwack, and where the nearside wheel of a south-bound lorry, for all its squealing brake-power, ran over the man's pelvis with an audible crunch.

Others on that scene showed, perhaps for the first time in their lives, a desperate courage born of the hour: figures knelt by the dying man, and coats were laid over his crushed body; a young man with greasy shoulder-length hair took upon himself the duties of a traffic policeman; a doctor was on his way from the Summertown Health Centre on the corner; the ambulance and police were already being summoned.

But Morse felt his stomach tighten and twist in a spasm of pain. A light sweat had broken out on his forehead, and he thought he was going to vomit as he averted his eyes and hurried away. The sense of his inadequacy and cowardice disgusted him, but the physical sickness prowling in his bowels drove him on, farther and farther up the road, past the Summertown shops, and at last to his home. Even the Levite had taken a quick look before passing by on the other side.

What it was about road accidents that threw him so completely off balance, Morse had never quite been able to understand. Many a time he had been on the scene of a murder, and examined a brutally mutilated corpse. With an ugly distaste, certainly; but with nothing worse. Why was it, then? Perhaps it was something to do with the difference between death and the *process* of dying, certainly of dying in a writhing agony after a road accident. Yes, it was the *accidental* angle of things; the flukey, fortuitous nature of it all; the 'if only' of being just a few yards, just a few inches even, from safety; of being just a second, just a fraction of a second, earlier – or later. It was all that Lucretian business about the random concourse of the atoms, hurtling headlong through the boundless void, colliding occasionally like billiard balls, colliding like a car against a motor-bike. All so pointless, somehow; all so cruelly haphazard. Occasionally Morse considered the ever-decreasing possibility of having a family himself, and he knew that he might be able to face some terrible illness in those he loved; but never an accident.

In the distance sounded the urgent two-toned siren of an ambulance, like some demented mother wailing for her children.

Morse picked up his one pint of milk and shut the door of his bachelor flat behind him. Not the best of starts to a holiday! He selected Richard Strauss's *Vier Letzte Lieder*; but a sudden thought flashed through his mind, and he put the record down again. In the Randolph he had quickly read through cutting number four, the newspaper account of the inquest on Lawson; little of interest there, he'd thought. But had he been right? He read it through again now. The poor fellow had obviously been a terrible sight, his body violently crushed by his fall, his skull – Yes! That is what had clicked in Morse's mind as he had lifted the lid of the record-player. If he himself had been unwilling to look at the face of a dying motor-cyclist, had those two witnesses looked as closely as they should have done at that sadly shattered skull? All he needed now was a little information from the official report of the coroner's hearing; and, knowing the coroner very well, he could get that little information straight away – that very afternoon.

Ten minutes later he was asleep.

CHAPTER NINE

AVOIDING THE MAN'S look, Ruth Rawlinson finished her second Martini and stared at the slice of lemon at the bottom of her glass.

'Another?'

'No, I mustn't. Really. I've had two already.'

'Go on! Enjoy yourself! We only live once, you know.'

Ruth smiled sadly. It was just the sort of thing her mother kept saying: 'You're missing out on life, Ruthie dear. Why don't you try to meet more people? Have a good time?' Her mother! Her grumbling, demanding, crippled mother. But still her mother; and she, Ruth, her only child: forty-one years old (almost forty-two), a virgin until so recently, and then not memorably deflowered.

'Same again, then?' He was on his feet, her glass held high in his hand.

Why *not?* She felt pleasantly warm somewhere deep down inside her, and she could always go to bed for a few hours when she got home. Monday afternoon was her mother's weekly bridge session, and nothing short of a nuclear attack on north Oxford could ever disturb those four mean old women as they grubbed for penalty points and overtricks at the small green-baize table in the back room.

'You'll have me drunk if you're not careful,' she said.

'What do you think I'm trying to do?'

She knew him fairly well now, and she watched him as he stood at the bar in his expensively cut suit: a few years older than herself, with three teenage children and a charming, intelligent, trusting wife. And he wanted *her*.

Yet for some reason she didn't want him. She couldn't quite bear the thought of being intimate with him – not (she reminded herself) that she really knew what intimacy was all about . . .

Her eyes wandered round the room once more, in particular to a point in the farthest corner of the room. But Morse had gone now, and for some unfathomable reason she knew she had wanted him to stay – just to *be* there. She'd recognized him, of course, as soon as she'd walked in, and she had been conscious of his presence all the time. Could she get into bed with *him*? It was his eyes that fascinated her; bluey-grey, cold – and yet somehow vulnerable and lost. She told herself not to be so silly; told herself she was getting drunk.

As she slowly sipped the third Martini, her companion was busily writing something on the back of a beer-mat.

'Here we are, Ruth. Be honest with me – please!'

She looked down at what he had written:

Tick the box which
in your opinion is nearest

to your inclinations. Will
you let me take you to bed

this week?	❏
next week?	❏
this year?	❏
next year?	❏
sometime?	❏
never?	❏

It made her smile, but she shook her head slowly and helplessly. 'I can't answer that. You know I can't.'

'You mean it's "never"?'

'I didn't say that. But – you *know* what I mean. You're married, and I know your wife. I respect her. Surely—'

'Just tick one of the boxes. That's all.'

'But—'

'But you'll disappoint me if you tick the last one, is that it? Go on, then. Disappoint me. But be honest about it, Ruth. At least I shall know where I stand.'

'I like you – you know that. But—'

'You've got plenty of choice.'

'What if none of the answers is the right one?'

'One of 'em must be right.'

'No.' She took out her own pen and wrote in a single word before 'sometime': the word 'perhaps'.

Unlike Morse, she didn't sleep that afternoon. She felt fresh and alive, and would have done a few odd jobs in the garden but for the persistent drizzle. Instead she revised the lines for her part in the play. Friday was looming frighteningly near, and the cast was rehearsing at 7.30 p.m. that evening. Not that a tuppenny-ha'penny play at a church social was all that grand; but she was never happy about doing even the smallest things half-heartedly – and they always had a good audience.

Morse himself woke up with a shudder and a grunt at 3 p.m., and slowly focused upon life once more. The newspaper cuttings still lay on the arm of his chair, and he collected them together and put them back in their envelope. Earlier in the day he had allowed things to get out of perspective. But no longer. He was on holiday, and he was going to *have* a holiday. From his bookshelf he hooked out a thick volume; and just as the Romans used to do it with the Sibylline Books, just as the fundamentalists still do it with the Holy Scriptures – so did Morse do it with the *A.A. Hotels of Britain.* He closed his eyes, opened the book at random, and stuck his index finger half-way down the left-hand page. There she was. Derwentwater: *Swiss Lodore Hotel.* Keswick, three miles S. along the ... He rang the number immediately. Yes, they had a single room with private bath. How long for? Four or five nights, perhaps. All right. He'd be leaving straight away, and be there about – oh, about nine or ten. Good.

Evesham – about an hour, if he was lucky. Along the old Worcester Road. M5 and M6 – 80 m.p.h. in the fast lane. Easy! He'd be there in time for a slap-up meal and a bottle of red wine. Lovely. *That's* what holidays were all about.

CHAPTER TEN

THE REVEREND KEITH MEIKLEJOHN exuded a sort of holy enthusiasm as he stood at the door of the church hall. Obviously there was going to be a big audience, and in between the unctuous Good evenings, how nice of you to comes, he debated the wisdom of fetching some of the old chairs from the store-room. It was only 7.20 p.m., but already the hall was two-thirds full. He knew why, of course: it was the Sunday School infant classes' tap-dance troupe, with its gilt-edged guarantee of attracting all the mums and aunts and grandmas. 'Hello, Mrs Walsh-Atkins. How very nice of you to come. Just a few seats left near the front...' He despatched two reluctant choirboys for the extra chairs, and was ready with his beam of ecclesiastical bonhomie for the next arrival. 'Good evening, sir. How nice of you to come. Are you a visitor to Oxford or—?'

'No, I live here.'

The newcomer walked into the hall and sat down at the back, a slightly sour expression on his face. He gave five pence to the pretty pigtailed girl who came up to him and stuck the programme in his pocket. What a day! Almost six hours from Keswick to the Evesham exit: single-line traffic north of Stoke; a multiple pile-

70

up just after Birmingham, with all lanes closed for almost an hour on the south-bound carriageway; flood warnings flashing for the last thirty miles and the juggernaut lorries churning up spray like speed-boats... And what a so-called holiday! On fine days (he had little doubt) the view from his bedroom at the Swiss Lodore would have been most beautiful; but the mist had driven down from the encircling hills, and it was as much as he could do to spot the grass on the lawn below his window, with its white chairs and tables – all deserted. Some of his fellow-guests had taken to their cars and driven (presumably) in search of some less-bedraggled scenery; but the majority had just sat around and read paperback thrillers, played cards, gone swimming in the heated indoor pool, eaten, drunk, talked intermittently, and generally managed to look rather less miserable than Morse did. He could find no passably attractive women over-anxious to escape their hovering husbands, and the few who sat unattended in the cocktail-lounge were either too plain or too old. In his bedroom Morse found a leaflet on which was printed Robert Southey's 'How the Waters Come Down at Lodore'; but he felt that even a poet laureate had seldom sunk to such banality. And anyway, after three days, Morse knew only too well how the waters came down at Lodore: they came down in bucketfuls, slanting incessantly in sharp lines from a leaden sky.

On Friday (it was 7 April) *The Times* was brought into his room with his early-morning tea; and after looking at the weekend weather forecast he decided to

leave immediately after breakfast. It was as he was taking
out his chequebook at the reception desk that the
folded white leaflet fluttered to the floor: he had
pocketed it absent-mindedly from the literature set out
on the table at the entrance to St Frideswide's, but it
was only now that he read it.

CONCERT

At the Church Hall St Aldates
Friday, April 7th, at 7.30 p.m.

TAP-DANCE TROUPE (Sunday School)
GILBERT & SULLIVAN MEDLEY (Church Choir)
A VICTORIAN MELODRAMA (Drama Group)
Entrance Fee 20p. Programme 5p.

ALL WELCOME
(Proceeds in aid of the Tower Restoration Fund)

It was that last line, pregnant with possibilities, that
had monopolized Morse's thoughts as he drove the
Lancia south. Were the crenellations really crumbling
after all? *Had* they crumbled, when Lawson looked his
last over the familiar landmarks of the city? Whenever
possible, juries were keen to steer away from 'suicide'
verdicts, and if the tower had been at all unsafe the
point would have been a crucial one. What Morse really
needed was the coroner's report: it would all be there.
And it was to the coroner's office that Morse had

immediately driven when he finally reached Oxford at 4.30 p.m.

The report, apart from the detailed descriptions of Lawson's multiple mutilations, was vaguer than Morse had hoped, with no mention whatsoever of the parapet from which Lawson had plummeted to earth. Yet there was one section of the report that firmly gripped his interest, and he read it through again. 'Mrs Emily Walsh-Atkins, after giving formal evidence of identification, said that she had remained alone for some minutes in the church after the service. She then waited for about five minutes outside the church, where she had arranged to be picked up by taxi: the service had finished slightly earlier than usual. At about 8.10 a.m. she heard a terrible thud in the churchyard and had looked round to find Lawson's body spread-eagled on the railings. Fortunately two police officers had soon appeared on the scene and Mr Morris' (Morris!) 'had taken her back inside the church to sit down and recover . . .' Morse knew that he would have little mental rest until he had seen Mrs W.-A., and it was that lady who was the immediate cause of his attendance at the Church Concert. (Was she the *only* reason, Morse?) He had just missed her at the Home for Ageing Gentlefolk, but they knew where she had gone.

Meiklejohn had finished his long-winded, oily introduction, the lights had been switched off, and now the stage curtains were jerkily wound back to reveal the Tap-Dance Troupe in all its bizarre glory. For Morse the whole thing was embarrassingly amusing; and he was quite unprepared for the wild applause which greeted the final unsynchronized kneelings of the eleven little girls, plumed plastic headgear and all, who for three minutes or so had braved inadequate rehearsal, innate awkwardness, and the appallingly incompetent accompaniment of the pianist. To make matters worse, the troupe had started with a complement of twelve, but one small child had turned left instead of right at a crucial point in the choreography, and had promptly fled to the wings, her face collapsing in tearful misery. Yet still the audience clapped and clapped, and was not appeased until the appearance of the troupe's instructress, alias the piano player, leading by the hand the unfortunate, but now shyly smiling, little deserter – the latter greeted by all as if she were a prima ballerina from the Sadler's Wells.

The Gilbert and Sullivan selections were excellently sung, and Morse realized that the St Frideswide's choir contained some first-rate talent. This time, fortunately, the piano was in the hands of an infinitely more able executant – Mr Sharpe, no less, former deputy to Mr Morris (that name again!). Morris . . . the man who had been on the scene when Josephs was murdered; had been on the scene, too, when Lawson was – when Lawson was found. Surely, surely, it shouldn't be at all difficult to trace him? Or to trace Mrs Brenda Josephs? They must be somewhere; must be earning some money; must have insurance numbers; must have a house . . . With clinical precision the choir cut off the last chord from the finale of *The Mikado*, and their turn was complete – greeted by appreciative if comparatively short-lived applause.

It took a good five minutes for the Victorian melodrama to materialize; minutes during which could be heard the squeaking and bumping of furniture, during which the curtains were twice prematurely half opened, and during which Morse once more looked through the coroner's digest on Lawson's death. There was this fellow Thomas's evidence, for example: 'He had just parked his car in St Giles and was walking down towards Broad Street when he noticed someone on the tower of St Frideswide's. He could not recall seeing anyone standing there before, but it was not unusual to see people looking out over Oxford from St Mary's in the High, or from Carfax tower. He thought that the figure was dressed in black, looking down, his head leaning over the parapet . . .' That was all, really. Only later had he heard of the morning's tragedy and had reluctantly rung up the police – at his wife's suggestion. Not much there, but the man must have been the very last person (Morse supposed) to see Lawson alive. Or was he? He might just have been the first – no, the second – person to see Lawson *dead*. Morse found the key words again: 'looking down, his head leaning over the parapet . . .' How high *were* those parapets? No more than three feet or so, surely. And why bring Lawson's head into it? Why not just 'leaning over the parapet'? And why 'looking down'? Was a man about to leap to his death likely to be all that worried about the place he was going to land? A minister, surely – more than most of his fellow-mortals – might be expected to seek a little consolation from more ethereal realms, whatever the depths of his despair. But if . . . if Lawson had been dead already; if someone had—

The melodrama was under way at last, and in Morse's view a more crudely amateurish production could seldom have merited a public presentation. The play appeared to have been chosen to embrace the largest possible cast, and to allow to all of its participants the briefest possible exposure on the boards, in order to minimize their breathtaking incompetences. The bearded one-armed hero, who at least had learned his lines and spoke them audibly, clumped around in a pair of squeaky army boots, and at one point conducted a crucial telephone conversation by speaking into the ear-piece – of an incongruously modern-looking instrument at that; whilst one of the numerous housemaids was every other line reduced to referring to a copy of her part pasted on the underside of her dustpan. The only feature which prevented the whole thing from degenerating into a farcical shambles was the performance of the heroine herself, a young blonde who acted with a charm and sophistication hopelessly at variance with the pathetically inadequate crew around her. She appeared to know everyone else's part, and covered their lapses and stumbles with impressive aplomb. She even managed, at one stage, to prevent one of the butlers (blind fool! thought Morse) from tripping over an intervening chair as he carried in her ladyship's tea. Mercifully many of the lines (as originally written) must have been extremely amusing, and even voiced by these clowns could elicit a little polite laughter; and when the final curtain drew its veil over the proceedings there seemed to Morse not the slightest sign of embarrassed

relief amongst the audience. Perhaps all church concerts were the same.

The Vicar had earlier announced that tea would
be served at the end of the entertainment, and Morse
felt certain that Mrs W.-A. would not be leaving without a cup. All he had to do was find out which one
she was. He looked around in vain for Miss Rawlinson, but it seemed clear that she'd given the evening a
miss – enough of a penance, no doubt, her scrubbing
the pews. But he felt a certain disappointment ...
People were leaving the hall fairly quickly now, but
Morse decided to wait a minute or two. He took out
his programme and looked at it vaguely, but with no
real purpose other than that of seeming not to be
lonely.

'I hope you'll have a cup of tea with us?' Even at this
late stage Meiklejohn was not neglecting his pastoral
duties.

Tea? It had never occurred to Morse that he might
be drinking tea at 9 p.m. 'Yes; thank you. I wonder if
you happen to know a Mrs Walsh-Atkins. I want—'

'Yes, yes. This way. Wonderful concert, wasn't it?'

Morse mumbled inaudibly and followed his guide
into the crowded vestibule where a stout lady was
coaxing a dark-brown liquid from a formidable urn.
Morse took his place in the queue and listened to the
conversation of the two women in front of him.

'You know, it's the fourth time now he's been in one
of them. His dad would have been ever so proud of
him.'

'No one would ever suspect he was blind, would they? Coming on the way he does and all that.'

'It's lots of rehearsal that does it, you know. You have to sort of picture where everything is—'

'Yes. You really must be proud of him, Mrs Kinder.'

'They've asked him to be in the next one, anyway, so he must be all right, mustn't he?'

So the poor devil *had* been blind after all. And learning a part and stepping out on to the stage had probably been about as much of an ordeal as for a sighted person walking through a swamp of crocodiles. Morse suddenly felt very moved, and very humbled. When it came to his turn, he slipped a fifty-pence piece on to the tea-money plate, and hoped that nobody had noticed. He felt oddly out of place there. These were good people, who rejoiced in the simple ties of family and Christian fellowship; who thought of God as a father, and who never in a month of Sabbaths could begin to understand the aberrations of the new theology which thought of Him (if it thought of Him at all) as the present participle of the verb 'to be'. Morse sipped his tea self-consciously, and once more took out his programme and looked for the name of Her Ladyship's butler, whose mother (with what sweet justification!) was feeling so happy and proud. But once again he was interrupted. Meiklejohn was at his shoulder, and with him a diminutive old lady munching a digestive biscuit.

'Mr – er?'

'Morse.'

'You said you wanted to meet Mrs Walsh-Atkins?'

Morse stood above her, acutely conscious of her smallness, and suggested they should sit down back in the hall. He explained who he was, why he was there, and what he wanted to know; and she readily told him of her own part in that dreadful day's events when she'd found Lawson dashed to pieces from the tower, repeating virtually verbatim the words she had used at the inquest.

Nothing! Morse had learned nothing. Yet he thanked her politely and asked if he could fetch her another cup of tea.

'One's enough for me these days, Inspector. But I must have left my umbrella somewhere. If you would be kind enough to . . .'

Morse felt his scalp tingling in the old familiar way. They were seated at a small table at the back of the hall, and there was the umbrella, large as life, lying diagonally across it. There could be little doubt about it: *the old lady must be going blind.*

'Do you mind me asking how old you are, Mrs Walsh-Atkins?'

'Can you keep a secret, Inspector?'

'Yes.'

'So can I,' she whispered.

Whether Morse's decision to patronize the cocktail-lounge of the Randolph was determined by his thirst, or by some wayward wish to find out if Miss Rawlinson might be there, he didn't stop to think. But he recognized no one, left after only one pint, and caught a bus outside the Taylorian. Back home, he poured himself a large neat whisky and put on *Vier Letzte Lieder*. Marvellous. 'Melismatic', as it said on the sleeve . . .

It was time for an early night, and he hung up his jacket in the hallway. The programme stuck out of one of the pockets and, third time lucky, he opened it and read it.

'Her Ladyship's Butler – Mr John Kinder.' And then his pulse raced as he looked at the top of the cast: 'Her Ladyship, the Hon. Amelia Barker-Barker – Miss Ruth Rawlinson.'

CHAPTER ELEVEN

MEDIUMS AND CLAIRVOYANTS claim enhanced scope for their talents if they can be physically present in a room where the absent ones – the missing or the plain dead – may have left a few stray emanations behind. Murderers, likewise, have the reputation of nursing an uncontrollable urge to revisit the scene of death, and on Sunday morning Morse found himself wondering whether the murderer of Josephs had ever set foot in St Frideswide's again since the day of his crime. He thought that the answer was probably 'yes', and it was one of the very few positive thoughts he had managed to generate since Friday evening. Somehow his mind had gone completely stale, and on the Saturday he had firmly resolved to abandon all idea of further investigation into a mysterious affair which was none of his business anyway. In the morning he had consulted the Sibyl once more, but had drawn the line at Inverness. In the afternoon he had wasted two idle hours in front of the television set watching the racing from Doncaster. He was restless and bored: there were so many books he could read, so many records he could play – and yet he could summon up no enthusiasm for anything. What *did* he want? His listless mood persisted through to Sunday morning, when not even the few erotic titbits in the *News of the World* could cheer him. He sprawled gloomily in his armchair, his eyes vaguely scanning the multi-coloured spines along the bookshelves. Baudelaire might match his mood, perhaps? What was that line about the prince in 'La Fleurs du Mal'? 'Riche, mais impuissant, jeune et pourtant très vieux . . .' And quite suddenly Morse felt better. Bloody nonsense! He was neither impotent nor senile – far from it! It was time for action.

He rang the number and she answered.

'Hello?'

'Miss Rawlinson?'

'Speaking.'

'You may not remember me. I – I met you in St Frideswide's last Monday.'

'I remember.'

'I was – er – thinking of going to church this morning—'

'Our church, you mean?'

'Yes.'

'You'd better get a move on – it starts at half-past ten.'

'Oh, I see. Well – er – thank you very much.'

'You're very interested in us all of a sudden, Inspector.' There was a suggestion of friendly amusement in her voice, and Morse wanted to keep her on the phone.

'Did you know I came to the social on Friday evening?'

'Of course.' Morse felt a silly juvenile joy about that 'of course'. Keep going, lad!

'I – er – I didn't see you afterwards. In fact I didn't realize that it was you in the play.'

'Amazing what a blonde wig does, isn't it?'

'Who is it?' Someone called behind her voice.

'Pardon?' said Morse.

'It's all right. That was my mother – asking who you are.'

'Oh, I see.'

'Well, as I say, you'd better hurry up if you're going—'

'Are *you* going? Perhaps I could give you—'

'No, not this morning. Mother's had one of her asthma attacks, and I can't leave her.'

'Oh.' Morse hid his disappointment beneath a cheerful farewell, and said 'Bugger it!' as he cradled the phone. *He* was going, though. It wasn't Ruth Rawlinson he wanted to see. He just wanted to get the feel of the place – to pick up a few of those stray emanations. He told himself that it didn't matter two hoots whether the Rawlinson woman was there or not.

Looking back on his first church attendance for a decade, Morse decided that it was quite an experience. St Frideswide's must, he thought, be about as 'spikey' as they come in the Anglican varieties. True, there was no Peter's Pence at the back of the church, no bulletin from the pulpit proclaiming the infallibility of his Holiness; but in other respects there seemed little that separated the church from the Roman fold. There'd been a sermon, all right, devoted to St Paul's humourless denunciation of the lusts of the flesh, but the whole service had really centred round the Mass. It had not started all that well for Morse who, two minutes late, had inadvertently seated himself in the pew reserved for the churchwarden, and this had necessitated an awkward, whispered exchange as the people knelt to confess their wrongdoings. Fortunately, from his vantage-point at the rear, Morse was able to sit and stand and kneel in concert with the rest, although many of the crossings and genuflections proved equally beyond his reflexes as his inclinations. What amazed him more than anything was the number of the cast assembled around the altar, each purposefully pursuing his part: the celebrant, the deacon, the sub-deacon, the incense-swinger and the boat-boy, the two acolytes and the four torch-bearers, and conducting them all a youngish, mournful-faced master of ceremonies, his hands sticking out horizontally before him in a posture of perpetual prayer. It was almost like a floor show, with everyone so well trained: bowing, crossing, kneeling, rising, with a synchronized discipline which (as Morse saw it) could profitably have been emulated by the Tap-Dance Troupe. To these manoeuvres the equally well-disciplined congregation would match its own reactions, suddenly sitting, as suddenly on its feet again, and occasionally giving mouth to mournful responses. The woman seated next to Morse had soon spotted him for the greenhorn that he was, and was continually thrusting the appropriate page of the proceedings under his nose. She herself sang in a shrill soprano, and was so refined in her diction that the long 'o' vowels issued forth as bleating 'ew's: thus, all the 'O Lords' became 'You Lords', and three times at the start of the service, whilst Meiklejohn walked briskly up and down the aisles sprinkling everything in sight with holy water, she had implored the Almighty to wash her from her sins and make her waiter yea waiter than snew. But there was one thing in Morse's favour – he knew most of the hymns; and at one point he thought he almost managed to drown the 'Hewly Hewly Hewly' on his right. And he learned something, too. From Meiklejohn's notices for the week's forthcoming attractions, it was clear that this Mass business was rather more complicated than he'd imagined. There must be three types, it seemed – 'low', 'high' and 'solemn'; and if, as Morse suspected, the low variety wasn't all that posh, if no choir was involved – no organist even? – then what in heaven's name was Morris doing in church when the unhappy Lawson dashed himself to pieces from the tower? People perhaps did sometimes go to church because they wanted to but ... Anyway, it might be worthwhile finding out a bit more about those different masses. And there was something else; something very suggestive indeed. With the exception of Morse himself, all the congregation partook of the blessed bread and the blessed wine, ushered quietly and firmly to the chancel-rails by that same churchwarden who had so nearly lost his seat, and who – doubtless by venerable tradition – *was himself the very last to receive the sacrament.* Josephs had been churchwarden. Josephs must have been the last to kneel at the chancel-rails on the evening of his death. Josephs had drunk some of the communion wine that same night. And Josephs – so the pathologist said – had finished up with some very queer things in his stomach. Was it possible? Was it possible that Josephs had been poisoned at the altar? From his observation of the final part of the ritual, it was clear to Morse that any celebrant with a chalice in his hands could wreak enormous havoc if he had the inclination to do so, for when he'd finished *he could get rid of every scrap of evidence.* Nor did he need any excuse for this, for it was part of the drill: rinse the cup and wipe it clean and stick it in the cupboard till the next time. Yes. It would be tricky, of course, with all those other stage-hands standing around, like they were now; but on the evening of Josephs' murder, the cast must surely have been very much smaller. Again, it was something worth looking into. There was another snag, though, wasn't there? It seemed that the celebrant himself was called upon to drain the dregs that were left in the chalice, and to do it in front of the whole congregation. But couldn't he just pretend to do that? Pour it down the piscina later? Or, again, there might have been nothing left in the chalice at all . . .

There were so very many possibilities . . . and Morse's fancies floated steeple-high as he walked out of the cool church into the sunlit reach of Cornmarket.

CHAPTER TWELVE

IT WAS SOME relief for Morse to recognize the fair countenance of Reason once more, and she greeted him serenely when he woke, clear-headed, on Monday morning, and told him that it would be no bad idea to have a quiet look at the problem itself before galloping off towards a solution. Basically there were only two possibilities: either Lawson had killed Josephs, and thereafter committed suicide in a not surprising mood of remorse; or else some unknown hand had killed Josephs and then compounded his crime by adding Lawson to his list. Of these alternatives, the first was considerably the more probable; especially so if Josephs had in some way been a threat to Lawson, if the dagger found in Josephs' back had belonged to Lawson, and if Lawson himself had betrayed signs of anxiety or distress in the weeks preceding Josephs' death, as well as in the days that followed it. The trouble was that Morse had no one to talk to. Yet someone, he felt sure, knew a very great deal about his three 'ifs', and at 9.45 a.m. he found himself knocking rather hesitantly on the door of number 14 Manning Terrace. Such hesitancy was attributable to two causes: the first, his natural diffidence in seeming on the face of it to be so anxious to seek out the company of the fair Ruth Rawlinson; the second, the factual uncertainty that he was actually knocking on the right door, for there were two of them, side by side; the one to the left marked 14B, the other 14A. Clearly the house had been divided – fairly recently by the look of it – with one of the doors (Morse presumed) leading directly to the upper storey, the other to the ground floor.

'It's open,' shouted a voice behind 14A. 'I can't get any farther.'

For once, Sod's Law had been inoperative, and he had chosen right. Two steps led up to the narrow carpeted passage which served as a hallway (the staircase was immediately behind the boarded-up wall to the left, and the conversion had left little room for manoeuvre here), and at the top of these steps sat Mrs Alice Rawlinson in her wheelchair, a rubber-tipped walking-stick held firmly across her lap.

'What d'you want?' Her keen eyes looked up at him sharply.

'I'm sorry to bother you – Mrs Rawlinson, isn't it?'

'I said what d'you want, Inspector.'

Morse's face must have betrayed his astonishment, and the old lady read his thoughts for him. 'Ruthie told me all about you.'

'Oh. I just wondered if—'

'No, she's not. Come in!' She worked her chair round in an expertly economical two-point turn. 'Close the door behind you.'

Morse obeyed quietly, and found himself pushed brusquely aside as he tried to help her through the door at the end of the passage. She waved him to an upright armchair in the neatly furnished sitting-room, and finally came to rest herself only about four feet in front of him. The preliminaries were now completed, and she launched into the attack immediately.

'If you want to cart my daughter off for a dirty week-end, you can't! We'd better get that straight from the start.'

'But Mrs Raw—' He was silenced by a dangerously close wave of the stick. (Belligerent old bitch! thought Morse.)

'I disapprove of many aspects of the youth of today – young men like yourself, I mean – especially their intolerable lack of manners. But I think they're quite right about one thing. Do you know what that is?'

'Look, Mrs Raw—' The rubber ferule was no more than three inches from his nose, and his voice broke off in mid-sentence.

'They've got enough sense to have a bit of sex together before they get married. You agree?'

Morse nodded a feeble acquiescence.

'If you're going to live with someone for fifty years—' She shook her head at the prospect. 'Not that I was married for fifty years . . .' The sharp voice had drifted a few degrees towards a more wistful tone, but recovered immediately. 'As I say, though. You can't have her. I need her and she's my daughter. I have the prior call.'

'I do assure you, Mrs Rawlinson, I hadn't the slightest intention of—'

'She's had men before, you know.'

'I'm not sur—'

'She was a very lovely girl, was my Ruthie.' The words were more quietly spoken, but the eyes remained shrewd and calculating. 'She's not a spring chicken any more, though.'

Morse decided it was wise to hold his peace. The old girl was going ga-ga.

'You know what her trouble is?' For a distasteful moment Morse thought her mind must be delving into realms of haemorrhoids and body-odour; but she sat there glaring at him, expecting an answer.

Yes, he knew full well what Ruth Rawlinson's trouble was. Too true, he did. Her trouble was that she had to look after this embittered old battle-axe, day in and day out.

'No,' he said. 'You tell me.'

Her lips curled harshly. 'You're lying to me, Inspector. You know her trouble as well as I do.'

Morse nodded. 'You're right. I don't think I could stick you for very long.'

Now her smile was perfectly genuine. 'You know, you're beginning to sound like the man Ruthie said you were.' (Perhaps, thought Morse, she's not so ga-ga after all?)

'You're a bit formidable sometimes, aren't you?'

'All the time.'

'Would Ruth have married – but for you?'

'She's had her chances – though I didn't think much of her choices.'

'Real chances?'

Her face grew more serious. 'Certainly one.'

'Well.' Morse made as if to rise, but got no farther.

'What was *your* mother like?'

'Loving and kind. I often think of her.'

'Ruthie would have made a good mother.'

'Not too old now, is she?'

'Forty-two tomorrow.'

'Hope you'll bake her a cake,' muttered Morse.

'What?' The eyes blazed now. 'You don't understand, either, do you? Bake? Cook? How can I do anything like that? I can't even get to the front door.'

'Do you try?'

'You're getting impertinent, Inspector. It's time you went.' But as Morse rose she relented. 'No, I'm sorry. Please sit down again. I don't get many visitors. Don't deserve 'em, do I?'

'Does your daughter get many visitors?'

'Why do you ask that?' The voice was sharp again.

'Just trying to be pally, that's all.' Morse had had his fill of the old girl, but her answer riveted him to the chair.

'You're thinking of Josephs, aren't you?'

No, he wasn't thinking of Josephs. 'Yes, I was,' he said, as flatly as his excitement would allow.

'He wasn't her sort.'

'And he had a wife.'

She snorted. 'What's that got to do with it? Just because you're a bachelor yourself—'

'You know that?'

'I know a lot of things.'

'Do you know who killed Josephs?'

She shook her head. 'I don't know who killed Lawson, either.'

'I do, Mrs Rawlinson. He killed himself. You'll find the information in the coroner's report. It's just the same as cricket, you know: if the umpire says you're out, you're out, and you can check it up in the papers next morning.'

'I don't like cricket.'

'Did you like Josephs?'

'No. And I didn't like Lawson, either. He was a homosexual, you know.'

'Really? I hadn't heard of any legal conviction.'

'You're surely not as naïve as you sound, Inspector?'

'No,' said Morse, 'I'm not.'

'I hate homosexuals.' The stick lifted menacingly, gripped tight in hands grown strong from long years in a wheelchair. 'I'd willingly strangle the lot of 'em.'

'And I'd willingly add you to the list of suspects, Mrs Rawlinson, but I'm afraid I can't. You see, if someone killed Lawson, as you're suggesting, that someone must have gone up the church tower.'

'Unless Lawson was killed in the church and *someone else* carried him up there.'

It was an idea; and Morse nodded slowly, wondering why he hadn't thought of it himself.

'I'm afraid I shall have to kick you out, Inspector. It's my bridge day, and I always spend the morning brushing up on a few practice hands.' She was winning every trick here, too, and Morse acknowledged the fact.

Ruth was fixing the lock on her bicycle when she looked up to see Morse standing by the door and her mother sitting at the top of the steps behind him.

'Hello,' said Morse. 'I'm sorry I missed you, but I've

had a nice little chat with your mother. I really came to ask if you'd come out with me tomorrow night.' With her pale face and her untidy hair, she suddenly seemed very plain, and Morse found himself wondering why she'd been so much on his mind. 'It's your birthday, isn't it?'

She nodded vaguely, her face puzzled and hesitant.

'It's all right,' said Morse. 'Your mother says it'll do you good. In fact she's very pleased with the idea, aren't you, Mrs Rawlinson?' (One trick to Morse.)

'Well, I – I'd love to but—'

'No buts about it, Ruthie! As the Inspector says, I think it would do you the world of good.'

'I'll pick you up about seven, then,' said Morse.

Ruth gathered up her string shopping bag, and stood beside Morse on the threshold. 'Thank you, Mother. That was kind of you. But' (turning to Morse) 'I'm sorry. I can't accept your invitation. I've already been asked out by – by someone else.'

Life was a strange business. A few seconds ago she'd looked so ordinary; yet now she seemed a prize just snatched from his grasp, and for Morse the day ahead loomed blank and lonely. As it did, if only he had known, for Ruth.

CHAPTER THIRTEEN

'WHAT THE 'ELL do *you* want?' growled Chief Inspector Bell of the City Police. A fortnight in Malaga which had coincided with a strike of Spanish hotel staff had not brought him home in the sweetest of humours; and the jobs he had gladly left behind him had (as ever) not gone away. But he knew Morse well: they were old sparring partners.

'The Spanish brothels still doing a roaring trade?'

'Had the wife with me, didn't I?'

'Tell me something about this Lawson business.'

'Damned if I will. The case is closed – and it's got nothing to do with you.'

'How're the kids?'

'Ungrateful little buggers. Shan't take 'em again.'

'And the Lawson case is closed?'

'Locked and bolted.'

'No harm in just—'

'I've lost the key.'

'All kids are ungrateful.'

'Especially mine.'

'Where's the file?'

'What d'you want to know?'

'Who killed Josephs, for a start.'

'Lawson did.'

'Morse blinked in some surprise. 'You mean that?'

Bell nodded. 'The knife that killed Josephs belonged to Lawson. The woman who charred for him had seen it several times on his desk in the vicarage.'

'But Lawson was nowhere near Josephs when—' Morse stopped in his tracks, and Bell continued.

'Josephs was just about dead when he was knifed: acute morphine poisoning, administered, as they say, at the altar of the Lord. What about that, Morse? Josephs was a churchwarden and he was always last at the altar-rail, and he finished up with some pretty queer things in his belly, right? It seems pretty obvious, then, that . . .' It was a strange experience for Morse. *Déjà vu.* He found himself only half-listening to Bell's explanation – no, not Bell's, his own explanation. '. . . rinse the utensils, wipe 'em clean, stick 'em in the cupboard till next time. Easy! Proof, though? No.'

'But how did Lawson—?'

'He's standing in front of the altar, waiting for the last hymn to finish. He knows Josephs is counting up the collection in the vestry as he always does, and Lawson's expecting him to be lying there unconscious; dead, probably, by now. But suddenly Josephs shouts for help, and Lawson comes swooping down the aisle in his batman outfit—'

'Chasuble,' mumbled Morse.

'—and covers him up under his what's-it; he keeps the others – there aren't many of 'em, anyway – away from the vestry, sends for help, and then when he's alone he sticks his knife in Josephs' back – just to make sure.'

'I thought the collection was pinched.'

Bell nodded. 'There was one of those down-and-out fellows at the service: Lawson had helped him occasionally – put him up at the vicarage, given him his old suits – that sort of thing. In fact, this fellow had been kneeling next to Josephs at the communion-rail—'

'So *he* could have put the stuff in the wine.'

Bell shook his head. 'You should go to church occasionally Morse. If he had done, Lawson would have been poisoned just like Josephs, because the minister has to finish off what's left of the wine. You know, I reckon your brain's getting addled in your old age.'

'Someone still pinched the collection,' said Morse feebly.

'Oh yes. And I'm sure it was this fellow – Swan, or something like that, his name was. He just saw the money in the vestry and – well, he just nicked it.'

'I thought you said Lawson kept all the others outside.'

'For a start, yes. He had to.'

Morse looked far from convinced, but Bell sailed happily on. 'A reasonably well-educated fellow, by all accounts. We put out a description of him, of course, but . . . They all look much of a muchness, those sort of fellows: none of 'em shave or get their hair cut. Anyway, he'd only be up for petty larceny if we found him. Two or three quid, at the outside – that's all he got. Funny, really. If he'd had a chance to go through Josephs' pockets, he'd have found nearly a hundred.'

Morse whistled softly. 'That means that Lawson couldn't have gone through his pockets, either, doesn't it? They tell me the clergy aren't exactly overpaid these days, and Lawson couldn't exactly have been rolling in—'

Bell smiled. 'Lawson was hellish lucky to get the chance to knife him – let alone go through his pockets. But that's neither here nor there. Lawson *was* rolling in it. Until a few weeks before he died, his deposit account at the bank stood at over £30,000.'

This time Morse's whistle was loud and long. 'Until a few weeks . . .?'

'Yes. Then he took his money out. Almost all of it.'

'Any idea—?'

'Not really.'

'What did the bank manager have to tell you?'

'He wasn't allowed to tell me anything.'

'What *did* he tell you?'

'That Lawson had told him he was going to make an anonymous donation to some charity, and that's why he wanted cash.'

'Some bloody donation!'

'Some people are more generous than others, Morse.'

'Did he take out all this cash before, or after, Josephs was murdered?'

For the first time Bell seemed slightly uneasy. 'Before, actually.'

Morse was silent for a short while. The new pieces of evidence were not fitting at all neatly. 'What was Lawson's motive for killing Josephs?'

'Blackmail, perhaps?'

'Josephs had some hold over him?'

'Something like that.'

'Any ideas?'

'There were a few rumours.'

'Well?'

'I prefer facts.'

'Was Lawson buggering the choirboys?'

'You always did put things so nicely.'

'What facts, then?'

'Lawson had made out a cheque for £250 to Josephs a couple of weeks earlier.'

'I see,' said Morse slowly. 'What else?'

'Nothing.'

'Can I look through the files?'

'Certainly not.'

Morse spent the next hour in Bell's office looking through the files.

Considering the limited number of personnel available, the investigations into the deaths of Josephs and Lawson had been reasonably thorough, although there were a few surprising omissions. It would have been interesting, for example, to read the evidence of every single member of the congregation present when Josephs died, but it seemed that several of them had been only casual visitors – two American tourists amongst them – and Lawson had quite innocently informed them that perhaps they needn't stay. Understandable, no doubt – but very careless and quite improper. Unless ... unless, thought Morse, Lawson wasn't over-anxious for all of them to tell the police what they'd seen? It was sometimes just those little details, just those little inconsistencies ... Of the statements that were available, all cleanly set out, all neatly typed, only one arrested Morse's attention: the one, duly signed in the dithery hand of Mrs Emily Walsh-Atkins, attesting to the identification of Lawson.

'Did you interview this old girl?' asked Morse, pushing the statement across the table.

'Not personally, no.'

So far Bell had shown himself a jump or two ahead all round the course, but Morse thought he now saw himself coming through pretty fast on the rails. 'She's as blind as a bloody bat, did you know that? What sort of identification do you think this is? I met her the other night and—'

Bell looked up slowly from the report he'd been reading. 'Are you suggesting that fellow we found draped over the railings *wasn't* Lawson?'

'All I'm suggesting, Bell, is that you must have been pretty hard up for witnesses if you had to rely on her. As I say, she's—'

'She's as blind as a bat – almost your own words, Morse; and, if I remember rightly, exactly the words of my own Sergeant Davies. But don't be too hard on the old dear for wanting to get into the act – it was the most exciting thing that ever happened to her.'

'But that doesn't mean—'

'Hold your horses, Morse! We only needed one identification for the coroner's court, so we only *had* one. Right? But we had another witness all ready, and I don't think *he's* as blind as a bat. If he is, he must have one helluva job when he play the organ in six sharps.'

'Oh, I see.' But Morse didn't see. What was Morris doing at St Frideswide's that morning? Ruth Rawlinson would know, of course. Ruth . . . Huh! Her birthday today, and she would be all dolled up for a date with some lecherous lout . . .

'Why was Morris at church that morning?'

'It's a free country, Morse. Perhaps he just wanted to go to church.'

'Did you find out if he was playing the organ?'

'As a matter of fact, I did, yes.' Bell was thoroughly enjoying himself again – something he'd seldom experienced in Morse's company before. 'He *was* playing the organ.'

After Morse was gone, Bell stared out of his office window for several minutes. Morse was a clever beggar. One or two questions he'd asked had probed a bit deeper than was comfortable; but most cases had a few ragged ends here and there. He tried to switch his mind over to another channel but he felt hot and sticky; felt he might be sickening for something.

Ruth Rawlinson had lied to Morse – well, not exactly lied. She did have an assignation on the evening of her birthday; but it wouldn't last for long, thank goodness! And then? And then she could meet Morse – if he still wanted to take her out.

At 3 p.m. she nervously flicked through the *m*s in the blue Oxford Area Telephone Directory, and found only one 'Morse' in north Oxford: Morse, E. She didn't know his Christian name, and she vaguely wondered what the 'E' stood for. Irrationally, as she heard the first few rings, she hoped that he wasn't in; and then, as they continued, she prayed that he was.

But there was no answer.

CHAPTER FOURTEEN

FROM THE CITY Police H.Q. Morse walked up past Christ Church to Cornmarket. To his left he noticed that the door of Carfax tower stood open, and beside it a notice inviting tourists to ascend and enjoy a panoramic view of Oxford. At the top of the tower he could see four or five people standing against the skyline and pointing to some of the local landmarks, and a teenage youth actually sitting on the edge, with one of his boots wedged against the next parapet. Morse, feeling a twinge of panic somewhere in his bowels, lowered his eyes and walked on. He joined the small bus-queue just outside Woolworth, thinking again of what he'd just been reading: the life-histories of Josephs and Lawson, the accounts of their deaths, the subsequent investigations. But for the moment the filters of his brain could separate out no new nugget of precious information, and he turned towards St Giles and looked up at the tower of St Frideswide's. No one up there, of course ... Just a minute! Had anyone been up there – recently? Suddenly a curious thought came into his mind – but no, it must be wrong. There'd been something in Bell's file about it: 'Each November a group of volunteers go up to sweep the leaves.' It had just been a thought, that's all.

A Banbury Road bus nudged into the queue, and Morse sat upstairs. As they passed St Frideswide's he looked up again at the tower and made a guess at its height: eighty, ninety feet? The trees ahead of him in St Giles had that long-distance look of green about them as the leaves began to open; and the bus, as it pulled into the lay-by outside the Taylorian Institute, was scraping against some of their budded branches, when something clicked in Morse's mind. How tall were the trees here? Forty, fifty feet? Not much more, certainly. So how in the name of gravity did the autumnal leaves ever manage to dance their way to the top of St Frideswide's tower? Wasn't there perhaps a simple answer, though? They *didn't.* The November leaf-sweeping brigade had no need to go up to the main tower at all: they just cleared the lower roofs over the aisle and the Lady Chapel. That must be it. And so the curious thought grew curiouser still: since the time of Lawson's death, when doubtless Bell's minions had sieved every leaf and every fragment of stone, had *anyone* been up to the roof of the tower?

The bell pinged for the bus to stop at the Summertown shops; and simultaneously another bell rang in Morse's mind, and he joined the exodus. In Bell's notes (it was all 'bells' now) there'd been a few tactful mentions of Josephs' weakness for gambling on the horses, and the intelligent early suggestion (before Bell's visit to Josephs' bank manager) that the £100 or so found in the dead man's wallet might have had a fairly simple provenance – the licensed betting-office in Summertown.

Morse pushed open the door and immediately registered some surprise. It was more like a branch of Lloyds Bank than the traditional picture of a bookmaker's premises. A counter faced him along the far wall, with a low grille running the length of it, behind which two young women were taking money and stamping betting-slips. Round the three other walls the racing pages of the daily newspapers were pinned, and in front of them were placed black plastic chairs where clients could sit and study the form guides and consider their own fancies or the tipsters' selections. There were about fifteen people there, all men – sitting or standing about, their minds keenly concentrated on the state of the going, the weights and the jockeys, their ears intent on the loudspeaker which every few minutes brought them the latest news of the betting direct from the courses. Morse sat down and stared vacantly at a page of the *Sporting Chronicle*. To his right, a smartly dressed Chinaman twisted the knob on a small machine affixed to the wall and tore off a betting-slip. And from the corner of his eye Morse could see exactly what he wrote: '3.35 Newmarket – £20 win – The Fiddler'. Phew! Surely most of the punters here had to be satisfied with a modest fifty pence or so each way? He turned his head and watched the Chinaman at the pay-in counter, four crisp fivers fanned out neatly in his right hand; watched the girl behind the grille, as she accepted the latest sacrifice with the bland indifference of a Buddhist deity. Two minutes later the loudspeaker woke up again, and without enthu-

siasm an impersonal voice announced the 'off';
announced, after a period of silence, the order of the
runners at the four-furlong marker; then the winner,
the second, the third – The Fiddler not amongst them.
To Morse, who as a boy had listened to the frenetically
exciting race-commentaries of Raymond Glendenning,
the whole thing seemed extraordinarily flat, more like
an auctioneer selling a Cézanne at Sotheby's.

The Chinaman resumed his seat beside Morse, and
began to tear up his small yellow slip with the exaggerated delicacy of one who practises the art of origami.

'No luck?' ventured Morse.

'No,' said the Chinaman, with a polite oriental
inclination of the head.

'You lucky sometimes?'

'Sometime.' Again the half-smile, the gentle inclination of the head.

'Come here often?'

'Often.' And, as if to answer the query on Morse's
face, 'Me pretty rich man, you think so?'

Morse took the plunge. 'I used to know a fellow who
came in here most days – fellow called Josephs. Used to
wear a brown suit. About fifty.'

'Here now?'

'No. He died about six months ago – murdered,
poor chap.'

'Ah. You mean Harree. Yes. Poor Harree I know
heem. We often talk. He murdered, yes. Me verree
sorree.'

'He won quite a bit on the horses, I've heard. Still,
some of us are luckier than others.'

'You wrong. Harree verree unluckee man. Always just not there quite.'

'He lost a lot of money, you mean?'

The Chinaman shrugged. 'Perhaps he rich man.' His narrow eyes focused on the 4.00 card at Newmarket, his right hand reaching up automatically for the knob on the wall machine.

Probably Josephs had been losing money pretty consistently, and not the sort of money he could hope to recoup from the unemployment exchange. Yet he'd got money from somewhere, by some means.

Morse considered a little wager of his own on the Chinaman's next selection, but squint as he would he couldn't quite see the name, and he left and walked thoughtfully up the hill. It was a pity. A few minutes after Morse had let himself into his flat, the little Chinaman stood smiling a not particularly inscrutable smile at the pay-out counter. He hadn't really got his English syntax sorted out yet, but perhaps he'd coined as fitting an epitaph for Harry Josephs as any with those five disjointed adverbs: 'Always just not there quite.'

CHAPTER FIFTEEN

'NO, I'M SORRY, Inspector – he isn't.' It was ten past seven and Mrs Lewis regretted the interruption to *The Archers*: she hoped that Morse would either come in or go away. 'Oxford are playing tonight, and he's gone to watch them.'

The rain had been falling steadily since tea-time, and still pattered the puddles in the Lewises' front drive. 'He must be mad,' said Morse.

'It's working with you, Inspector. Are you coming in?'

Morse shook his head and a raindrop dripped from his bare head on to his chin. 'I'll go and see if I can find him.'

'You must be mad,' muttered Mrs Lewis.

Morse drove carefully through the rain up to Headington, the windscreen-wipers sweeping back and forth in clean arcs across the spattered window. It was these damned holidays that upset him! Earlier this Tuesday evening he had sat in his armchair, once again in the grip of a numbing lethargy that minute by minute grew ever more paralysing. The Playhouse offered him a Joe Orton farce, hailed by the critics as a comedy classic. No. The Moulin Rouge announced that the torrid

Sandra Bergson was leading a sexy, savage, insatiable all-girl gang in *On the Game*: an X trailer, no doubt, advertising a U film. No. Every prospect seemed displeasing, and even women, temporarily, seemed vile. Then he'd suddenly thought of Sergeant Lewis.

It had been no problem parking the Lancia in Sandfield Road, and Morse now pushed through the stiff turnstile into the Manor Road ground. Only a faithful sprinkling of bedraggled spectators standing along the west-side terrace, their umbrellas streaked with rain; but the covered terrace at the London Road end was tightly packed with orange-and-black-scarved youngsters, their staccato 'Ox-ford – clap-clap-clap' intermittently echoing across the ground. One row of brilliant floodlights was suddenly switched on, and the wet grass twinkled in a thousand silvery gleams.

A roar greeted the home team, yellow-shirted, blue-shorted, leaning forward against the slanting rain, and kicking and flicking a series of white footballs across the sodden pitch until they shone like polished billiard balls. Behind him, as Morse turned, was the main stand, under cover and under-populated; and he walked back to the entrance and bought himself a transfer ticket.

By half-time Oxford were two goals down, and in spite of repeated scrutinies of those around him, Morse had still not spotted Lewis. Throughout the first half, when the centre of the pitch and the two goal-mouths had churned up into areas of squelchy morass reminiscent of pictures of Passchendaele, Morse's thoughts had given him little rest. An improbable, illogical, intuitive notion was growing ever firmer in his mind –

a mind now focused almost mesmerically on the tower of St Frideswide's; and the fact that he himself was quite unable to check his forebodings served only to reinforce their probability. He needed Lewis badly – there could be no doubt of that.

Greeted by a cacophony of whistles and catcalls, his black top and shorts shining like a skindiver's suit, the referee came out to inspect the pitch again, and Morse looked at the clock by the giant scoreboard: 8.20 p.m. Was it really worth staying?

A firm hand gripped his shoulder from behind. 'You must be mad, sir.'

Lewis clambered over the back of the seat and sat himself down beside his chief.

Morse felt indescribably happy. 'Listen, Lewis. I want your help. What about it?'

'Any time, sir. You know me. But aren't you on—?'

'*Any* time?'

A veil of slow disappointment clouded Lewis' eyes. 'You don't mean—?' He knew exactly what Morse meant.

'You've lost this one, anyway.'

'Bit unlucky, weren't we, in the first half?'

'What are you like on heights?' asked Morse.

Like the streets around the football ground, St Giles was comparatively empty, and the two cars easily found parking-spaces outside St John's College.

'Fancy a beefburger, Lewis?'

'Not for me, sir. The wife'll have the chips on.'

Morse smiled contentedly. It was good to be back in harness again; good to be reminded of Mrs Lewis' chips. Even the rain had slackened, and Morse lifted his face and breathed deeply, ignoring Lewis' repeated questions about their nocturnal mission.

The large west window of St Frideswide's glowed with a sombre, yellow light, and from inside could be heard the notes of the organ, muted and melancholy.

'We going to church?' asked Lewis; and in reply Morse unlatched the north door and walked inside. Immediately on their left as they entered was a brightly painted statue of the Virgin, illumined by circles of candles, some slim and waning rapidly, some stout and squat, clearly prepared to soldier on throughout the night; and all casting a flickering kaleidoscopic light across the serene features of the Blessed Mother of God.

'Coleridge was very interested in candles,' said Morse. But before he could further enlighten Lewis on such enigmatic subject-matter a tall, shadowy figure emerged from the gloom, swathed in a black cassock.

'I'm afraid the service is over, gentlemen.'

'That's handy,' said Morse. 'We want to go up the tower.'

'I beg your pardon.'

'Who are you?' asked Morse brusquely.

'I am the verger,' said the tall man, 'and I'm afraid there's no possibility whatsoever of your going up to the tower.'

Ten minutes later with the verger's key, and the verger's torch, and the verger's warning that the whole thing was highly irregular, Morse found himself on the first few steps of the ascent – a narrow, steep, scalloped stairway that circled closely upwards to the tower above. With Lewis immediately behind he shone the torch ahead of him, and, increasingly breathless from exertion and apprehension, gritted his teeth and climbed. Fifty-five, fifty-six, fifty-seven . . . On the sixty-third step a narrow window loomed on the left, and Morse shut his eyes, hugging the right-hand wall ever more closely; and ten steps higher, steps still religiously counted, he reached the inexorable conclusion that he would climb one step higher, make an immediate U-turn, descend to the bottom, and take Lewis for a pint in the Randolph. A cold sweat had broken out on his forehead, and the planes registering the vertical and horizontal realities were merging and sliding and slanting into a terrifying tilt. He craved only one thing now: to stand four-square on the solid ground outside this abominable tower and to watch the blessedly terrestrial traffic moving along St Giles. To stand? No, to sit there; to lie there even, the members of his body seeking to embrace at every point the solid, fixed contours of the flat and comforting earth.

'Here you are, Lewis. You take the torch. I'm – I'm right behind you.'

Lewis set off ahead of him, easily, confidently, two steps at a time, upwards into the spiralling blackness; and Morse followed. Above the bell chamber, up and up, another window and another dizzying glimpse of the ground so far below – and Morse with a supreme effort of will thought only of one step upwards at a time, his whole being concentrating itself into the purely physical activity of lifting each leg alternately, like a victim of locomotor ataxia.

'Here we are, then,' said Lewis brightly, shining the torch on a low door just above them. 'This must be the roof, I think.'

The door was not locked and Lewis stepped through it, leaving Morse to sit down on the threshold, breathing heavily, his back tight against the door-jamb and his hands tight against his clammy forehead. When finally he dared to look about him, he saw the tessellated coping of the tower framed against the evening sky and then, almost fatally, he saw the dark clouds hurrying across the pale moon, saw the pale moon hurrying behind the dark clouds, saw the tower itself leaning and drifting against the sky, and his head reeled vertiginously, his gut contracted, and twice he retched emptily – and prayed that Lewis had not heard him.

From the north side of the tower Lewis looked down and across the broad, tree-lined expanse of St Giles. Immediately below him, some eighty or ninety feet, he guessed, he could just make out the spiked railing that surrounded the north porch, and beyond it the moonlit graves in the little churchyard. Nothing much of interest. He shone the torch across the tower itself. Each of the four sides was about ten or twelve yards in length, with a gully running alongside the outer walls, and a flat, narrow walk, about a yard in width, between these walls and the leaded roof which rose from each side in a shallow pyramid, its apex some eight or nine feet high, on which a wooden post supported a slightly crooked weathervane.

He walked back to the door. 'You all right, sir?'

'Yes, fine. Just not so fit as you, that's all.'

'You'll get a touch of the old Farmer Giles sitting there, sir.'

'Find anything?'

Lewis shook his head.

'You looked all round?'

'Not exactly, no. But why don't you tell me what we're supposed to be looking for?' Then, as Morse made no reply: 'You *sure* you're all right, sir?'

'Go and – go and have a look all the way round, will you? I'll – er – I'll be all right in a minute.'

'What's wrong, sir?'

'I'm scared of bloody heights, you stupid sod!' snarled Morse.

Lewis said nothing more. He'd worked with Morse many times before, and treated his outbursts rather as he had once treated the saddeningly bitchy bouts of temper from his own teenage daughters. Nevertheless, it still hurt a bit.

He shone the torch along the southern side of the tower and slowly made his way along. Pigeon-droppings littered the narrow walk, and the gully on this side was blocked somewhere, for two or three inches of water had built up at the south-east corner. Lewis took hold of the outer fabric of the tower as he tried to peer round the east side, but the stonework was friable and insecure. Gingerly he leaned his weight against the slope of the central roofing, and shone the torch round. 'Oh Christ!' he said softly to himself.

There, stretched parallel to the east wall, was the body of a man – although even then Lewis realized that the only evidence for supposing the body to be that of a man was the tattered, sodden suit in which the corpse was dressed, and the hair on the head which was not that of a woman. But the face itself had been picked almost clean to the hideous skull; and it was upon this non-face that Lewis forced himself to shine his torch again. Twice in all – but no more.

Chapter Sixteen

At lunch-time on the following day, Morse sat alone in the Bulldog, just opposite Christ Church, and scanned an early copy of the *Oxford Mail*. Although the main headline and three full columns of the front page were given over to COMPONENTS STRIKE HITS COWLEY MEN, 'Body Found on Church Tower' had been dramatic enough news to find itself halfway down the left-hand column. But Morse didn't bother to read it. After all, he'd been sitting there in Bell's office a couple of hours previously when one of the *Mail's* correspondents had rung through and when Bell's replies had been guarded and strictly factual: 'No, we don't know who he is.' 'Yes, I did say a "he".' 'What? Quite a long time, yes. Quite a long time.' 'I can't say at the minute, no. They're holding the post-mortem this afternoon. Good headline for you, eh? P.M. THIS P.M.' 'No, I can't tell you who found him.' 'Could be a link-up, I suppose, yes.' 'No, that's the lot. Ring up tomorrow if you like. I might have a bit more for you then.' At the time Morse had felt that this last suggestion was a bit on the optimistic side, and he still felt so now. He turned to the back page and read the sports headline: UNITED COME UNSTUCK ON PITCH LIKE GLUE. But he didn't

115

read that account, either. The truth was that he felt extremely puzzled, and needed time to think.

Nothing had been found in the dead man's pockets, and the only information imparted by the dark-grey suit, the underclothing, and the light-blue tie was 'Burton', 'St Michael' and 'Munro Spun' respectively. Morse himself had declined to view what Bell had called 'a sticky, putrescent mess', and had envied the perky *sang-froid* of the police surgeon who reported that whoever he was he wasn't quite such a gruesome sight as some of the bodies they used to fish out of the water at Gravesend. One thing was clear. It was going to be a tricky job to identify the corpse: tricky for Bell, that was. And Bell had not been in the best of humours as he'd glared across the table at Morse and reminded him that he *must* have some idea who the fellow was. It was Morse who had taken Lewis to the exact spot, wasn't it? And if he was pretty sure he was going to find a corpse he must have got a jolly good idea whose corpse it was!

But Morse hadn't – it was as simple as that. A peculiar combination of circumstances had concentrated his thoughts on to the tower of St Frideswide's, and all he'd done (whatever Bell suspected) was to obey a compelling instinct which had proved too strong even for his chronic acrophobia. But he'd not expected to find a corpse up there, had he? Or had he? When Lewis had shouted the grim discovery over the roof to him, Morse's mind had immediately jumped to the shadowy figure of the tramp and his miserably thin pickings from the collection-plate. All along he'd felt that it should have been comparatively easy for the police to pick up such a character. People like that had to depend almost entirely on charitable and welfare services of some kind, and were usually well known to the authorities wherever they went. Yet extensive enquiries had led nowhere, and might there not have been a very very simple reason for that?

Morse bought himself another pint and watched the glass as the cloudy sedimentation slowly cleared; and when he sat down again his brain seemed to have cleared a little, too. No; it wasn't the tramp they'd found, Morse felt sure of that. It was the clothes, really – especially that light-blue tie. Light-blue . . . Cambridge . . . graduates . . . teachers . . . Morris . . .

Bell was still in his office.

'What happened to Paul Morris?' asked Morse.

'Buggered off with Josephs' wife, like as not.'

'You don't *know*?'

Bell shook his head. He looked tired and drawn. 'We tried, but—'

'Did you find *her*?'

Again Bell shook his head. 'We didn't push things too far. You know how it is. What with Morris teaching at the same school as his son and—'

'His *what*? You didn't tell me Morris had a son!'

Bell sighed deeply. 'Look, Morse. Whadya want from me? You find me another body last night, and I'm deeply grateful, aren't I? That'll be another half-dozen of my lads out of circulation. And I've just had a call to say somebody's been fished out of the river at Folly Bridge, and we've got more trouble with some squatters down in Jericho.' He took out a handkerchief and sneezed heavily. 'And I'm sickening for the flu, and you want me to go chasing after some fellow who was known to be seein' Josephs' missus pretty regularly long before—'

'Really?' said Morse. 'Why didn't I read that in the report?'

'Come off it!'

'He could have killed Josephs. Jealousy! Best motive of the lot.'

'He was sittin' – playin' the bleedin' organ – when—' Bell sneezed noisily again.

Morse settled back in his chair, for some unfathomable reason looking very pleased with himself. 'You still think it really *was* Lawson you found on the railings?'

'I told you, Morse, we had two identifications.'

'Oh yes. I remember. One from a blind woman and one from the man who ran away with Brenda Josephs, wasn't it?'

'Why don't you go home?'

'You know,' said Morse quietly, 'when you've finished with your squatters, you'd better get a squad of lads to dig up old Lawson's coffin, because I reckon – just reckon, mind – that *you might not find old Lawson in it.*' Morse's face beamed with a mischievous pleasure, and he got up to go.

'That's a bloody fool's thing to say.'

'Is it?'

'Not all that easy, either.' It was Bell who was enjoying himself now.

'No?'

'No. You see, they cremated him.'

The news appeared to occasion little surprise or disappointment on Morse's face. 'I knew a minister once—'

'Well, well!' mumbled Bell.

'—who had one of his feet amputated in the First World War. He got it stuck in a tank, and they had to get him out quick because the thing was on fire. So they left his foot there.'

'Very interesting.'

'He was very old when I knew him,' continued Morse. 'One foot already in the grave.'

Bell pushed his own chair back and got up. 'Tell me about it some other time.'

'He was in a discussion one day about the respective merits of burial and cremation, and the old boy said he didn't mind two hoots what they did with him. He said he'd sort of got a foot in *both* camps.'

Bell shook his head in slow bewilderment. What the hell was *that* supposed to mean?

'By the way,' said Morse. 'What was the name of Paul Morris' son?'

'Peter, I think. Why—?'

'But Morse left without enlightening Bell on the point.

*

P.M. THIS P.M., Bell had said; and as he drove the Lancia up to Carfax the initials kept repeating themselves to his mind: post-mortem, post meridiem, prime minister, Paul McCartney, Post Master, putrifying mess, Perry Mason, Provost Marshal, Peter Morris ... The lights were red at the end of Cornmarket, and as Morse sat waiting there for them to change he looked up yet again at the tower of St Frideswide's looming overhead, and at the great west window which only last night had glowed in the dark when he and Lewis ... On a sudden impulse he pulled round the corner into Beaumont Street and parked his car outside the Randolph. A uniformed young flunkey pounced upon him immediately.

'You can't leave your car here.'

'I can leave the bloody car where I like,' snapped Morse. 'And next time you speak to me, lad, just call me "sir", all right?'

The north porch was locked, with a notice pinned to it: 'Due to several acts of wanton vandalism during the past few months, we regret that the church will now be closed to the public from 11 a.m. to 5 p.m. on weekdays.' Morse felt he would have liked to recast the whole sentence, but he satisfied himself by crossing through 'due' and writing 'owing'.

CHAPTER SEVENTEEN

MORSE RAPPED BRISKLY on the door marked 'Enquiries', put his head round the door, and nodded 'Hello' to a nice-looking school secretary.

'Can I help you, sir?'

'Headmaster in?'

'Is he expecting you?'

'Doubt it,' said Morse. He walked across the narrow office, tapped once on the study door and entered.

Phillipson, headmaster of the Roger Bacon School, was only too pleased to be of help.

Paul Morris, it seemed, had been a music master of the first water. During his short stay at the school he'd been popular both with his teaching colleagues and with his pupils, and his G.C.E. O Level and A Level results had been encouragingly good. Everyone had been mystified – for a start anyway – when he'd left so suddenly, without telling a soul; right in the middle of term, too, on (Phillipson consulted his previous year's diary) 26 October, a Wednesday. He had turned up for school perfectly normally in the morning and presumably gone off, as he often did on Wednesdays, to have lunch at home. And that was the last they'd seen of him. His son, Peter, had left the school just after lessons finished at a quarter to four, and that was the last they'd seen of *him*. The next day several members of staff had pointed out that both of them were absent from school, and no doubt someone would have gone round to the Morris residence if it hadn't been for a call from the Oxford City Police. It seemed that some anonymous neighbour had tipped them off that Morris and his son had left Kidlington and gone off to join a woman ('I suppose you know all about this, Inspector?') – a Mrs Josephs. Inspector Bell had called personally to see Phillipson and told him that a few enquiries had already been made, and that several of Morris' neighbours had seen a car answering the description of Mrs Josephs' Allegro parked somewhere nearby several times during the previous months. In fact, the police had learned from other sources that in all probability Morris and Mrs Josephs had been lovers for some time. Anyway, Bell had asked Phillipson to soft-pedal the whole thing; make up some story about Morris having to be away for the rest of the term – death of one of his parents – anything he liked. Which Phillipson had done. A temporary stand-in had taken over Morris' classes for the remainder of the autumn term, and a new woman appointed from January. The police had visited the house that Morris had rented furnished, and found that most of the personal effects had been taken away, although for some reason a fair number of books and an expensive record-player had been left behind. And that was all, really. Phillipson had heard nothing more from that day to this. To the best of his knowledge no one had received any communication from Morris at all. He had not applied for a reference, and perhaps, in the circumstances, was unlikely to do so.

Not once had Morse interrupted Phillipson, and when finally he did say something it was totally irrelevant. 'Any sherry in that cupboard, Headmaster?'

Ten minutes later Morse left the headmaster's study and leaned over the young secretary's shoulder.

'Making out a cheque for me, miss?'

'"Mrs"; Mrs Clarke.' She wound the yellow cheque from the typewriter carriage, placed it face downwards on her desk, and glared at Morse defiantly. His lack of manners when he'd come in had been bad enough, but—

'You look pretty when you're cross,' said Morse.

Phillipson called her through to his study. 'I've got to go out, Mrs Clarke. Take Chief Inspector Morse along to the first-year-sixth music group, will you? And wash up these glasses when you get back, please.'

Tight-lipped and red-cheeked, Mrs Clarke led the way along the corridors and up to the music-room door. 'In there,' she said.

Morse turned to face her and laid his right hand very gently on her shoulder, his blue eyes looking straight into hers. 'Thank you, Mrs Clarke,' he said quietly. 'I'm awfully sorry if I made you angry. Please forgive me.'

As she walked back down the steps, she felt suddenly and marvellously pleased with life. Why had she been so silly? She found herself wishing that he would call her back about something. And he did.

'When do the staff get their cheques, Mrs Clarke?'

'On the last Friday in the month. I always type them the day before.'

'You weren't typing them just now, then?'

'No. We're breaking up tomorrow, and I was just typing an expenses cheque for Mr Phillipson. He had a meeting in London yesterday.'

'I hope he's not on the fiddle.'

She smiled sweetly. 'No, Inspector. He's a very nice man.'

'You're very nice, too, you know,' said Morse.

She was blushing as she turned away, and Morse felt inordinately envious of Mr Clarke as he watched the secretary's legs disappearing down the stairs. Last Friday in the month, she'd said. That would have been 28 October, and Morris had left two days before his cheque was due. Very strange!

Morse knocked on the music-room door and entered.

Mrs Stewart stood up immediately and made as if to turn off the record-player; but Morse held up his right hand, waved it slightly, and sat down on a chair by the wall. The small class was listening to Fauré's *Requiem;* and with an almost instant ecstasy Morse closed his eyes and listened again to the ethereal sweep of the 'In Paradisum': *aeternam habeas requiem* . . . 'that thou mayest have eternal rest' . . . Too quickly the last notes died away into the silence of the room, and it occurred to Morse that rather too many people had all too recently had a premature dose of that eternal rest thrust forcibly upon them. The score stood at three at the minute; but he had a grim foreboding that soon it might be four.

He introduced himself and his purpose, and was

soon surveying the seven girls and the three boys who were in the first year of their A Level music course. He was making enquiries about Mr Morris; they'd all known Mr Morris; there were various business matters which had to be cleared up, and the police weren't sure where Mr Morris had gone to. Did any of them know anything at all about Mr Morris that might just possibly be of any help? The class shook their heads, and sat silent and unhelpful. So Morse asked them a lot more questions, and still they sat silent and unhelpful. But at least two or three of the girls were decidedly decorative – especially one real honey at the back whose eyes seemed to flash the inner secrets of her soul across the room at him. Morris must have looked at her lustfully just once in a while? Surely so . . .

But he was getting nowhere slowly, that was obvious; and he changed his tactics abruptly. His target was a pallid-looking, long-haired youth in the front row. 'Did you know Mr Morris?'

'Me?' The boy swallowed hard. 'He taught me for two years, sir.'

'What did you call him?'

'Well, I – I called him "Mr Morris".' The rest of the class smirked silently to each other, as if Morse must be a potential idiot.

'Didn't you call him anything else?'

'No.'

'You never called him "sir"?'

'Well, of course. But—'

'You don't seem to realize the seriousness of this

125

business, lad. So I'll have to ask you again, won't I? What else did you call him?'

'I don't quite see what you mean.'

'Didn't he have a nickname?'

'Well, most of the teachers—'

'What was his?'

It was one of the other boys who came to the rescue. 'Some of us used to call him "Dapper".'

Morse directed his gaze towards the new voice and nodded wisely. 'Yes. So I've heard. Why was it, do you think?'

It was one of the girls now, a serious-looking soul with a large gap between her front teeth. 'He alwayth drethed very nithely, thir.' The other girls tittered and twittered amongst themselves, and nudged each other knowingly.

'Any more contributions?'

It was the third boy who took up the easy theme. 'He always wore a suit, you see, sir, and most of the staff – well' (more sniggering) 'well, you know, most of 'em have beards, the men, I mean' (a great guffaw from the class now) 'and wear jeans and sweaters and all that. But Mr Morris, he always wore a suit and looked – well, smart, like.'

'What sort of suits did he wear?'

'Well' (it was the same boy) 'sort of dark, you know. Party suits, sort of thing. So, well, we called him "Dapper" – like we said.'

The bell rang for the end of the lesson, and several members of the class began to gather their books and file-cases together.

'What about his ties?' persisted Morse. But the psychological moment had passed, and the colour of Morris' ties seemed to have faded from the collective memory.

As he walked up the drive to his car, Morse wondered if he ought to talk to some of the staff; but he hadn't quite enough to go on yet, and decided it would be better to wait for the pathologist's report.

He had just started the engine when a young girl appeared at the driving-window. 'Hello, beautiful,' he said. It was the girl from the back row, the girl with the radar eyes, who leaned forward and spoke. 'You know you were asking about ties? Well, I remember one tie, sir. He often wore it. It was a light-blue tie. It sort of went with the suits he used to wear.'

Morse nodded understandingly. 'That's most helpful. Thank you very much for telling me.' He looked up at her and suddenly realized how tall she was. Strange how all of them looked about the same size when they were sitting down, as if height were determined not so much from the bottom to the shoulder as by the length of the legs – in this case by the length of some very beautiful legs.

'Did you know Mr Morris well?'

'Not really, no.'

'What's your name?'

'Carole – Carole Jones.'

'Well, thank you, Carole. And good luck.'

Carole walked thoughtfully back to the front entrance and made her way to the next lesson. She wondered why she so often felt so attracted to the older men. Men like this inspector fellow; men like Mr Morris ... Her mind went back to the time they'd sat in the car together; when his hand had lightly touched her breasts, and when her own left hand had gently pushed its way between the buttons of his white shirt – beneath the light-blue tie he'd worn that day; the time when he'd asked her to his house, when he'd answered the door and told her that an unexpected visitor had just arrived and that he'd get in touch with her again – very soon.

But he never had.

CHAPTER EIGHTEEN

MORSE WAS STILL asleep the next morning when his bedside phone rang. It was Superintendent Strange of the Thames Valley Police H.Q.

'I've just had a call from the City Police, Morse. You still in bed?'

'No, no,' said Morse. 'Decorating the lavatory, sir.'

'I thought you were on holiday.'

'A man's got to use his leisure hours profitably—'

'Like clambering over church roofs at the dead of night, you mean.'

'You heard?'

'Heard something else, too, Morse. Bell's got flu. And since you seem to have taken over the case already I just wondered whether you'd like to sort of – take over the case. Officially, I mean.'

Morse shot upright in bed. 'That's good news, sir. When—?'

'From now. It'll be better if you work from St Aldates. All the stuff's there, and you can work from Bell's office.'

'Can I have Lewis?'

'I thought you'd already got him.'

Morse's face beamed with pleasure. 'Thank you, sir. I'll just slip a few clothes on and—'

'Decorating in your pyjamas, Morse?'

'No. You know me, sir. Up with the lark—'

'And to bed with the wren. Yes, I know. And it wouldn't be a bad thing for morale here if you got to the bottom of things, would it? So what about getting out of bed?'

Five minutes later Morse got through to Lewis and reported the good news. 'What are you doing today, old friend?'

'My day off, sir. I'm going to take the wife over to—'

'Were you?' The change of tense was not lost on Lewis, and he listened cheerfully to his instructions. He'd been dreading another visit to his ancient mother-in-law.

The Lancia took only one and a half hours to cover the eighty-odd miles to Stamford in Lincolnshire, where the Lawson clan had lived for several generations. The speedometer had several times exceeded 85 m.p.h. as they drove along, up through Brackley, Silverstone and Towcester, then by-passing Northampton and twisting through Kettering before looking down from the top of Easton Hill on to the town of Stamford, its grey stone buildings matching the spires and towers of its many old churches. *En route* Morse had cheerfully sketched in the background of the St Frideswide's murders; but the sky had grown overcast and leaden, and the sight of thousands of dead elm trees along the Northamptonshire roads seemed a sombre reminder of reality.

'They say those trees commit suicide,' Lewis had

ventured at one point. 'They secrete a sort of fluid to try to—'

'It's not always easy to tell suicide from murder,' muttered Morse.

By late afternoon the two men had uncovered a fairly solid body of information about the late and (it seemed) little-lamented Lionel Lawson. There had been two Lawson brothers, Lionel Peter and Philip Edward, the latter some eighteen months the younger. Both had won scholarships to a public school some ten miles distant, and both had been weekly boarders, spending their Saturday evenings and Sundays during term-time with their parents, who ran a small local business specializing in the restoration of ancient buildings. Academically (it appeared) the two boys were more than competent, with Philip potentially the abler – if also the lazier and less ambitious. After leaving school each of them had spent eighteen months on National Service; and it was during his time in the Army that Lionel, always the more serious-minded of the two, had met a particularly persuasive psalm-singing padre, and been led to the conviction that he was called to the ministry. After demobilization, he had studied hard on his own for a year before gaining acceptance at Cambridge to read theology. During this period Philip had worked for his father for a few years, but seemingly with little enthusiasm; and finally he had drifted away from home, occasionally revisiting his parents, but with no firm purpose in life, no job, and with little prospect of discovering either. Five years ago Mr Lawson senior and his wife had been killed in the Zagreb air crash whilst returning from a holiday in southern Yugoslavia, and the family business had been sold, with each of the two sons inheriting about £50,000 net from the estate.

For most of the day Morse and Lewis had worked separately, each pursuing a different line of enquiry; and it was only on the last visit, to the ex-headmaster of the Lawson boys' public school, that they came together again.

Doctor Meyer's speech was that of an old schoolmaster, deliberate, over-latinized with an apparent dread of imprecision. 'He was a clever boy, young Philip. With a modicum of dedication and perseverance – who knows?'

'You've no idea where he is now?'

The old man shook his head. 'But Lionel, now. He worked like a Trojan – although exactly why the Trojans are proverbially accredited with a reputation for industriousness has always been a mystery to me. His ambition was always to win a scholarship to Oxford, but—' He broke off suddenly as if his memory could take him no farther along that avenue of recollection. But Morse was clearly anxious to push him past a few more trees.

'How long was Lionel in the sixth form?'

'Three years, as I recall it. Yes, that's right. He took his Higher School Certificate at the end of his second year, and got it all right. He took the Oxford entrance examination just after that, in the Michaelmas term, but I had little real hope for him. His mind was not quite – not quite alpha potential. They wrote to me about him, of course. They said they were unable to offer him a place, but the boy's work had not been without merit. They advised him to stay on for a further year in the sixth and then to try again.'

'Was he very disappointed?'

The old man eyed Morse shrewdly and relit his pipe before replying. 'What do you think, Inspector?'

Morse shrugged his shoulders as if the matter were barely of consequence. 'You said he was ambitious, that's all.'

'Yes,' replied the old man slowly.

'So he stayed on another year?'

'Yes.'

Lewis shuffled a little uncomfortably in his chair. At this rate of progress they wouldn't be home before midnight. It was as if Morse and Meyer were at the snooker table, each of them playing his safety shots. Your turn, Morse.

'He took his Higher again?'

Meyer nodded. 'He didn't do quite so well as in the previous year, if I remember rightly. But that is not unusual.'

'You mean he was more worried about preparing for his Oxford entrance?'

'That was probably the reason.'

'But he didn't make it to Oxford?'

'Er – no.'

Something seemed to be puzzling Morse, Lewis could

see that. Was he on to something? But it appeared not. Morse had got to his feet and was pulling on his coat. 'Nothing else you can tell me about him?'

Meyer shook his head and prepared to see his visitors out. He was a short man, and now well over eighty; yet there was still an air of authority in his bearing, and Lewis could well understand (what he'd heard earlier in the day) that Meyer had ruled his school with a rod of iron, and that pupils and staff alike had trembled at his coming.

'Nothing at all?' repeated Morse as they stood at the door.

'There's nothing more I can tell you, no.'

Was there slightly more emphasis on the 'can' than there need have been? Lewis wasn't sure. He was lost as usual anyway.

For the first part of their return journey, Morse seemed rapt in thought; and when he finally did say something Lewis could only wonder what those thoughts had been.

'What was the exact day when Lionel Lawson left school?'

Lewis looked through his notebook. 'November the eighth.'

'Mm.' Morse nodded slowly. 'Tell me when you spot a phone-box.'

When, ten minutes later, Morse got back into the car, Lewis could see that he was very pleased with himself.

'Are you letting me in on this one, sir?'

'Of course!' Morse looked sideways at his sergeant in mild surprise. 'We're partners, aren't we? We do things together, you and me. Or "you and I" as I've no doubt old man Meyer would say. You see, young Lionel Lawson was an ambitious little swot, right? He's not been over-endowed by the Almighty with all that much up top, but he makes up for it by sheer hard work. More than anything else he wants to go up to Oxford. And why not? It's a fine ambition. Let's just recap on Master Lionel, then. He tries once – and he fails. But he's a sticker. He stays on for another year – another year of grind on his set books and the rest of it, and all the time he's being groomed by his masters for his entrance exam. I shouldn't think he's too bothered about not doing so well in his other exams that summer – he's set his sights on higher things. Remember he's already done three years in the sixth form, and he goes back in the autumn term because that's when the entrance exams are always taken. He's all ready for the final furlong – agreed?'

'But he didn't make it.'

'No, you're right. But he didn't *fail* to get in, Lewis – and that's the interesting point. Lawson, L., left school on November the eighth, you tell me. And I'll tell *you* something. That year the entrance papers were sat in the first week of December – I just rang up the Registry at Oxford – *and Lawson, L., didn't sit the examination.*'

'Perhaps he changed his mind.'

'And perhaps somebody changed it for him!'

A light flickered dimly in the darkness of Lewis' mind. 'He was expelled, you mean?'

'That's about it, I reckon. And that's why old man Meyer was so cagey. He knew a good deal more than he was prepared to tell us.'

'But we have no real evidence—'

'Evidence? No, we haven't. But you've got to use a bit of imagination in this job, Lewis, haven't you? So let's use a bit. Tell me. Why do boys usually get expelled from public schools?'

'Drugs?'

'They had no drugs in those days.'

'I don't know, sir. I never went to a public school, did I? There was none of that Greek and Latin stuff for me. We had enough trouble with the three Rs.'

'It's not the three Rs we're worried about now, Lewis. It's the three Bs: bullying, beating and buggery! And Lawson, L., from what we've learned of him, was a quietly behaved little chap, and I doubt he got expelled for bullying or beating. What do you think?'

Lewis shook his head sadly: he'd heard this sort of thing before. 'You can't just – you can't just make up these things as you go along, sir. It's not fair!'

'As you wish.' Morse shrugged his shoulders, and the needle on the speedometer touched 90 m.p.h. as the Lancia skirted Northampton on the eastern bypass.

CHAPTER NINETEEN

BACK IN OXFORD at about 4.30 p.m. that same afternoon, two men were walking slowly down Queen Street from Carfax. The elder, and slightly the taller of the two, a growth of greyish stubble matting his long vacant face, was dressed in an old blue pin-striped suit which hung loosely on his narrow frame. In his right hand he carried a bull-necked flagon of Woodpecker cider. The younger man, bearded and unkempt, anywhere in age (it seemed) between his mid-forties and mid-fifties, wore a long army-issue greatcoat, buttoned up to the neck, its insignia long since stripped off or lost. He carried nothing.

At Bonn Square they turned into the circle of grass that surrounds the stone cenotaph, and sat down on a green-painted bench beneath one of the great trees girdling the tiny park. Beside the bench was a wire waste-paper basket, from which the younger man pulled out a copy of the previous day's edition of the *Oxford Mail.* The elder man unscrewed the liquor with great deliberation and, having taken a short swig of its contents, wiped the neck of the bottle on his jacket sleeve before passing it over. 'Anything in the paper?'

'Nah.'

Shoppers continuously criss-crossed one another in the pedestrian precinct in front of the park, many of them making their way down the covered arcade between the light-beige brickwork of the Selfridges building and the duller municipal stone of the public library. A few casual glances swept the only two people seated on the park benches – glances without pity, interest or concern. Lights suddenly blazed on in the multi-storeyed blocks around and the evening was ushered in.

'Let's look at it when you've finished,' said the elder man, and immediately, without comment, the paper changed hands. The bottle, too, was passed over, almost rhythmically, between them, neither man drinking more than a mouthful at a time.

'This is what they were talking about at the hostel.' The elder man pointed a thin grubby finger at an article on the front page, but his companion made no comment, staring down at the paving stones.

'They've found some fellow up the top of that tower, you know, just opposite—' But he couldn't quite remember what it was opposite to, and his voice trailed off as he slowly finished the article. 'Poor sod!' he said finally.

'We're all poor sods,' rejoined the other. He was seldom known to communicate his thoughts so fully, and he left it at that, hunching himself down into his greatcoat, taking a tin of shredded tobacco from one of its large pockets and beginning to roll himself a cigarette.

'P'haps you weren't here then, but a fellow got hisself murdered there last – when was it now? – last ... Augh! Me memory's going. Anyway, a few days later the minister there, he chucks hisself off the bloody tower! Makes you think.'

But it was not apparent that the younger man was given cause to think in any way. He licked the white cigarette-paper from left to right, repeated the process, and stuck the ill-fashioned cylinder between his lips.

'What was his name? Christ! When you get older your memory ... What was his name?' He wiped the neck of the bottle again and passed it over. 'He knew the minister there ... I wish I could think of ... He was some sort of relation or something. Used to stay at the vicarage sometimes. What *was* his name? You don't remember him?'

'Nah. Wasn't 'ere then, was I?'

'He used to go to the services. Huh!' He shook his head as if refusing credence to such strange behaviour. 'You ever go to church?'

'Me? Nah.'

'Not even when you was a lad?'

'Nah.'

A smartly dressed man carrying a briefcase and umbrella walked past them on his way from the railway station.

'Got a coupla bob for a cup o' tea, mister?' It was a long sentence for the younger man, but he could have saved his breath.

'I've not seen him around at all recently,' continued

the other. 'Come to think of it, I've not seen him since the minister chucked hisself . . . Were you there when the police came round to the hostel?'

'Nah.'

The elder man coughed violently and from his loose, rattling chest spat out a gob of yellowish phlegm on to the paving. He felt tired and ill, and his mind wandered back to his home, and the hopes of his early years . . .

'Gizz the paper 'ere!' said his companion.

Through thin purplish lips the elder man was now whistling softly the tune to 'The Old Folks at Home', lingering long over the melody like a man whose only precious pleasure now is the maudlin stage of drunkenness. 'Wa-a-ay down upon the—' Suddenly he stopped. 'Swan-something. *Swanpole* – that was it! Funny sort of name. I remember we used to call him Swanny. Did you know him?'

'Nah.' The younger man folded the *Oxford Mail* carefully and stuck it through the front of his coat. 'You oughta look after that cough o' yours,' he added, with a rare rush of words, as the elder man coughed up again – revoltingly – and got to his feet.

'I think I'll be getting along. You coming?'

'Nah.' The bottle was now empty, but the man who remained seated on the bench had money in his pockets, and there may have been a glint of mean gratification in his eyes. But those eyes were shielded from public view behind an incongruous pair of dark glasses, and seemed to be looking in the opposite direction as the elder man shuffled unsteadily away.

It was colder now, but the man on the bench was

gradually getting used to that. It was the first thing he'd discovered. After a time you learn to forget how cold you are: you accept it and the very acceptance forms an unexpected insulation. Except for the feet. Yes, except for the feet. He got up and walked across the grass to look at the inscriptions on the stone obelisk. Among the buglers and privates whose deeds were commemorated thereon, he noticed the odd surname of a young soldier killed by the mutineers in Uganda in 1897: the name was Death.

CHAPTER TWENTY

AT 4.30 P.M. ON the Friday of the same week, Ruth Rawlinson wheeled her bicycle through the narrow passageway and propped it against the side of the lawn-mower in the cluttered garden-shed. Really, she must tidy up that shed again soon. She took a white Sainsbury carrier bag from the cycle-basket, and walked back round to the front door. The *Oxford Mail* was in the letter-box, and she quietly withdrew it.

Just a little bit today, but still on page one:

CORPSE STILL UNIDENTIFIED

POLICE still have no positive clue about the identity of the body found on the tower-roof of St Frideswide's Church. Chief Inspector Morse today repeated that the dead man was probably in his late thirties, and revealed that he was wearing a dark-grey suit, white shirt and light-blue tie. Anyone who may have any information is asked to contact the St Aldates Police Station, Oxford 49881. Enquiries have not as yet established any link with the still unsolved murder of Mr Harry Josephs in the same church last year.

Ruth's body gave an involuntary little jerk as she read the article. 'Anyone who may have . . .' Oh God! She had information enough, hadn't she? Too much information; and the knowledge was weighing ever more heavily upon her conscience. And was Morse in charge now?

As she inserted the Yale key, Ruth realized (yet again) how sickeningly predictable would be the dialogue of the next few minutes.

'Is that you, Ruthie dear?'

Who else, you silly old crow? 'Yes, Mother.'

'Is the paper come?'

You know it's come. Your sharp old ears don't miss a scratch, do they? 'Yes, Mother.'

'Bring it with you, dear.'

Ruth put the heavy carrier bag down on the kitchen-table, draped her mackintosh over a chair and walked into the lounge. She bent down to kiss her mother lightly on an icy cheek, placed the newspaper on her lap, and turned up the gas fire. 'You never have this high enough, you know, Mother. It's been a lot colder this week and you've got to keep yourself warm.'

'We've got to be careful with the bills, dear.'

Don't start on that again! Ruth mustered up all her reserves of patience and filial forbearance. 'You finished the book?'

'Yes, dear. *Very* ingenious.' But her attention was fixed on the evening paper. 'Anything more about the murder?'

'I don't know. I didn't know it was a murder anyway.'

'Don't be childish, dear.' Her eyes had pounced

upon the article and she appeared to read it with ghoulish satisfaction.

'That man who came here, Ruthie – they've put him in charge.'

'Have they?'

'He knows far more than he's letting on – you mark my words.'

'You think so?'

The old girl nodded wisely in her chair. 'You can still learn a few things from your old mother, you know.'

'Such as what?'

'You remember that tramp fellow who murdered Harry Josephs?'

'Who said he murdered—?'

'No need to get cross, dear. You know you're interested. You still keep all the newspaper clippings, I know that.'

You nosey old bitch! 'Mother, you must *not* go looking through my handbag again. I've told you before. One of these days—'

'I'll find something I shouldn't? Is that it?'

Ruth looked savagely into the curly blue line of flame at the bottom of the gas fire, and counted ten. There were some days now when she could hardly trust herself to speak.

'Well, that's who it is,' said her mother.

'Pardon?'

'The man up the tower, dear. It's the tramp.'

'Bit elegantly dressed for a tramp, wouldn't you say, Mother? White shirt and a—'

'I thought you said you hadn't seen the paper, dear.' The charge was levelled with a silky tongue.

Ruth took a deep breath. 'I just thought you'd like to find it for yourself, that's all.'

'You're beginning to tell me quite a few little lies, Ruthie, and you've got to stop it.'

Ruth looked up sharply. What was that supposed to mean? Surely her mother couldn't know about . . .? 'You're taking nonsense, Mother.'

'So you don't think it *is* the tramp?'

'A tramp wouldn't be wearing clothes like that.'

'People can change clothes, can't they?'

'You've been reading too many detective stories.'

'You could kill someone and then change his clothes.'

'Of course you couldn't.' Again Ruth was watching her mother carefully. 'Not just like that anyway. You make it sound like dressing up a doll or something.'

'It would be difficult, dear, I know that. But, then, life is full of difficulties, isn't it? It's not impossible, that's all I'm saying.'

'I've got two nice little steaks from Sainsbury's. I thought we'd have a few chips with them.'

'You could always change a man's clothes *before* you killed him.'

'What? Don't be so silly! You don't identify a body by the clothes. It's the face and things like that. You can't change—'

'What if there's nothing left of his face, dear?' asked Mrs Rawlinson sweetly, as if reporting that she'd eaten the last piece of Cheddar from the pantry.

Ruth walked over to the window, anxious to bring the conversation to a close. It was distasteful and, yes, worrying. And perhaps her mother wasn't getting quite so senile after all . . . In her mind's eye Ruth still had a clear picture of the 'tramp' her mother had been talking of, the man she'd known (though she'd never actually been told) to be Lionel Lawson's brother, the man who had usually looked exactly what he was – a worthless, feckless parasite, reeking of alcohol, dirty and degraded. Not quite always, though. There had been two occasions when she'd seen him looking more than presentable: hair neatly groomed, face shaven freshly, finger-nails clean, and a decently respectable suit on his back. On those occasions the family resemblance between the two brothers had been quite remarkable . . .

'. . . if they ask me, which doubtless they won't—' Mrs Rawlinson had been chattering non-stop throughout, and her words at last drifted through to Ruth's consciousness.

'What would you tell them?'

'I've *told* you. Haven't you been listening to me, dear? Is there something wrong?'

Yes, there's a lot wrong. You, for a start. And if you're not careful, mother dear, I'll strangle you one of these days, dress you up in someone else's clothes, carry your skinny little body up to the top of the tower, and let the birds have a second helping! 'Wrong? Of course there isn't. I'll go and get tea.'

Rotten, black blotches appeared under the skin of the first potato she was peeling, and she took another from the bag she had just bought – a bag marked with the words 'Buy British' under a large Union Jack. Red, white and blue ... And she thought of Paul Morris seated on the organ-bench, with his red hood, white shirt and blue tie; Paul Morris, who (as everyone believed) had run off with Brenda Josephs. But he hadn't, had he? Someone had made very, very sure that he hadn't; someone who was sitting somewhere – even now! – planning, gloating, profiting, in some way, from the whole dreadful business. The trouble was that there weren't many people left. In fact, if you counted the heads of those that *were* left, there was really only one who could conceivably ... Surely not, though. Surely Brenda Josephs could have nothing to do with it, could she?

Ruth shook her head with conviction, and peeled the next potato.

CHAPTER TWENTY-ONE

ALTHOUGH HER HUSBAND (unbeknown to her) had borrowed on the mortgage of their house in Wolvercote, Mrs Brenda Josephs was now comfortably placed financially, and the nurses' hostel in the General Hospital on the outskirts of Shrewsbury provided more than adequate accommodation. On Paul's specific instructions, she had not written to him once, and she had received only that one letter from him, religiously guarded under the lining of her handbag, much of which she knew by heart: '... and above all don't be impatient, my darling. It will take time, perhaps quite a lot of time, and whatever happens we must be careful. As far as I can see there is nothing to worry us, and we must keep it that way. Just be patient and all will be well. I long to see you again and to feel your beautiful body next to mine. I love you, Brenda – you know that, and soon we shall be able to start a completely new life together. Be discreet always, and do nothing until you hear from me again. Burn this letter – now!'

Brenda had been working since 7.30 a.m. on the women's surgical ward, and it was now 4.15 p.m. Her

Friday evening and the whole of Saturday were free, and she leaned back in one of the armchairs in the nurses' common room and lit a cigarette. Since leaving Oxford her life (albeit without Paul) had been fuller and freer than she could ever have hoped or imagined. She had made new friends and taken up new interests. She had been made aware, too, happily aware, of how attractive she remained to the opposite sex. Only a week after her appointment (she had given, as her referee, the name of the matron for whom she had worked prior to her nursing at the Radcliffe) one of the young married doctors had said to her, 'Would you like to come to bed with me, Brenda?' Just like that! She smiled now as she recollected the incident, and an unworthy thought, not for the first time, strayed across the threshold of her mind. Did she *really* want Paul all that badly now? With that son of his, Peter? He was a nice enough young boy, but . . . She stubbed out her cigarette and reached for the *Guardian*. There was an hour and a half to wait before the evening meal, and she settled down to a leisurely perusal of the day's news. Inflation figures seemed mildly encouraging for a change; but the unemployment figures were not, and she knew only too well what unemployment could do to a man's soul. Middle East peace talks were still taking place, but civil wars in various parts of Africa seemed to be threatening the delicate balance between the superpowers. In the Home News, at the bottom of page three, there was a brief item on the discovery of a body on the tower of an Oxford church; but Brenda didn't reach it. The young doctor sat down beside her, unnecessarily but not distressingly close.

'Hello, beautiful! What about us doing the crossword together?'

He took the paper from her, folded it over to the crossword, and unclipped a biro from the top pocket of his white coat.

'I'm not much good at crosswords,' said Brenda.

'I bet you're good in bed, though.'

'If you're going to—'

'One across. Six letters. "Girl takes gun to district attorney." What's that, do you think?'

'No idea.'

'Just a minute! What about BRENDA? Fits, doesn't it? Gun – "bren"; district attorney – "D.A." Voilà!'

Brenda snatched the paper and looked at the clue: 'Girl in bed – censored.' 'You're making it up,' she laughed.

'Lovely word "bed", isn't it?' He printed the letters of 'Brenda' on the margin of the paper, and then neatly ringed the three letters 'b', 'e', 'd' in sequence. 'Any hope for me yet?'

'You're a married man.'

'And you ran away.' He underlined the three remaining letters 'r', 'a', 'n', and turned impishly towards her. 'No one'll know. We'll just nip up to your room and—'

'Don't be silly!'

'I'm not silly. I can't help it, can I, if I lust after you every time I see you in your uniform?' His tone was light and playful, but he suddenly became more serious as the door opened and two young nurses came in. He spoke softly now. 'Don't get cross with me if I keep trying, will you? Promise?'

'Promise,' whispered Brenda.

He wrote BANNED into the squares for 1 Across, and read out the clue for 1 Down. But Brenda wasn't listening. She didn't wish to be seen sitting so closely to the young doctor as this, and soon made up an excuse to go to her room, where she lay back on her single bed and stared long and hard at the ceiling. The door was locked behind her, and no one would have known, would they? Just as he'd said. If only ... She could hardly bring herself to read her own thoughts. If only he'd just walk up the stairs, knock on the door and ask her again in his simple, hopeful, uncomplicated way, she knew that she would invite him in, and lie down – just as she lay there now – gladly unresistant as he unfastened the white buttons down the front of her uniform.

She felt tired, and the room was excessively stuffy – the radiator too hot to touch. Gradually she dozed off, and when she awoke her mouth was very dry. Something had woken her; and now she heard the gently reiterated knock-knock at the door. How long had she slept for? Her watch told her it was 5.45 p.m. She fluffed her hair, straightened her uniform, lightly smeared on a little lipstick and, with a little flutter of excitement in her tummy, walked across to the door of her room, newly painted in dazzling white gloss.

It was lying by the same door that a member of the cleaning staff found her the next morning. Somehow she had managed to crawl across from the centre of the small room; and it was clear that her fingers had groped in vain for the handle of the door, for the lower panels were smeared with the blood coughed up from her throat. No one seemed to know exactly where she came from, but the letter the police found beneath the lining of her handbag suggested strongly that she was, or had been, on the most intimate terms with a man called 'Paul', who had given his address only as 'Kidlington', and who had urged the recipient to burn the evidence immediately.

CHAPTER TWENTY-TWO

IT WAS ON Saturday morning, and in the middle of page two of the long-delayed post-mortem report on the corpse found on the tower, that Morse came to the conclusion he might just as well be reading the *Chinese People's Daily*. He appreciated, of course, the need for some technical jargon, but there was no chance whatsoever for a non-medical man to unjumble such a farrago of physiological labellings. The first paragraph had been fairly plain sailing, though, and Morse handed the report over to Lewis:

The body is that of an adult Caucasian male, brachycephalic. Height: 5 ft 8½ in. Age: not easy to assess with accuracy, but most likely between 35 and 40. Hair: light brown, probably cut a week or so before death. Eyes: colouring impossible to determine. Teeth: remarkably good, strongly enamelled, with only one filling (posterior left six). Physical peculiarities: none observable, although it cannot be assumed that there were no such peculiarities, since the largest patch of skin, taken from the lower instep (left), measures only . . .

Lewis passed the report back, for he had little wish to be reminded too vividly of the sight picked out so recently by the narrow beam of the verger's torch. Moreover, his next job promised to be quite gruesome enough for one morning, and for the next half-hour he sifted through the half-dozen transparent plastic bags containing the remnants of the dead man's clothes. Morse himself declined to assist in the unsavoury operation and expressed only mild interest when he heard a subdued whistle of triumph from his subordinate.

'Let me guess, Lewis. You've found a label with his name and telephone number.'

'As good as, sir.' In a pair of tweezers, he held up a small rectangular bus-ticket. 'It was in the breast-pocket of the jacket – 30p fare on 26 October. I reckon the fare from Kidlington to Oxford's about 30p—'

'Probably gone up by now,' muttered Morse.

'—and surely' (Lewis' eyes suddenly sparkled with excitement) 'that was the day when Paul Morris disappeared, wasn't it?'

'Never my strong point – dates,' said Morse.

For the moment, however, nothing was going to dampen Lewis' enthusiasm. 'Pity his teeth were so good, sir. He's probably not been near a dentist for years. Still, we ought to be able to—'

'You're taking an awful lot for granted, you know. We neither of us have the slightest proof about who the fellow is, agreed? And until—'

'No, we haven't. But there's not much sense in closing our eyes to the obvious.'

'Which is?'

'That the man we found is Paul Morris,' replied Lewis with firm confidence.

'Just because a young girl in one of his classes says he used to wear a dark suit—'

'And a blue tie.'

'—and a blue tie, all right, that makes him Paul Morris, you say? Lewis! You're getting as bad as I am.'

'Do you think I'm wrong?'

'No, no. I wouldn't say that. I'm just a little more cautious than you, shall we say?'

This was ridiculous. Morse, as Lewis knew only too well, was a man prepared to take the most prodigious leaps into the dark; and yet here he was now – utterly blind to the few simple facts that lay staring him in the face in broad daylight. Forget it, though!

It took Lewis no more than ten minutes to discover that Paul Morris had been a patient at the Kidlington Health Centre, and after a little quiet but urgent pressure the senior partner of that consortium was reading through the details on his medical card.

'Well?' asked Morse, as Lewis cradled the receiver.

'Fits pretty well. Thirty-eight years old, five feet nine inches, light-brown hair—'

'Fits a lot of people. Medium height, medium colouring, medium—'

'Don't you *want* to find out who he is?' Lewis stood up and looked down at Morse with unwonted exasperation in his voice. 'I'm sorry if all this doesn't fit in with any clever little theory you've thought up, but we've got to make some sort of start, haven't we?'

Morse said nothing for a few moments, and when he did speak his quiet words made Lewis feel ashamed of the tetchiness which had marked his own.

'Surely you can understand, can't you, Lewis, why I'm hoping that rotting corpse isn't Paul Morris? You see, if it is, I'm afraid we'd better start looking round pretty quickly, hadn't we? We'd better start looking round for yet another corpse, my old friend – a corpse aged about twelve.'

Like Bell, the landlord of 3 Home Close, Kidlington, had flu, but he gave Morse a sneezy blessing to look over the property, rented out (since Morris left) to a young married couple with one baby daughter. But no one answered Lewis' repeated knockings. 'Probably shopping,' he said as he sat down again next to Morse in the front of the police car.

Morse nodded and looked vaguely around him. The small crescent had been built some time in the early 1930s – a dozen or so red-brick, semi-detached properties, now beginning to look their age, with the supports of their slatted wooden fences virtually sopped and sapped away. 'Tell me, Lewis,' he said suddenly. 'Who do *you* think murdered Josephs?'

'I know it's not a very original idea, sir, but I should think it must have been this down-and-out fellow. Like as not he decided to pinch the collection-money, and Josephs got in his way, and he knifed him. Another possibility—'

'But why didn't Josephs yell the place down?'

'He did try to shout for help, sir, if you remember. Couldn't make himself heard above the organ, perhaps.'

'You could be right, you know,' said Morse, almost earnestly, as if he'd suddenly woken up to the fact that the obvious way of looking at things wasn't necessarily the wrong one. 'What about Lawson? Who killed him?'

'You know better than I do, sir, that the majority of murderers either give themselves up or commit suicide. There's surely not much doubt that Lawson committed suicide.'

'But Lawson didn't kill Josephs, did he? You just said—'

'I was going on to say, sir, that there was another possibility. I don't think Lawson himself actually killed Josephs, but I think he may have been *responsible* for killing him.'

'You do?' Morse looked across at his subordinate with genuine interest. 'I think you'd better take it a bit more slowly, Lewis. You're leaving me a long way behind, I'm afraid.'

Lewis allowed himself a mild grin of modest gratification. It wasn't often that Morse was the back-marker – just the opposite in fact: he was usually about three or four jumps ahead of his stable-companion. 'I think there's more than a possibility, sir, that Lawson got this down-and-out fellow to kill Josephs – probably by giving him money.'

'But why should Lawson want to kill Josephs?'

'Josephs must have had some hold over him.'

'And Lawson must have had some hold on this down-and-out fellow.'

'How right you are, sir!'

'Am I?' Morse looked across in a semi-bewildered way at his sergeant. He remembered how when he was taking his eleven-plus examination he was seated next to a boy renowned for his vacuous imbecility, and how this same boy had solved the tenth anagram whilst Morse himself was still puzzling over the third.

'As I see it,' continued Lewis, 'Lawson must have been looking after him all ways: meals, clothes, bed, everything.'

'He must have been like a sort of brother to him, you mean?'

Lewis looked at Morse curiously. 'Bit more than that, wasn't he, sir?'

'Pardon?'

'I said it was a bit more than being like a brother to him. He *was* a brother, surely.'

'You mustn't believe every piece of gossip you hear.'

'And you mustn't automatically disbelieve it, either.'

'If only we had a bit more to go on, Lewis!' And then the truth hit him, as it usually did, with a flash of blinding simplicity. Any corroboration he'd wanted had been lying under his nose since his visit with Lewis to Stamford, and a shiver of excitement ran along his scalp as at last he spotted it. 'Swanpole' had appeared several times in Bell's files as the probable name of the man who had been befriended by the Reverend Lionel

Lawson, the man who had so strangely disappeared after the murder of Josephs. But, if all the rumours were right, that man's real name was Philip Edward Lawson, and whether you were a rather timid little fellow trying your eleven-plus question-paper, or whether you were a souring middle-aged detective sitting in a panda-car, *Swanpole was an anagram of P. E. Lawson.*

'I reckon this'll be mother and infant,' said Lewis under his breath. And indeed the heavily pregnant, dowdily dressed young woman dragging a two-year-old child along the pavement duly announced that she herself was the present occupier of 3 Home Close and that this was her daughter, Eve. Yes, she said, since the landlord had no objections, they could come in and have a look round the house. With pleasure.

Morse declined the offer of a cup of tea, and went out into the back garden. Clearly someone had been very busy, for the whole plot showed every evidence of a systematic and recent digging-over; and in the small garden-shed the tines of the fork and the bottom half of the spade were polished to a silvery smoothness.

'I see your husband's keen on growing his own veg,' said Morse lightly, as he wiped his shoes on the mat by the back door.

She nodded. 'It was all grass before we came, but, you know, with the price of things these days—'

'Looks as if he's been doing a bit of double-digging.'

'That's it. Took him ages, but he says it's the only way.'

159

Morse, who hardly knew a sweet pea from a broad bean, nodded wisely, and gratefully decided he could forget about the garden.

'Mind if we have a quick look upstairs?'

'No. Go ahead. We only use two of the bedrooms – like the people who was here before us did. But – well, you never know . . .' Morse glanced down at her swollen belly and wondered how many bedrooms she might need before her carrying days were over.

Young Eve's bower, the smallest of the bedrooms, was redolent of urine, and Morse screwed up his nose in distaste as he cursorily bent down over the uncarpeted floorboards. A dozen Donald Ducks on the newly decorated walls seemed to mock his aimless investigations, and he quickly left the room and closed the door behind him.

'Nothing in either of the other rooms, sir,' said Lewis, joining Morse on the narrow landing, where the walls had been painted in a light Portland beige, with the woodwork cleanly finished off in white gloss. Morse, thinking the colours a good match, looked up at the ceiling – and whistled softly. Immediately above his head was a small rectangular trap-door, some 3 feet by 2½ feet, painted as lovingly as the rest of the woodwork.

'You got a step-ladder?' Morse shouted downstairs.

Two minutes later Lewis was poking his head over the dusty beams and shining a torch around the rafters. Here and there a little of the early afternoon light filtered through ill-fitting joints in the tiles, yet the surprisingly large roof-space seemed dismal and darkly silent as Lewis took his weight on his wrists, gently levered himself up into the loft, and warily trod from beam to beam. A large trunk occupied the space between the trap-door and the chimney-stack, and as Lewis opened the lid and shone his torch on the slightly mildewed covers of the books inside a black, fat-bellied spider scurried its way out of reach. But Lewis was no arachnophobe, and quickly satisfying himself that the trunk was packed only with books he prodded around amid the rest of the débris: a furled Union Jack on a long blue pole, its colours faded now and forlorn; an old camp-bed probably dating from the Baden-Powell era; a brand-new lavatory-pan, patched (for some unfathomable purpose) with strips of gummed brown paper; an antiquated carpet-sweeper; two rolls of yellow insulation material; and a large roll of something else – surely? – pushed up tight between the beams and the roof-angle. Bending forward as low as he could, and groping in front of him, Lewis managed to reach the bundle, where his finger-tips prodded something soft and where his torch-light shone on to a black shoe sticking out of one end, the toe-cap filmed with a layer of grey dust.

'Anything there?' Lewis heard the quiet urgent voice from below, but said nothing. The string tying the bundle together broke as he tugged at it, and there unrolled before him a collection of good-quality clothes: trousers, shirts, underclothes, socks, shoes and half a dozen ties – one of them a light Cambridge blue.

Lewis' grim face appeared suddenly framed in the darkened rectangle. 'You'd better come up and have a look, sir.'

They found another roll of clothes then, containing very much the same sort of items as the first. But the trousers were smaller, as indeed were all the other garments, and the two pairs of shoes looked as if they might have fitted a boy of about eleven or twelve. There was a tie, too. Just the one. A brand-new tie, with alternate stripes of red and grey: the tie worn by the pupils of the Roger Bacon Comprehensive School.

Chapter Twenty-Three

A GOOD MANY of the gradually swelling congregation were acid-faced spinsters of some fifty or sixty summers, several of whom glanced round curiously at the two strangers who sat on the back row of the central pews, next to the empty seat now clearly marked CHURCH-WARDEN. Lewis both looked and felt extraordinarily uncomfortable, whilst Morse appeared to gaze round him with bland assurance.

'We do what everybody else does, understand?' whispered Morse, as the five-minute bell ceased its monotonous melancholy toll, and the choir set out in procession from the vestry and down the main aisle, followed by the incense-swinger and the boat-boy, the acolytes and torch-bearers, the master of ceremonies, and three eminent personages, similarly but not identic-ally dressed, the last wearing, amongst other things, alb, biretta and chasuble – the ABC of ecclesiastical rig as far as Morse as yet had mastered it. In the chancel, the dramatis personae dispersed to their appropriate stations with practised alacrity, and suddenly all was order once more. Ruth Rawlinson, in a black, square choir-hat, took her place just beneath a stone-carved angel and the assembled choir now launched into the

Mass. During this time the churchwarden had slipped noiselessly into his seat, and handed Morse a little scrap of paper: 'Setting, *Iste Confessor* – Palestrina'; at which Morse nodded wisely before passing it on to Lewis.

At half-time, one of the eminent personages temporarily doffed his chasuble and ascended the circular steps of the pulpit to admonish his flock against the dangers and follies of fornication. But Morse sat throughout as one to whom the admonition was not immediately applicable. Once or twice earlier his eyes had caught Ruth's, but all the female members of the choir were now sheltered from view behind a stout octagonal pillar, and he leaned back and contemplated the lozenge-shaped panes of stained glass – deepest ruby, smoky blue and brightest emerald – his mind drifting back to his own childhood, when he had sung in the choir himself . . .

Lewis, too, though for different reasons, very soon lost all interest in fornication. Being, in any case, the sort of man who had seldom cast any lascivious glances over his neighbour's wife, he let his mind wander quietly over the case instead, and asked himself once more whether Morse had been right in his insistence that another visit to a church service would be certain to spark off a few flashes of association, 'to give the hooked atoms a shake', as Morse had put it – whatever that might mean . . .

It took some twenty minutes for the preacher to exhaust his anti-carnal exhortations; after which he descended from the pulpit, disappeared from view through a screen in the side of the Lady Chapel, before re-emerging, chasuble redonned, at the top of the main chancel. This was the cue for the other two members of the triumvirate to rise and to march in step towards the altar where they joined their brother. The choir had already picked up their Palestrina scores once more, and amid much genuflexion, crossing and embracing the Mass was approaching its climactic moment. 'Take, eat, this is my body,' said the celebrant, and his two assistants suddenly bowed towards the altar with a perfect synchronization of movement and gesture – just as if the two were one. Yes, just as if the two were one ... And there drifted into Morse's memory that occasion when as a young boy he'd been taken to a music-hall show with his parents. One of the acts had featured a woman dancing in front of a huge mirror, and for the first few minutes he had been unable to fathom it out at all. She wasn't a particularly nimble-bodied thing, and yet the audience had seemed enthralled by her performance. Then his mind had clicked: the dancer wasn't in front of a mirror at all! The apparent reflection was in reality another woman; dancing precisely the same steps, making precisely the same gestures, dressed in precisely the same costume. There were two women – not one. So? So, if there had been two dancers, could there not have been two priests on the night when Josephs was murdered?

The kittiwake was soaring once again ...

Five minutes after the final benediction, the church was empty. A cassocked youth had finally snuffed out the last candle in the galaxy, and even the zealous Mrs Walsh-Atkins had departed. *Missa est ecclesia.*

165

Morse stood up, slid the slim red *Order of Service* into his raincoat pocket, and strolled with Lewis into the Lady Chapel, where he stood reading a brass plaque affixed to the south wall.

In the vaults beneath are interred the terrestrial remains of Jn. Baldwin Esq., honourable benefactor and faithful servant of this parish. Died 1732. Aged 68 yrs. Requiescat in pace.

Meiklejohn smiled without joy as he approached them, surplice over his left arm. 'Anything else we can do for you, gentlemen?'

'We want a spare set of keys,' said Morse.

'Well, there *is* a spare set,' said Meiklejohn, frowning slightly. 'Can you tell me why—?'

'It's just that we'd like to get in when the church is locked, that's all.'

'Yes, I see.' He shook his head sadly. 'We've had a lot of senseless vandalism recently – mostly school-children, I'm afraid. I sometimes wonder . . .'

'We shall only need 'em for a few days.'

Meiklejohn led them into the vestry, climbed on to a chair, and lifted a bunch of keys from a hook underneath the top of the curtain. 'Let me have them back as soon as you can, please. There are only four sets now, and someone's always wanting them – for bell-ringing, that sort of thing.'

Morse looked at the keys before pocketing them: old-fashioned keys, one large, three much smaller, all of them curiously and finely wrought.

'Shall we lock the door behind us?' asked Morse. It was meant to be lightly jocular, but succeeded only in sounding facetious and irreverent.

'No, thank you,' replied the minister quietly. 'We get quite a lot of visitors on Sundays, and they like to come here and be quiet, and to think about life – even to pray, perhaps.'

Neither Morse nor Lewis had been on his knees throughout the service; and Lewis, at least, left the church feeling just a little guilty, just a little humbled: it was as if he had turned his back on a holy offering.

'C'm on,' said Morse, 'we're wasting good drinking time.'

At 12.25 p.m. the same day, a call from the Shrewsbury Constabulary came through to the Thames Valley Police H.Q. in Kidlington, where the acting desk sergeant took down the message carefully. He didn't *think* the name rang any bells, but he'd put the message through the appropriate channels. It was only after he'd put the phone down that he realized he hadn't the faintest idea what 'the appropriate channels' were.

CHAPTER TWENTY-FOUR

MORSE WAS LINGERING longer than usual, and it was Lewis who drained his glass first.

'You feeling well, sir?'

Morse put the *Order of Service* back in his pocket, and finished his beer in three or four gargantuan gulps. 'Never better, Lewis. Fill 'em up.'

'Your round, I think, sir.'

'Oh.'

Morse leaned his elbows beside the replenished pints and continued. 'Who murdered Harry Josephs? That's the key question really, isn't it?'

Lewis nodded. 'I had a bit of an idea during the service—'

'No more ideas, please! I've got far too many already. Listen! The prime suspect's got to be the fellow Bell tried to trace. Agreed? The fellow who'd stayed several times at Lawson's vicarage, who was at the church when Josephs was murdered, and who disappeared afterwards. Agreed? We're not *quite* certain about it, but there's every chance that this fellow was Lionel Lawson's brother, Philip Lawson. He's hard up and he's a wino. He sees some ready cash on the collection-plate and he decides to pinch it. Josephs tries to stop him, and gets a knife in the back for his trouble. Any problems?'

'How did Philip Lawson come to have the knife?'

'He'd seen it lying around the vicarage, and he decided to pocket it.'

'Just on the off chance?'

'That's it,' said Morse, as he turned unblinking towards Lewis.

'But there were only a dozen or so people at the service, and the collection wouldn't have come to more than a couple of quid.'

'That's it.'

'Why not wait till one of the Sunday-morning services? Then he'd have the chance of fifty-odd quid.'

'Yes. That's true.'

'Why didn't he, then?'

'I dunno.'

'But no one actually *saw* him in the vestry.'

'He skipped it as soon as he'd knifed Josephs.'

'Surely someone would have seen him – or heard him?'

'Perhaps he just hid in the vestry – behind the curtain.'

'Impossible!'

'Behind the door to the tower, then,' suggested Morse. 'Perhaps he went up to the tower – hid in the bell-chamber – hid on the roof – I dunno.'

'But that door was locked when the police arrived – so it says in the report.'

'Easy. He locked it from the inside.'

'You mean he had – he had the key?'

'You say you read the report, Lewis. Well? You must have seen the inventory of what they found in Josephs' pockets.'

The light slowly dawned in Lewis' mind, and he could see Morse watching him, a hint of mild amusement in the inspector's pale-blue eyes.

'You mean – they didn't find any keys,' he said at last.

'No keys.'

'You think he took them out of Josephs' pocket?'

'Nothing to stop him.'

'But – but if he looked through Josephs' pockets, why didn't he find the money? The hundred quid?'

'Aren't you assuming,' asked Morse quietly, 'that that was all there was to find. What if, say, there'd been a *thousand*?'

'You mean—?' But Lewis wasn't sure what he meant.

'I mean that everyone, *almost* everyone, Lewis, is going to think what you did: that the murderer didn't search through Josephs' pockets. It puts everyone on the wrong scent, doesn't it? Makes it look as if it's petty crime – as you say, a few pennies off the collection-plate. You see, perhaps our murderer wasn't really much worried about *how* he was going to commit the crime – he thought he could get away with that. What he didn't want was anyone looking too closely at the *motive*.'

Lewis was growing increasingly perplexed. 'Just a minute, sir. You say he wasn't much worried about how he murdered Josephs. But how *did* he? Josephs was poisoned as well as stabbed.'

'Perhaps he just gave him a swig of booze – doctored booze.'

Again Lewis felt the disconcerting conviction that Morse was playing a game with him. One or two of the points the chief had just made were more like those flashes of insight he'd learned to expect. But surely Morse could do better than this? He could do better himself.

'Josephs could have been poisoned when he took communion, sir.'

'You think so?' Morse's eyes were smiling again. 'How do you figure that out?'

'I reckon the churchwarden is usually the last person to take communion—'

'Like this morning, yes.'

'—and so this tramp fellow is kneeling there next to him and he slips something into the wine.'

'How did he carry the poison?'

'He could have had it in one of those rings. You just unscrew the top—'

'You watch too much television,' said Morse.

'—and sprinkle it in the wine.'

'It would be a whitish powder, Lewis, and it wouldn't dissolve immediately. So the Rev. Lionel would see it floating on top. Is that what you're saying?'

'Perhaps he had his eyes closed. There's a lot of praying and all that sort of thing when—'

'And Josephs himself? Was he doing a lot of praying and all that sort of thing?'

'Could have been.'

'Why wasn't Lawson poisoned, then? It's the minister's

171

job to finish off any wine that's left and, as you say, Josephs was pretty certainly the last customer.'

'Perhaps Josephs swigged the lot,' suggested Lewis hopefully; and then his eyes irradiated a sudden excitement. 'Or perhaps, sir – or perhaps the two of them, the two Lawson brothers, were in it together. That would answer quite a lot of questions, wouldn't it?'

Morse smiled contentedly at his colleague. 'You know, Lewis, you get brighter all the time. I think it must be my company that does it.'

He pushed his glass across the table 'Your turn, isn't it?'

He looked around him as Lewis waited patiently to be served: it was half past one and Sunday lunch-time trade was at its peak. A man with a rough beard, dressed in a long ex-army coat, had just shuffled through the entrance and was standing apprehensively by the bar; a man in latish middle age, it seemed, wearing that incongruous pair of sunglasses, and grasping an empty flagon of cider in his hand. Morse left his seat and walked over to him.

'We met before, remember?'

The man looked slowly at Morse and shook his head. 'Sorry, mate.'

'Life not treating you so good?'

'Nah.'

'Been roughing it long?'

'Last back-end.'

'You ever know a fellow called Swanpole?'

'Nah. Sorry, mate.'

'Doesn't matter. I used to know him, that's all.'

'I knew somebody who did,' said the tramp quietly. 'Somebody who knew the fellah you was just talking about.'

'Yes?' Morse fumbled in his pockets and pushed a fifty-pence piece into the man's hand.

'The old boy I used to go round with – 'e mentioned that name recently. "Swanny" – that's what they called 'im, but 'e's not round these parts any more.'

'What about the old boy? Is he still around?'

'Nah. 'E's dead. Died o' pneumonia – yesterday.'

'Oh.'

Morse walked back thoughtfully to the table, and a few minutes later watched a little sadly as the landlord showed the tramp the way to the exit. Clearly there was no welcome for the poor fellow's custom here, and no cider slowly to be sipped on one of the city's benches that Sunday afternoon; not from this pub anyway.

'One of your pals?' grinned Lewis, as he placed two more pints on the table.

'I don't think he's got any pals.'

'Perhaps if Lawson were still alive—'

'He's just the man we've got to talk about, Lewis – suspect number two. Agreed?'

'You mean he suddenly disappeared from in front of the altar, murdered Josephs, and then came back and carried on with the service?'

'Something like that.'

The beer was good, and Lewis leaned back, quite happy to listen.

'Come on, sir. I know you're dying to tell me.'

'First, let's just follow up your idea about the

173

poisoned chalice. There are too many improbabilities
in the way you looked at it. But what if the Rev. Lionel
himself put the morphine in the wine? What then?
After his brother's had a swig, he can pretend that the
chalice is empty, turn round to the altar, slip in the
powder, pour in a drop more wine, give it a quick stir –
no problem! Or else he could have had two chalices –
one of 'em already doctored – and just put the one
down and pick up the other. Easier still! Mark my
words, Lewis. If it was either of the two brothers who
poisoned Josephs, I reckon the odds are pretty heavily
on the Rev. Lionel.'

'Let me get it straight, sir. According to you, Lionel
Lawson tried to kill Josephs, only to find that someone
had done a far neater job a few minutes later – with a
knife. Right?' Lewis shook his head. 'Not on, sir, is it?'

'Why not? The Rev. Lionel knows that Josephs'll go
straight to the vestry, and that in a few minutes he's
going to be very dead. There's one helluva dose of
morphine in the communion wine and the strong
probability is that Josephs is going to die all nice and
peaceful like, because morphine poisoning isn't a pain-
ful death – just the opposite. In which case, Josephs'
death may well pose a few problems; but no one's going
to be able to pin the murder on the Rev. Lionel. The
chalice has been carefully washed out and dried, in
strict accord with ecclesiastical etiquette – a wonderful
example of a criminal actually being encouraged to
destroy the evidence of his crime. Beautiful idea! But
then things began to go askew. Josephs must have
guessed that something was desperately wrong with

him, and before he collapsed in the vestry he just managed to drag himself to the curtains and shout for help – a shout that all the congregation heard. But someone, *someone*, Lewis, was watching that vestry like a hawk – the Rev. Lionel himself. And as soon as he saw Josephs there he was off down the aisle like an avenging Fury; and he was down there in the vestry before anyone else had the nous or the guts to move; and once inside he stabbed Josephs viciously in the back, turned to face the congregation, and told 'em all that Josephs was lying there – murdered.' (Morse mentally congratulated himself on an account that was rather more colourful and dramatic than Bell's prosaic reconstruction of exactly the same events.)

'He'd have got blood all over him,' protested Lewis.

'Wouldn't have mattered much if he'd been wearing the sort of outfit they were wearing this morning.'

. Lewis thought back to the morning service and those deep-crimson vestments – the colour of dark-red blood . . . 'But why finish Josephs off with a knife? He'd be almost dead by then.'

'Lionel was frightened that Josephs would accuse him of doing the poisoning. Almost certainly Josephs would have guessed what had happened.'

'Probably everyone else would, too.'

'Ah! But if you stabbed Josephs in the back as well, people are going to ask who did *that*, aren't they?'

'Yes. And they're going to think that was Lawson, too. After all, it was Lawson's knife.'

'No one knew that at the time,' said Morse defensively.

'Did Bell think that's how it happened?'

Morse nodded. 'Yes, he did.'

'And do *you*, sir?'

Morse seemed to be weighing the odds in the mental balance. 'No,' he said finally.

Lewis leaned back in his chair. 'You know, when you come to think of it, it's a bit improbable that a minister's going to murder one of his own congregation, isn't it? That sort of thing doesn't happen in real life.'

'I rather hope it does,' said Morse quietly.

'Pardon, sir?'

'I said I rather hope it *does* happen. You asked me if Lionel Lawson killed Josephs in a particular way, and I said I didn't think so. But I reckon it *was* Lionel Lawson who killed Josephs, though in a rather more simple way. He just walked down to the vestry, knifed poor old Harry Josephs—'

'And then he walked back!'

'You've got it!'

Lewis' eyes rolled towards the tobacco-stained ceiling and he began to wonder if the beer had not robbed the inspector of his wits.

'With all the congregation watching him, I suppose.'

'Oh, no. They didn't see him.'

'They didn't?'

'No. The service at which Josephs was killed was held in the Lady Chapel. Now, if you remember, there's an archway in the screen separating this chapel from the central chancel, and I reckon that after the bread and wine had been dished out Lawson took a few of the utensils across from the altar in the Lady Chapel to the main altar – they're always doing that sort of thing, these priests.' (Lewis was hardly listening any more, and the landlord was wiping the tables, collecting glasses and emptying the ashtrays.) 'You want to know how he performed this remarkable feat, Lewis? Well, as I see it, the Rev. Lionel and his brother had got everything worked out, and that night the pair of 'em were all dressed up in identical ecclesiastical clobber. Now, when the Rev. Lionel walked out of the Lady Chapel for a few seconds, it wasn't the Rev. Lionel who walked back! There are only a few prayerful old souls in the congregation, and for that vital period the man standing in front of the altar, kneeling there, praying there, *but never actually facing the congregation*, is brother Philip! What do you think, Lewis? You think anyone looking up could have suspected the truth?'

'Perhaps Philip Lawson was bald.'

'Doubt it. Whether you go bald depends on your grandfather.'

'If you say so, sir.' Lewis was growing increasingly sceptical about all this jiggery-pokery with duplicate chalices and chasubles; and, anyway, he was anxious to be off home. He stood up and took his leave.

Morse remained where he was, the forefinger of his left hand marrying little droplets of spilt beer on the table-top. Like Lewis, he was far from happy about his possible reconstructions of Josephs' murder. But one idea was growing even firmer in his mind: there must have been some collaboration somewhere. And, like as not, that collaboration had involved the two brothers.

But how? For several minutes Morse's thoughts were chasing round after their own tails. For the thousandth time he asked himself where he ought to start, and for the thousandth time he told himself that he had to decide who had killed Harry Josephs. All right! Assume it was the Rev. Lionel – on the grounds that *something* must have driven him to suicide. But what if it wasn't Lionel who had thrown himself from the tower? What if it was Philip who had *been* thrown? Yes, that would have been very neat ... But there was a virtually insuperable objection to such a theory. The Rev. Lionel would have to dress up his brother's body in his own clothes, his own black clerical front, his dog-collar – everything. And that, in such a short space of time after the morning service, was plain physically impossible! But what if ...? Yes! What if Lionel had somehow managed to persuade his brother to change clothes? Was it possible? Phew! Of course it was! It wasn't just possible – it was eminently probable. And why? *Because Philip Lawson had already done it before.* He'd agreed to dress up in his brother's vestments so that he could stand at the altar whilst Josephs was being murdered! Doubtless he'd been wonderfully well rewarded for his troubles on that occasion. So why not agree to a second little charade? Of course he would have agreed – little thinking he'd be dressing up for his own funeral. But with one seemingly insuperable problem out of the way another one had taken its place: two people had positively identified the body that had fallen from the tower. Was that a real problem, though? Had Mrs Walsh-Atkins really had the stomach to look all that carefully at a face that was as smashed and bleeding as the rest of that mutilated body? Had her presence outside the church just been an accidental fluke? Because someone else had been there, had he not? Someone all ready to testify to the identity – the false identity – of the corpse: Paul Morris. And Paul Morris had subsequently been murdered because he knew too much: knew, specifically, that the Reverend Lionel Lawson was not only still in the land of the living, but was also a murderer, to boot! A double-murderer. A triple-murderer . . .

'Do you mind drinking up, sir?' said the landlord. 'We often get the police round here on Sunday mornings.'

CHAPTER TWENTY-FIVE

ON THE SAME day, just after eight o'clock in the evening, a middle-aged man, his white shirt open at the neck, sat waiting in a brightly lit, well-furnished room. He was lounging back on a deep sofa, its chintz covers printed in a russet-and-white floral design, from which, smoking a king-sized Benson & Hedges cigarette, he vaguely watched the television. She was a little late tonight; but he had no doubts that she would come, for she needed him just as much as he needed her. Sometimes, he suspected, even more so. A bottle of claret, already opened, and two wineglasses stood on the coffee-table beside him, and through the half-opened bedroom door he could see the hypotenuse of white sheet drawn back from the pillows.

Come on, girl!

It was eight-ten when the key (she had a key – of course she did!) scraped gently in the Yale lock and she entered. Although a steady drizzle persisted outside, her pale-blue mackintosh seemed completely dry as she slipped it from her shoulders, folded it neatly across its waist, and put it over the back of an armchair. The white cotton blouse she wore was drawn tight across her breasts, and the close-fitting black skirt clung to the curve of her thighs. She said nothing for a while; merely looked at him, her eyes reflecting no affection and no joy – just a simmering animal sensuality. She walked across the room and stood in front of him – provocatively.

'You told me you were going to stop smoking.'

'Sit down and stop moaning, woman. Christ! You make me feel sexy in that outfit.'

The woman did exactly as she was told, almost as if she would do anything he asked without demur; almost as if she thrived on the brusque crudity of his commands, There were no tender words of preliminary love-play on either side, yet she sat close to him as he poured two full glasses of wine, and he felt the pressure of her black-stockinged leg (good girl – she'd remembered!) against his own. In token of some vestigial respect they clinked their glasses together, and she leaned back against the sofa.

'Been watching the telly all night?' Her question was commonplace, uninterested.

'I didn't get back till half past six.'

She turned to look at him for the first time. 'You're a fool going out like that. Especially on Sundays. Don't you realize—?'

'Calm down, woman! I'm not a fool, and you know it. Nobody's seen me slipping out of here yet. And what if they did? Nobody's going to recognize me now.' He leaned across her and his fingers deftly unfastened the top button of her blouse. And then the next button.

As always with this man, the woman experienced that curious admixture of revulsion and attraction –

compulsive combination! Until so very recently a virgin, she was newly aware of herself as a physical object, newly conscious of the power of her body. She lay back passively as he fondled her far beyond the point which a few months previously would have been either pleasing or permissible; and she seemed almost mesmerized as he pulled her up from the sofa and led the way through to the bedroom.

Their coitus was not exceptionally memorable – certainly not ecstatic; but it was satisfactory and satisfying. It usually was. As usual, too, the woman now lay between the sheets silently, feeling cheap and humiliated. It was not only her body that was naked, but her soul, too; and instinctively she drew the top of the sheet up to her neck and prayed that for a little while at least he would keep his hands and eyes away from her. How she despised him! Yet not one half, not one quarter as much as she had learned to despise herself.

It had got to stop. She hated the man and the power he had come to wield over her – yet she needed him, needed the firm virility of his body. He had kept himself wonderfully fit . . . but, then, that wasn't . . . wasn't surprising . . . not really . . . not really . . .

Briefly she fell asleep.

He spoke to her as she stood by the door, the mackintosh loosely over her shoulders. 'Same time on Wednesday?'

Once more the humiliation of it all settled heavily upon her, and her lip was shaking as she replied.

'It's got to stop! You know it has!'

'Stop?' His mouth was set in a conceited sneer. 'You couldn't stop. You know that as well as I do.'

'I can stop seeing you whenever I like, and there's nothing you or anybody else—'

'Isn't there? You're in this as deeply as I am – don't you ever forget that!'

She shook her head, almost wildly. 'You said you'd be going away. You promised!'

'And I shall be. I'll be going very soon now, my girl, and that's the truth. But until I do go I keep seeing you – understand? I see you when I want, as often as I want. And don't tell me you don't enjoy it, because you do! And you know you do.'

Yes, she knew it, and she felt her eyes prickling with hurt at his cruel words. How could she do this? How could she hate a man so much – and yet allow him to make love to her? No! it just couldn't go on like this! And the solution to all her troubles was so childishly simple: she just had to go and see Morse, that was all; tell him everything and face the consequences, whatever they were. She still had a bit of courage left, didn't she?

The man was watching her carefully, half-guessing what was going through her mind. He was used to taking swift decisions – he always had been; and he saw his next moves as clearly as if he were a grandmaster playing chess with a novice. He had known all along that he would have to deal with her sooner or later; and, although he had hoped it would be later, he realized now that the game must be finished quickly.

For him, sex had always come – would always come – a poor second to power.

He walked over to her, and his face for once seemed kind and understanding as he placed his hands so very lightly on her shoulders, his eyes looking searchingly into hers.

'All right, Ruth,' he said quietly. 'I'll not be a nuisance to you any more. Come and sit down a minute. I want to talk to you.' Gently he took her arm and led her unresisting to the sofa. 'I won't make any more demands on you, Ruth – I promise I won't. We'll stop seeing each other, if that's what you really want. I can't bear to see you unhappy like this.'

It had been many weeks since he had spoken to her in such a way, and for a while, in the context of her wider grief, she felt infinitely grateful for his words.

'As I say, I'll be going away soon and then you can forget me, and we can both try to forget what we've done. The wrong we've done – because it *was* wrong, wasn't it? Not about us going to bed together – I don't mean that. That was something lovely for me – something I shall never regret – and I'd hoped . . . I'd hoped it was lovely for you, too. But never mind that. Just promise me one thing, Ruth, will you? If you ever want to come to me – while I'm here, I mean – please come! Please! You know I'll be wanting you – and waiting.'

She nodded, and the tears trickled down her cheeks at the bitter-sweet joy of his words as he cradled her head against his shoulder and held her firmly to him.

She stayed there for what seemed to her a long, long time; yet for him it was little more than a functional interspace, his cold eyes staring over her shoulder at the hateful wallpaper behind the television. He would have to kill her, of course: that decision had been taken long ago anyway. What he was quite unable to understand was the delay. Surely the police were not so stupid as they seemed? Nothing so far – *why*? – about the Shrewsbury murder. Nothing definite about the body on the tower; Nothing at all about the boy . . .

'Your mother all right?' He asked it almost tenderly.

She nodded and sniffed. It was time she was back home with that mother of hers.

'Still cleaning the church?'

She nodded again, continued her sniffing, and finally broke away from him.

'Mondays, Wednesdays and Fridays?'

'Just Mondays and Wednesdays now. I'm getting a bit slack in my old age.'

'Still in the mornings?'

'Mm. I usually go about ten. And I've been going for a drink in the Randolph when I've finished, I'm afraid.' She laughed nervously, and blew her nose loudly into her sopping handkerchief. 'I could do with a quick drink now if—'

'Of course.' He fetched a bottle of Teacher's whisky from the sideboard and poured a good measure into her wineglass. 'Here you are. You'll feel better soon. You feel better *now*, don't you?'

'Yes, I do.' She took a sip of the whisky. 'You – you remember when I asked you whether you knew anything about – about what they found up on the church tower?'

'I remember.'

'You said you hadn't any idea at all—'

'And I hadn't – haven't. Not the faintest idea. But I expect the police will find out.'

'They just say they're – they're making enquiries.'

'They've not been bothering you again, have they?'

She breathed deeply and stood up. 'No. Not that I could tell them anything about *that*.'

For a moment she thought of Morse with his piercing eyes. Sad eyes, though, as if they were always looking for something and never quite finding it. A clever man, as she realized, and a nice man, too. Why, oh why, hadn't someone like Morse found her many years ago?

'What are you thinking about?' His voice was almost brusque again.

'Me? Oh, just thinking how nice you can be when you want. That's all.'

She wanted to get away from him now. It was as if freedom beckoned her from behind the locked door, but he was close behind her and his hands were once again fondling her body; and soon he had forced her to the floor where, within a few inches of the door; he penetrated her once again, snorting as he did so like some animal, whilst she for her part stared joylessly at a hair-line crack upon the ceiling.

186

CHAPTER TWENTY-SIX

'THEY TELL ME you can start a fibroblast from the commercial banger,' said Morse, rubbing his hands delightedly over the crowded plate of sausages, eggs and chips which Mrs Lewis had placed before him. It was half past eight on the same Sunday evening.

'What's a fibroblast?' asked Lewis.

'Something to do with taking a bit of tissue and keeping it alive. Frightening really. Perhaps you could keep a bit of somebody alive – well, indefinitely, I suppose. Sort of immortality of the body.' He broke the surface of one of his eggs and dipped a golden-brown chip into the pale-yellow yolk.

'You won't mind if I have the telly on?' Mrs Lewis sat down with a cup of tea, and the set was clicked on. 'I don't really care what they do to me when I'm gone, Inspector, just as long as they make absolutely certain that I'm dead, that's all.'

It was an old fear – a fear that had prompted some of the wealthier Victorians to arrange all sorts of elaborate contraptions inside their coffins so that any corpse, revivified contrary to the expectations of the physicians, could signal from its subterranean interment immediate intelligence of any return to consciousness. It was a fear, too, that had driven Poe to write about such things with so grisly a fascination; and Morse refrained from mentioning the fact that those whose most pressing anxiety was they might be lowered living into their graves could have their minds set at rest: the disturbing medical truth was they quite certainly *would* be so lowered.

'What's on?' mumbled Morse, his mouth full of food.

But Mrs Lewis didn't hear him. Already, Svengali-like, the television held her in its holy trance.

Ten minutes later Lewis sat checking his football pools from the *Sunday Express*, and Morse leaned back on the sofa and closed his eyes, his mind preoccupied with death and people being lowered . . . lowered into their graves . . .

Where – where was he?

Morse's head and shoulders jerked backwards, and he blinked himself awake. Lewis was still engrossed in the back page of the *Sunday Express*, and on the television screen a head butler was walking sedately down some stairs to a wine-cellar.

That was it! Silently Morse cursed himself for his own stupidity. The answer had stared him in the face that very same morning: 'In the vaults beneath are interred the terrestrial remains . . .' A wave of excitement set his senses tingling as he stood up and drew back the edge of the curtain from the window. It was dark now, and the pane was spattered with fine drizzle.

Things could wait, surely? What on earth was going to be gained by another nocturnal visit to a dark, deserted church that couldn't wait until the light of the morning? But inevitably Morse knew that he couldn't wait and wouldn't wait.

'Sorry about this, Mrs Lewis, but I shall have to take the old man away again, I'm afraid. We shouldn't be long, though; and thanks again for the meal.'

Mrs Lewis said nothing, and fetched her husband's shoes from the kitchen. Lewis himself said nothing, either, but folded the newspaper away and resigned himself to the fact that his Lit-plan permutations had once more failed to land him a fortune. It was the 'bankers' that always let him down, those virtual certainties round which the plan had to be constructed. Like this case, he thought, as he pulled on his shoes: no real certainties at all. Not in his own mind anyway; and from what Morse had said at lunch-time no real certainties in *his* mind, either. And where the Dickens, he wondered, were they off to now?

As it happened, the church was neither dark nor deserted, and the main door at the north porch creaked open to reveal a suffused light over the quiet interior.

'Do you think the murderer's here, sir – confessing his sins?'

'I reckon somebody's confessing something,' muttered Morse.

His ears had caught the faintest murmurings and he pointed to the closed curtains of the confessional, set into the north wall.

Almost immediately an attractive young woman emerged, her sins presumably forgiven, and with eyes averted from the two detectives click-clacked her way out of the church.

'Nice-looking girl, sir.'

'Mm. She may have what you want, Lewis; but do you want what she's got?'

'Pardon, sir?'

The Reverend Canon Meiklejohn was walking silently towards them on his rubber-soled shoes, removing a long, green-embroidered stole from round his neck.

'Which of you wants to be first, gentlemen?'

'I'm afraid I've not been sinning much today,' said Morse. 'In fact there's many a day when I hardly get through any sinning at all.'

'We're all sinners, you know that,' said Meiklejohn seriously. 'Sin, alas, is the natural state of our unregenerate humanity—'

'Is there a crypt under the church?' asked Morse.

Meiklejohn's eyes narrowed slightly. 'Well, yes, there is, but – er – no one goes down there. Not as far as I know anyway. In fact I'm told that no one's been down there for ten years or so. The steps look as if they've rotted away and—'

Again Morse interrupted him. 'How can we get down there?'

Meiklejohn was not in the habit of being spoken to

so sharply, and a look of slight annoyance crossed his face. 'I'm afraid you can't, gentlemen. Not now anyway. I'm due at Pusey House in about—' He looked down at his wristwatch.

'You don't really need me to remind you what we're here for, do you, sir? And it's not to inspect your Norman font, is it? We're investigating a murder – a series of murders – and as police officers we've every right to expect a bit of co-operation from the public. And for the minute *you're* the public. All right? Now. How do we get down there?'

Meiklejohn breathed deeply. It had been a long day and he was beginning to feel very tired. 'Do you really have to talk to me as if I were a naughty child, Inspector? I'll just get my coat, if you don't mind.'

He walked off to the vestry, and when he returned Morse noticed the shabbiness of the thick, dark overcoat; the shabbiness, too, of the wrinkled black shoes.

'We shall need this,' said Meiklejohn, pointing to a twenty-foot ladder against the south porch.

With a marked lack of professionalism, Morse and Lewis manœuvred the long ladder awkwardly out of the south door, through the narrow gate immediately opposite, and into the churchyard, where they followed Meiklejohn over the wet grass along the south side of the outer church wall. A street lamp threw a thin light on to the irregular rows of gravestones to their right, but the wall itself was in the deepest gloom.

'Here we are,' said Meiklejohn. He stood darkly over a horizontal iron grille, about six feet by three feet, which rested on the stone sides of a rectangular shaft cut into the ground. Through the grille-bars, originally painted black but now brown-flaked with rust, the torch-light picked out the bottom of the cavity, about twelve feet below, littered with the débris of paper bags and cigarette-packets. To the side of the shaft furthest from the church wall was affixed a rickety-looking wooden ladder, and parallel to it an iron hand-rail ran steeply down. Set just beneath the church wall was a small door: the entrance to the vaults.

For a minute or so the three men looked down at the black hole, similar thoughts passing through the mind of each of them. Why not wait until the sane and wholesome light of morning – a light that would dissipate all notions of grinning skulls and gruesome skeletons? But no. Morse put his hands beneath the bars of the grille and lifted it aside easily and lightly.

'Are you sure no one's been down here for ten years?' he asked.

Lewis bent down in the darkness and felt the rungs of the ladder.

'Feels pretty firm, sir.'

'Let's play it safe, Lewis. We don't really want any more corpses if we can help it.'

Meiklejohn watched as they eased down the ladder, and when it was resting firmly on its fellow Lewis took the torch and slowly and carefully made his way down.

'I reckon someone's been down here fairly recently, sir. One of the steps near the bottom here's broken, and it doesn't look as if it happened all that long ago.'

'Some of these hooligans, I expect,' said Meiklejohn to Morse. 'Some of them would do anything for what they call a "kick". But look, Inspector, I really must be going. I'm sorry if I – er . . .'

'Forget it,' said Morse. 'We'll let you know if we find anything.'

'Are you – are you expecting to find something?'

Was he? In all honesty the answer was 'yes' – he was expecting to find the body of a young boy called Peter Morris. 'Not really, sir. We just have to check out every possibility, though.'

Lewis' voice sounded once more from the black hollow. 'The door's locked, sir. Can you—?'

Morse dropped his set of keys down. 'See if one of these fits.'

'If it doesn't,' said Meiklejohn, 'I'm afraid you really will have to wait until the morning. My set of keys is just the same as yours and—'

'We're in, Meredith,' shouted Lewis from the depths.

'You get off, then, sir,' said Morse to Meiklejohn. 'As I say, we'll let you know if – er – if . . .'

'Thank you. Let's just pray you don't, Inspector. This is all such a terrible business already that—'

'Goodnight, sir.'

With infinite pains and circumspection Morse eased himself on to the ladder, and with nervously iterated entreaties that Lewis make sure he was holding 'the bloody thing' firmly he gradually descended into the shaft with the slow-motion movements of a trainee tight-rope walker. He noted, as Lewis had just done, that the third rung from the bottom of the original wooden ladder had been snapped roughly in the middle, the left-hand half of it drooping at an angle of some forty-five degrees. And, judging from the yellowish-looking splintering at the jagged fracture, someone's foot had gone through the rung comparatively recently. Someone fairly heavy; or someone not so heavy, perhaps – with an extra weight upon his shoulder.

'Do you think there are any rats down here?' asked Morse.

'Shouldn't think so. Nothing to feed on, is there?'

'Bodies, perhaps?' Morse thought yet again of leaving the grim mission until the morning, and experienced a little shudder of fear as he looked up at the rectangle of faint light above his head, half-expecting some ghoulish figure to appear in the aperture, grinning horridly down on him. He breathed deeply.

'In we go, Lewis.'

The door creaked whiningly on its rusted hinges as inch by inch Lewis pushed it open, and Morse played his torch nervously to one side and then to the other. It was immediately clear that the main supporting pillars of the upper structure of the church extended down to the vaults, forming a series of stone recesses and dividing the subterranean area into cellar-like rooms that seemed (at least to Lewis) far from weird or spooky. In fact the second alcove on the left could hardly have been less conducive to thoughts of some skeletal spectre haunting these nether regions. For within its walls, dry-surfaced and secure, was no more than a large heap of coke (doubtless for the church's earlier heating system) with a long-handled spatulate instrument laid across it.

'Want a bit of free coke, sir?' Lewis was leading the way, and now took the torch from Morse and shone it gaily around the surprisingly dry interior. But as they progressed deeper into the darkness it became increasingly difficult to form any coherent pattern of the layout of the vaults, and Morse was already hanging back a little as Lewis shone the torch upon a stack of coffins, one piled on top of another, their lids warped and loose over the shrunken, concave sides.

'Plenty of corpses here,' said Lewis.

But Morse had turned his back and was staring sombrely into the darkness. 'I think it'll be sensible to come back in the morning, Lewis. Pretty daft trying to find anything at this time of night.' He experienced a deeper shudder of fear as he grew aware of something almost tangibly oppressive in the dry air. As a young boy he'd always been afraid of the dark, and now, again, the quaking hand of terror touched him lightly on the shoulder.

They retraced their way towards the entrance, and soon Morse stood again at the entrance to the vaults, his forehead damp with cold sweat. He breathed several times very deeply, and the prospect of climbing the solid ladder to the ground above loomed like a glorious release from the panic that threatened to engulf him. Yet it was a mark of Morse's genius that he could take hold of his weaknesses and almost miraculously transform them into his strengths. If anyone were going to hide a body in these vaults, he would feel something (surely!), at least *something*, of this same irrational fear of the dark, of the dead, of the deep-seated terror that forever haunted the subconscious mind? No one, surely, would venture too far, alone and under the cover of night, into these cavernous, echoing vaults? His foot kicked a cigarette-packet as he walked past the heap of coke, and he picked it up and asked Lewis to shine the torch on it. It was a golden-coloured empty packet of Benson & Hedges, along the side of which he read: 'Government health warning. Cigarettes can seriously damage your health. Middle tar.' When had the Government decided to stipulate such a solemn warning to cigarette addicts? Three, four, five years ago? Certainly not – what had Meiklejohn said? – ten years!

'Have a look under the coke, will you?' said Morse quietly.

Five minutes later Lewis found him. He was a young boy, aged about eleven or twelve, well preserved, just over five feet in height, and dressed in school uniform. Round his neck was a school tie, a tie tightened so viciously that it had dug deep into the flesh around the throat; a tie striped alternately in the regulation red and grey of the Roger Bacon School, Kidlington.

In the Pending file of the duty-sergeant's tray at Thames Valley H.Q., there still lay the handwritten message taken down from Shrewsbury.

CHAPTER TWENTY-SEVEN

LEWIS REACHED BELL'S office at 9.15 a.m. the following morning, but Morse had beaten him to it and was sitting behind the desk shouting into the phone with a livid fury.

'Well, get the stupid bugger, then. Yes! *Now.*' He motioned Lewis to take a seat, the fingers of his left hand drumming the desk-top in fretful impatience.

'You?' he bellowed into the mouthpiece at last. 'What the hell do you think you're playing at? It's been sitting under your bloody nose since yesterday lunchtime! And all you can do is to sit on that great fat arse of yours and say you're sorry. You'll be sorry, my lad – you can be sure of that. Now, just listen to me carefully. You'll go along to the Super's office as soon as I give you permission to put that phone down, and you tell him exactly what you've done and exactly what you've *not* done. Is that understood?'

The unfortunate voice at the other end of the line could only have mumbled something less than propitiatory, and Lewis sat almost fearfully through the next barrage of abuse.

'What are you going to tell him? I'll tell you what you're going to tell him, my lad. First, you tell him you deserve the bloody V.C. All right? Second, you tell him it's about time they made you chief constable of Oxfordshire. He'll understand. Third, you tell him you're guilty of the blindest bloody stupidity ever witnessed in the history of the force. That's what you tell him!' He banged down the phone and sat for a minute or so still seething with rage.

Sensibly Lewis sat silent, and it was Morse who finally spoke. 'Mrs Josephs was murdered. Last Friday, in a nurses' hostel in Shrewsbury.'

Lewis looked down at the threadbare carpet at his feet and shook his head sadly. 'How many more, sir?'

Morse breathed deeply and seemed suddenly quite calm again.

'I dunno.'

'Next stop Shrewsbury, sir?'

Morse gestured almost hopelessly. 'I dunno.'

'You think it's the same fellow?'

'I dunno.' Morse brooded in silence and stared blankly at the desk in front of him. 'Get the file out again.'

Lewis walked across to one of the steel cabinets. 'Who was on the other end of the rocket, sir?'

Morse's face broke into a reluctant grin. 'That bloody fool, Dickson. He was sitting in as duty-sergeant yesterday. I shouldn't have got so cross with him really.'

'Why did you, then?' asked Lewis, as he put the file down on the desk.

'I suppose because I ought to have guessed, really – guessed that she'd be next on the list, I mean. Perhaps I was just cross with myself, I dunno. But I know one thing, Lewis: I know that this case is getting out of hand. Christ knows where we are; I don't.'

The time seemed to Lewis about right now. Morse's anger had evaporated and only an irritable frustration remained to cloud his worried features. Perhaps he would welcome a little bit of help.

'Sir, I was thinking when I got home last night about what you'd been saying in the Bulldog. Remember? You said that Lawson, the Reverend Lawson, that is, might just have walked straight down—'

'For God's sake, Lewis, come off it! We're finding corpses right, left and centre, are we not? We're in the biggest bloody muddle since God knows when, and all you can do is to—'

'It was you who said it – not me.'

'I *know* – yes. But leave me alone, man! Can't you see I'm trying to think? *Somebody's* got to think around here.'

'I was only—'

'Look, Lewis. Just forget what I said and start thinking about some of the *facts* in the bloody case. All right?' He thumped the file in front of him viciously. 'The facts are all in here. Josephs gets murdered, agreed? All right. Josephs gets murdered. The Reverend Lionel Lawson jumps off the bloody tower. Right? He jumps off the bloody tower. Morris senior gets murdered and gets carted off to the same bloody tower. Right? Exit Morris senior. Morris junior gets strangled and gets carted off down the crypt. Right? Why not just accept these facts, Lewis? Why fart around with all that piddling nonsense about – Augh! Forget it!'

Lewis walked out, making sure to slam the door hard behind him. He'd had just about enough, and for two pins he'd resign from the force on the spot if it meant getting away from this sort of mindless ingratitude. He walked into the canteen and ordered a coffee. If Morse wanted to sit in peace – well, let the miserable blighter! He wouldn't be interrupted this side of lunch-time. Not by Lewis anyway. He read the *Daily Mirror* and had a second cup of coffee. He read the *Sun* and had a third. And then he decided to drive up to Kidlington.

There were patches of blue in the sky now, and the overnight rain had almost dried upon the pavements. He drove along the Banbury Road, past Linton Road, past Belbroughton Road, and the cherry- and the almond trees blossomed in pink and white, and the daffodils and the hyacinths bloomed in the borders of the well-tended lawns. North Oxford was a lovely place in the early spring; and by the time he reached Kidlington Lewis was feeling slightly happier with life.

Dickson, likely as not, would be in the canteen. Dickson was almost always in the canteen.

'I hear you got a bit of a bollocking this morning,' ventured Lewis.

'Christ, ah! You should have heard him.'

'I did,' admitted Lewis.

'And I was only standing in, too. We're so short here that they asked me to take over on the phone. And then this happens! How the hell was I supposed to know who she was? She'd changed her name anyway, and she only *might* have lived in Kidlington, they said. Huh! Life's very unfair sometimes, Sarge.'

'He can be a real sod, can't he?'

'Pardon?'

'Morse. I said he can be a real—'

'No, not really.' Dickson looked far from down-hearted as he lovingly took a great bite from a jam doughnut.

'You've not been in to the Super yet?'

'He didn't mean that.'

'Look, Dickson. You're in the force, you know that – not in a play-school. If Morse says—'

'He didn't. He rang me back half an hour later. Just said he was sorry. Just said forget it.'

'He didn't!'

'He bloody did, Sarge. We had quite a pally little chat in the end, really. I asked him if I could do anything to help, and d'you know what he said? Said he just wanted me to find out from Shrewsbury C.I.D. whether the woman was killed on Friday. That's all. Said he didn't give a monkey's whether she'd been knifed or throttled or anything, just so long as she was killed on Friday. Funny chap, ain't he? Always asking odd sort of questions – never the questions you'd think he'd ask. Clever, though. Christ, ah!'

Lewis stood up to go.

'It wasn't a sex murder, Sarge.'

'Oh?'

'Nice-looker, they said. Getting on a little bit, but it seems quite a few of the doctors had tried to get off with her. Still, I've always thought those black stockings are sexy – haven't you, Sarge?'

'Was she wearing black stockings?'

Dickson swallowed the last of his doughnut and wiped his fingers on his black trousers. 'Don't they all wear—?'

But Lewis left him to it. Once more he felt belittled and angry. Who was supposed to be helping Morse anyway? Himself or Dickson? Aurrgh!

It was 11.45 a.m. when Lewis re-entered St Aldates Police Station and walked into Bell's office. Morse still sat in his chair, but his head was now resting on the desk, pillowed in the crook of his left arm. He was sound asleep.

CHAPTER TWENTY-EIGHT

MRS RAWLINSON WAS getting more than a little anxious when Ruth had still not arrived home at five minutes to one. She suspected – knew, really – that Ruth's visits to the Randolph were establishing themselves into a regular lunch-time pattern, and it was high time she reminded her daughter of her filial responsibilities. For the moment, however, it was the primitive maternal instinct that was paramount; and increasingly so as the radio news finished at ten past one with still no sign of her daughter. At a quarter past one the phone rang, shattering the silence of the room with a shrill, abrupt urgency, and Mrs Rawlinson reached across for the receiver with a shaking hand, incipient panic welling up within her as the caller identified himself.

'Mrs Rawlinson? Chief Inspector Morse here.'

Oh my God! 'What is it?' she blurted out. 'What's happened?'

'Are you all right, Mrs Rawlinson?'

'Yes. Oh, yes. I – I just thought for a moment . . .'

'I assure you there's nothing to worry about.' (But didn't *his* voice sound a little worried?) 'I just wanted a quick word with your daughter, please.'

'She's – she's not in at the moment, I'm afraid. She—' And then Mrs Rawlinson heard the key scratching in the front door. 'Just a minute, Inspector.'

Ruth appeared, smiling and fresh-faced, round the door.

'Here! It's for you,' said her mother as she pushed the receiver into Ruth's hand, and then leaned back in her wheelchair, luxuriating in a beautifully relieved anger.

'Hello?'

'Miss Rawlinson? Morse here. Just routine, really. One of those little loose ends we're trying to tie up. I want you to try to remember, if you can, whether the Reverend Lawson wore spectacles.'

'Yes, he did. Why—?'

'Did he wear them just for reading or did he wear them all the time?'

'He always wore them. Always when I saw him anyway. Gold-rimmed, they were.'

'That's very interesting. Do you – er – do you happen to remember that tramp fellow? You know, the one who sometimes used to go to your church?'

'Yes, I remember him,' replied Ruth slowly.

'Did he wear spectacles?'

'No-o, I don't think he did.'

'Just as I thought. Good. Well, that's about all, I think. Er – how are you, by the way?'

'Oh, fine; fine, thanks.'

'You still engaged on your – er – your good works? In the church, I mean?'

'Yes.'

'Mondays and Wednesdays, isn't it?'

'Ye-es.' It was the second occasion she'd been asked the same question within a very short time. And now (she knew) he was going to ask her what time she usually went there. It was just like hearing a repeat on the radio.

'Usually about ten o'clock, isn't it?'

'Yes, that's right. Why do you ask?' And why did she suddenly feel so frightened?

'No reason, really. I just – er – I just thought, you know, I might see you again there one day.'

'Yes. Perhaps so.'

'Look after yourself, then.'

Why couldn't *he* look after her? 'Yes I will,' she heard herself say.

'Goodbye,' said Morse. He cradled the phone and for many seconds stared abstractedly through the window on to the tarmacadamed surface of the inner yard. Why was she always so tight with him? Why couldn't she metaphorically open her legs for him once in a while?

'You ask some very odd questions,' said Lewis.

'Some very important ones, too,' replied Morse rather pompously. 'You see, Lawson's specs were in his coat pocket when they found him – a pair of gold-rimmed specs. It's all here.' He tapped the file on the death of the Reverend Lionel Lawson which lay on the desk in front of him. 'And Miss Rawlinson said that he always wore them. Interesting, eh?'

'You mean – you mean it wasn't Lionel Lawson who—'

'I mean exactly the opposite, Lewis. I mean it *was* Lionel Lawson who chucked himself off the tower. I'm absolutely sure of it.'

'I just don't understand.'

'Don't you? Well, it's like this. Short-sighted jumpers invariably remove their specs and put 'em in one of their pockets before jumping. So any traces of glass in a suicide's face are a sure tip-off that it wasn't suicide but murder.'

'But how do you know Lawson was short-sighted. He may have been—'

'Short-sighted, long-sighted – doesn't matter! It's all the same difference.'

'You serious about all this?'

'Never more so. It's like people turning their hearing-aids off before they have a bath or taking their false teeth out when they go to bed.'

'But the wife never takes hers out when she goes to bed, sir.'

'What's your wife got to do with it?'

Lewis was about to remonstrate against the injustice of such juvenile logic, but he saw that Morse was smiling at him. 'How do you come to know all this stuff about suicides anyway?'

Morse looked thoughtful for a few seconds. 'I can't remember. I think I read it on the back of a match-box.'

'And that's enough to go on?'

'It's something, isn't it? We're up against a very clever fellow, Lewis. But I just can't see him murdering

Lawson, and then very carefully taking off his specs and putting 'em back in their case. Can you?'

No, Lewis couldn't see that; couldn't see much at all. 'Are we making any progress in this case, sir?'

'Good question,' said Morse. 'And, as one of my old schoolmasters used to say, "Having looked that problem squarely in the face, let us now pass on." Time we had a bit o' lunch, isn't it?'

The two men walked out of the long three-storey stone building that forms the headquarters of the Oxford Constabulary, up past Christ Church, across Carfax, and turned into the Golden Cross, where Morse decided that, for himself at least, a modicum of liquid refreshment was all that would be required. He had always believed that his mind functioned better after a few beers, and today he once again acted on his customary assumption. He should, he realized, be off to Shrewsbury immediately; but the prospect of interviewing hospital porters and nurses and doctors about times and places and movements and motives filled him with distaste. Anyway, there was a great deal of routine work to be done in Oxford.

Lewis left after only one pint, and Morse himself sat back to think. The flashing shuttles wove their patterns on the loom of his brain, patterns that materialized in different shapes and forms, but patterns always finally discarded. After his third pint, there was nothing to show for his cerebrations except the unpalatable truth that his fanciful theories, all of them, were futile, his thinking sterile, his progress nil. Somewhere, though, if only he could think where, he felt convinced that he had missed something – something that would present him with the key to the labyrinth. Yes, that's what he needed: the key to the— He had the key to the *church*, though. Was it there, in the church itself, that he had overlooked some simple, obvious fact that even at this very second lay waiting to be discovered?

CHAPTER TWENTY-NINE

MORSE RELOCKED THE door in the north porch after him, conscious that he must try to look upon the interior of the church somehow differently. Previously he had gazed vaguely across the pews, his mind wafted away to loftier things by the pervasive sickly sweet smell of the incense and the gloomy grandeur of the stained-glass windows. Not so now. He fingered through half a dozen devotional tracts, neatly stacked side by side on a wall-ledge just inside the door to the left; he examined a sheaf of leaflets to be filled in by those who wished to be added to the electoral roll; he drew back a curtain just behind the font and noticed a bucket, a scrubbing-brush and two sweeping-brushes. This was much better – he felt it in his bones! He examined postcards (6p each), which carried exterior views of the church taken from several angles, large close-ups of the famous font (much admired, it seemed, by all save Morse), and full frontal photographs of one of the grinning gargoyles on the tower (how on earth had anyone taken those?); then he turned his attention to a stack of Guides to St Frides-wide's (10p each), and another stack of Parish Notes (2p each) in which details of the current month's activities were fully listed; then, beside the west wall, he noted again the heaps of prayer books with their dull-red covers and the heaps of hymn-books with their— He suddenly stopped, experiencing the strange conviction that he had already overlooked the vital clue that he'd been looking for. Was it something he'd just seen? Something he'd just heard? Something he'd just smelt? He went back to the door, retraced his few steps around the porchway, and then duplicated as far as he could his exact actions since entering the church. But it was no use. Whatever it was – if it was anything – was still eluding his grasp. Maddeningly. Slowly he paced his way up the central aisle and there stood still. The hymns from the previous evening's service were there, white cards with their red numbers, slotted into a pair of hymn-boards, one on either side of him. Odd! Why hadn't they been taken down? Was that one of Ruth Rawlinson's jobs? The bucket and the scrubbing-brush looked as if they had been used very recently, almost certainly by Ruth herself that very morning. Had she forgotten the hymn-boards? Or was that the job of the Vicar? Or one of the choir? Or one of the supernumerary assistants? For someone had to look after such matters. Come to think of it, someone had to decide the hymns, the psalms, the collects, epistles and gospels and the rest. Morse knew nothing about it, but he presumed that it was all laid down in some great holy book available for the guidance of the clergy. Must be. Like all those saints' days and other religious festivals. No one could carry all that stuff around in his head. What was more, someone would have to keep some sort of record of all the services every week – surely so! – especially when you had as many services as—*That* was it! He walked quickly back to the north porch and picked up a copy of the Parish Notes, and stared with curious excitement at the front page:

CHURCH OF ST FRIDESWIDE, OXFORD

SERVICES

Sundays Mass and Holy Communion 8 a.m.

10.30 a.m. (High) and 5.30 p.m.

Evening Service 6 p.m.

Weekdays Mass on Tuesdays and Fridays 7.30 a.m.

On Feast Days 7.30 a.m. and 7.30 p.m.

(Solemn)

CONFESSIONS

Tuesdays, Fridays and Saturdays, all at midday.

Or by arrangement with the clergy.

CLERGY

The Revd Canon K. D. Meiklejohn (Vicar),

St Frideswide's Vicarage.

The Revd Neil Armitage (Curate),

19 Port Meadow Lane.

APRIL

1st   In Octave of Easter

2nd LOW SUNDAY. Preacher at 10.30 a.m.

The Bishop of Brighton. Annual Parish

Meeting 6.15 p.m.

3rd ST RICHARD OF CHICHESTER

Mass at 8 a.m. and 7.30 p.m.

4th	Holy Hour 11 a.m.
5th	Mothers' Union 2.45 p.m.
6th	Deanery Synod 7.45 p.m.
8th	Holy Hour 5 to 6 p.m.
9th	EASTER II . . .

So it went on, through the whole month, with one major Feast Day (Morse noted) in two of the other three weeks. But so what? Was there anything here that was of the slightest interest or value? The name 'Armitage' was new to Morse, and he suspected that the Curate was probably a fairly recent acquisition, and had almost certainly been one of the three wise men in the purple vestments. Still, with all those services on the programme, there'd be need of a helping hand, wouldn't there? It would be a pretty hefty assignment for one poor fellow, who presumably was entrusted, in addition, with the pastoral responsibilities of visiting the lame and the sick and the halt and the blind. My goodness, yes! Meiklejohn would certainly need a co-labourer in such an extensive vineyard. And then a little question posed itself to Morse's mind, and for a second or two the blood seemed to freeze in his cheeks. *Did Lawson have a curate?* It should be easy enough to find out, and Morse had a peculiar notion that the answer might be important, though exactly *how* important he had, at this point, no real idea at all.

He pocketed the Parish Notes, and turned back into the church. A long tasselled rope barred access to the altar in the Lady Chapel, but Morse stepped irreverently over it and stood before the heavily embossed and embroidered altar-cloth. To his immediate left was the arched opening to the main altar, and slowly he walked through it. In a niche to the left of the archway was an Early English piscina, and Morse stopped to look at it carefully, nodding slowly as he did so. He then turned left, made his way along the high carved screen which separated the Lady Chapel from the main nave, skipped lightly across the entrance to the Lady Chapel, and came to a halt outside the vestry. For some reason he looked quite pleased with himself and nodded his head again several times with a semi-satisfied smile.

He stood where he was for several minutes looking around him once more; and, indeed, had he but realized it, he was now within a few yards of the clue that would smash some of his previous hypotheses into a thousand pieces; but for the moment the Fates were not smiling upon him. The north door was opened and Meiklejohn entered, carrying a carton of electric light-bulbs, in the company of a young man balancing an extending ladder on his shoulder.

'Hello, Inspector,' said Meiklejohn. 'Discovered anything more yet?'

Morse grunted non-commitally, and decided that the investigation of the vestry could, without any cosmic ill-consequence, be temporarily postponed.

'We're just going to change the bulbs,' continued Meiklejohn. 'Have to do it, you know, every three or four months. Quite a few have gone already, I'm afraid.'

Morse's eyes travelled slowly up to the tops of the walls where, about forty feet above the floor he could see a series of twin electric-light bulbs, each pair set about twenty feet apart. Meanwhile the ladder had been propped up beneath the nearest lights, and in a progressively more precarious stutter of elongations the two men were pushing the ladder even higher until the slimly converging top of the third extension now rested about two or three feet below the first pair of bulbs.

'I'm afraid,' said Morse, 'that I just haven't got the stomach to stop and witness this little operation any further.'

'Oh, it's not so bad, Inspector, as long as you're careful. But I must admit I'm always glad when it's over.'

'He's a better man than I am,' said Morse, pointing to the young man standing (rather nervously?) on the second rung and gently manœuvring the ladder on to a more firmly based vertical.

Meiklejohn grinned and turned to Morse quietly. 'He's about as bad as you are – if not worse. I'm afraid I have to do the job myself.'

And may the good Lord be with you, thought Morse, as he made his rapid exit, completely forgetting that he was debtor to church funds to the sum of 2p; forgetting, too, that there was a most important question he had yet to put to the daredevil incumbent of St Frideswide's.

In all there were twenty bulbs to change, and as always the job was taking an unconscionably long time to complete. To any observer of the scene, it would have appeared that the young man who stood dutifully with his foot placed firmly on the bottom rung of the ladder seemed quite incapable of raising his eyes above the strict horizontal as Meiklejohn repeatedly ascended to the dizzy heights above him where, standing on the antepenultimate rung, he would place his left hand for support against the bare wall, stretch up to twist out one of the old bulbs, place it carefully in his coat pocket, and then insert one of the new bulbs with an upward thrust of his right arm which virtually lifted his body into unsupported space. With the merest moment of carelessness, with the slightest onset of giddiness, the good vicar would have lost his precarious balance and plunged to his death on the floor so far below; but mercifully the task was now almost complete, and the ladder was in place below the last pair of bulbs when the door (which had remained unlocked) creaked open to admit a strange-looking man whose beard was unkempt, who was dressed in a long, shabby greatcoat, and who wore an incongruous pair of sunglasses. For a moment or two he looked about him, unaware of the presence of the other two men. The afternoon had grown dull and the electricity had been turned off whilst the bulbs were being changed.

'Can I help you?' asked Meiklejohn.

'What?' The man started nervously. 'Cor, you frightened me, guv.'

'Please do have a look around. You're most welcome.'

'Sorright. I just – I just wanted to – er . . .'

'I can show you around myself in a minute if you can—'

'Nah. Sorright, guv.' He shuffled out, and Meikle-john raised his eyebrows to the young man. The ladder was ready again now and he put his right hand up to the rung just above his head – and then stopped.

'You remember my predecessor here – poor Mr Lawson? He had a way with these down-and-outs, they tell me. Often used to have one or two of them staying with him for a few days. You probably know that anyway. Perhaps I should make more of an effort than I do. Still, we're all different, Thomas. Just as the good Lord made us.' He smiled, rather sadly, and began to climb. 'Perhaps poor Mr Lawson wasn't very good at changing light-bulbs, eh?'

Thomas managed a ghostly-weak smile in response and took up his guardian rôle on the bottom rung, his eyes once more averted from the fast-disappearing soles of the vicar's black shoes. Funny, really! He'd joined St Frideswide's church just over a year ago (he was an undergraduate at Hertford College) and he remem-bered the previous vicar very well indeed. He thought he remembered other things, too. For example, he thought he remembered the tramp who'd just walked in. Hadn't he seen him in church once or twice?

CHAPTER THIRTY

THE DECISION TO travel to Shrewsbury was taken, momentarily and arbitrarily, when Morse had walked out of the church on his way back to St Aldates; and as Lewis drove the police car round the Woodstock Road roundabout and headed out on to the A34 both men were mentally calculating the possible time schedule. It was already 4.20 p.m. Two hours, say, to get there – if the traffic was reasonable; two hours actually there; another two hours back. So, with a bit of luck, they could be back in Oxford by about 10.30 p.m.

Morse, as was his wont, spoke little in the car, and Lewis was quite happy to give his whole attention to the motoring. They had started in time to miss the diurnal mass exodus from Oxford which begins at about a quarter to five and continues its semi-paralytic progress for almost another hour. It was good fun, too, driving in a conspicuously marked POLICE car. As always other road-users immediately became punctilious about speed restrictions as they spied the pale-blue and white car in their mirrors, and ostentatiously shunned the slightest suspicion of sub-standard driving, behaving with a courtesy and care that were wildly at variance with their customary frenetic aggression.

So it was now.

Lewis turned left off the A34 through Chipping Norton, up through Bourton-on-the-Hill, through-Moreton-in-Marsh, and then, with the Vale of Evesham opening out in a vast panorama before them, down the long, steep hill into Broadway, its houses of mellowed Cotswold stone gleaming a warm yellow in the late afternoon sun. At Evesham, Morse insisted that they took the road to Pershore, in which town he enthused lovingly over the red-brick houses with their white-painted window-frames; and at Worcester he directed Lewis along the Bromyard Road.

'I've always thought,' said Morse, as they turned north from Leominster on to the A49, 'that this is one of the prettiest roads in England.'

Lewis sat silent. It was also a pretty long way round, and at this rate it would be about seven before they reached Shrewsbury. Yet as they drove past Church Stretton it seemed to Lewis that Morse was perhaps right; and even more so as they left the Long Mynd behind them, when the sun, still hovering over the Welsh hills far off on the western horizon, suffused the early evening sky with a fiery glow and turned the white clouds to the softest shade of purple.

It was half past seven when finally the two Oxford detectives were seated in the Superintendent's office at the Salop Police H.Q.; and it was half past eight when they emerged. Morse had said little, and Lewis less, and neither man felt that the meeting was of more than routine value. There were no grounds for suspecting anyone, and not the slightest whisper of a likely motive.

The dead woman had been quietly popular with her fellow-nurses, slightly less quietly popular with the surgeons and housemen, and it was difficult to believe that even Florence Nightingale herself could have found too many faults with her efficient and experienced nursing. One of the doctors had spoken to her the previous evening, had sat in the nurses' common room with her doing a crossword puzzle; but, although he was probably the last person (apart from the murderer) to see her alive, there was no reason whatsoever to suspect that he'd had anything to do with her death. But somebody had. Somebody had strangled her brutally with her own belt and left her for dead on the floor by the side of her bed, from where she had later managed to crawl to the door of her room to try desperately to call for help. But no one had heard her, and no one had come.

'I suppose we'd better see her?' said Morse dubiously, as they all trooped out of the Superintendent's office.

In the cream-tiled police morgue, a constable pulled out a sliding container from a stainless-steel structure, and turned back the sheet from the face – white, waxy-textured and washed, the lolling bloodshot eyes bearing their chilling witness to the agony of her death. At the base of her neck and running up to her right ear was the hideous groove left by the belt.

'Probably left-handed,' muttered Lewis, 'if he strangled her from the front, that is.' He turned towards Morse as he spoke, and noticed that the great man had his eyes shut.

Five minutes later Morse was looking immeasurably happier as he sat in the anteroom surveying the contents of the murdered woman's pockets and handbag.

'We should be able to check the handwriting easily enough,' said Lewis, as he saw Morse studying the letter from Kidlington.

'We hardly need to, do we?' said Morse, putting it to one side and turning to the other contents of the handbag. There were two pocket diaries, a lady's handkerchief, a leather purse, three luncheon vouchers, and the usual bric-à-brac of feminine toiletry: perfume, nail-file, comb, hand-mirror, eye-shadow, lipstick and tissues.

'Was she wearing much make-up when you found her?' asked Morse.

The Superintendent frowned slightly and looked less than comfortable. 'I think she was wearing some, but – er . . .'

'I thought you said she'd just come off duty. They don't let 'em slink round the wards all tarted up, surely?'

'You think she might have been expecting somebody?' Morse shrugged his shoulders. 'Possibility, isn't it?'

'Mm.' The Superintendent nodded thoughtfully, and wondered why he hadn't thought of that himself; but Morse had brushed aside the cosmetics as if whatever interest they might momentarily have exercised over him was now a thing of the past.

The purse contained six one-pound notes, about fifty pence in small change, and a local bus timetable. 'No driving licence' was Morse's only comment, and the

Superintendent confirmed that as far as they knew she'd had no car since coming to work at the hospital.

'She was pretty anxious to cover up her tracks, Super. Perhaps,' he added quietly, 'perhaps she was frightened that somebody would find her.' But again he seemed to lose interest in the line of thought upon which he had embarked, and proceeded to turn his attention to the two slim diaries, one for the current, one for the previous year.

'She wasn't exactly a Samuel Pepys, I'm afraid,' said the Superintendent. 'The odd jotting here and there, but not much to go on as far as I can see.'

Mrs Brenda Josephs had certainly started off the two years with admirable intentions, and the first few days of each of the two Januarys were fairly fully documented. But, even then, such *aide-mémoire* entries as her 'Six fish fingers' or '8.30 Nurses' Social' seemed hardly likely to lead the Salop or the Oxon constabulary very much nearer to the apprehension of her murderer. The expression on Morse's face was mildly sour as he flicked rather aimlessly through the pages, and in truth he found little to hold his attention. On the day of Brenda's death he noticed the single entry 'Periods due'; rather pathetic, but of little consequence.

Lewis, who hitherto had felt his contribution to the visit to have been less than positively constructive, picked up the diary for the previous year and examined it with his usual exaggerated care. The writing was neatly and clearly charactered, but for the most part so small that he found himself holding the diary at arm's length and squinting at it lop-sidedly. Against virtually every Sunday throughout the year up to mid-September were the letters 'SF', and these same letters were repeated at irregular intervals and on irregular weekdays throughout the the same period. 'SF'? The only thing he could think of was Science Fiction, but that was obviously wrong. There was something else, though. From July up until late September there was a series of 'P's, written (almost imperceptibly) in pencil in the ruled blue lines which separated the days of the month from each other. And the day was always a Wednesday.

'What does "SF" stand for, sir?'

'Saint Frideswide's,' said Morse without a moment's thought.

Yes. That must be it. Harry Josephs (as Lewis now recalled) had been disqualified from driving, and it was his wife's duty to take him down to the church in her own car. That fitted all right. Sunday mornings for the big service of the week, and then, at intermittent intervals, the mid-week days whenever some prestigious saint or other held an anniversary. That was it. No doubt about it.

'What does "P" stand for, sir?'

Morse reeled them off with the fluency of a man who had devoted too many hours of his life to the solving of crosswords: 'soft', 'president', 'prince', 'page', 'participle'.

'Nothing else?'

'Phosphorus?'

Lewis shook his head. 'Probably the initial of someone's name. It's a capital "P".'

'Let's have a look, Lewis.'

'Could be "Paul", sir? Paul Morris?'

'Or Peter Morris – if she's a paedophile.'

'Pardon?'

'Nothing.'

'Always on Wednesdays, though, sir. Perhaps she suddenly decided she wanted to see him more often—'

'And her old man was in the way and so she bumped him off?'

'I've heard of odder things. She said she'd nipped off to the pictures that night, didn't she?'

'Mm.' Morse's interest appeared to be engaged at last. 'How much does it cost to go to the pictures these days?'

'Dunno, sir. A quid? One-fifty?'

'Expensive for her, wasn't it? She couldn't have been there much more than an hour, at the most.'

'*If* she went, sir. I mean, she mightn't have gone to the pictures at all. She might have just crept quietly back into the church and—'

Morse nodded. 'You're quite right. She probably had the best motive of the lot of 'em. But you're forgetting something. The door creaks like hell.'

'Only the north door.'

'Really?' But Morse had clearly lost all interest in creaking doors, and Lewis found himself once more wondering why they'd bothered to come all this way. Nothing had been learned. No progress had been made.

'There's another "P", isn't there?' said Morse suddenly. 'We've forgotten Philip Lawson.'

Yes, Lewis had forgotten Philip Lawson; but where on earth was *he* supposed to fit into this particular picture?

The constable packed up Brenda Josephs' possessions, replaced them in their plastic bags, and redeposited the bags in a labelled cabinet. Morse thanked the Superintendent for his co-operation, shook hands with him, and got into the car beside Lewis.

It was on the Kidderminster road about six or seven miles south of Shrewsbury that a wave of chilling excitement, starting from the bottom of the back, gradually crept up to the nape of Morse's neck. He tried to conceal the agitation of his mind as he questioned Lewis. 'Did you say that Brenda Josephs marked off the days when she took her husband to church?'

'Looked like it, sir. And quite a few times apart from Sundays.'

'"SF", you said. She put "SF"?'

'That's about it, sir. As you said, it's "St Frideswide's". Not much doubt about that.' He turned suddenly and glanced at Morse, who was staring with extraordinary intensity into the outer darkness of the night. 'Unless, of course, you think it stands for something else?'

'No, no. It doesn't stand for anything else.' And then, very quietly, he said, 'Turn round, please. We're going back.'

The luminous dial on the fascia board showed half past ten, just gone, and things were running way behind even the most pessimistic schedule. But Lewis turned round at the earliest possible opportunity. He also was a man under authority.

The constable in the police mortuary reopened the cabinet and shook out the contents of the plastic bags once more. They were always a funny lot – these fellows from other forces.

Morse managed to keep his hand from shaking as he picked up the earlier of the two diaries and turned to the one specific page. And as he looked at the page the blood seemed to congeal in his jowls, and a slow smile of joyous satisfaction formed about his mouth.

'Thank you very much, Constable. Thank you very much. You don't think I could take this diary?'

'I don't know about that, sir. The Super's gone off now and—'

Morse held up his right hand like a priest delivering the benediction. 'Forget it! Doesn't matter!' He turned quickly to Lewis. 'See that?' He pointed to the space for Monday, 26 September, the day on which Harry Josephs had been murdered; and Lewis' forehead creased into a frown as he looked at it, and then looked at it again. The space was completely blank.

'You remember your Sherlock Holmes, Lewis?' But whether or not Lewis was familiar with the works of that great man was not immediately apparent, for clearly Morse himself had a good many passages of Holmesian dialogue by heart, and before Lewis could reply he proceeded to recite one:

' "Is there any point to which you would wish to draw my attention?"

' "To the curious incident of the dog in the night-time."

' "The dog did nothing in the night-time."

'"That was the curious incident."'

'I see,' said Lewis, seeing not.

'How fast will she go?' asked Morse as he clambered into the police car once more.

'About ninety – bit more – on the straight.'

'Well, put the flasher on and start the siren up. We must get back to Oxford quickly, all right?'

The car sped through the darkened countryside, down through Bridgnorth and Kidderminster, along the old Worcester Road to Evesham, and then in an almost incredibly short time back to Oxford. An hour and a half – almost to the minute.

'Back to the station, is it?' asked Lewis as he turned into the Northern Ring Road.

'No. Take me straight home, Lewis. I'm tired out.'

'But I thought you said—'

'Not tonight, Lewis. I'm dead beat.' He winked at Lewis and slammed the door of the Ford behind him. 'Good fun, wasn't it? Sleep tight! We've got work to do in the morning.'

Lewis himself drove off home happily. His honest soul had very few vices – but fast driving was certainly one of them.

Chapter Thirty-One

Perhaps the events of the past few days had disturbed the Reverend Keith Meiklejohn rather less than they should have done; and being an honest man the realization of this was worrying to him. It was true that, inducted as he had been only in the previous November, he had not known the Morris family personally, and could not therefore be expected to react too keenly to the tragic discoveries of what (if rumour were to be believed) were the bodies of father and son. Yet as he sat in his study at 9.30 a.m. on Tuesday morning he knew that his compassion should have been engaged more deeply, and he wondered about himself; wondered about his church, too.

Meiklejohn was a robust, well-built man, forty-one years of age and happily unmarried. His childhood had been spent in a family household brimming with evangelical piety, and one forever frequented by inveterate god-botherers and born-again Baptists. From his earliest years the promises of eternal life and the terrors of the lake that burneth with fire and brimstone had been as real to him as liquorice allsorts and the landscape of his Dorset home. In his early youth, whilst his classmates discussed the prospects of their favourite football teams or the merits of their new racing bikes, young Keith had grown zealous over matters ecclesiastical and theological and by the age of sixteen the way ahead was quite clear: he was destined to take holy orders. As a young curate he had at first been moderately low-church in his views on the liturgy and the sacraments; but gradually he had been more and more attracted towards the doctrines of the Oxford Movement, and at one point he had come within a communion wafer of conversion to the Roman Church. But all that was in the past. With a new-found balance, he discovered he could tread the tight-rope of High Anglicanism with security and confidence, and it was pleasing to him that his congregation appeared to think well of him for doing so. His predecessor, Lionel Lawson, had not (it seemed) found universal favour with an ecclesiastical stance that was decidedly more middle-and-leg than middle-and-off. In fact, when Lawson's curate, some five years earlier, had been promoted to a parish of his own there had been no request to the Bishop for a replacement, and Lawson himself had coped single-handed with the manifold duties of St Frideswide's parish. Inevitably, of course, there had been cuts in services, and it was Meiklejohn's resolve to restore as soon as possible the daily masses at 11.15 a.m. and 6.15 p.m. which were a wholly necessary feature (as he saw things) of a church that was dedicated to the glory of God.

Yet, as he sat at the ancient roll-top desk, the page over which his pen had been poised for several minutes remained blank. It was high time he preached again on transubstantiation: a tricky issue, of course, but one that was vital for the spiritual health of the brethren. But could that sermon wait, perhaps? His limp-leather copy of the Holy Writ lay open before him at the book of Hosea. A marvellous and memorable piece of writing! It was almost as if the Almighty himself had not really known what to do with his people when their goodness and mercy were as evanescent as the mists or the early dews that melted away in the morning sun. Was the Church in danger of losing its love? For without love the worship of God and the care of the brethren was little more than sounding brass and tinkling cymbals ... Yes, a possible sermon was just beginning to shape itself nicely. Not too forcefully expressed: nothing to smack too strongly of the stamping pulpit-thumper. But then another verse caught his eye from an earlier chapter of the same prophecy: 'Ephraim is joined to idols; let him alone.' Another striking verse! Idolaters were, after all, those within the Church – not those outside it. Those who worshipped, but who worshipped a false representation of God. And not just the golden calf, either. There was always a danger that other representations could get in the way of true worship: yes – he had to admit it! – things like incense and candles and holy water and crossings and genuflections, and all the sheer apparatus of ceremonial which could perhaps clog up the cleansing power of the Holy Spirit. It was possible, too – only too easy, in fact – to be blinded to the spiritual health of the Church by the arithmetical aggregation of its membership, especially when he considered (as he did with pride) the undoubted increase in the numbers attending divine worship since his own arrival. The records showed that there had been times under Lawson's régime when attendance had been just a little disappointing; and indeed some occasions in mid-week when it had been difficult to muster much of a congregation at all! But God didn't just count heads – or so Meiklejohn told himself; and he pondered again the central problem that had dominated his earlier thinking: should he not be more concerned than he was about the spiritual health of his church?

He was still undecided about the text of his next sermon, the page still blank beneath his pen, the disturbing words of the prophet Hosea still lying before him, when the door-bell rang.

Had it been the will of Providence that he had been pondering the state of St Frideswide's soul? At the very least, it was an uncanny coincidence that his visitor was soon asking him the very same questions he had been asking himself; asking them pretty bluntly, too.

'You had a big congregation last Sunday, sir.'

'About usual, Inspector.'

'I've heard that you get even more people than Lawson did.'

'Perhaps so. Certainly in the week, I think.'

'The crowds are flocking back, so to speak?'

'You make it sound like a football match.'

'Bit more interesting than the last football match I saw, I hope.'

'And one doesn't have to queue up at the turnstiles, Inspector.'

'You keep a fairly accurate record of the congregations, though?'

Meiklejohn nodded. 'I've continued my predecessor's practice in that respect.'

'Not in all respects?'

Meiklejohn was aware of the Inspector's blue eyes upon him. 'What are you trying to say?'

'Was Lawson lower-church in his views than you are?'

'I didn't know him.'

'But he was?'

'He had views, I believe, which were – er . . .'

'Lower-church?'

'Er – that might be a way of putting it, yes.'

'I noticed you had three priests in church on Sunday morning, sir.'

'You've still got quite a lot to learn about us, Inspector. There were myself and my curate. The sub-deacon need not be in holy orders.'

'Three's a bit more than the usual ration, though, isn't it?'

'There are no ration-books when it comes to divine worship.'

'Did Lawson have a curate?'

'For the first part of his time here, he did. The parish is a large one, and in my view should always have a curate.'

'Lawson was on his own, then – for the last few years?'

'He was.'

'Did you ever hear, sir, that Lawson might have been a fraction too fond of the choirboys?'

'I – I think it quite improper for you or for me to—'

'I met his former headmaster recently,' interrupted Morse, a new note of authority in his voice. 'I felt he was concealing something, and I guessed what it was: the fact that Lionel Lawson had been expelled from school.'

'You're sure of that?'

Morse nodded. 'I rang the old boy up today and put it to him. He told me I was right.'

'Expelled for homosexuality, you say?'

'He refused to confirm that,' said Morse slowly. 'He also refused to deny it, I'm afraid, and I'll leave you to draw your own conclusions. Look, sir. I want to assure you that whatever you may have to tell me will be treated in the strictest confidence. But it's my duty as a police officer to ask you once again. Have you heard any rumours that Lawson was at all inclined to that sort of thing?'

Meiklejohn looked down at his feet and picked his words with uneasy care. 'I've heard one or two rumours, yes. But I don't myself think that Lawson was an active homosexual.'

'Just a passive one, you mean.'

Meiklejohn looked up, and spoke with quiet conviction: 'It is my view that the Reverend Mr Lawson was not a homosexual. I am, of course, sometimes wrong, Inspector. But in this case I think I am right.'

'Thank you,' said Morse, in the tone of a man who says 'Thank you for nothing'. He looked round the room at the bookshelves, lined with rows of theological works, the spines of most of them either dark-blue or brown. It was in this dark and sombre room that Lawson himself would have sat, probably for several hours each day, during his ten-year ministry at St Frideswide's. What had *really* gone wrong here? What strange tales of the human heart and the deep abyss of human consciousness could these walls and these books tell, if only they had tongues to speak to him? Could Meiklejohn tell him any more? Oh, yes, he could. There was just that one final question, the most vital question he would ask in the whole case. It was the question which had suddenly sprung to life in his mind the previous evening on the road just a few miles south of Shrewsbury.

He took from his pocket the now-crumpled Parish Notes for April.

'You print one of these every month?'

'Yes.'

'Do you' – this was it, and his mouth seemed suddenly to grow dry as he asked it – 'do you keep copies of them from previous years?'

'Of course. It's a great help in compiling the Parish Notes to have the previous year's copy. Not so much with the Easter period, of course, but—'

'Can I look at last year's Notes, please, sir?'

Meiklejohn walked over to one of the bookshelves and took out a loose-leafed folder. 'Which month's copy do you want?' His eyes reflected a shrewd intelligence. 'September, perhaps?'

'September,' said Morse.

'Here we are, yes. July, August . . .' He stopped and looked a little puzzled. 'October, November . . .' He turned back to January and went very carefully through the issues once more. 'It's not here, Inspector,' he said slowly. 'It's not here. I wonder . . .'

Morse was wondering, too. But – please! – it wouldn't be too difficult to find a copy somewhere, would it? They must have printed a few hundred – whoever 'they' were.

'Who prints these for you, sir?'

'Some little man in George Street.'

'He'd surely keep the originals, wouldn't he?'

'I'd have thought so.'

'Can you find out for me – straight away?'

'Is it that urgent?' asked Meiklejohn quietly.

'I think it is.'

'You could always check up from the church register, Inspector.'

'The *what*?'

'We keep a register in the vestry. Every service – I think it *is* a service you're looking for? – every service is recorded there. The time, the type of service, the minister officiating, the offertory – even the number of the congregation, although I must admit that's a bit of a rough guess sometimes.'

Morse allowed himself an exultant grin. His hunch had been right, then! The clue for which he'd been searching was where he'd always thought it would be – under his very nose inside the church itself. The next time he had a hunch, he decided, he would pursue it with a damned sight more resolution than he had done this one. For the moment, however, he said nothing. He was there – almost there anyway – and he felt the thrill of a man who knows that he has seven draws up on the football pools and is just going out to buy a sports paper to discover the result of the eighth match.

The two men walked down the wide staircase and into the hallway, where Meiklejohn took his coat from the clothes-stand, stained dark brown like almost every other item of furniture in the large, echoing vicarage.

'A lot of room here,' said Morse they stepped out into the street.

Again the Vicar's eyes flashed with intelligence. 'What you mean to say is that I ought to turn it into a hostel, is that it?'

'Yes, I do,' replied Morse bluntly. 'I understand your predecessor used to take in a few waifs and strays now and then.'

'I believe he did, Inspector. I believe he did.'

They parted at George Street, and Morse, in a state of suppressed excitement, and already fingering the heavy church-keys in his raincoat pocket, walked on down Cornmarket to St Frideswide's.

CHAPTER THIRTY-TWO

JUST AS MEIKLEJOHN had said, the bulky, leather-bound register stood on its shelf in the vestry, and Morse felt the same amalgam of anxiety and expectation with which as a schoolboy he had opened the envelopes containing his examination results: any second – and he would know. The pages of the register were marked in faded blue lines, about a third of an inch apart, with each line, stretched across the double page, quite sufficient to accommodate the necessary information. On the left-hand page were written the day, the date, and the time of the service, followed by some brief specification of the particular saint's day, feast day, et cetera; on the right-hand page the record was continued with details of the type of service celebrated, the number present in the congregation, the amount taken at the offertory, and lastly the name (almost always the signature) of the minister, or ministers, officiating. Doubtless in a church permeated by a more fervent evangelicalism, there would have been the biblical reference of the text which the preacher had sought to propound; but Morse was more than delighted with the information he found in front of him. The register had fallen open at the current month and he noted the last entry: 'Monday, 3rd April. 7.30 p.m. St Richard of Chichester. Low Mass. 19. £5.35. Keith Meiklejohn M.A. (Vicar).' Then he turned back a thickish wedge of the book's heavy pages. A little too far, though: July, the previous year. On through August, and his heart suddenly seemed to sink within him as the thought flashed into his mind that someone might well have torn out the page he was seeking. But no! There it was now, staring him in the face: 'Monday, 26th Sept. 7.30 p.m. The Conversion of St Augustine. Solemn Mass. 13. – . Lionel Lawson M A. (Vicar).' For several minutes Morse stared at the entry with a blank fixity. Had he been wrong after all? For there it was, all printed out in Lawson's own hand – the precise details of the service at which Josephs had been murdered: the date and time, the occasion, the type of service (which, of course, accounted for Paul Morris' presence); the number in the congregation, the offertory (the sum quite naturally unknown and unrecorded, except perhaps for a few brief seconds in Josephs' brain before he met his death), and then Lawson's signature. All there. All in order. What had Morse hoped to find there? Surely he had not expected the amount of the offertory to be recorded? That would have been an elementary mistake of such monumental stupidity on Lawson's part that if repeated in other aspects of his crime would have led to an arrest within a few hours by any even moderately competent detective. No. Morse had not been looking for any such mistake. The simple truth of the matter was that *he'd expected there to be no entry at all.*

The door at the north porch creaked open, and Morse felt a sudden brief surge of primitive fear as he stood alone in the silent church. Somewhere, perhaps somewhere very near, there was a murderer still at large, watching every latest development with a vicious, calculating mind; watching even now, perhaps, and sensing that the police might be hovering perilously close to the truth. Morse walked on tiptoe to the heavy red curtain which cloaked the entrance to the vestry and cautiously peered through.

It was Meiklejohn.

'This is what you want, Inspector,' he said breezily. 'You must excuse me, if you will. We've got a service here at eleven.'

He handed to Morse a single sheet of paper, printed on both sides in faded black ink, with rows of asterisks dividing up the Parish Notes for the previous September into a series of closely typed paragraphs, of which the first, in double columns, gave full details of that month's forthcoming (and, in one case, fatal) functions. Morse sat down in the back pew and looked down intently at the sheet.

He was still looking down at the sheet several minutes later when Mrs Walsh-Atkins made her careful way down the central aisle, passing her left hand from pew-head to pew-head as she progressed, until finally settling herself in her accustomed seat where she knelt down, her forehead resting on the crook of her left arm, for a further protracted audience with the Almighty. A few other faithful souls had come in, all of them women, but Morse had not heard their entrances, and it was clear to him that the hinges on the door at the south porch had received a more recent oiling than those of its fellow at the north porch. He registered the point, as if it might be of some importance.

Morse sat through the devotional service – literally 'sat'. He made no pretence to emulate the gestures and movements of the sprinkling of ageing ladies; but a neutral observer would have marked a look of faintly smiling contentment on his features long before Meiklejohn's solemn voice at last, at very long last, intoned the benediction.

'It *was* what you wanted, I hope, Inspector?' Meiklejohn was leaning forward over the low table in the vestry, writing down the details of the service in the register with his right hand, his left unfastening the long row of buttons down his cassock.

'Yes, it was, and I'm most grateful to you. There's just one more thing, sir. Can you tell me anything about St Augustine?'

Meiklejohn blinked and looked round. 'St Augustine? Which St Augustine?'

'You tell me.'

'There were two St Augustines. St Augustine of Hippo, who lived about A.D. 400 or thereabouts. He's chiefly famous for his *Confessions* – as you'll know, Inspector. The other one is St Augustine of Canterbury, who lived a couple of hundred years or so later. He's the one who brought Christianity to Britain. I've got several books you could borrow if—'

'Do you know when either of 'em was converted?'

'Converted? Er – no, I'm afraid I don't. In fact I

wasn't aware that there was any such biographical data – certainly not about our own St Augustine anyway. But as I say—'

'Which one of 'em do you celebrate here, sir?' Upon Meiklejohn's answer, as Morse now knew, hung all the law and prophets, and the light-blue eyes that fixed the Vicar were almost hostile in their unblinking anticipation.

'We've never celebrated either of them,' said Meiklejohn simply. 'Perhaps we should. But we can't have an unlimited succession of special days. If we did, none of them would be "special", if you follow me. "When everyone is somebody, then no one's anybody."'

Phew!

After Meiklejohn had left, Morse hurriedly checked the three previous years' entries for September in the register, and almost purred with pleasure. The institution of any celebration to mark the conversion of one or other of the great Augustines had only begun – if it had begun at all – in the September of the previous year. Under the Reverend Lionel Lawson!

As Morse was about to leave the church, he saw that Mrs Walsh-Atkins had finally risen from her knees, and he walked back to help her.

'You're a faithful old soul, aren't you?' he said gently.

'I come to all the services I can, Inspector.'

Morse nodded. 'You know, it's surprising really that you weren't here the night when Mr Josephs was murdered.'

The old lady smiled rather sadly. 'I suppose I must have forgotten to look at the Parish Notes that week.

That's one of the troubles of growing old, I'm afraid –
your memory just seems to go.'

Morse escorted her to the door and watched her as
she walked away up to the Martyrs' Memorial. Had he
wished, he could have told her not to worry too much
about forgetting things. At the very least there had
been no error of memory on her part over the Parish
Notes for the previous September. For in those same
notes, the notes which Meiklejohn had just found for
him, *there was not a single word about the service at which
Josephs would be murdered.*

Chapter Thirty-Three

Lewis had spent a busy morning. He had co-ordinated arrangements with the Coroner's Sergeant for the forth-coming inquests on the Morrises, *père et fils*; he had written a full report on the Shrewsbury trip; and he had just come back from acquainting a rapidly recovering Bell with the latest developments in the case when Morse himself returned from St Frideswide's, looking tense yet elated.

'What time does the *Oxford Mail* go to press, Lewis?'

'First edition about now, I should think.'

'Get me the editor on the blower, will you? Quick! I've got some news for him.'

Morse very hastily scribbled a few notes, and when Lewis handed him the phone he was ready.

'I want this in tonight's *Mail*, is that clear? Absolutely vital. And what's more it's got to go on the front page somewhere. Got your pencil ready? Here goes. Head-line: ARREST IMMINENT IN ST FRIDESWIDE'S MURDER HUNT. Got that? Good. Now, here's your copy. Exactly as I tell you. I don't want any sub-editor buggering about with so much as a comma. "The Oxford police today reported that their long investigation into the murder last September of Mr Harry Josephs is now

virtually complete stop The further deaths at St Frideswide's reported in these columns last week are now
known to be connected with the earlier murder comma
and the bodies .discovered comma one on the tower
and one in the crypt of the church comma have been
positively identified as those of Mr Paul Morris comma
formerly music-master of the Roger Bacon School
Kidlington comma and of his son Peter Morris comma
former pupil of the same school and a member of the
church choir stop The police confirmed also that a
woman found murdered last week in a nurses' genitive
plural hostel in Shrewsbury was Mrs Brenda Josephs
comma wife of Mr Harry Josephs stop Chief Inspector
Morse capital M-o-r-s-e of the Thames Valley Constabulary told reporters today that public response to earlier
appeals for information had been extremely encouraging comma and that evidence is now almost complete."
No. Change that last bit: "and that only one more key
witness remains to come forward before the evidence is
complete stop In any case an arrest is confidently
expected within the next forty hyphen eight hours
stop" End of copy. You got all that? Front page, mind,
and give it a good big headline – about the same size
type you use when Oxford United win.'

'When did that last happen?' asked the editor.

Morse put down the phone and turned to Lewis.
'And here's a little printing job for you. Get it typed
and stick it on the outside of the south door at St
Frideswide's.'

Lewis looked down at what Morse had written:
'Because of imminent danger from falling masonry

immediately above the inside of the porch, this door must on no account be opened until further notice'.

'Come back as soon as you've done that, Lewis. There are a few things I've got to tell you.'

Lewis stood up and tapped the note with his fingers. 'Why don't we just lock the door, sir?'

'Because there's only one lock on it, that's why.'

For once Lewis refused to rise to the bait, put a clean white sheet of paper into the typewriter carriage, and turned the ribbon to 'red'.

The hump-backed surgeon put his head round the door of Bell's office just after 3 p.m., and found Morse and Lewis in earnest conversation.

'Won't interrupt you, Morse. Just thought you ought to know we're not much forrader with that fellow you found up the tower. I dunno as we're ever going to be certain, you know.'

Morse seemed neither surprised nor overmuch interested. 'Perhaps you're getting too old for the job.'

'Not surprising, Morse, old son. We're all ageing at the standard rate of twenty-four hours *per diem*, as you know.'

Before Morse could reply, he was gone, and Lewis felt glad that the interruption was so brief. For once in the case he knew exactly (well, almost exactly) where they were and why they were there.

*

It was just after half past four when one of the paper-boys from the Summertown Newsagents turned into Manning Terrace on his racing-bicycle, the drop handlebars (in one of the stranger perversions of fashion) turned upward. Without dismounting he took a copy of the *Oxford Mail* from the canvas bag thrown over his shoulder, folded it expertly in one hand, rode up to the door of number 7, and stuck it through the letter-box. Four doors in a row next, all on the right-hand side, starting with number 14A, where Ruth Rawlinson was just inserting her Yale key after an afternoon's shopping in Oxford.

She took the paper from the boy, put it under her right arm, and carried the two fully laden shopping bags into the house.

'Is that you, Ruthie dear?'

'Yes, Mother.'

'Is the paper come?'

'Yes, Mother.'

'Bring it with you, dear.'

Ruth put her carrier bags down on the kitchen table, draped her mackintosh over a chair, walked into the lounge, bent down to kiss her mother lightly on the cheek, placed the newspaper on her lap, turned up the gas fire, almost commented on the weather, wondered why she hadn't already gone mad, realized that to-morrow was Wednesday – oh God! How much longer would she be able to stand all this – her mother, and him? Especially *him.* There was little enough she could do about her mother, but she could do something about him. She just wouldn't go – it was as simple as that.

'Ruth! Come and read this!' said her mother.

Ruth read through the front-page article. Oh my God!

The man seated on the deep sofa, its chintz covers designed in the russet-and-white floral pattern, was not surprised by the factual material reported in the front-page article, but he was deeply worried by its implications. He read the article through many, many times and always would his eyes linger on the same lines: 'only one more key witness remains to come forward before evidence is complete. In any case an arrest is confidently expected within the next forty-eight hours.' It was the piece about the 'key witness' which he found the more disturbing. Himself he could look after without help from anyone, but ... In a flash, as always, the decision was taken. Yes, it had to be tomorrow – tomorrow morning. It *would* be tomorrow morning.

It was not only Ruth Rawlinson, therefore, who had decided to miss the regular Wednesday-evening rendezvous. Someone else had now made exactly the same decision for her.

CHAPTER THIRTY-FOUR

AT FIVE MINUTES past ten the next morning, Ruth Rawlinson was not so wholly preoccupied with other things that she failed to notice and to admire the baskets of daffodils that bedecked the lamp-standards all the way along St Giles. But, if the morning was bright and sunny, her own mood was full of dark foreboding, for affairs were getting terrifyingly out of hand. Having been informed of the identities of the two bodies found at St Frideswide's, having learned of the death of Brenda Josephs, and knowing in any case far more than the police could know, her thoughts were in constant and grievous agitation. What was to stop her, at this very second, from cycling straight on through Cornmarket and down St Aldates to the Oxford City Police H.Q.? In any case, it was her duty to do so. It had always been her moral duty, but it was something more than that now: it was a personal cry for help as the walls began to close in around her. Five minutes earlier, when she had left Manning Terrace, her firm resolve had been to go to see Morse immediately and tell him the whole tragic tale. But that resolution was now crumbling, and she told herself that she needed a chance to think things out a little more clearly; a chance to brace herself emotionally, before plunging her own life, and thereby her mother's life, too, into utter ruin and desolation. Yes. She needed time – just a little more time. She propped her bicycle against the wall of the south porch, fastened the lock through the rear wheel, and then saw the notice on the door, pinned rather too high and typed in red capitals. Registering no particular surprise, Ruth Rawlinson walked round to the door at the north porch. It was open.

From the sub-manager's office on the top floor of the large store almost opposite, Lewis followed Ruth's progress with his binoculars – just as he had followed the progress of the others who had entered the church since 8.45 a.m., when the door at the north porch had first been unlocked. But they had been few, and his task had been far easier than he could have imagined. A flamboyantly dressed group of what looked from above like American tourists had gone in at 9.10 a.m.: ten of them. And at 9.22 a.m. ten of them had emerged into the sunlight and drifted off towards Radcliffe Square. At 9.35 a.m. a solitary white-haired lady had gone in, and had come out, her morning devotions completed, about ten minutes later. During the same time, a tall, bearded youth, carrying an extraordinarily large transistor radio, had gone in, only to make his exit some twenty seconds later, doubtless (as it appeared to Lewis) having mistaken the place for somewhere else. That was all – until Lewis recognized

Ruth Rawlinson. He'd accepted the offer of a cup of coffee five minutes after she'd gone in, but had kept his binoculars trained on the north entrance, even refusing to turn round to express his thanks. This, if Morse were right (and Lewis thought he was), could be the vital time. Yet half an hour later it hardly seemed as if it were going to be so. There had been no further visitors, if one discounted, that is, an innocent-looking white-haired terrier which had urinated against the west wall.

Some of the daffodils on the sides of the altar steps were now well past their prime, and Ruth picked them out, neatly rearranging the remainder, and mentally deciding to buy some more. She then walked boustro-phedon along the pews on either side of the main aisle, replacing on their hooks whatever loose hassocks had been left on the floor, flicking the pew-ledges with a yellow duster, and at the same time collecting a few stray hymn-books and prayer-books. At one point she peered curiously up at the stonework above the south porch, but was unable to identify any visible signs of impending collapse.

Morse watched her with mixed emotions. He watched her large eyes and her full sensitive lips, and he realized once again how attractive she could have been to him. Even her little mannerisms were potentially endearing: the way she would blow a stray wisp of hair away from her face; the way she would stand, her hands on her waist, with something approaching pride on her face after completing one of her humble tasks. And yet, at the same time, he was conscious that she was in far more imminent danger than the masonry above the south porch was ever likely to be. If he was right (which after 10.20 a.m. he was beginning to doubt somewhat), Ruth Rawlinson was not likely to die in her nightdress, but in the very church in which he was now sitting, carefully concealed behind the dull-red curtain of the confessional. His intermittent fears that she would decide to spring-clean his own observation-post had hitherto proved groundless; but now, arms akimbo, she was looking searchingly around her. Did it matter all that much, though, if she did find him? He could explain as best he could – even take her over to the Randolph for a drink, perhaps. Yet he was glad when he heard the tell-tale clatterings and the drumming of cold water into the bottom of the scrubbing-bucket.

Several members of the public had entered the church during this time, and at each clinking of the latch and creaking of the door Morse felt the tension rise within him – only to fall again as the visitors stared rather vacantly around them, fumbled through the church literature, and without exception departed again within ten minutes of their arrival. Lewis had seen them go in; seen them leave, too – the coffee long since cold at his elbow. But Morse's own vigilance was becoming progressively less keen, and he began to feel just a little bored. The only book within arm's reach was a stiff-backed bible, whose pages he now turned desultorily, thinking back as he did so to his youth. Something had gone sadly wrong somewhere with his own spiritual development, for he had almost completely lost his early ebullient faith and he now had to confess that when faced with the overwhelming difficulties of forming any coherent philosophy of life and death he had come to regard the teachings of the Church as so much gobbledegook. He could be wrong, of course. Probably *was* wrong – just as he was probably wrong about this morning. Yet it had seemed such a logical time – certainly the time *he* would have chosen had he found himself in the murderer's shoes.

At some point in his musings, he thought he had heard a twanging metallic noise, but only now did it register fully. Could it have been the north door being locked? If so, it must surely have been locked from the outside. Yes. Blast it! He'd forgotten that notice about the recent vandalism, and someone must have come and locked the place up. But surely that someone would have looked into the church first? There was Ruth in there, for a start, although she probably had a key herself. *Did* she have a set of keys? What about any others who were in the church? If Ruth hadn't got a key, they'd all be shut up in there, wouldn't they?

Morse was only too conscious how woolly and confused his thinking was becoming – when he suddenly froze in his seat. He heard a man's voice, very close to him. It said, 'Hello, Ruth!' That was all. Quite a pleasant voice by the sound of it, but it seemed to turn Morse's blood to ice. Someone must have locked the door all right. *From the inside.*

Chapter Thirty-Five

'WHAT ARE YOU doing in here?' she asked sharply. 'I didn't hear you come in.'

'No, you wouldn't would you? I've been here a long time. Up on the tower. It's cold up there; but you get a wonderful view, and I like looking down on things – and people.'

(Oh, Lewis! If only your eyes had not been focused quite so closely on the door!)

'But you must go! You can't stay here! You shouldn't be out at all!'

'You *worry* too much.' He laid a hand on her shoulder as they stood together in the central aisle, and pulled her towards him.

'Don't be silly!' she whispered harshly. 'I've told you – we agreed—'

'The door's locked, my beauty, have no fear. I locked it myself, you see. There's only the two of us here, so why don't we sit down for a little while?'

She pushed his hand from her. 'I've told you. It's got to finish.' Her lips were quivering with emotion, and she was very close to tears. 'I can't take any more of this. I just can't! You've got to go away from here. You've got to!'

'Of course I have. That's exactly what I've come to see you for – can't you understand that? Just sit down, that's all. Not too much to ask, is it, Ruth?' His voice was silkily persuasive.

She sat down and the man sat next to her, no more than ten feet or so from the confessional. (The man's heavy brown shoes, as Morse could now see, were of good quality, but appeared not to have been cleaned for many weeks.) For some time neither of them spoke as the man's left arm rested across the back of the pew, the hand lightly gripping her shoulder. (The finger-nails, as Morse could now see, were clean and well manicured, reminding him of a clergyman's nails.)

'You read the article,' she said flatly. It was not a question.

'We both read the article.'

'You must tell me the truth – I don't care what you say, but you must tell me the truth. Did you – ' (her voice was faltering now) ' – did you have anything to do with all that?'

'Me? You must be joking! You can't honestly believe that – surely you can't, Ruth!' (The man, as Morse could now see, wore a pair of dingy grey flannels, and above them a large khaki-green jumper, with leather shoulder-patches, reaching up to the neck in such a way that it was not clear whether or not he wore a tie.)

Ruth was leaning forward, her elbows on the top edge of the pew in front of her, her head in her hands. From the look of her she might well be praying, and Morse guessed that she probably was. 'You're not telling me the truth. You're *not*. It was *you* who killed them! All of them! I *know* you did.' She was a lost soul now, uncaring in the bitter depths of her misery as she buried her head in her hands. Morse, as he watched her, felt a profound and anguished compassion welling up within him; yet he knew that he must wait. The previous day he had guessed at the truth behind the grim succession of tragedies, and here and now that very same truth was working itself out, not more than a few yards away from him.

The man made no denial of the charges spoken against him, but his right hand seemed to be working round his throat, his face momentarily turned away. (The face, as Morse had already noticed, was that of a man in his late forties – or early fifties perhaps, for both the long, unkempt, blackish hair and the beard which covered his face were heavily streaked with white and grey.)

Here it all was, then – in front of him. It was all so very simple, too – so childishly simple that Morse's mind, as always, had refused to believe it and had insisted instead on trying to find (and, indeed, almost finding) the weirdest, most complex solutions. Why, oh, why, just for once in a while was he not willing to accept and come to terms with the plain, incontrovertible facts of any case – the facts that stared him point-blank in the face and simply shrieked out for a bit of bread-and-butter common sense and application? The man sitting here now, next to Ruth Rawlinson? Well, Morse? Of course it was! It was Lionel Lawson's brother – *Philip Lawson*; the man so despised in the stories of clever detection, the man so despised by Morse himself; the man who committed a not-very-clever crime for the very meanest of rewards; the layabout, the sponger and the parasite, who had bedevilled his long-suffering brother's life from their earliest schooldays together; the cleverer boy, the more popular boy, the favourite – the boy who had grown up without a thread of moral fibre in his being, the boy who had wasted his considerable substance on riotous living, and who had come back to prey once more upon his wretched brother Lionel; come back, with a complete knowledge of his brother's life and his brother's weaknesses; come back with threats of betrayal and public exposure – threats which Lionel had paid off with help and kindness and compassion and, doubtless, with money, too. And then – yes, and then came the time when Lionel himself, for once in his life, had desperately needed the help of his worthless brother, and was more than prepared to pay for it; the time when the two brothers had planned the execution and arranged the subsequent cover-up of Harry Josephs' murder, a murder planned meticulously at the very moment when Paul Morris had just opened the diapason stop on the organ, and was doubtless drowning the church with the last verse of 'Praise to the Holiest in the Height' or something. *fff*.

These were the thoughts that flashed across Morse's mind in that instant, with the multiple murderer sitting there just in front of him, his left arm still resting along the back of the pew, his right hand still fumbling with something round his neck; and Ruth still bending forward in her posture of semi-supplication, still so pathetically vulnerable.

Then, even as he watched, Morse felt his every muscle tense in readiness as the adrenalin coursed through his body. The fingers of the man's left hand were holding the narrower end of a tie; a dark navy-blue tie with broad diagonal scarlet stripes bordered by very much thinner ones of green and yellow; and as Morse watched the scene being enacted immediately before his eyes his mind came to a dead stop in its tracks, seemed to turn a reverse somersault and to land in a state of complete stupefaction.

But the time for thought was past; already the man's left hand had looped the tie round the woman's neck; already the right hand was moving to meet it – and Morse acted. It was ill luck that the low door of the confessional opened inwards, for he had to clamber awkwardly in the narrow space and by the time he was out the element of surprise was gone; and as the tourniquet was already tightening about Ruth's throat she cried a terrible cry.

'Keep your distance!' snarled the man, springing to his feet and dragging Ruth up with him, the tie cutting cruelly into her neck. 'You heard me! Keep it there! Not a step farther or else.'

Morse hardly heard him. He lunged desperately at the pair of them, and Ruth fell heavily in the central aisle as Morse seized the man's right arm and tried with all his considerable strength to twist it behind his back. But with almost ridiculous ease his adversary shook himself clear and stood there, a vicious hatred blazing in his eyes.

'I know you,' said Morse, panting heavily. 'And you know who I am, don't you?'

'Yes, I know you, you bastard!'

'There's no sense in trying anything – I've got my men all round the church—' (the words were coming out in a series of breathless snatches) 'there's no way for you to get out of here – no way at all – now – now please be sensible – I'm going to take you from here – there's nothing to worry about.'

For a while the man stood quite motionless, only his eyes roving about in their sockets as if weighing the situation with a frenetic logicality, as if searching for some desperate remedy. Then something seemed to snap in the man, as if the glaze that suddenly dilated the eyes had effaced the very last vestiges of any rational thought. He turned swiftly, almost athletically, on his heel, and with his descending peal of maniacal laughter echoing under the vaulted roof he ran to the back of the church and disappeared behind the curtains of the vestry.

At that point (as Lewis later protested) Morse could have chosen several more logical courses of action than the one which he in fact pursued. He could have gone to the door at the north porch and signalled Lewis immediately; he could have led Ruth from the church and locked the door behind him, with his quarry cornered and powerless; he could have sent Ruth, if sufficiently recovered, to get help, and himself stayed where he was, performing no more than a watchdog brief until that help arrived. But Morse did none of these things. He felt that strangely compelling and primitive instinct of the hunter for the hunted, and he walked almost boldly to the vestry where in a sudden flurry he flung the curtains aside on their rollers. No one was there. The only other doorway from the vestry led to the tower, and Morse walked across the parquet floor and tried the door. Locked. He took out his keys, selected the right one first time, unlocked the door and, standing cautiously to one side, pulled it open. On the lowest of the circular stone steps, he saw a man's greatcoat, long, shabby and dirty; and, placed neatly on top of it, a pair of dark sunglasses.

CHAPTER THIRTY-SIX

TRACERIES OF BLACKENED cobwebs lined the under-lintels of the stone steps above his head as step by step Morse ascended the circular stairway. He was conscious of no fear: it was as if his paranoiac acrophobia was temporarily suspended, subsumed by the saner, more immediate danger from the man somewhere above him. Up and up he climbed, the door to the bell-chamber just appearing on his right when he heard the voice from high above him.

'Keep going, Mr Morse. Lovely view from the top.'

'I want to talk to you,' shouted Morse. He put his hands out to the walls on either side of him and looked upwards towards the tower. For a second his balance threatened to desert him as he caught sight, through the small low window to his left, of the shoppers walking along Cornmarket, far, far below him. But a raucous laugh from above served only to restore his equilibrium.

'I only want to talk to you,' repeated Morse, and climbed another six steps. 'I only want to *talk* to you. As I told you, my men are outside. Be sensible, man. For Christ's sake, be sensible!'

But there was no reply.

Another window, again to his left, and the angle

down on to the stream of shoppers was now virtually vertical. Strangely, however, Morse realized that he could now look down without that wave of incipient panic. What for the life of him he was unable to do was to look across at the store almost opposite, where he knew that the faithful Lewis would still be watching the door at the north porch with his wonted, unwavering vigilance.

Another six steps. And another six steps.

'The door's open, Mr Morse. Not much farther.' Then again the almost insane laugh, but softer this time – and more menacing.

On the second step from the top of the tower and with the door (as the man had asserted) wide open, Morse stopped.

'Can you hear me?' he asked. He was breathing heavily, and he realized sadly how ill-conditioned he had allowed his body to become.

Again, there was no reply.

'It must have been heavy work carting a body up here.'

'I've always kept fit, Mr Morse.'

'Pity the ladder collapsed, though. You could have hidden 'em both in the crypt then, couldn't you?'

'Well, well! How observant we are!'

'Why did you have to kill the boy?' asked Morse. But if there was a reply a sudden tugging gust of wind cut across the words and whipped them away.

It was clear to Morse that the man was not concealed behind the tower door and after taking one further step he could now see him, standing facing him at the northern wall of the tower, about thirty feet away, on the narrow gully that divided the sides of the tower from the shallow central eminence. With a peculiarly detached inconsequentiality, Morse noticed how very large the weather-vane was, and for a second or two he wondered whether he would soon be waking from a terrifying dream.

'Come down. We can't talk here. Come on.' Morse's tone was gentle and persuasive. He knew the whole truth at last, and his one remaining duty was to get this man down safely. 'Come on. Come down. We can talk then.' Morse climbed the final stop, and felt the wind pulling at his thinning hair.

'We'll talk now, Mr Morse, or we won't talk at all. Do you understand what I mean?' The man hitched himself up and sat on the coping between two of the crenellations, his feet dangling loosely above the tower floor.

'Don't do anything stupid!' shouted Morse, his voice betraying a sudden panic. 'That solves nothing. That's no way out for you. Whatever else you are, you're not a coward.'

The last word seemed to strike a chord which could still vibrate with something of its former attunement, for the man jumped lightly down and his voice was steady now. 'You're right, Mr Morse. Dangerous sitting there like that, especially in the wind.'

'Come on!' Morse's mind was racing now. This was the time when it mattered so desperately that he said and did exactly the right things. He felt sure that there must be some suitable phrases in the psychiatrist's hand-book that would soothe the raging of a maddened lion; but his own brain was quite incapable of formulating any such irenic incantations. 'Come on,' he said again; then, as a minor variant, 'Come along.' And, in spite of the bankruptcy of these banal exhortations, Morse felt that he was adopting the right sort of approach, for there now seemed some hesitation in the other's manner, some indication of a slightly saner attitude.

'Come along,' repeated Morse, and took one slow step towards the man. Then another step. Then another. And still the man stood motionless, his back to the north wall of the tower. Only five or six yards now separated them, and Morse took yet a further step towards him. 'Come along.' He held out his hand as if to lend support to one who has passed the dangers of a long walk along a tight-rope, and now is only a few feet from final safety.

With a snarl on his bearded lips, the man launched himself at Morse and pinned him round the shoulders with a vicious vice-like power. 'No one's ever called me a coward,' he hissed. 'No one!'

Morse managed to grab hold of the man's beard with both hands and to force his head back inch by inch until they both lost their balance and fell heavily against the leaded slope of the central roofing. Morse felt himself pinned beneath the other man's body, his legs and shoulders utterly powerless. He felt strong hands at his throat, the thumbs digging deep into the flesh; and his own hands were now frantically gripping the man's wrists, temporarily staying the irresistible thrust, his lips stretched to their widest extremity over his gritted teeth, his eyes closed with a desperate tightness, as though somehow this might lend him a few extra seconds of time, an extra ounce of strength. The blood thudded in his ears like someone pounding against a heavy door that would admit no entrance, and from somewhere he heard what sounded like the tinkling crash of a broken milk bottle; and the noise registered coolly and clinically in his brain, as if his mind was now outside himself, contemplating events with an objective detachment that was wholly devoid of panic or fear. He saw the scene with such clearly focused clarity. He was driving through the night along the fast, straight, narrow stretch of road from Oxford to Bicester, a long stream of cars coming towards him, ever coming towards him, their twin headlights staggered slightly in a continuous double line of yellow circles, ever approaching – and then flashing past him. And now there was another vehicle coming straight towards him, coming on the wrong side of the road, its offside blinker flashing as it closed upon him. Yet (amazingly!) his hands remained firm and steady on the driving-wheel ... Perhaps that was one of death's most guarded secrets? Perhaps the fear of dying, perhaps even death itself, was nothing but a great deception after all ... The headlights turned to spinning yellow circles in his brain, and then as he opened his eyes he could see only the dull sky above him. His knees were drawn up under the man's stomach: but so oppressive was the weight upon him that he could gain no leverage at all. If only he could find the strength to co-ordinate his arms and his knees, there might just be the chance of unbalancing the man and turning him sideways, and thus for a few seconds relieving the overpowering pressure of the hands at his throat. But his strength was almost gone, and he knew that his body, any second now, would almost gladly capitulate as the aching muscles in his arms screamed out for rest. He was relaxing already, his head resting almost comfortably now against the cold surface of the central roofing. That weather-vane really was enormous! How on earth could anyone have carried such a weight up here, up the circling staircase, up and up and up, with such a great weight upon his shoulder?

The full realization of his situation registered for the last time, and for a few seconds longer his grip on the man's wrists held firm as he dredged up the very last drop of his energy. But he had nothing more to offer. His grip on the steering-wheel slowly relaxed and as he closed his eyes the lights from the oncoming cars were dazzlingly bright. He thought of the final words of Richard Strauss's last song: 'Ist dies etwa der Tod?'

Chapter Thirty-Seven

MORSE REALIZED THAT something miraculous had occurred. The body so inexorably pressing down upon him had become, in the self-same moment of time, both heavier and lighter; the grip at his throat both tighter and looser. The man groaned as if in some intolerable agony, and as he did so Morse's knees thrust him away, almost lightly and easily. The man reeled away towards the side of the tower where he frantically reached out to the nearest crenellation to stay himself. But his impetus was too great. The stonework crumbled away as his right hand jarred into it for support; and head first the man plunged over the parapet. Then was to be heard the diminuendo of a terrifying 'Yaooh' as the man's body fell somersaulting to the ground far below, and finally a deadly thump followed by the terrified shrieks of those passing by at the foot of the tower.

Lewis stood there still clutching the top end of a long brass candlestick. 'You all right, sir?'

Morse remained where he was, blissfully breathing in the heady air in mighty gulps. The pain in his arms was like raging toothache, and he spread them out beside him, lying there on the gently sloping roof like a man who is crucified.

'Are you all right?' It was another voice now, a gentler, softer voice, and slim, cool fingers pressed themselves against his wet forehead.

Morse nodded, and looked up at her face. He saw that there was a slight down of very fair hair upon her cheeks and light-brown freckles on either side of her nose. She was kneeling beside him, her large eyes brimming with happy tears. She held his head in her arms and pressed him closely to her for what to Morse seemed many days and many hours.

They said nothing to each other. When they slowly descended from the tower, she leading but only so little a way in front that their hands could remain firmly clasped, they still said nothing. When a few minutes later Lewis saw them they were sitting in the back pew of the Lady Chapel, her tear-stained face resting happily on his shoulder. And still they said nothing.

Lewis had seen the two men on the tower, had almost broken his own neck clambering down the five flights of stairs, had knocked several young ladies out of the way as he had run through the ground-floor cosmetic department, and finally, like some frustrated Fury, had hammered and hammered with his fists against the north door. The woman was still in there, he knew that, but it occurred to him that something might have happened to her; and in desperation he had hurled a large stone through the lowest and most convenient window with the dual purpose of making himself heard and of creating a possible means of entry. And the woman had heard him. The door was unlocked and, grabbing a candlestick from the shrine of the Blessed Virgin, he had taken the tower staircase three steps at a time and once on the roof he had smashed the candlestick with all his force across the middle of the back of Morse's bearded assailant.

Two duty-policemen were already on the scene when Lewis emerged. A ring of people, standing some four or five yards off, surrounded the dead body, and an ambulance, already summoned, was whining its way down St Giles from the Radcliffe Infirmary. Lewis had plucked a cassock from one of the hooks in the vestry, and now draped it over the dead man.

'Do you know who he is?' asked one of the policemen.

'I think so,' said Lewis.

'You all right?' The hump-backed police surgeon was the third person to have asked the same question.

'Fine. Few weeks on the Riviera and I'll be fine. Nothing serious.'

'Huh! That's what they all say. Whenever I ask my patients what their parents died of, they all say the same – "Oh, nothing serious".'

'I'd tell you if I wasn't all right.'

'You know, Morse, don't you, that every single person ever born has at least one serious illness in life – the last one?'

Mm. It was a thought.

Lewis came back into the church: things were almost ready outside. 'You all right, sir?'

'Oh, for Christ's sake!' said Morse.

Ruth Rawlinson still sat on the rear pew of the Lady Chapel, her eyes staring blankly ahead of her – composed, silent and passive.

'I'll see her home,' said Lewis quietly. 'You just—'

But Morse interrupted him. 'She can't go home, I'm afraid. You'll have to take her down to the station.' He breathed heavily and looked away from her. 'She's under arrest, and I want you personally to take her statement.' He turned to Lewis with inexplicable anger in his voice. 'Is that clear? You! Personally!'

Unspeaking and unresisting Ruth was led away to a police car by one of the constables; and after she was gone Morse, Lewis and the police surgeon followed.

The crowd outside, now standing three or four deep around the covered body, watched their emergence with deep interest, as if the principal protagonists in a drama had just walked on to the stage: the hump-backed, rather elderly man, who looked (had he been around in 1555) as if he might have viewed unmoved the sight of Ridley and Latimer as they had burned to death in front of Balliol, only a few hundred yards away; next, the placid-looking, rather thick-set man, who earlier had seemed to be in charge of all the operations but who now appeared to fade a little into the background as if he were in the presence of his superiors; and finally a slimmer, balding, pale-faced man with piercing eyes, in whose sombre mien – if in any of the trio's – lay the look of a natural authority.

They stood there, these three, over the covered body.

'You want to look at him, Morse?' asked the police surgeon.

'I've seen enough of him,' muttered Morse.

'His face is all right – if you're feeling squeamish.'

The surgeon pulled back the top of the cassock from the dead man's face, and Lewis looked down at it with great interest and intensity.

'So that's what he looked like, sir.'

'Pardon?' said Morse.

'Lawson's brother, sir. I was just saying that—'

'That's not Lawson's brother,' said Morse quietly; so quietly in fact that neither of the other men seemed to hear him.

The Book of Ruth

CHAPTER THIRTY-EIGHT

Statement given by Miss Ruth Rawlinson, 14A Manning Terrace, Oxford, dictated by Miss Rawlinson, signed by the same, and witnessed by Sergeant Lewis, Thames Valley Police (C.I.D.)

Perhaps it is easier to start twenty years ago. I was then in the first-year sixth at Oxford High School studying for my A Levels in English and History and Economics. The headmistress came into the class one morning and called me outside. She told me that I must be a brave girl because she had some very sad news for me. My father who worked as a printer with Oxford University Press had suffered a massive coronary thrombosis and had died within an hour of being admitted to the Radcliffe Infirmary. I remember a feeling of numbness more than anything and little real grief. In fact for the next few days I felt almost a sense of pride as the mistresses and the other girls treated me with a kindness I had never really known before. It was just as if I were a heroine who had suffered much misfortune with great fortitude. But that wasn't the case at all really. I didn't dislike my father but we had never been close to each other. A perfunctory kiss when I went up to bed or a pound note sometimes when I'd done well in examinations but he had shown little real interest and no real love. Perhaps it wasn't his fault. My mother had been struck down with multiple sclerosis and although at that time she was still reasonably mobile my father's first and every thought was for her welfare and happiness. He must have loved her very dearly and his death was a terrible blow to her. Almost from that day onwards she seemed to change. It was as if the woman she had been could never come to terms with such bereavement and therefore had to become a different person. Something happened to me too. I suddenly began to lose all pride in my school work and I began to lose all love for my mother. I suspected that she exaggerated her physical handicaps and all the cooking and washing and cleaning and shopping I did for her were accepted with less and less gratitude. I stayed on at school and took my A Levels the next year but I didn't apply for a university place although oddly enough my mother wanted me to. Instead I took a year's course at the Marlborough Secretarial College in the High and soon found that I had a real aptitude for the work. Even before I left the college I had been offered three posts and I finally accepted a very good offer from Oxford University Press as a personal and confidential secretary to a man who had known my father slightly. He was a very kind boss and a very clever man and the five years I spent with him were the happiest of my life. He was a bachelor and a year or so after starting with him he began to ask me out for an occasional meal or a visit to the Playhouse and I accepted. He never tried to take the slightest advantage of me and only when he used to take my arm through his as we walked to the car was there the slightest physical contact between us. Yet I fell in love with him – quite hopelessly as I thought. Then two things happened almost within a few days of each other. My boss asked me if I would marry him and there was a sudden sharp deterioration in my mother's condition. Whether these two things were connected it is impossible for me to say. I had told her about the proposal of marriage and she had told me what she thought about it in typically forthright terms. He was just a dirty old man looking for a bit of regular sex and look at the huge difference in our ages. Ridiculous! I should find myself some nice young man about my own age – that is if I had finally decided to leave her to rot away in some lonely home for chronic invalids. She worked herself up into a most distraught state and I realize that I am perhaps being less than fair in doubting her genuine shock at the news I had brought her. Anyway her G.P. told me that she was very poorly indeed and would have to go into hospital immediately. Then two more things happened almost at once. My mother returned home now needing a great deal of daily attention and I told my boss that I couldn't accept his proposal and that in the circumstances it would be better for me to leave. I remember the look of childlike sadness and disappointment in his eyes. When I left three weeks later he took me out for a marvellous meal at the Elizabeth and he talked quite happily all the evening. When he took me home and we sat in the car trying to say our very awkward farewells I turned to him and kissed him freely and lovingly on the mouth. From that day I grew my own shell round me just as my mother had grown hers. Doubtless I am much more like my mother than I would want to believe. Anyway mother had probably been quite right. When I left work I was twenty-four and my boss was forty-nine. I met him once or twice after that just casually in the street. We asked the usual polite questions and went our ways. He never married. Two years afterwards he died of a brain haemorrhage and I went to his funeral. Looking back on it I feel no deep regrets that we didn't marry but I shall always regret that I never offered to become his mistress. These facts may seem irrelevant but I mention them only in the hope that someone may be able to understand why things began to go wrong and not in order to exonerate myself in any degree for my own part in the terrible business that was to come.

I must now talk about money. With my own quite handsome little salary now cut off, our financial situation had to be considered carefully and my mother thought that my own C-grade pass in A Level Economics was a sure guarantee of prudence and wizardry in monetary matters. Soon therefore I came to have a very full knowledge of all our financial affairs and it wasn't long before my mother gladly handed over all the responsibility to me. There was no problem with the house since my father had taken out a combined mortgage and life-insurance policy on it. It was far too big for the two of us but its market value was now about ten times greater than when my father had bought it twenty-five years earlier and with his death it was ours. At that time too my mother had realizable assets of about £2,000 in various stock-market equities and my own deposit account with Lloyds stood at over £800. In addition my

mother had a small widow's pension accruing from a
policy my father had taken out with the Press and from
this time I also began to claim a dependency allowance
from the Department of Social Security. For the next ten
years or so I took on quite a lot of typing duties at home
– mostly theses for doctorates and manuscripts for
hopeful authors and that sort of thing. So we lived with
a reasonable degree of comfort and security. And then
two years ago came the stock-market slump and I was
persuaded to realize my mother's stock capital for less
than £500. If only I had held on for another six months
all would have been well or at least not half so disastrous
but there were great fears at the time of a complete
collapse in the market. As the shares plummeted even
lower in the weeks that followed it seemed that I had
been wise to act as I had done but the truth was that I
had been badly advised and that I had acted disastrously. I kept all this from my mother as best I could and
this was not difficult. She had no real knowledge about
financial affairs. Whilst my father was alive he had
managed his small resources with a shrewd competence and would never let my mother worry about such
things or enquire too closely into them. Since his death
the burden of responsibility had fallen on my own
slimmer shoulders and my mother fully expected that all
was still well. I was too ashamed of my own incompet-
ence to let her think otherwise. I decided then (and
remember this was only two years ago) to put all our
remaining assets into my one idea of a sound invest-
ment. I've already mentioned that our house was far too
big for the two of us and I had my plans for it. We would

divide the house into two with mother and myself living on tho ground floor and another family on the first floor. My idea was to partition the front hall so that the stairs to the upper floor led directly to a completely self-contained residence. The bathroom and toilet were already on that floor anyway and the only major reconstruction necessary was a kitchen sink upstairs and a small bathroom downstairs with a second front door so that there need be no sharing of keys or door-bells and no postal complications. A friend from St Frideswide's (yes I shall be coming to that soon) drew up some neat little plans for me and after finding out that no planning permission was required I asked for estimates. They all seemed to me surprisingly high but I decided we could just manage the lowest estimate of £1,500. So I went ahead and the work began a few months later with heaps of sand and piles of bricks and builders' planks appearing in the front driveway. Everything was going well until a year last February when my mother received a letter from an old friend of hers who had heard of a marvellous clinic in Switzerland which specialized in the treatment and care of multiple sclerosis. No magical cures were promised but there were glowing reports from satisfied clients and the brochure included with the letter gave full details of the three-week course together with technicolour pictures of the clinic itself overlooking Lake Thun with the snowy summits of the Alps behind and the foothills alive with saxifrage and eidelweiss. The cost was £630 which included the return air fare from Heathrow to Basel and transport to and from the clinic. Never before this time had I fully understood the terrible tyranny of money. If I had it my mother could go. If I didn't she couldn't go. There were no gradations of merit or need. I was rather sceptical about any treatment for my mother's illness but the clinic was obviously a reputable one and I knew that a period abroad would do my mother some good. She had not stirred out of the house for more than eighteen months and often couldn't even be bothered to get out of bed and into her wheelchair. But now for the first time in years she had taken a firm decision herself. She wanted to go and was excited at the prospect. She went. Although I spent the three weeks of her absence working as hard and as long as I could as a temporary typist by day and as a waitress in the evenings I found the time exhilarating and I once more discovered some of the joy of living. But things were not working out at all well. The builders were finding unexpected snags and I received a letter from the head of the firm saying that if the work was to be properly carried out the estimate would have to be increased by £350. My mother's return did nothing to help of course and when it was discovered that the waste pipes on the ground floor would quite definitely have to be replaced I was compelled to ask the builders to lay off work for a few weeks since I was unable to meet the next monthly instalment. By the middle of the summer I was at my wits' end. It was then I went to see the Reverend Lionel Lawson.

CHAPTER THIRTY-NINE

Statement given by Miss Ruth Rawlinson (continued)

The first time I had been in St Frideswide's was as a girl in the High School choir when we had sung the Stainer Crucifixion with the Oxford augmented choirs. Several of us sang there again especially when the choir was short of sopranos and contraltos for the Palestrina masses. So I got to know some of the people there and began to feel quite at home. Soon I became a regular member of the choir not because I had any deep conviction about High Anglicanism but because I enjoyed having a different ambit of action and acquaintances. There was an old woman there who cleaned the church every morning of the week – a woman so crippled with arthritis that the carrying of mops and buckets was in itself a positive affirmation of her faith and will. I got to know her well and one day I asked her about herself and she said ever so simply and happily that she hoped God would one day reward her for what she was doing but that if He decided she was not worthy then she still wished to praise and glorify Him for the blessings he had given her. Instead of feeling surprised or cynical about this I felt myself most profoundly moved and when she died I vowed that I would try to take upon myself at least some part of her good works. And so I found myself scrubbing and polishing and the rest and discovering just a little bit of the fulfilment in life that the old woman had experienced. In the course of this self-imposed pennance I naturally got to know Lionel Lawson quite well and as I say it was to him that I went for help and advice when I could no longer cope with our financial crisis. I had one of the great surprises of my life when he told me that if all I was worrying about was money I could and should forget my worries immediately. He asked me what I needed and when I told him he sat down at his desk (where I noticed a paper-knife in the form of a crucifix) and wrote out a cheque for £500. It was just like a miracle and when I told him that I had no idea of when I could repay him or how I could thank him enough he just said that he might be in trouble himself one day and if he was he'd like to know that I would try to help him in any way I could. Of course I promised that I would do absolutely anything for him, and I remember clearly how at the time I hoped and prayed that I would one day be able to do some really big favour for him in return. As I was leaving the vicarage that day I saw a man coming out of the kitchen downstairs. For a moment I didn't recognize him although his face looked familiar. He was rather shabbily dressed but he was freshly shaven and his hair had been recently trimmed. I knew that Lionel had a few of the men from the Church Army Hostel to stay with him for a day or two and sometimes he would persuade them to come along to church services. Then I recognized him. He was much the same age and build as Lionel but the last time I'd seen him he'd had a week or so's growth of stubble on his face and his hair had been long and dirty. It was only later that I learned that this man was Lionel's brother Philip.

It was shortly after this time that Harry Josephs came into my life. One way and another tensions were growing between various members of the church at the end of last summer. It was then that I first heard a nasty rumour about Lionel possibly liking the company of choirboys rather more than he should but I couldn't bring myself to believe it. Even now I am quite convinced that if Lionel was in some way homosexually inclined his weakness was a very gentle and a completely passive one. But there was another rumour almost everyone seemed to have heard about to the effect that Paul Morris the church organist was very much too fond of Harry Josephs' wife Brenda who almost always brought Harry to the services. Harry himself had been disqualified from driving for some reason. Brenda was often seen talking to Paul although she herself would rarely stay in the church for a service and one of the women in the congregation told me she had once seen them holding hands. I must admit that although I had no direct evidence to go on I began to suspect more and more that this second rumour might be true. And then I knew it was true because Harry Josephs told me so. The first time he had called at my home there were the three of us because mother happened to be up that day and he was very pleasant and polite and he stayed for about two hours. After that he called quite regularly always in the morning and we took to sitting together in the lounge when mother was in bed. In some ways he reminded me a bit of my old boss because he made no attempt at all to take the slightest advantage of me. Not then anyway. But he couldn't hide the fact that he was a lonely and disappointed man and before long he told me that he knew all about his wife's affair with Paul Morris. At first I think he must have come to see me just to find a little sympathy because he never once asked my opinion of what he should do. But then one day as we walked to the front door he just turned to me and told me that he found me attractive and that he would love to go to bed with me. Of course I felt a little bit flattered and certainly I had no moral scruples about the situation. We had been drinking sherry together and I was feeling rather more vivacious and daring than I normally do. What was I to say? I was still a virgin. I was forty-one. I had turned down the only man I had so far fallen in love with. I knew that life was passing me by and that if I didn't get to know something about sex fairly soon I never would. Not that I said any of this to Harry. In other circumstances I think I would have reminded him that he was married and that I liked and respected his wife too much to think of anything between us. As it was I think I just smiled and told him not to be so silly. He didn't say anything else but he looked so dejected and humiliated as he stood at the front door that I suddenly felt terribly sorry for him. Immediately to our right was the newly installed door to 14B which had just been painted Cambridge blue. I had the key in my pocket and I asked him if he'd like to have a look at the flat. He made love to me on the mattress of the unmade bed in the back room. It wasn't a particularly happy initiation for me but I experienced little regret. In fact I almost felt a sense of satisfaction and for the next few months we made love together once a week. As I became a little more practised in the physical side of it all I found myself enjoying the act of sex itself more and more. But I knew that something was sadly wrong because I felt so shoddy and cheap after it was over and I began to hate myself for wanting sex at all. I tried to stop it but looking back I think my try was half-hearted. The man seemed to have some power over me and I began living more and more on my nerves. I started worrying about my mother finding out although she seemed to suspect nothing. I started worrying about the neighbours too but goodness knows why because the houses on either side of us were multi-occupied with an ever-changing stream of temporary tenants or undergraduates. Above all I was worried about myself. The truth was that I now needed Harry more than he needed me and he knew this. Whatever agonies of self-reproach I suffered after he was gone I knew that I would be thinking all the time about our next meeting. I began to hate him as well as myself. He was like a drug to which I was fast becoming an addict.

It is perhaps important for you to know all this if you are to understand what happened to me later.

CHAPTER FORTY

Statement given by Miss Ruth Rawlinson (continued)

One Wednesday morning in early September my mother had a bad attack and I decided I had to put off my cleaning visit from the Wednesday morning to the Wednesday evening. But I had keys to the church and could get in whenever I wanted to so a break in my regular routine didn't matter. I locked the door behind me (I almost always used the south door because I could leave my bicycle in the porch there) and I was cleaning the confessional when I heard the north door being unlocked. Paul Morris and Lionel Lawson's brother (as I now knew) Philip came in. For some reason I felt frightened and I sat quietly where I was. I couldn't hear anything they said but it was clear to me that Paul was being blackmailed and that he couldn't and wouldn't pay up very much longer. I didn't understand too much of what was going on and I felt confused and worried. I just kept sitting where I was and I'm not sure exactly what happened next. But a few minutes later it was clear to me that Paul must have gone and that Lionel himself had come into the church because I could now hear the two brothers talking to one another. Again I didn't catch too much of what they were saying but the little I managed to pick up hit me like a thunderbolt. They were talking about murdering Harry Josephs. I was so astounded that the scrubbing-brush I was holding fell clattering to the floor – and they found me. Philip Lawson left almost immediately and then Lionel talked to me for a long long time. I am not prepared even now to disclose everything he told me then but the simple fact is that he begged me for my co-operation. He reminded me of course of my earlier promise to him and he offered to write me a cheque for £5,000 immediately (£5,000!) if I would do as he asked. He said that this payment was for me to keep the upstairs flat free so that his brother Philip could live there for what was likely to be no more than a month at the outside. I felt completely dumbfounded and could hardly begin to realize the implications of all this. At home things were going from bad to worse. The £500 loan from Lionel had all gone and although the flat was now virtually ready our own part of the house was living on borrowed time. According to the builders the whole of the ground floor badly needed rewiring and the water tank was corroded and likely to burst any day. To cap it all the gas central-heating had broken down completely only that very week after a few days of fitful functioning. I had not taken into account either the decoration of the con-verted kitchen upstairs and the only estimate I'd had on that was a horrifying £200. Just imagine my feelings then! But there was something else. I should have mentioned it much earlier but since it is the one thing in the whole case which inescapably incriminates me you will perhaps understand my reluctance – my refusal almost – to mention it. Lionel explained to me that I could now discharge my obligation to him and that this would involve me in the telling of one lie. No. Even now I am not being quite truthful. He made me swear on my most solemn honour I would tell this one lie. He emphasized repeatedly that it would only be one lie – it would involve me in nothing more than that and he insisted that it would be perfectly simple for me to carry out. I didn't care! I was desperately glad to be able to help him and I agreed without a second's hesitation. My mind was in a complete whirl as I left the church that evening. Of Harry Josephs I tried not to think at all. I suppose I almost managed to persuade myself that I had misheard the whole thing. But of course I hadn't. I knew that for some reason or other Harry Josephs was going to die and that my own commitment to tell one simple lie was quite certainly going to be associated with that (for me) not unwelcome event. Where did Philip Lawson fit in? I couldn't then be sure but if money was involved with me surely it would be involved with him too. The conviction gradually grew in my mind that Lionel had hired his brother to murder Harry Josephs and if this was the case my own part in the business – my own lie – would have something to do with being with a certain person at a certain time. An alibi. Yes. I began to feel convinced that such was the case – and again I didn't care! During this time I felt no burden of conscience. It was money now that played the tyrant. Sex was no longer the dominating force and even if it had been I had plenty of opportunity. Several times I had met a man in the Randolph cocktail-bar who showed he was obviously attracted towards me. He was a sales consultant for some prestigious firm and I had little doubt that the room he had in the Randolph would leave little to ask for in terms of physical comfort. I suspect he had taken up with another woman but it was me that he really wanted. At this time too I was becoming increasingly mean with money. Now I had far more than ever before in my whole life. I found myself not even offering to pay for any drinks and accepting expensive meals and generally being an utterly selfish parasite. I bought no new clothes no perfume no special tit-bits for meals. As I grew mean with money I grew mean in other ways too. The same week I rang Harry Josephs and told him that our weekly date was off because my mother was very ill again. Lying like that was ridiculously easy for me now. Good practice! At home the boiler they said could just about be repaired and so I refused to buy a new one. I regarded the first rewiring estimate as ridiculously high so I got a local odd-job man in to do it for half the price. Not that he made a wonderful success of it. I decided to redecorate the upstairs kitchen myself and I found I thoroughly enjoyed doing it. For years I had put 50p in the collection-plate each Sunday morning. Now I put in 20p. But I still cleaned the church. It was my one pennance and I seemed to take more pride than ever in my self-imposed duties. You will think all of this very strange yet it is exactly how I felt and acted. From the way I have just been talking I am conscious that I have made it sound as if it all took place over a long time. But of course it didn't. It was only just over three weeks until the 26th September.

On that day the five of us met at 7 p.m. at St Frideswide's: Brenda Josephs and Paul Morris and

Lionel Lawson and Philip Lawson and myself. The doors were locked and I received my instructions. The candles were to be lit in the Lady Chapel and prayer books set out as if for thirteen members of a congregation – including the churchwarden's pew! I think that last thing was the worst of all really. Paul was playing something on the organ and he seemed to me to look more strained than any of us. Brenda was standing by the font dressed in a smart two-piece green suit and looking quite expressionless. Lionel was busying himself with what appeared to be the usual preparations for a mass – his face quite normal as far as I could tell. Lionel's brother was just as spruce as when I had last seen him and was sitting in the vestry drinking from a bottle which Lionel had no doubt provided for him. At about 7.15 Lionel asked Brenda and myself to go and stand up at the altar in the Lady Chapel and to stay there until he told us. Almost immediately we heard the key being fitted into the north door and Harry Josephs walked in carrying a fairly large brown-paper parcel under his arm. He looked flushed and excited and it was obvious that he had been drinking quite heavily. He saw the pair of us and nodded – but whether to me or to Brenda I couldn't tell. We sat down on the steps of the altar and I think that both of us were trembling. Then the organ suddenly stopped and Paul came through and pressed his hand lightly on Brenda's shoulder before walking up towards the vestry. For several minutes we could hear the men's mumbled voices and then there was a scuffling of feet followed by a dull low sort of moan. When Lionel fetched us he was dressed in surplice and cope. He was breathing heavily and looked very shaken. He said that when the police came I was to tell them that there had been about a dozen or more in the congregation mostly American visitors and that I had heard Harry cry out for help from the vestry during the playing of the last hymn. Whether Brenda was still with me I can't remember. I just walked slowly down to the vestry in a daze. I could see him clearly. He lay there quite still in his brown suit and the cassock he always wore in church with Lionel Lawson's paper-knife stuck deep in his back.

Of the other deaths in this nightmarish business I know nothing at all. But I am convinced that Lionel himself committed suicide unable to face what he had done. I am only too glad that at least he cannot be accused of the murders of Brenda Josephs and the Morrises. As I now finish this long statement my thoughts are with my mother and I beg of you to look after her for me and to tell her – but I can't think what you can tell her. I suppose it will have to be the truth.

Signed: Ruth Rawlinson

'Well?'

Morse put down the statement and looked at Lewis with some distaste. He had been away from the station for more than six hours and had left word of his whereabouts to no one. It was now 8 p.m., and he looked tired.

'Whoever typed that isn't very fond of commas, is she?'

'She's a jolly good girl, sir. Wish we had her up at Kidlington.'

'She can't spell "penance".'

'She can take about 130 words a minute, though.'

'Did Miss Rawlinson speak as fast as that?'

'Pretty fast, yes.'

'Strange,' said Morse.

Lewis looked at his chief with an air of weary puzzlement. 'Clears the air a bit, doesn't it, sir?'

'That?' Morse picked up the statement again, separated the last few sheets, tore them across the middle, and deposited them in the wastepaper basket.

'But you can't just tear—'

'What the hell? The factual content of those pages isn't worth a sheet of lavatory paper! If she's decided to persist in her perjury, she'll get twice as long! Surely you can see that, man?'

Lewis saw very little. He'd been pleased with his day's work – still was; but he, too, felt very tired now and shook his head without bitterness. 'I reckon I could do with a bit of rest, sir.'

'Rest? What the hell are you talking about? You save my life for me and all you want to do is indulge in a bit of Egyptian P.T. Rubbish! We're going to celebrate, you and me.'

'I think I'd rather—'

'But don't you want to hear what I've been up to, old friend?' He looked slyly for a minute at Lewis, and then smiled – a smile which but for a slight hint of sadness could have been called wholly triumphant.

The Book of Revelation

CHAPTER FORTY-ONE

THE FRIAR BACON stands a little way back from the A40 Northern Ring Road, its name commemorating the great thirteenth-century scientist and philosopher, and its beer pleasing to the critical palate of Chief Inspector Morse. The sign outside this public house depicts a stout, jolly-looking man in Franciscan habit, pouring out what appears at first glance to be a glass of Guinness, but what on closer scrutiny proves to be a quantity of some chemical liquid being poured from one glass phial to another. Well, that's what Morse said. Inside they ordered beer and sat down. And then Morse spoke as follows.

'There are some extremely odd points in this case, Lewis – or rather there were – each of them in itself suggestive but also puzzling. They puzzled all of us, and perhaps still do to some extent, because by the time we'd finished we'd got no less than five bodies on our hands and we were never in a position to learn what any of the five could have told us. So, if first of all we look for motive, it's likely to be little more than intelligent guesswork, although we've got some little bits of evidence here and there to help us on our way. Let's start with Harry Josephs. He's getting desperately short of money, and what little he manages to get hold of he promptly donates to his bookmaker. Unbeknown to his wife he borrows money from his insurance company against his house – and he's soon through that, too. Then – as I strongly suspect, Lewis – he starts embezzling church funds, of which there are temptingly large sums and to which he has easy access. Then – I'm guessing again – Lionel Lawson must have found out about this; and if he reports the matter we've got the humiliating prospect of a highly respected ex-officer caught pilfering from the till. It would surely be the last straw for a man who's already lost his job and his money, and who's in real danger of losing his wife as well. Then take Lionel Lawson. Rumours are beginning to spread about him – nasty rumours about his relations with the choirboys, and someone soon made him very much aware of them – pretty certainly Paul Morris, whose son Peter was actually in the choir. Again we've got the prospect of public humiliation: a highly respected minister of the C. of E. caught interfering with the choirboys. Then there's Paul Morris himself. He's having what he hopes is a discreet affair with Harry Josephs' wife, but rumours are beginning to spread about that, too, and it's not very long before Harry gets to know what's going on. Next we come to Ruth Rawlinson. She's got her eyes and ears open more than most, and very soon she gets to know a great deal – in fact a great deal more than is good for her. But she's got a good many problems herself, and it's directly because of them that she becomes caught up in the case. Last, there's Lawson's brother, Philip, who as far

as I can see only comes permanently on to the Oxford
scene last summer. He's been an idle beggar all his life,
and he still was then – absolutely on his uppers and
looking yet again to his brother for help. Lionel has
him to stay at the vicarage, and it isn't long before the
old tensions begin to mount again. By the way, Lewis,
I'm not making that last bit up, but I'll come back to it
later. What have we got then? We've got enough
miscellaneous motives here for a multitude of murders.
Each of those involved has some cause to fear at least
one of the others, and at the same time some hope he
might profit from it all. There's enough potential
blackmail and hatred to boil up into a very, very ugly
situation. The only thing needed to set the whole
reaction off is a catalyst, and we know who that catalyst
was – the Reverend Lionel Lawson. It's he who's got
the one priceless asset in the case – money: about forty
thousand pounds of it. What's more, this money means
very little to him personally. He's perfectly happy to
struggle along on the miserable little stipend he's
allowed by the mean-minded Church Commissioners,
because whatever weaknesses he may have the love of
money is not among 'em. So, he carefully tests the ice,
and after a few tentative steps he finds that the ice on
the pond is thick enough to hold all of 'em. What does
he offer? To his brother Philip – money, and the chance
to perpetuate his dissolute life-style for a few more years
to come. To Josephs – money, and the chance to clear
up his financial affairs and get away to start a new life
somewhere else, minus his wife. To Morris – again,
doubtless, money, if that's what Morris wanted; but he

can also probably ensure that Morris gets Brenda Josephs as well, and the chance for both of 'em to get away and start a new life together, with a healthy bank balance into the bargain. To Ruth Rawlinson – money, and the chance to settle once and for all her chronic anxiety over her domestic problems. So Lionel Lawson sets up his scheme, with the others as his willing accomplices. He fixes up a bogus service to celebrate some non-existent feast – and then the deed is done. The witnesses happily perjure themselves and at the same time vouch for one another's alibis. Lionel is standing at the altar, Paul Morris is playing the organ, Ruth Rawlinson is sitting in the congregation, and Brenda Josephs is across the road at the cinema. If they all stick to their stories, they're all in the clear. All the suspicion, of course, is going to fall on brother Philip; but Lionel has told him – and probably told everyone else – that everything has been most carefully arranged for him: within a few minutes of the murder, he will have caught a train from Oxford station and will be on his way to some pre-arranged hotel booking, with several thousand pounds in his pocket for his troubles. And for all that a little suspicion is a cheap price to pay, wouldn't you say?'

Morse finished his beer and Lewis, who for once had beaten him to it, walked up to the bar. It was quite clear to him, as Morse had said, that there was a whole host of motives in the case interlocking and (if Morse were right) mutually complementary and beneficial. But where did all this *hatred* against Harry Josephs spring from? All right, the lot of them were getting into a terrible mess, but (again, if Morse were right) money seemed to be coping quite adequately with all their problems. And why, oh, why, all this peculiar palaver in the church? It all seemed a ridiculously complicated and quite unnecessary charade. Why not just kill Josephs and dump his body somewhere? Between them that would have been infinitely simpler, surely? And what about the actual murder itself? Morphine poisoning *and* a knife in the back. No. It didn't really add up.

He paid for the beer and walked circumspectly back to their table. He wouldn't be thanked if he slopped as much as a cubic millimetre on to the carpet.

Morse took a mighty swallow from his beer and continued. 'We've now got to ask ourselves the key question: how can we account for enough hatred – on somebody's part – against Harry Josephs? Because unless we can answer that question we're still groping about in the dark. And closely connected with it we've got to ask ourselves why there was all this clumsy kerfuffle at the phoney service, and also why Josephs was killed twice over. Well, let's deal with the last question first. I'm sure you've heard of those firing squads when you get, say, four men with rifles, all quite happy to shoot the poor fellow tied to the post, but three of 'em have blanks up the barrel and only one has a live bullet. The idea is that none of 'em will ever know which one actually fired the fatal shot. Well, I thought that something of the sort may have happened here. There were three of 'em, remember, and let's say none of 'em is too keen on being solely responsible for **the killing. Now, if Josephs, as well as being poisoned** and stabbed, had also been bashed on the head, I reckon the evidence would have pointed strongly to my being right. But we learned from the post-mortem that there were two causes of death, and not three. Somebody gives Josephs morphine in some red wine; and then somebody, either the same somebody or somebody else, stabs him in the back. Why bother to kill him twice over? Well, it may well be that two of 'em *were* involved in the actual murder; a division of labour could have been agreed for the reason I've just mentioned. But there was a far more important reason than that. Are you ready for a bit of a shock, Lewis?'

'Ready for anything, sir.'

Morse drained his glass. 'By Jove, the beer's good here!'

'It's your turn, sir.'

'Is it?'

The landlord had come through into the lounge-bar, and for a few minutes Lewis could hear him discussing with Morse the crass stupidity of the selectors of the England football team.

'These are on the house,' said Morse, planting the two pints carefully on the Morrells' beer-mats. (For a man proposing to treat his junior officer for services rendered, he seemed to Lewis to be getting away with things extremely lightly.) 'Where was I now? Ah, yes. You didn't ask me where I'd been today, did you? Well, I've been up to Rutland again.'

'Leicestershire, sir.'

Morse appeared not to hear. 'I made one bad blunder in this case, Lewis. Only one. I listened too much to rumour, and rumour's a terrible thing. If I tell everybody that you're having an affair with that comma-less typist of yours, you'd suddenly find yourself trying like hell to prove you weren't – even though there was absolutely no truth in it. Like they say, you throw enough mud and some of it'll stick. Well, I reckon that's what happened with Lionel Lawson. If he was a homo-sexual, he must have been one of the very mildest variety, I think. But once the charge had been sug-gested he found himself in the middle of a good deal of suspicion, and I was one of those prepared to think the worst of him. I even managed to convince myself, without the slightest shred of evidence, that when he was expelled from school it must have been because he was buggering about with some of the younger lads there. But suddenly I began to wonder. What if I'd been quite wrong? What if Lionel Lawson's old headmaster wasn't too unhappy about letting me believe what I did – *because the truth of the matter was far worse?* I thought I knew what this truth was, and I was right. Today I met Meyer again, as well as Lionel's old housemaster. You see, the Lawson brothers were an extremely odd mixture. There was Lionel the elder brother, a hard-working, studious swot, not too gifted academically, struggling along and doing his best, bespectacled even then, lacking in any confidence – in short, Lewis, a bit of a bore all round. And then there was Philip, a clever little beggar, with all the natural gifts any boy could ask for – a fine brain, good at games, popular, good-looking, and yet always idle and selfish. And the parents dote on – guess who? – young, glamour-pants

Philip. It doesn't require much imagination to see the situation from Lionel's point of view, does it? He's jealous of his brother – increasingly and, finally, furiously jealous. From what I've been able to learn there was a young girl mixed up in it all, when Lionel was eighteen and Philip a year or so younger. She wasn't a brilliant looker by all accounts – but she was Lionel's girl. Until, that is, Philip decided to step in; and probably for no other reason than to spite his brother he took her away from him. It was from that point that the whole of the tragedy dates. At home, one weekend, *Lionel Lawson tried to kill his brother*. He tried to use the kitchen-knife, and in fact he wounded him quite seriously – *in the back*. Things were hushed up as far as possible and the police were quite happy to leave the situation in the hands of the school and the parents. Some arrangement was worked out, with both the boys being taken away from the school. No charge was brought, and things, so it seemed, settled down. But the records couldn't be altered, could they, Lewis? The fact was that at the age of eighteen Lionel Lawson had tried unsuccessfully to murder his brother. So if, as I said, we're looking for any festering, insatiable hatred in this case, then we've found it: the hatred that existed between Lionel Lawson and his younger brother.'

It was all very interesting and suggestive, Lewis could see that; but he couldn't really see how it affected many of the problems in the present case. Morse was going on, though, and the shock he'd spoken of was imminent.

'At first I thought that Lionel Lawson had killed

Harry Josephs and had then faked his own suicide by dressing up his brother in clerical get-up and chucking him from the top of the tower. What could be neater? All you'd want was someone who would agree to a wrong identification of the body, and such a person was readily available in Paul Morris, a man who would have profited twofold from the murder of Josephs: first, by pocketing a considerable sum of money; and, second, by having Josephs' wife for himself. But you made the point to me yourself, Lewis, and you were absolutely right: it's one helluva job to dress up a dead man in someone else's clothes. But it's not an *impossible* job, is it? Not if you're all prepared for the difficulties and if you've got plenty of time. But in this particular instance you were right, I'm convinced of that. It was Lionel Lawson, not his brother Philip, who fell from the tower last October. In his own conscience Lionel must have realized that he'd done something so terrible and so unforgivable that he just couldn't live with it any longer. So he took his spectacles off, put them in their case – and jumped. And while we're on this identification business, Lewis, I must confess I had my fair share of doubts about whether the body we found on the tower really was Paul Morris. If it wasn't, the possibilities were staggeringly interesting. But, although we've no satisfactory identification as yet, you can take my word for it that it *was* Paul Morris. Yes, indeed. And so at long last I began to shelve all these fanciful theories, and I just looked at the simple possibility that all of us had completely ignored from the very beginning. Ruth Rawlinson herself came very near to telling the truth and giving the game away in that ridiculous statement of hers when she said that she was prepared to tell one lie – *one lie*. She told us, as you'll remember, that this lie was about the service in St Frideswide's that never took place, and about her silence in the plotting of Harry Josephs' murder. But listen, Lewis! That wasn't the real lie at all. The real lie was about something else: she lied about the identification of the body lying dead in St Frideswide's vestry that night in September! *That* was her one big lie. Because, you see, the body found murdered that night was not the body of Harry Josephs at all! *It was the body of Lionel Lawson's brother – Philip Lawson.*'

CHAPTER FORTY-TWO

Extract from the transcript of proceedings held on 4 July at Oxford Crown Court against Miss Ruth Isabel Rawlinson on the charges of perjury and conspiracy, Mr Gilbert Marshall, Q.C., prosecuting for the Crown, Mr Anthony Johns, Q.C., acting for the defence.

Marshall: Let us turn, if we can, away from these rather nebulous areas of motive, and come to the events of last September, specifically to the evening of Monday the twenty-sixth of that month. The Court will be glad, I know, to hear your own explanation of the events which took place that unholy night.

Morse: It is my view, sir, that a conspiracy had been formed to murder Mr Philip Lawson, and that this conspiracy involved the Reverend Lionel Lawson, Mr Paul Morris and Mr Harry Josephs. I am quite sure in my own mind that the statement made by the defendant about the events of that evening is substantially correct. Correct, that is, as far as it goes, since I am convinced that Miss Rawlinson was not in a position to know the detailed sequence of events, being neither an active party in, nor an actual witness to, the murder itself.

Marshall: Try to confine yourself to the question, Inspector, will you? It is for the Court to determine the degree of the defendant's involvement in this crime — not for you. Please continue.

Morse: If I were to guess the sequence of events that night, sir, it would have to be something like this. Lionel Lawson was able somehow to persuade his brother Philip that it would be greatly to his advantage to be in the church at a certain time that evening. It would have been no great problem to persuade him to drink a glass of red wine whilst they waited there – wine that had already been doctored with morphine. The fact that the man found dead at the church that night could have died, or certainly would have died, of morphine poisoning was clearly established by the post-mortem findings; but the provenance of the morphine itself was never discovered, in spite of extensive police enquiries. However, there was one of the three men who had earlier had direct and daily access to a complete pharmacopoeia, a man who had worked for eighteen months as a chemist's assistant in Oxford. That man, sir, was Harry Josephs. And it was Josephs who, in my view, not only suggested but actually administered the lethal dose of morphine in the wine.

Marshall: Can you tell us why, if the man was already dead, it was necessary to stab him into the bargain?

Morse: I don't think he was already dead, sir, although I agree he would have been unconscious fairly soon after drinking the wine. Whatever happened, though, he had to be dead when the police arrived, because there might always be the outside chance of his recovering and telling the police what he knew. Hence the knife. And so if I may say so, sir, the key question is not why he was stabbed in the back – but why he was given morphine. And in my considered view the reason was this: it was absolutely vital from Lionel Lawson's point of view that his brother's clothes should be changed, and you can't stab a man in the back and then change his clothes without removing the knife and stabbing him again. By arrangement, Josephs had changed from the brown suit which by all accounts he always wore and brought it with him to the church that night. Without any doubt, I should think, the suit was wrapped up in the brown-paper parcel which Miss Rawlinson mentions in her statement. The police would obviously examine the dead man's clothes in the minutest detail, and an actual change of clothes would be the one certain way of making the deception appear absolutely authentic. And so, when Philip Lawson had slumped unconscious in the vestry, his own clothes were removed and Josephs' clothes put on him – a difficult and lengthy job, I should imagine, but there were three of them to do it and time was very much on their side. Then they dressed him in Josephs' cassock and the moment of truth had now arrived for Lionel Lawson. I suspect that he asked the other two to leave him, and then he completed a task which he had attempted once before and in which he had failed so disastrously. He looked down on the brother he had hated for so long, and he stabbed him in the back with his paper-knife. As I say, I don't myself think that Philip Lawson was dead at that point, and the defendant's statement tends to confirm this view, since what she heard must almost certainly have been the dying man's final groans. The police were summoned immediately, the body wrongly identified, both by the defendant and by Paul Morris, and I think you know the rest, sir.

Marshall: Doesn't all this seem to you an extraordinarily complicated business, Inspector? To me, at least, it seems quite ludicrously so. Why didn't the Reverend Lionel Lawson just murder his brother himself?

Judge: It is my duty to remind prosecuting counsel that it is not the Reverend Mr Lawson who is on trial in this court, and it is improper for the witness to answer the question in the form in which it has been phrased.

Marshall: Thank you, m'lord. Will the witness please explain to the Court why, in his view, the Reverend Mr Lawson, supposing him to have been responsible for his brother's death, did not proceed in this matter in a significantly more simple manner?

Morse: In my opinion, sir, two things were absolutely imperative for the Reverend Lawson. First that his brother should die – a matter which, as you suggest, he could perhaps have coped with single-handedly all right if he'd tried. But the second imperative need was far trickier, and one which he could never have coped with by himself, however hard he tried. He had to have someone who was willing to be identified as the dead man and who was also prepared to disappear immediately from the Oxford scene. Let me explain, sir, why I think this was so. Philip Lawson had let it be known to several people, including the defendant, for example, that he was Lionel Lawson's brother. So if he had been murdered and identified as the man who had often been seen at the vicarage, in the church, and so on, it would only have been a matter of time before the police discovered his true identity. And once that was known other facts would have been swift to follow. An attempt had already been made upon the man's life once before – with a knife – by his elder brother. Police enquiries would very quickly have been channelled in the right direction and virtually certain suspicion would have centred on the Reverend Lawson. As I say, sir, it was absolutely vital not only that Philip Lawson should die but also that he should be wrongly identified. As the Court now knows, he was indeed wrongly identified – as Harry Josephs; and Harry Josephs himself disappeared from the scene, although as it happens he didn't disappear very far. That same night he moved into the upstairs flat at 14B Manning Terrace, and he lived there until he died. He'd taken Philip Lawson's clothes from the church and no doubt the idea was that he should destroy them. But for various reasons Josephs grew restless—

Marshall: Before you go on with your evidence, Inspector, I must ask you if it is your view that the defendant's relations with Mr Josephs had ever been in any way more – shall we say? – more intimate than merely providing him with the daily necessities of living?

Morse: No.

Marshall: You are aware, no doubt, of the evidence before the Court from an earlier witness of several visits by Mr Josephs to Manning Terrace during the course of last summer?

Morse: I am, sir.

Marshall: And it is your view that these visits were of a purely – er – purely social nature?

Morse: It is, sir.

Marshall: Please continue, Inspector.

Morse: I think the idea must have been for Josephs to stay where he was until the dust had settled and then to get right away from Oxford somewhere. But that again has to be guesswork. What is certain is that he very soon learned that the Reverend Lionel Lawson had committed suicide and—

Marshall: I'm sorry to interrupt you again, but is it your view that in that death, at least, the late Mr Josephs could have had no hand whatsoever?

Morse: It is, sir. News of Lawson's death, as I say, would have been a big shock to Josephs. He must have wondered what on earth had gone wrong. Specifically he must have wondered many times whether Lawson had left a note and, if so, whether the note in any way incriminated himself and the others. Quite apart from that, though, Josephs had been dependent on Lawson. It was Lawson who had arranged his present hide-out and it was Lawson who was arranging his impending departure from Oxford. But now he was on his own, and he must have felt increasingly isolated. But again that's guesswork. What is clear is that he started going out into Oxford during the early winter months. He wore Philip Lawson's old clothes, with the long dirty great-coat buttoned up to the neck; he wore a pair of dark glasses; he grew a beard; and he found that he could merge quite anonymously into the Oxford background. It was about this time, too, I think, that he must have realized that there was now only one other person who knew exactly what had taken place in the vestry that September evening; and that person was Paul Morris, a man who had robbed him of his wife, a man who was probably going to live with her after the end of the school term, and a man who had done very nicely out of the whole thing, without actually doing very much at all himself. It is my own view, by the way, sir, that Paul Morris may not have been quite so eager to get away with Mrs Josephs as he had been. But Josephs himself could have no inkling of that, and his hatred of Morris grew, as did his sense of power and his rediscovered capacity for the sort of action he had once known as a captain in the Royal Marine Commandos. On some pretext or other Josephs was able to arrange a meeting with Paul Morris at St Frideswide's, where he killed him and hid his body – though probably not, at that point, on the roof of the tower. Remember that no keys had been found in the clothing of the man murdered in the vestry; and it is clear that Josephs kept them for himself, and was therefore able to use the church for the murders of Paul Morris and his son Peter. Not only that, though. He was compelled to use the church. He was disqualified from driving, and without a licence, of course, he couldn't even hire a car. If he'd had a car, he would probably have tried to dispose of the bodies elsewhere; but in this respect, at least, he was a victim of circumstance. Later the same day – at tea-time in fact – he also arranged to meet Peter Morris, and there can be little doubt that the young boy was also murdered in St Frideswide's. I'm pretty sure his first idea was to hide both bodies in the crypt, and as soon as it was dark he put the boy in a sack and opened the door at the south porch. Everything must have seemed safe enough and he got to the grilled entrance to the crypt in the south churchyard all right – it's only about fifteen yards or so from the door. But then something happened. As he was carrying the body down, the ladder snapped and Josephs must have had an awkward fall. He decided that he couldn't or daren't repeat the process with a much bigger and heavier body; so he changed his plans and carried Paul Morris' body up to the tower roof.

Marshall: And then he decided to murder his wife?

Morse: Yes, sir. Whether at this point he knew exactly where she was; whether he had actually been in touch with her; whether he was able to find out anything from Paul Morris – I just don't know. But once the bodies – or just one of them – were found, he was going to make absolutely sure that *she* didn't talk, either; and, in any case, with Paul Morris now out of the way, his jealous hatred was directing itself ever more insanely against his wife. For the moment, however, he had a dangerous job on his hands. He had to get to the Morrises' house in Kidlington and try to make everything there look as if they'd both left in a reasonably normal manner. It was no problem getting into the house. No keys were found on either of the Morrises, although each of them must have had a latch-key. Once inside—

Marshall: Yes, yes. Thank you, Inspector. Could you now tell the Court exactly where the defendant fits into your scheme of things?

Morse: I felt reasonably certain, sir, that Miss Rawlinson would be safe only so long as she herself had no knowledge of the identities of the bodies found in St Frideswide's.

Marshall: But as soon as she did – tell me if I am wrong, Inspector – Josephs decided that he would also murder the defendant?

Morse: That is so, sir. As you know, I was an eye-witness to the attempted murder of Miss Rawlinson, and it was only at that point that I was convinced of the true identity of the murderer – when I recognized the tie he tried to strangle her with: the tie of the Royal Marine Commandos.

Marshall: Yes, very interesting, Inspector. But surely the defendant was always just as much of a threat to the murderer as Brenda Josephs was? Don't you think so? And, if she was, why do you think he treated the two women so differently?

Morse: I believe that Josephs had grown to hate his wife, sir. I made the point earlier in my evidence.

Marshall: But he didn't feel the same hatred towards the defendant – is that it?

Morse: I don't know, sir.

Marshall: You still wish to maintain that there was no special relationship between the defendant and Mr Josephs?

Morse: I have nothing to add to my earlier answer, sir.

Marshall: Very well. Go on, Inspector.

Morse: As I say, sir, I felt convinced that Josephs would attempt to kill Miss Rawlinson almost immedi-ately, since it must have been clear to him that things were beginning to move very fast indeed, and since Miss Rawlinson was the only person left, apart from himself, who knew something of the truth – far too much of it, he must have felt. So my colleague, Sergeant Lewis, and myself decided we would try to bring the murderer out into the open. We allowed a slightly inaccurate report on the case to appear prominently in the *Oxford Mail* with the sole purpose of making him suspect that the net was already beginning to close on him. I thought that wherever he was – and remember that I had no idea whatsoever that he was living in the same house as Miss Rawlinson – he was almost certain to use the church once more. He would know exactly the times when Miss Rawlinson would be cleaning there, and he had his plans all ready. In fact, he got to church very early that morning, and managed to ruin the precautions which we had so carefully taken.

Marshall: But fortunately things worked out all right, Inspector.

Morse: I suppose you could say that. Thanks to Sergeant Lewis.

Marshall: I have no more questions.

Johns: I understand, Inspector, that you heard the conversation between my client and Mr Josephs before the attempt to strangle her was made.

Morse: I did.

Johns: In that conversation, did you hear anything which might be considered by the Court to be mitigating evidence in the case against my client?

Morse: Yes. I heard Miss Rawlinson say that she—

Judge: Will the witness please speak up for the Court?

Morse: I heard Miss Rawlinson say that she had decided to go to the police and make a full statement of all she knew.

Johns: Thank you. No further questions.

Judge: You may stand down, Inspector.

CHAPTER FORTY-THREE

'WHAT BEATS ME,' said Bell, 'is how many crooks there are around – in a church, too! I always thought those sort of people walked straight down the middle of the paths of righteousness.'

'Perhaps most of them do,' said Lewis quietly.

They were sitting in Bell's office just after the verdict and sentence had been passed on Miss Ruth Rawlinson. Guilty; eighteen months' imprisonment.

'It still beats me,' said Bell.

Morse was sitting there, too, silently smoking a cigarette. He either smoked addictively or not at all, and had given up the habit for ever on innumerable occasions. He had listened vaguely to the mumbled conversation, and he knew exactly what Bell had meant, but . . . His favourite Gibbon quotation flashed across his mind, the one concerning the fifteenth-century Pope John XXIII, which had so impressed him as a boy and which he had committed to memory those many years ago: 'The most scandalous charges were suppressed; the vicar of Christ was only accused of piracy, murder, rape, sodomy, and incest.' It was no new thing to realize that the Christian church had a great deal to answer for, with so much blood on the hands of its temporal administrators, and so much hatred and bitterness in the hearts of its spiritual lords. But behind it all, as Morse knew – and transcending it all – stood the simple, historical unpalatable figure of its founder – an enigma with which Morse's mind had wrestled so earnestly as a youth, and which even now troubled his pervasive scepticism. He remembered his first visit to a service at St Frideswide's, and the woman singing next to him: 'Wash me, and I shall be whiter than snow.' Wonderful possibility! The Almighty, as it were, wiping the slate clean and not just forgiving, but forgetting, too. And it was forgetting that was the really hard thing. Morse could find it even in his own cynical soul to forgive – but not to forget. How could he forget? For a few blissful moments on that day in St Frideswide's he had felt such a precious affinity with a woman as he had felt only once before; but their orbits, his and hers, had crossed too late in the day, and she, like all other lost souls, like the Lawsons and Josephs and Morris, had erred and strayed from the ways of acceptable human behaviour. But how could his mind not be haunted by the revelations she had made? Should he go to see her now, as she had asked? If he *was* to see her, it would have to be very soon.

Dimly and uninterestedly his mind caught up with the conversation once more: 'Doesn't reflect very well on me, does it, Sergeant? I'm in charge of the case for months, and then Morse here comes along and solves it in a fortnight. Made me look a proper Charley, if you ask me.' He shook his head slowly. 'Clever bugger!'

Lewis tried to say something but he couldn't find the right words. Morse, he knew, had the maddeningly brilliant facility for seeing his way through the dark labyrinths of human motive and human behaviour, and he was proud to be associated with him; proud when Morse had mentioned his name in court that day. But such matters weren't Lewis' forte; he knew that, too. And it was almost a relief – after Morse – to get back to his usual pedestrian and perfunctory duties.

Morse heard his own name mentioned again and realized that Bell was talking to him.

'You know, I still don't understand—'

'Nor do I,' interrupted Morse. Throughout the case he had made so many guesses that he could find no mental reserve to fabricate more. The words of St Paul to the Corinthians were writ large in his brain: 'There is a manifestation and there is a mystery'; and he felt sure that whatever might be puzzling Bell was not likely to be one of the greater mysteries of life. Wasn't one of the real mysteries the source of that poison which had slowly but inexorably dripped and dripped into Lionel Lawson's soul? And that was almost as old as the seed of Adam himself, when Cain and Abel had presented their offerings before the Lord . . .

'Pardon?'

'I said the pubs'll soon be open, sir.'

'Not tonight for me, Lewis. I – er – I don't feel much like it.'

He got up and walked out of the office without a further word, Lewis staring after him in some be-wilderment.

'Odd bugger!' said Bell; and for the second time

318

within a few minutes Lewis felt he had to agree with him.'

Obviously Ruth had been crying, but she was now recovered, her voice dull and resigned. 'I just wanted to thank you, Inspector, that's all. You've been – you've been so kind to me, and – and I think if anyone could ever understand me it might have been you.'

'Perhaps so,' said Morse. It was not one of his more memorable utterances.

'And then—' She sighed deeply and a film of tears enveloped her lovely eyes. 'I just wanted to say that when you asked me out that time – do you remember? – and when I said – when I—' Her face betrayed her feelings completely now, and Morse nodded and looked away.

'Don't worry about it. I know what you're going to say. It's all right. I understand.'

She forced herself to speak through her tears. 'But I *want* to say it to you, Inspector. I want you to know that—' Again, she was unable to go on; and Morse touched her shoulder lightly, just as Paul Morris had touched Brenda Josephs lightly on the shoulder on the night of Philip Lawson's murder. Then he got up and made his way quickly out along the corridor. Yes, he understood – and he forgave her, too. But, unlike the Almighty, he was unable to forget.

*

Mrs Emily Walsh-Atkins had been called upon to identify the battered corpse of Harry Josephs. (It was Morse's idea.) She had done so willingly, of course. What an exciting time this last year had been! And the goldfish flashed its tail almost merrily in her mind as she recalled her own part in the tragic events which had centred upon her chosen church. Her name had appeared once more in the *Oxford Mail* – in the *Oxford Times*, too – and she had cut out the paragraphs carefully, just as Ruth Rawlinson before her, and kept them in her handbag with the others. One Sunday morning during the hot summer which followed these events, she prayed earnestly for forgiveness for her sins of pride, and the Reverend Keith Meiklejohn, standing benignly beside the north porch, was kept waiting even longer than usual until she finally emerged into the bright sunshine.

Mrs Alice Rawlinson had been taken to the Old People's Home in Cowley immediately after her daughter's arrest. When Ruth was freed, after serving only eleven of her eighteen months' sentence, the old lady returned to 14A Manning Terrace, still going strong and looking good for several years to come. As she was helped into the ambulance on her way home, one of the young housemen was heard to murmur that anyone who predicted how long a patient had got to live was nothing but a bloody fool.

*

A few books had been found in Harry Josephs' upstairs flat at 14B Manning Terrace; and after the case was over these had been given to Oxfam, and were slowly sold, at ridiculously low prices, at the second-hand charity bookshop in north Oxford. A seventeen-year-old boy (by some curious coincidence, a boy named Peter Morris) bought one of them for five pence in the early summer. He had always been interested in crime, and the large, fat, glossy volume entitled *Murder Ink* had immediately attracted his attention. That same night whilst browsing through the assorted articles, he came to a piece about suicides on page 349, heavily underlined in red biro: *Myopic jumpers invariably remove their eyeglasses and put them in a pocket before jumping.*

CHAPTER FORTY-FOUR

MORSE TOOK HIS holidays later the following year and decided, again, to go to the Greek islands. Yet somehow his passport remained unrenewed in its drawer, and one sunny morning in mid-June the chief inspector caught a bus down from north Oxford into the city. For an hour he wandered contentedly around the Ashmolean where amongst other delights he stood for many minutes in front of the Giorgione and the Tiepolo. Just before midday he walked across to the cocktail-bar at the Randolph and bought a pint of beer, for he would never lend his lips to anything less than that measure. Then another pint. He left at half past twelve, crossed Cornmarket, and walked into St Frideswide's. The north door creaked no longer, but inside the only sign of life was the flickering candles that burned around the statue of the Virgin. The woman he was seeking was not there. As once before, he decided to walk up to north Oxford, although this time he witnessed no accident at the Marston Ferry crossroads. Reaching the Summertown shops, he called into the Dew Drop, drank two further pints of beer, and continued on his way. The carpet-shop, from which Brenda Josephs had once observed her husband, had now been taken over by an insurance firm, but otherwise little seemed to have changed. When he came to Manning Terrace, Morse turned into it, paused at one point for a second or two, and then continued along it. At number 14A he stopped, knocked briskly on the door, and stood there waiting.

'You!'

'I heard you'd come home.'

'Well! Come in! Come in! You're the first visitor I've had.'

'No, I won't do that. I just called by to tell you that I've been thinking a lot about you since you've been – er – away, and you'd blush if I told you what happened in my dreams.'

'Of course I wouldn't!'

'Don't take any notice of me – I've had too much beer.'

'*Please* come in.'

'Your mother's there.'

'Why don't you take me to bed?'

Her large eyes held his, and in that moment a sparkling mutual joy was born.

'Can I use your "gents"?'

'There's one upstairs – it's a "ladies", too.'

'Upstairs?'

'Just a minute!'

She was back almost immediately with a Yale key labelled 14B in her hand.

'Hadn't you better tell your mother—?'

'I don't think so,' she said, and a slow smile spread across her lips as she closed the door of 14A quietly behind her and inserted the key into 14B.

Morse's eyes followed her slim ankles as she climbed the carpeted stairs ahead of him.

'Bedroom or lounge?'

'Let's go into the lounge a few minutes first,' said Morse.

'There's some whisky here. Do you want a drink?'

'I want you.'

'And you can have me. You know that, don't you?'

Morse took her in his arms as they stood there, and kissed her tenderly on her sweet, full lips. Then, as if the moment were too unbearably blissful to be prolonged, he pressed her body tightly to him and laid his cheek against hers.

'I dreamed about you, too,' she whispered in his ear.

'Did I behave myself?'

'I'm afraid so. But you're not going to behave yourself now, are you?'

'Certainly not.'

'What's your Christian name?' she asked.

'I'll tell you afterwards,' said Morse quietly, as his fingers lingered lightly on the zip at the back of her brightly patterned summer dress.